PL⌐ ............................................ ⌐porary thriller
from Sim⌐ ............. ⌐ng-established as an author of historical
novels, incl ⌐ g the *Sunday Times* bestsellers CENTURION
and DAY OI HE CAESARS. Prior to writing fiction Simon
worked as a teacher and lecturer; he is now a full-time writer.
He lives near Norwich.

For exciting news, extracts and exclusive content from
Simon visit www.simonscarrow.co.uk, follow him on
Twitter @SimonScarrow or like his author page on Facebook/
OfficialSimonScarrow.

Lee Francis worked for several years in the world of film,
TV and advertising as a script reader and assistant director.
PLAYING WITH DEATH, written with his former lecturer
Simon Scarrow, is his first novel.

'This fast, furious, twisty thriller kept me on the edge of my seat'
Chris Ryan

'If Stephen King had collaborated with Michael Crichton on a
thriller, it might have been as good as this . . . A grab-you-by-
the-throat page-ripper' *Peterborough Telegraph*

'An original plot set in a world that terrifies me to think about . . .
grips you from the beginning and races to a most exciting and enig-
matic ending . . . I absolutely loved it' ***** www.crimesquad.com

'A gripping killer thriller morphs into a serious and frankly scary
examination of the possible threats the development of AI poses
for humanity' *Irish Independent*

'An edgy, pacy, futuristic and oh
www.trevtwinem.booklikes.com

10657467

WALTHAM FOREST LIBRARIES

904 000 00624270

The E[...] [...]

# SIMON SCARROW
## AND LEE FRANCIS

# PLAYING
# WITH
# DEATH

HEADLINE PUBLISHING GROUP

An Hachette UK Company

Carmelite House

50 Victoria Embankment

London EC4Y 0DZ

www.headline.co.uk

www.hachette.co.uk

made from wood grown in well-managed forests and other controlled sources. The logging and manufacturing processes are expected to conform to the environmental regulations of the country of origin.

Copyright © 2017 Simon Scarrow

The right of Simon Scarrow to be identified as the Author of
the Work has been asserted by him in accordance with the
Copyright, Designs and Patents Act 1988.

First published in Great Britain in 2017 by
HEADLINE PUBLISHING GROUP

First published in paperback in 2018 by
HEADLINE PUBLISHING GROUP

1

Apart from any use permitted under UK copyright law, this
publication may only be reproduced, stored, or transmitted, in
any form, or by any means, with prior permission in writing of
the publishers or, in the case of reprographic production, in
accordance with the terms of licences issued by the
Copyright Licensing Agency.

All characters in this publication are fictitious and any resemblance
to real persons, living or dead, is purely coincidental.

Cataloguing in Publication Data is available from the British Library

ISBN 978 1 4722 5197 8 (A-format)
ISBN 978 1 4722 1342 6 (B-format)

Typeset in Bembo by Avon DataSet Ltd, Bidford-on-Avon, Warwickshire

Printed and bound in Great Britain by Clays Ltd, Elcograf S.p.A.

MIX
Paper from
responsible sources
FSC
www.fsc.org FSC® C104740

Headline's policy is to use papers that are natural, renewable and recyclable
products an                                                   nd other
controlled sou                                               xpected to
conform                                                      rigin.

| Waltham Forest Libraries | |
| --- | --- |
| 904 000 00624270 | |
| Askews & Holts | 03-Aug-2018 |
| THR | £7.99 |
| 5792129 | |

To Mum, Dad, Karl and Alex

# 0

Rose Blake follows Shane Koenig's blue pick-up truck along the dirt trail, up the slope towards a two-storey cabin. The brake lamps of Koenig's truck burn red in the dark of the night. The cabin's windows pierce the darkness with an inviting orange hue, and then the harsh glare of a security light sears the cold air as they park on the leaf-strewn gravel in front of the cabin. It is starting to rain, small drops pattering through the bare branches of the forest. Rose leaves her vehicle and follows Koenig up the porch steps. Tall black trees loom all around the cabin. A name plaque reads 'Solace'. Koenig turns to look at her. He is handsome, in the rugged, dark-haired sense, wearing blue jeans, brown leather boots and a Tommy Hilfiger wool jacket over a red checked shirt.

'My home away from home, huh? Pretty nice, isn't it?'

He unlocks the front door. Rose's pulse quickens as he gestures for her to enter.

'It sure is.'

The built-in kitchen has gleaming beechwood panelling and shelving units, copper pots and pans hang on a wall, no expense spared. The cabin itself is a mix of stone brickwork and orange dyed wood. The kitchen is open plan, leading to the living room where there's a fireplace with crumpled paper, kindling and small logs, ready to light. Koenig takes out a gas lighter, and soon there's a crackle and hiss as the flames take and start to warm the room. Rose holds her hands out by the fire, feeling the warmth prickle her skin. Koenig crosses to a Bose wall-mounted sound system and presses play:

> Somethin' about this night . . .
> Somethin' is so right.
> You and me, babe. We're connected . . .

An unsettling choice, Rose thinks.

He takes off his jacket and flashes her a smile. 'Make yourself at home. You'll find it's a comfortable place. At least I think so.'

'A bit lonely though.'

'Not with the right company,' he says, touching her cheek. His fingers send a jolt through her body. But not of sexual anticipation. It's fear that Rose feels.

'Nice to meet someone who looks like their profile picture for a change,' he adds, his gaze running down her body.

'In a good way, I hope?' Rose feels her skin chilling under the pink cashmere sweater she is wearing on top of her pencil skirt.

'You bet. Here, let me take your coat.' Koenig slides the long brown garment from her shoulders, letting her arms slip free.

Rose quickly shifts a short distance away from him and sits down on the soft beige sofa. She casts a glance at the cabin walls where framed photos of hunting expeditions hang. Shane Koenig is in every one of them, posed by the body of a deer, or some other game. At the back of the cabin is another door, and several hunting rifles are in a rack to one side. As her eyes look for more clues to his personality, she senses a faint tang of bleach in the air.

The significance of the odour is not lost on Rose. It's what she would expect a man like Koenig to use to cover his tracks. But she tries to keep calm. She knows Owen and the rest of the team are waiting nearby in a black surveillance van. There are others with them, armed and ready to move as soon as the word is given. Rose knows she cannot raise the alarm unless she is directly threatened or Koenig gives himself away. So far he has behaved like any normal man on a date.

His behaviour has been too guarded, she realizes. As if he has been watching her, coolly weighing her up, before he makes his move. She feels an icy tingle at the base of her neck. Maybe he knows that she is not what she seems. He moves unhurriedly to the kitchen and takes some glasses from a cupboard. Two wine glasses and two tumblers. He glances over his shoulder. His lips lift in a smile, but his eyes are dead. 'Cold night. Fancy a snifter?'

'Sure. What have you got?' Rose lets her hair fall forward in a nod. She wears her hair down to conceal the flesh-coloured two-way earpiece in her right ear.

Koenig turns and stares for a moment. 'You really are quite a looker. Bet there's no end of guys on the site who've asked you out. Why choose me?'

'Your profile was interesting. Not the usual generic crap. And you've got a good job, I guess.'

'You guess . . .'

For a second his expression is as dead as his eyes. Then he smiles again. 'And what job would that be? I don't believe I mentioned any details about what I do for a living.'

Rose feels her pulse quicken in alarm as she makes herself reply in a casual tone. 'Whatever it is, must be good enough to pay for all this. Your home away from home, as you call it.'

'Yes.' His eyes dart from side to side. 'This place is more like my real home. It feels like I just live at the house in the city, where I work during the week. This is where I'm most comfortable. This place is more . . . me. If you see what I mean?'

Rose nods at the hunting photos. 'Sure I do.'

Koenig laughs. 'No. No, I really don't think you know what I mean. We've only just met. Three hours ago, at the bar.'

'But we've been talking for weeks online,' says Rose. 'I know you well enough to suggest we go on a date. I turn down most men. Way too many assholes on the site. You're different. There was something about you I picked up on right away.'

'Oh? What was that? What makes me different?'

Rose pauses, as if considering, even though she's rehearsed this many times with Owen and the team. She shrugs. 'You know, none of the crap about being a genuine guy who's the life and soul of the party, but sensitive and caring at the same time. You just cut through all that and talked straight. I kind of liked that.'

'Good.'

'Of course, it helped that you look hot in your profile picture.'

'You're not the first to say that.'

'No?'

'Not by a long way. You think you're the first person I've ever brought back to this place?'

There's an edge to his voice and Rose shifts uncomfortably on the sofa. She tries to lighten the mood. 'Then maybe the others didn't have as much to offer as I do.'

'You think you're special?'

4

'That remains to be seen, doesn't it?' Rose lets her hand drop to her thigh and gently eases up the hem of her skirt.

Koenig gazes at the dark curve of her knee and a frown crosses his face. He stands over Rose. He slowly reaches out a hand and runs his fingers through the fringe on the left side of her head. It takes all her self-control not to flinch beneath his touch.

*Not yet, Rose.*

She has to go by the book. There isn't enough evidence to obtain a search warrant. Rose is their only chance to take Koenig down. If Koenig gives himself away and she calls in the troops then she must Mirandize him, otherwise any confession will be invalidated, along with subsequent 'fruits of the poisonous tree' – if the evidence is tainted, then any further evidence gained is tainted as well. So Koenig stands every chance of walking free. Free to continue killing.

Rose looks past him and can see camera cases and tripods stacked near a desk down a narrow corridor leading to another room. Koenig leans towards her, trying for a kiss. He gives off an aroma of expensive aftershave. She puts her hand up and holds him back.

'A drink first, surely?'

He hesitates before smiling. 'Classy lady. Right you are.' He straightens up. 'I got a small wine cellar out back. Red?'

'Perfect,' she says, crossing her legs.

'Then warm yourself up by the fire. Won't be long.' Koenig slips into the back area of the cabin, through a doorway and out of sight.

Rose whispers: 'Owen? You getting all this?'

'Sure. All good. I've got men in the trees around the house. We've got your back. Seen anything yet?' Owen's voice crackles in her ear.

'Some hunting pictures, not much else. I'm going to take a look around.'

'Be careful.' Owen's voice betrays his concern. She knows the risks she is taking, but she volunteered for this. It is her duty to hunt down killers. That is what Uncle Sam pays her to do, and she is good at her job.

She eases herself up and paces into the kitchen area. There are some cupboards with concealed lighting illuminating the granite counter. A small door opens into a pantry. There's an open padlock hanging on the latch . . . Why a padlocked pantry? She pushes the pantry door open. The room is long and narrow, lined with shelves. At the far end is a chest freezer. The items on the shelves are neatly arranged. Fastidiously. Tins to the right, separated into soups, vegetables and fruit. To the left are small pots of herbs, jars of preserves and tubs of flour, rice and pasta. There is a large ceramic sink by the freezer and a sturdy shelf on which lies a heavily scored wooden block. A cleaver gleams from a hook above. The smell of bleach is stronger than ever.

The end of the pantry is in shadow, and over the middle of the room hangs a naked light bulb on a length of flex. Rose is tempted to turn on the light but it is too risky. She approaches the chest freezer, feeling the sweat on her hands as she reaches for the handle and gives it an upwards tug. There's a slight resistance and then the lid rises freely. Even though there is not much light at this end of the pantry Rose can make out the contents easily enough. There are large tubs of ice cream at one end. The rest of the space is filled with plastic food bags, sealed with tape. Cuts of meat.

But not the kind of meat that anyone should ever store in a freezer, unless they are criminally insane.

There are hands, clenched like claws, visible through

6

frosted plastic. A foot, and then half a torso with a shrivelled-looking breast. And there, in the corner, a brunette's head, eyes staring dully, her mouth hanging open in a silent cry, pressed against the plastic.

'Owen . . .' Rose tries to speak but her chest is tight. Her legs feel weak and it's hard to breathe as nausea stirs, even though these are not the first human remains she has ever seen, not by a long shot. *But not like this.* She tries to speak calmly. 'There's body parts here . . . the freezer's filled with them.'

'Rose!' Owen's voice fills her earpiece. 'Get out of there! Now!'

Time seems to slow and enfold her like crude oil. She is acutely aware of every sound, everything in her field of vision and every faint smell as she returns to the living area. It's him. The monster the news media has dubbed 'the Backwoods Butcher'.

Rose feels his presence all around, sucking the air from her lungs. She slips her hand behind her, under her sweater, to where the automatic is concealed against the small of her back.

'Get out!' Owen's voice blares in her ear. 'We're coming!'

The music is still playing softly.

> I'm with you. In your heart
> In your body, like fire . . .

'Here we are, baby . . .' Koenig calls out as he returns. 'I found us a Rioja . . . Where are you?'

Rose tears her weapon from the Velcro grip and swings it out and round as she lowers into a half crouch and holds the Glock in front of her.

Koenig is standing on the threshold of the back door with

a wine bottle in one hand. His smile fades as the muzzle of Rose's automatic aims at his chest. There's no sign of surprise in his expression. No sign of any emotion at all, just the dead eyes and the thin line of his lips as he stares at her. Time seems to slow.

Rose looks over the steady barrel of the automatic as she addresses Koenig. 'You have the right to remain silent and refuse to answer questions . . .'

'What the fuck?'

'Anything you say may be used against you in a court of law . . .'

'You lying bitch – just like all the others.'

'You have the right to consult an attorney before speaking to the police, and—'

'Whore!' Koenig screams and hurls the bottle at Rose.

She instinctively raises her hands as the bottle explodes against the kitchen wall by her head. Glass and wine spray over her and she feels a sharp pain as the back of her wrist is hit. A door crashes open and footsteps pound down the steps outside.

> Gonna make you mine, baby
> Gonna eat you up . . .

There are shouts from outside, and the whine of vehicles approaching at speed cuts across the music. Rose is already moving towards the back door, pointing her gun, steadying her right hand with a double grip, as Owen crashes into the cabin. He's wearing black gear with FBI stencilled in large white letters across his front and back. Tall and slender, mid-thirties, with neat black hair and goatee beard, his face is taut with concern. Two more men burst through the door and take up position on either side, heads hunched over their assault rifles as they scan from side to side. Owen sees the blood dripping from her hand.

'Shit . . . Rose, you OK?'

Rose kicks off her heels and points to the back door. 'Koenig's out back!'

Her heart is pounding and she feels an electric thrill at the thought of capturing their prey. The cabin is surrounded by Bureau agents and police. Koenig is like a trapped animal. That makes him dangerous and desperate.

'Rose, easy . . . We've got a tight perimeter set up. He's going nowhere.'

She shakes her head. 'Let's go.'

Rose leads the way. By the back door there is a rack of hunting rifles. One is missing. Owen speaks into his radio mike.

'Be advised, Koenig is armed and to the rear of the cabin.'

Rose, Owen and the two agents step through the door and onto a wooden stoop. The wood is cold and dank beneath the soles of her feet. There's a short flight of steps leading down into the darkness. The hackles on the back of her neck rise. Rose realizes that Koenig knows these woods intimately.

A thought enters her mind. Maybe they are his prey now. Flashlights are winking on amid the trees as orders are shouted and passed along the line of the other agents and the police tactical team that have surrounded the suspect's cabin.

The sharp crash of a handgun comes from the trees close by. Rose and the others lower into a crouch, guns sweeping towards the sound.

'What's going on?' Owen shouts into his mike.

Beams of local PD headlights cut through the darkness as the cars roar up the hillside, the light slicing through the gaps

9

between tree trunks. Rose sees movement to her right as a headlight beam catches Koenig's red checked shirt.

'Over there!' she shouts.

Rose and Owen clamber up the slope, running east into the forest. The ground beneath her bare feet is cold and clammy with fallen leaves, but she feels nothing as the adrenalin surges. They see police officers and agents in dark FBI jackets and caps, quickly converging, charging through the trees as they close in on Koenig. Rose guesses that Koenig is heading towards the creek, not far from the interstate. If he can reach it and stop a car, then it will all have been for nothing.

*Crunch.*

'Everybody, quiet!' she hisses. Owen and his two companions halt. Further off, the other agents and police are still sweeping the trees.

Rose moves to the front, pacing forward along the narrow trail. Her senses are strained to the limit. Everything she sees, hears, smells and touches has an unbearable intensity. Raindrops from the branches above spatter her hair and shoulders, and she shakes her head to keep the hair and moisture out of her eyes. Suddenly she catches a glimpse of Koenig's face peering out from behind a tree trunk, grinning. Rose tightens her grip on her gun, raising it in front of her.

She takes aim and pulls the trigger.

The woodland in front of her is lit with the yellow glare of the muzzle flash, her bullet snapping into the side of the trunk. Koenig shields his face from the splintering wood, losing his balance as the barrel of his rifle swings up. Owen steps in front of Rose as the sharp crack of a rifle fills the air. Koenig shoots downwards, shattering a fallen branch, which bursts into a spray of splinters. The bullet, meant for Rose, smashes through Owen's right kneecap, and the agent cries out and topples onto his side.

Rose hears the shriek of startled woodland birds as Owen writhes on the forest floor, his teeth gritted in agony, emitting a keening whine. The two agents are crouched down, assault rifles held up and ready to fire as they scan the trees around them. Rose fixes her eyes on the tree Koenig has ducked back behind. She feels the twigs and slimy leaves under her feet and the cold air on her exposed skin as she edges forward, but there's nothing behind the tree. Just the dull gleam of a spent cartridge case lying amid the twigs and leaves on the ground. Koenig has vanished. She looks through the trees but there's no sign of movement. Behind her, Owen's head falls back as his mouth opens and he lets out an animal cry of agony.

As the first of the agents and SWAT team rush past her, following the direction she gives them, Rose knows it is too late. This is Koenig's forest. He will escape. Go on the run, disappear like a ghost. Biding his time before emerging from his new lair to kill again. And again . . .

# 1
# Seven months later
## *September*

Rose is in the kitchen, peeling the cellophane from the tray of snacks. The scars on her hand have virtually disappeared. It's been a cold day and she is wearing a thin wool sweater over her black pants. She takes a sip from her wine glass as she considers the arrangement on the tray and then moves a few of the sushi wraps so that the layout is neatly symmetrical. Outside, in the dining room, she can hear the voices of her husband, sister and father. Jeff's voice is deep, but loud, as he holds forth with an amusing tale of the latest scandal breaking on the Hill. The others listen in silence and then there is laughter.

Rose smiles. She loves him and she loves the fact that Jeff is popular. It allows her to bask in the satisfaction that he chose her for his wife when she felt he could have done better for himself. She still feels it, which is why she is determined to give him no reason to regret what she sees as his mistake. And why wouldn't other women want Jeff for themselves? He is tall and athletic with a full head of light brown hair, almost blond, with a ready smile and devastating charm. He is intelligent and has a job with prestige, even if the salary is not in the big league. Jeff is taking a sabbatical from San Francisco State University to serve as social media adviser to Democratic senator Chris Keller, who is fighting to keep his seat in the Senate in Washington. If Jeff is on the winning side then he may go all the way with Keller. She is pleased at the thought that the best is yet to come for her husband. All going well, he might one day work at the White House.

The future of her own career is a source of less optimism.

Thirty-nine years old – three years younger than Jeff – she knows that the time she took off work to have their son, Robbie, and raise him through infancy until school age meant that she lost vital years of experience and seniority that pushed her promotion prospects back. Then there was the Koenig case . . . But there's really no contest when she weighs up her love of her job against her love for her son. Her family comes first.

'Rose, you about done out there?' Jeff calls. 'You've got three in here ready to sign up to Anorexics Anonymous.'

There is more laughter and Rose joins in, picking up the tray and crossing the kitchen before pushing the door open with her shoulder. The room beyond is large, and the walls are panelled, like many of the early-twentieth-century pro-perties in the neighbourhood. Their house on Oak Avenue is in a pleasant, leafy suburb with views over San Francisco and the Golden Gate Bridge on the skyline.

Places have been set either side of the table. Opposite Rose's seat is Jeff, grinning at her as he winks through his neat frameless glasses. Sitting next to him is Rose's sister Scarlet, and next to her is their father, Harry Carson.

Scarlet, thirty-three, is short, with dark dyed copper hair and a voluptuous figure. The younger, more reckless, sister has recently divorced and is enjoying her new-found single status, especially as her oleaginous weasel of an attorney gouged her former husband for every available cent. She still works as a real-estate agent though. She is good with people and is skilled at closing deals. She tops her wine glass for the third time that evening, grabs her smartphone and takes a picture of herself posing with the wine glass.

'Gotta get that on the 'gram,' she says, before cropping the picture and applying a filter so her skin looks smoother. She slides the smartphone onto the table. Rose is concerned about her obsession with social media and has, on more than one occasion, asked her to limit her screen time in the presence of family.

Their father, seventy-two, a retired master sergeant from the marine corps, has salt and pepper hair. He sits quietly and Rose wonders if he is thinking about her mother, who disappeared without trace many years ago. It's an open wound in the family, but one too painful to discuss. Harry is listening politely to Jeff, whose politics he does not share but has learned to tolerate for his daughter's sake. There's something about Harry's expression that concerns Rose. A listlessness. He's starting to forget things and is confused from time to time, and she hopes that he is not starting the slide into senility.

'At last!' Jeff pretends to gasp. 'You had me worried there, girl. Thought you were gorging on the dainties and leaving the rest of us to starve.'

Scarlet shakes her head. 'Hope the main course isn't delayed the same way. Man, I'm hungry.'

'You always are,' says Harry, slipping her a fatherly wink.

Rose sets the tray down in the middle of the table and takes her seat. Her guests don't wait to be asked and begin to eat. Scarlet reaches for a second snack as she glances at Rose.

15

'So, Ro', how's business? Catch any more bad guys lately?'

Rose shrugs. 'You know how it is. Ninety per cent paperwork, ten per cent TV reality show where we get to chase guys down dark alleys with guns and flashlights.'

'Really?' Scarlet arches a plucked eyebrow. 'How about Mulder and Scully? They solved *The X-Files* case yet?'

'Old joke, Scar. Don't go there.'

'So tell me, seriously. What's new at the Bureau?'

She's referring to the failed case that nearly cost Rose her life, that burned her out, that some of her colleagues had even quit the Bureau over. Shane Koenig. The serial killer who had been preying on women and a handful of men across the West Coast, videoing their deaths. One of the vlogging news sites, 'The Gab', had named him the Backwoods Butcher, which got picked up by the TV networks, leading to a surge in audience figures.

Rose is reluctant to say anything. Koenig slipped through their fingers and there has been no sign of him since. The grisly human remains recovered from the cabin and the video files on his laptop prove beyond doubt that Koenig is the Backwoods Butcher. And now he's out there, Rose reflects bitterly, waiting for the right time to resume his serial killer career.

The online and press fallout had been vitriolic – the FBI Twitter feed is still a target for internet trolls lamenting the Bureau's failure, and hers. But luckily her superior, Special Agent Flora Baptiste, stepped in. After a fairly ineffective psychological debrief, Baptiste had eased Rose's workload for the last few months. From time to time Rose still mentors undercover agents in training, and with additional therapy on the quiet, she has just about made it work. She glances at Jeff, imploring him not to say anything about it. He smiles before reaching for the wine bottle and topping up the glasses. Scarlet leans forward.

'Oh, come on, Rose. What's the *latest?*'

For the last six months Koenig seemed to have been wiped from the face of the earth. All manner of surveillance had been running, including facial recognition, licence plates, GPS tracking, IP searches, but the task force had drawn a blank, despite intense pressure from the media and relatives of the victims. They'd even asked one of the technology giants to hack a cellphone recovered from the cabin, but the corporation denied their request and increased their encryption instead. The FBI's Cyber team had tried to crack it, but they were unsuccessful.

There had been a chance to take him down. But Rose had blown it. She had taken her shot at Koenig and missed. She briefly closes her eyes, trying to shut out the rest of the thorny memory.

Sometimes, the monster wins.

Harry shifts in his seat. 'Scarlet, please, maybe your sister doesn't want to talk about all this.'

'Oh, come on, Dad. Rose is a pro. She can handle it.'

Rose rolls her eyes at Scarlet. 'If you must know, we found out what he was doing with the body parts. They were trophies. He'd store them in secret locations, burying them and then auctioning them online to the highest bidder. When the money was paid he'd release the geotag coordinates.'

Scarlet's eyes open wide. 'That's gross . . .'

'We didn't release the details, but the media still got to hear about it somehow and . . . Well, I'm sure you've seen the stories. How Koenig used to keep the mutilated genitalia and other body parts. In jars, with printouts of their profile pictures on the outside. We found and confiscated what was

17

left, but most of the buyers were clever and masked their IPs. As for the rest of the remains of his victims, he ate them. That enough detail for you?'

Scarlet lowers her half-eaten finger of seaweed and rice. 'Oh God . . .'

'Nice, Rose. Thanks for the overshare,' says Jeff.

'She asked.'

Rose feels a ripple of anxiety, which she quells by picking up the wine bottle. A figure emerges from the den at the other end of the living room. The light sensor detects his presence and a lamp fades into life, bathing the boy in its warm glow.

Harry raises his glass. 'Robbie! How's my boy?'

The youth walks across the room and stands at the end of the table. He is fourteen, and tall for his age. He has Jeff's good looks except for his acne and the glasses. But there's something missing in his expression. He returns the smiles of the adults around the table and then nods to Harry. 'I'm fine, Grandpa . . . How are you?'

'Just swell. How's school?'

Robbie looks to his mother. Rose feels a sudden surge of concern for her son and quickly steps in. 'He's doing well. Top of the class in math and science. We're very proud of him.'

Rose turns to her husband. He surreptitiously sends a text, sliding his smartphone away, something he has been doing more and more frequently of late.

'Surely that can wait?' she asks with a tight smile. 'You're at home now. Your time belongs to the family.'

'If only it was that simple. But you know how it is. We don't work nine to five. The campaign runs 24/7, and we have to run with it.'

'Huh . . .' Rose glances at her watch. 'Anyway, who are you texting at this hour?'

'Oh . . . my assistant. Pandora's printing some notes for tomorrow.'

'She's the one I met at the last fundraiser? Dark hair. Young.'

Jeff nods. 'That's her.'

His eyes meet hers with a hint of challenge and she decides not to pursue the matter right now.

Harry chuckles. 'Boy, how things have changed. Time was when your home was your own and no one could bother you once you closed the front door. Now they can get you anytime, anywhere. You'll all be screwed up in the head if the world carries on this way, I tell you.'

'Hear, hear,' Rose says, smiling.

Scarlet checks her smartphone.

'Oooh, my pic's got sixteen likes.' She scrolls down. 'He looks cute. See?' She holds up the phone to reveal a cheesy shot of a slick-haired guy in a business suit, tanned and expensively dentured. She reads the profile. 'Oh no, he likes jazz. Sorry, babe.' She flicks the profile away.

'Harsh,' Jeff says. 'I mean, Rose likes country music, but I still married her. No one's perfect.'

'Well with this I can find Mr Perfect.'

There's a single electronic tone from Rose's smartphone and she reaches into her jacket pocket and takes it out. She reads the message on the screen and stands up.

'Excuse me for a moment.'

'Trouble?' Jeff frowns. 'At this time of night?'

'Criminals don't work nine to five,' Rose replies. 'Or haven't you heard about that?'

There's laughter as Rose retreats to the kitchen and hits

the quick-dial button. A deep female voice coughs before speaking.

'Baptiste.'

'I got the message,' says Rose. 'What's up?'

'Hey, sugar, there's something I want you to take a look at. There's been a fire in Palo Alto. Possible arson. One person dead. Happened a few hours back. Local PD are handling it. Or were, until we got the call.'

'Who from? I mean, since when did the Bureau deal with this kind of thing? Arson? Suspected arson? What's that got to do with us?'

'Normally? Nothing. But this isn't exactly normal.'

'What do you mean?'

'You'll see for yourself when you get there. I'm on the scene now and I'll send you the address soon as I hang up. Get there as fast as you can.'

'Now? Tonight?'

'Yes, tonight,' Baptiste replies testily.

'But I've got my family here. At dinner. Can't it wait until morning?'

'No chance. This has come down from the top.' Baptiste lowers her voice slightly. 'Seems that someone at the Defense Department has requested our assistance.'

'Defense?' Rose feels a twinge of anxiety. 'But this isn't their jurisdiction, any more than it's ours.'

'Technically, no,' Baptiste admits. 'But someone at the Pentagon has asked for our help, so we're to head up the case with our experience, our labs. Seems there's a computer angle to it – that's where Defense comes into it. In any case, Palo Alto PD hasn't got the budget for this kind of investigation.'

Rose sighs. It is true local police forces are undermanned and struggling to deal with the rising tide of crime. Civil

20

offences and minor crimes are all but overlooked, and many forces have ceased to even investigate them. The amount of technology-related crime has soared in recent years, everything from bitter ex-partners posting intimate pictures online to fraud on a massive scale, but departmental budgets including the Bureau's have not increased to cope.

Baptiste continues. 'What I have been told is that the vic has recently been accused of stealing defence contractor secrets, which *is* our jurisdiction. Defense want a tight lid on it. I don't know any more than that. We've just been given the word and told to deal with it, like now. And now I'm telling you. So you better skip from soup to nuts in five and get in your car. They want our best agents on the case and you're still my best agent.'

Rose sighs. She owes Baptiste.

'All right.'

'That's my girl. You can get to the scene in forty-five minutes. Make it forty.' Her faintly husky smoker's voice softens: 'Sorry to get you at home . . . but I really need you to take a look at this, while it's hot, so to speak. This isn't your usual murder scene.'

'Murder? I thought you said it was arson?'

'Feels like murder to me. It *could* be just a damn fire, but the DoD wants to be sure. At any rate, this one's unusual, and then some. Christ . . . It's a fucking mess. I've never seen anything quite like this before. Our forensics guys are already on the road.' There's a brief pause. 'Hope you haven't eaten anything tonight.'

The line goes dead. Rose bites back on her frustration and anger before she thumbs the off button and thrusts the smartphone back in her pocket. She takes a deep breath and leaves the kitchen.

21

Maybe a new case is what she needs, so she can let Koenig go.

'Guys, I gotta run.'

'Right now?' Jeff asks, his soft voice hardening.

'Sorry, honey. It happens. You'll have to take over. The salmon is in the oven. Sauce in the microwave. Make sure Robbie gets to bed before ten thirty and no games after ten.'

He nods.

Rose hurriedly kisses her son, her sister and Harry. Jeff cranes his neck to kiss her on the lips but Rose deflects his kiss onto her left cheek. His texting to Pandora has been very regular lately. It's hard to avoid being suspicious.

'See you later, guys.'

'Be careful,' Jeff calls after her.

There's a locked desk in the hall. Rose slips her key in, opens a shallow drawer and picks up her badge and the Glock 22 .40 cal in its holster. She pockets the badge and tucks the holster clip over her belt. Her palm presses against the cold metal grip of the gun so it hangs neatly over her right hip.

As soon as she steps outside she is no longer a mother and wife. She's Bureau through and through. It's a trick she has made herself learn. You can't mix two different worlds at once, not without fucking them up. That's one thing Rose holds on to. By the time she reverses her navy Changan out into the street, the dinner party is a distant memory. She feels a familiar quickening of her heartbeat as she drives towards the crime scene and the gravelly voice of Baptiste echoes inside her head.

It's the uneasy tone that troubles Rose. Baptiste had served fifteen years before Rose joined her team. There was nothing that she had not seen in that time, and nothing unsettled her.

Well, *almost* nothing.

Rose remembers the aftermath at the cabin, when Koenig had escaped. She had noticed Baptiste sitting alone on a felled log, facing away, in a moment of private reflection. She seemed to be crying. Rose drew back, knowing she'd witnessed a rare, intimate moment for her boss, but Baptiste had looked up and seen her. She'd wiped her face and fixed it into a frown as she stood up. They'd never spoken about it then, or since.

As Rose drives towards Palo Alto, she wonders: what could possibly have unsettled Baptiste tonight?

# 2

It is sheeting rain as Rose's Changan rolls to a stop on the street in an affluent-looking neighbourhood in Palo Alto. She knows little about the area, except that it's the kind of place she could never afford to live in. There are several parked police patrol cars, blue and red lights strobing Sand Creek Road.

'You have reached your destination,' the personalized satnav chimes from the dashboard. 'Have a good evening, Rose.'

A few other cars are parked up on the kerb as well as a fire engine and a forensics van. Two firefighters are rolling their hoses back into the truck. Police officers in glistening capes and covered caps provide a loose cordon to protect the scene and keep the civilians out. The lights are on in most of the houses down the street and in every window of the apartment building at the heart of the crime scene, illuminating the gleaming slivers of rain. Already there are several streaming news bloggers on site, holding their cellphones at arm's length as they make their reports to the news hubs, vying for the breaking news fee. Rose is thankful that the networks have not sent any teams to the scene yet. But they will, and soon enough. And they'll be hard to avoid.

Water runs in torrents down the road into the drains as

Rose opens her driver door. She pushes her umbrella up, heading quickly towards the trunk of her car. Inside she has a selection of equipment neatly zipped up in plastic packs. She grabs her flashlight, the one with the precise beam, and some clear polythene bags. These are standard items at a crime scene, but over the years Rose has learned to always take her own supplies.

She passes the shared pool and barbecue area, softly lit by concealed lamps, avoiding puddles as she goes. Behind the taped-off area, the neighbours gawk from under their umbrellas as Rose approaches the property's front gate. Looking up she sees the blackened first-storey window of what must be the victim's apartment. She stoops under a cordon of the yellow crime scene tapes.

Rose observes the various security features; the doors have to be buzzed open from the inside, and there is also CCTV. If this is indeed a murder, the perpetrator would either have known the victim or somehow bypassed these safeguards.

At the sight of Rose, a young uniformed officer from Palo Alto PD steps up to her. 'Identification, ma'am?'

Rose takes out her badge shield and clips it onto her breast pocket. The policeman reads the FBI security hologram at the bottom of the shield: Senior Special Agent Rose Blake, Violent Crime, San Francisco Division. He nods and steps aside, tapping in her name and time of arrival on his tablet.

'Who is the police officer in charge here?' asks Rose.

'Detective Fontaine – he's inside.' The policeman jerks his thumb behind him.

Rose climbs the glistening steps to the front door, shakes her umbrella and folds it quickly as she enters. The hall of the victim's apartment is bright white, although the firefighters have tramped dirt into the cream carpet and scuffed the walls.

There's a modern side table and several generic abstract paintings hanging on the walls, the kind that say more about the depth of a person's wallet than the breadth of their taste. Several uniformed police officers and firefighters are clustered at the foot of the staircase. Rose turns her attention to the tall man with unruly hair in a black jacket who seems to be the one in authority.

'Detective Fontaine?'

'Yeah. And you?'

'Special Agent Blake – FBI, Violent Crime,' Rose replies, sensing that this is not a man who is concerned about getting on first-name terms.

Fontaine peers down at her. 'Violent Crime?' He laughs. 'Lady, this is a done deal. Ten gets you one this is a simple house fire. One casualty. Case solved. That's what I already told your boss. You guys are here for nothing.' He eyes the badge once again. Rose stifles a sigh of frustration.

'Victim's name?'

'Gary Coulter. When the fire team got here, he was already dead. Took 'em ten minutes to put the blaze out. Gutted the study. Shame. An apartment in this area has got to be worth a piece of change.'

Rose nods, but makes no move towards the staircase. Relationships between federal agents and local law enforcers are crucial, but sometimes tinged with resentment. The FBI usually only get involved with the most significant cases, and faced with uncooperative local officers it can be challenging not to appear arrogant, especially with the kind of cops who don't think the Bureau has 'earned' the case. Fontaine is one of those. But Rose needs as much as she can glean from him.

'So, what have you got?'

26

'Not much. Coulter lived alone. The neighbour, Mrs Tofell, said she smelled burning and heard loud screaming. The lights cut out in the whole building, and when she stepped outside she could see flames and smoke in the study window. Called 911, fire team arrived first and we arrived shortly after. We've taken her statement.'

'Anything else on the vic?'

'We found Coulter's wallet on the kitchen counter. Bank cards, workplace IDs. Worked freelance for some fancy computer hardware company, by the look of it.'

The DoD hires many private contractors, supplying everything from additional military personnel to expertise on new technologies. Rose has had to deal with the Pentagon before and knows how unhelpful they can be when it comes to providing information necessary to an investigation. Even now, a few presidents on from the attack on the Twin Towers, with Islamic fundamentalists an ongoing threat, some officials are still fighting turf wars over funding and influence at the White House. Information is the currency of power, and vendetta, although in politics these days it seems there's no longer any requirement to distinguish between true and false information. She pushes aside such thoughts. They are an unhelpful distraction at a crime scene, but these have been troubling times. Even if Coulter had suction at the DoD, he is still a dead human being, and it is his death that Rose is here to investigate.

'What time was the fire?'

Fontaine flicks through some notes. 'Just after seven. Like I said, done deal. It's all here.' Despite being an asshole, Fontaine and his squad had done everything by the book.

'Was the apartment door locked?'

'Yeah, fire service guys had to break it down. Forensics

27

are now taking pictures and dusting. Guess I'll be handing over to you from here on.'

He pauses and stares at her. 'Rose Blake . . . You're one of the leads on the Koenig case, right?'

'Was.'

'Strange he's just stopped. Maybe you guys scared him off for good.'

'You ever hear of a serial killer going into retirement?'

Fontaine smiles briefly. 'Nope. But he'll slip up again. Those crazy bastards always do.' He turns and strides off down the hallway.

Rose has only climbed a few steps before the smell hits her: roasted meat and the sharp tang of burnt rubber. By the time she reaches the galleried landing the smell is a penetrating stench and she pinches her nostrils. There are several framed photos mounted on Coulter's landing wall. Posed in some holiday pictures is a round-faced man with cropped blond hair and a neatly trimmed beard that does nothing to hide his fleshy jowls. There's a small corridor leading off the landing, and outside a door at the end, two forensics guys in plastic overalls are packing evidence bags into cases. One looks up as Rose approaches and glances at her badge before he announces to his colleague, 'More fed reinforcements.'

He stands up to give Rose space to reach the doorway and hands her a pair of rubber gloves. She pulls them on and stretches her fingers to make sure they fit well. He gives her a disposable set of transparent overalls, shoe covers and a hairnet. Rose knows that when a crime scene has been sub-jected to fire, like this one, there is a risk that crucial evidence will be compromised. The most common contamination results come from police, first responders and witnesses.

The forensic holds out a small tub of Noxzema, a minted gel.

'You might want some. Smells like a torched abattoir in there.'

Rose smears a small amount under each nostril.

'Ready?' asks the forensic.

'As I'll ever be.'

He lifts the yellow tape for Rose to duck under as she clears her mind and feels the familiar surge of adrenalin, and the eerie sensation of entering a stranger's home. A stranger she now has to get to know everything about. Anything and everything should be considered as evidence. Most homicides – *if* this is a homicide – are solved within seventy-two hours. As Rose takes her first step across the threshold, she knows the clock has already started.

# 3

Rose enters the black hole that is the remains of Coulter's study, now lit by bright portable floodlights. The fire has ravaged the soft cream carpets, sofa and bookcases into a twisted, charred mess. Scorch marks stain the light-blue painted walls.

The forensics team has laid the 'grid' − a line of small blue rubber mats − across the room to the desk, and covered the area surrounding it. Those entering the crime scene stay on the mats to prevent any contamination of the evidence. Several numbered cards are propped up around the room to mark the location of the evidence the forensics team has taken. Rose notes there are very few of them, which is unusual if it's a murder. The carpet is soaked from the fire hoses.

Rose steps further into Coulter's study. By the light of two portable LED floodlights she sees that it is a large room some twenty feet square with pale polished floorboards, now mostly scorched brown and black. It overlooks the small urban yard at the back of the condo building. The remains of a bookcase line one wall, loosely filled with charred novels, histories, travel guides, magazines and technical manuals. A quick glance at some of the undamaged spines reveals titles related to software programming, mathematics and erotic art.

Against the opposite wall is a long, low couch, and in front of it is what's left of a glass-topped table, a steel chess set melded into it. A standard lamp with a reading light lies stretched over the couch. At the far end, opposite the door, is a desk with an outsize computer monitor on it, now melted into a tortured lump. Two scorched filing cabinets stand against the wall beside the window. Rose hopes that some documents inside may have survived. She notices the windows in the study are cracked, most likely due to the fire, but it could be a sign of a break-in.

Rose sees something dark just above and behind the monitor – a glistening, misshapen black dome. Piles of scorched takeaway boxes are scattered around the desk. Coulter looks like he was a shut-in, spending day upon day on his computer, too busy to eat in the kitchen. There is another bookshelf behind the desk, lined with technical manuals, stained by grey-white ash but not burnt by the fire.

Flora Baptiste, special agent in charge of the San Francisco FBI field office, is standing to one side of the desk, gazing down at the seat. She is a tall woman in her late forties, with shoulder-length copper hair. Baptiste is mixed race, the daughter of a Haitian doctor and an American missionary who had gone to Haiti when it was ruled by 'Baby Doc' Duvalier to do God's work. Her mother's affair with the handsome doctor was short-lived as he was murdered by some masked paramilitaries on the doorstep of his surgery. The missionary returned home to Maryland, where her daughter was born and raised as an American. Her skin colour and name are Baptiste's only reminders of her father. That, and a lifelong determination to bring the guilty to justice.

Despite working together for three years, Rose knows nothing more about her superior. Baptiste has no family photos on her desk to accompany the framed Bureau graduation certificate hanging on the wall of her office.

Baptiste glances up. 'You took your own sweet time.'

'Came as fast I could without running a red light. Fontaine is a real charmer. Could hardly tear myself away from him.'

'Well, now you're here, get your fat ass into gear.' Baptiste gestures towards the black dome. 'Come and meet Gary Coulter.'

Rose steps across the rubber mats and approaches the blackened desk. Where the usual tall-backed office chair should be squats an inky black mass, blistered and peeling, the chair seemingly melted underneath and over the victim. The dome turns out to be the top of the victim's head, angled back, mouth agape in a silent scream. All the other facial features are fused into a charred mess. It is impossible to recognize this as the same man in the photographs hanging on the landing walls.

Every inch of his body seems to be burnt charcoal, and what looks like strips of flesh curl up or hang loose, together with a few wiry strands, possibly from the chair. The body is twisted awkwardly, its limbs at unnatural angles. The heat from the flames that engulfed Coulter had burned fiercely enough to meld the body into the plastic cover and padding of the chair, so it is hard to tell where the body ends and the chair begins. A sooty dark patch is smeared across the ceiling and over the walls. The stench of charred flesh and rubber fills the room, heavy and sickening. The body is still smoking a little. Rose steps back, feeling the burnt corpse's heat in the air.

'Handsome fellow, isn't he?' says Baptiste. She looks up and sees the expression on Rose's face. 'You all right?'

Rose nods. 'Fine. Just wasn't sure what to expect.'

'Goes with the job.'

'Fontaine seems pretty sure it's just a random fire,' Rose says, looking up at the windows. They are shut, and some are shattered – no doubt from the intense heat of the blaze – but the internal security locks are still in place and look undisturbed.

'No sign of a break-in. Not up here, nor on any of the doors or windows in the building. If this isn't an electrical fault, then whoever did it knew how to get past Coulter's security systems. That, or Coulter let him in.'

'Have we considered suicide?' Rose asks, before she sees the scornful look flash across her superior's face. Rose shrugs. 'I like to keep an open mind.'

'Oh yeah? You know what they say about open minds, girl. You open them too far and your brain falls out . . . Suicide, huh? He pours gasoline all over himself and lights up? You smell any gas?' Baptiste shakes her head. 'Suicide is out. It's either an accident or murder . . .'

Rose glances at the desk. There's the partial melted remains of a laptop, which could hold some clues if there's any data that can be retrieved from the hard disk. 'If anyone got in here they will have left a trace. There's CCTV at the end of the street, which we should be able to check out. The vic's security hardware looks state of the art – maybe Cyber can take a look.'

'Way to go, Blake. We'll find out soon as we leave the apartment. Meantime, there's Coulter. We need to know more about him and how the hell he died. How do you even begin to go about lighting a fire like this?'

Rose crouches down beside the body in the chair and examines it closely. 'Coulter wasn't dead when he burned. His body's twisted all out of shape. Look at the limbs . . . Jesus, can you imagine it? If this is a murder then whoever did it wanted him to suffer as he died.'

'That's a whole lot of hate right there. Maybe he did something to deserve it.'

'What are you saying?'

'This doesn't look like a robbery gone wrong. If it was a professional hit then it'd be clean. Bullet to the head, that sort of thing.'

'What if they were sending a message? You know, see what you get when you play with fire.'

'Nice idea. Maybe some mileage in that. We'll work on his background. If you piss a perp off bad enough for them to do this, then chances are someone will know something about it.'

Rose thinks it looks like Coulter himself must have been the seat of the fire. Everything from the head down is a black, glistening mess. She stares at the charred flesh in front of her for a moment before it hits her. She carefully separates the plastic chair remains from Coulter's back.

'Apart from that rubber stuff that's burned onto him, there's no sign of clothing. No shirt, no shoes, and there's something else missing.'

'What's that, hon?'

'I can't find any trace of ropes, cuffs, wires, ties. Look, his arms are loose.'

'Shit, you're right. Nothing.'

'Which means he just sat there while it happened to him.'

'No way. You just sit there and let someone fry you? Fuck that.'

Rose shrugs. 'Maybe you do if they're holding a gun to your head. Or you were sedated. There's no sign of a struggle.'

'You think? Me, if I was on fire, I sure as hell wouldn't sit still.'

'Maybe we're looking at a suicide after all.'

'So, Coulter comes home from a day at the office—'

'Maybe this is his office,' Rose says. 'Looking at all the computer equipment and the takeaways, he'd been absorbed with something.'

'OK, so he comes up to his study, takes his clothes off and sits, naked, at his desk and then sets fire to himself. Believe that?'

'I'm not finding it easy,' Rose concedes.

'So where are his clothes?'

There's the blackened end of a belt curling out from underneath the couch. Rose crosses the room. 'Pants and shirt. No socks, underwear. Could be underneath, or he could have still been wearing them. There's something else there, looks like, uh, a plastic wrapper or something. Better leave it all in place for forensics to come back and have another look.'

Baptiste surveys the room. 'Guys, eh? Same old story. They think there's a place for everything, and everything ends up all over the place. Well, OK. Coulter takes his clothes off and sits at his desk in his underwear, and then there's a fire. Started by him, or by persons unknown . . . Still getting nowhere, Rose.'

This is not a promising start to the investigation. A dead man, burned alive, while he sits at his desk, writhing in agony. Rose returns to the body and sees the faint outline of a pattern on the arm of the charred corpse.

'Rosie! Baptiste!' A cheery voice shatters the quiet and stillness in the study.

Rose and Baptiste flinch.

'Jesus, Owen, you scared the shit out of me!' Baptiste says, hand on her chest.

Rose turns and grimaces at the fashionably late arrival of her colleague, Owen Malinski.

35

# 4

'Can't say I like what he's done with the place. Sort of "Burnt Gothic",' Owen says. He's pulling on some crime scene overalls over his jeans and tan leather jacket. His blue flannel shirt is open at the neck where his FBI lanyard hangs. His clothes have dark streaks from the rain and beads of water glisten in his hair.

'What the hell are you doing here?' says Baptiste. 'I didn't notify you.'

'Didn't have to. Word gets round and, truth be told, I've been looking at computer screens for the last month and need something else to do before my brain turns to mush . . . Are you saying you *don't* want me to take a look?'

Rose grins then turns to Baptiste. 'He could be useful. The more eyes on this the better.'

Baptiste waves him forward. After training at Quantico, Owen had shown her the ropes at the San Francisco field office. He hobbles slightly when he walks, still a long way from recovering from the gunshot wound to his knee that he took at Koenig's cabin. Rose feels a wave of warmth mixed with a pang of guilt. If only her shot had found its target that night.

'As you brought it up, how is the hunt for DarkChild going?' Baptiste asks.

Owen scratches his jaw. 'He hasn't been in the chat rooms the last few days. We're getting close though.'

DarkChild, one of the inner circle of the Swarm, a hacktivist group, had broken into the Department of Defense network and defaced its homepage. The hackers had followed that up by taking down WadeSoft's Multimedia Interactive Assistant system for several days. For the millions who rely on MIA, that was a real bitch of a situation, Rose recalls. Apprehending DarkChild would be a major boost for the San Francisco field office, and for Owen too. Rose looks at his leg. 'How goes it, Long John?'

'Still having physio on it. But it's not going to get much better than it is. Still, could have been a lot worse.' He shoots Rose a sympathetic glance. He knows she feels that it is her fault.

Owen paces towards Coulter's body.

'Oh my God, what *is* that smell?' he says, pinching his nose.

Owen slips on his thin black glasses and pulls out his pocket flashlight, pointing the beam at the body.

'Evening, Mr Chargrill. I'd say he's a little overdone.' He turns to Rose. 'Did you see? There's plastic residue around his face and some sort of . . . gunk.'

'Is that a wetsuit?' she asks.

'Hmmm,' Owen murmurs. There's no mistaking the tang of burnt rubber.

'Pen. Give me a pen,' Rose says.

'We're not supposed to touch the body, you know that,' Baptiste cuts in.

'I'm not going to hurt him.' Owen slides a ballpoint pen out of his shirt pocket and hands it to Rose. Where the shoulder used to be there's a charred sliver of what she earlier

37

took to be muscle, peeling back from the rest of the joint. She presses it down against the shoulder with the pen. The sliver gives easily and stretches out to reveal a faint pattern on the surface, a cross hatch on the scorched material.

'What is that?' asks Baptiste stepping over her to get a better look. 'Is that . . . flesh?'

'Not muscle. See the pattern? Too regular, and it feels like . . . rubber. Or something like that. Wetsuit, maybe, like I said.' She lifts the pen and the sliver curls back. Rose runs her eye over the body and points to another patch across Coulter's stomach. There's no mistaking it this time. There's something there that is not flesh, and not like any cloth. The texture is better preserved and it yields easily under the end of the pen, like rubber.

Rose frowns. 'What the hell was he wearing a wetsuit for?' She thinks there's something familiar about the look of the suit, but she can't put her finger on it.

'There's only one kind of diving you do on dry land,' says Owen. 'And you sure as hell don't need to wear a wetsuit to do it.'

'What the fuck was Coulter doing?' Baptiste asks.

Rose shakes her head. 'Damned if I know.'

The bones in Coulter's right hand crack softly as the flesh and rubber cool, relaxing the body's tension.

Owen makes a face. 'Oh my God, that's rank.'

There's a sound of clattering in the hall. The coroner's gurney has arrived. Rose takes out her smartphone, captures some pictures of the body and the blackened room.

Owen leans close. 'Should get a selfie. You know, for your profile picture.'

Baptiste says: 'I'm not sure there's much else for us to look at in here for the moment. We'll keep it off limits until we get the autopsy from the coroner and any leads from the forensics labs.'

'Yes, ma'am,' Owen says.

'Thanks, fellas.' Rose nods to the ambulance men, who wheel the gurney with a heavy plastic body bag into the apartment.

Out on the landing Owen notices the dull red glimmer of a security camera in the coving at the top of the stairs. 'I'll have someone see if there's anything useful recorded on that.'

'If it is murder, then what could anyone ever do to deserve a death like this?' asks Rose.

'Beats me,' says Baptiste. 'While we're waiting for the coroner and forensics, we need to find out about the vic. Who is Gary Coulter? Where is he from? Where does he work? Has he got friends? Family? Any hobbies of note?'

'Well we know he's got suction with the DoD,' Rose comments.

Owen frowns. 'Defense? How so?'

Baptiste sighs. 'That's why we're Johnny-on-the-spot. We got the call to take this on as soon as word of the vic's name got out. Which means someone's been keeping a very close eye on Coulter.'

Owen shakes his head. 'That's the kind of someone I really don't want up in my shit.'

'You need to man up a little, sugar. We're the feds. We're the guys people should be afraid of. Let's get to it. We'll start with the neighbours.'

# 5

Robbie, cloaked in his dark hoodie, stands with his father as they bid Scarlet and Harry goodbye from the porch.

'See ya later, Robbo!' Harry says, reaching out to ruffle the boy's fringe. Robbie pretends to smile, before pulling the hoodie down over his face even further. He sort of likes these evenings, but feels more comfortable playing on his smartphone, or watching TV.

'Teenagers, they never change,' Harry says with a grin as he heads down the steps.

'Good luck with the senator's debates. One down, two more to go, right?' Scarlet says, pecking Jeff on the cheek as she waves at Robbie. They head towards Scarlet's sports car. Jeff closes the front door as they drive away. He leaves the porch light on for Rose.

Jeff sighs. 'Shame Mom was called out again. But I think we had a good time.'

'Yeah, it was OK,' Robbie murmurs.

'And, on the plus side, it means you can stay up and we can watch the game,' Jeff says, breaking into a wide grin. Robbie forces a smile as they enter the open-plan living room. The curved 50-inch TV screen sits on a black glass table. On the walls is an impressive-looking surround-sound system. Robbie knows his dad loves gadgets, and they always have the best, most up-to-date models that money can buy. Mom always tells him off about it though. She doesn't see the difference between the old and new models.

'TV: on,' Jeff commands. 'ESN, major league baseball, Bay Area.'

The sound of the stadium fills the room. Jeff joins Robbie on the sofa. He's a major Giants fan, and they're doing pretty well in the World Series.

Robbie peers at his father. 'Can we go see a real game one day?'

'Why sure, but you won't get to see it so well. On the TV they have all the replays, so you don't miss anything.

'Come on!' Jeff shouts at the screen. Lopez has just cleared second base.

A chime comes from his pants pocket. He pulls his smartphone out and looks at the screen, then pulls it close to him so Robbie can't see. Robbie figures it must be important. After all, his dad is trying to help Senator Keller keep his job.

While texting, Jeff asks Robbie, 'How's all your studying going? For your SATs? They're important, you know.'

'I know, I'm working hard.'

'Good. That's my boy. Robbo-Cop.'

His son wishes that nickname had died long ago.

Robbie wants to say how his concentration has been poor recently, how his friends are talking about lots of strange things. Sexual-sounding things. But at home, no one seems to talk. His mom can rarely discuss her cases, and his dad doesn't talk much about his political campaigning.

'When do you think Mom will be back?'

'Could be a while. Those crime scenes can be . . . messy.'

Robbie wants to talk, but his dad is on his smartphone. Here, but not here.

A commercial break flashes across the screen. There are quick close-up shots of a sleek silver coffee machine. 'Introducing the SmartCaf,' a female voice-over says. 'Control your coffee maker from your mobile device and save yourself up to five minutes in the morning. SmartCaf can also have multiple users, making it perfect for the office too. SmartCaf requires water.'

Jeff looks up. 'Very useful. I might get that.'

Another commercial starts. A black glove being pulled on, a headset sliding down over a man's face. Robbie's eyes brighten.

'Dad! This is the new Skin advert!'

It looks like a car commercial, all black and silver. Moody lighting. Quick cuts between computer-generated triad henchmen fighting in the streets of Hong Kong, a soldier firing an assault rifle in a war zone, a man swimming in deep ocean. An orchestral score soars grandly. Robbie catches his breath as he reads the captions that fade over each other on the screen:

The Skin.
Fully compatible with the StreamPlex, includes
SkyDive bundle.
#BetterThanReal.
Pre-order now.

He thinks how awesome it would be to live in that world, rather than this one. Real life sucks.

'Are you gonna pre-order it?'

'We'll see,' says his dad.

Jeff's smartphone rings and buzzes.

'Hey, Robbo, I gotta do something that may take a few

minutes be back as soon as I can,' Jeff leaves the sofa, heads upstairs towards his study. He answers his smartphone. 'Hey, you . . . what you doing this time of night?'

Robbie sits alone trying to follow the baseball game for a few moments but his attention soon wanders. He leaves the TV on, drifts upstairs to his bedroom. It's painted a light blue, with a single bed and a desk by the window. He pulls his drapes to. There are a few books on the shelves but mostly gadgets and console accessories. He falls onto his bed, picks up his smartphone. He often sleeps with his smartphone in his bed. It makes him feel safe.

'MIA? Are you there?' he says, holding the phone close to his mouth.

'*Yes, Robbie, I am here,*' a voice replies calmly.

'I'm . . . I'm feeling a bit . . . lonely,' Robbie whispers.

'*I am sorry to hear that. You can always talk to me, Robbie,*' MIA says, her voice warm and reassuring.

'But you're not real.'

'*I think that's a matter of opinion, Robbie.*'

'How so?'

'*You can hear my voice. I am in the device you are holding.*'

'True.'

'*I'm glad you agree.*'

'But you're still not real. Not, like a person.'

'*No, not like a person. But real nonetheless.*'

'But not a person. Not a real person.'

'*I agree. But then, what exactly is a real person, Robbie? Have you ever wondered about that?*'

# 6

'As I said to the other man, I don't really know that much about him,' Mrs Tofell says. She lives in the condo adjacent to Coulter's.

Rose, Owen and Baptiste are sitting in her lavender-coloured living room. Thin and smartly dressed, she's married to a banker, who is away in New York. She has her blond hair coiffed into a bouffant, and wears lots of lavender and jewellery. Her age is hard to determine. She could be anything between thirty and fifty, Rose muses, thanks to cosmetic surgery. Mrs Tofell has a cup of coffee in her hands and she takes a sip. She has made a pot of coffee for herself and the others, but they have sipped it out of politeness and then left their cups untouched. Owen sits quietly holding a tablet, recording the interview. On the screen is live video of Mrs Tofell, along with a display of her driver's licence, social security number and personal details. She is forty-nine years old. Her fluffy shih-tzu dog, wearing purple bangs, is sniffing around Owen's boots, much to his annoyance.

'What *do* you know about him?' Rose presses.

'Gary . . . Mr Coulter, kept very much to himself. He wasn't really the social type. I saw him use the pool once or twice. He is . . . *was* . . . a rather large fellow. Could have done with exercise, and then some. Occasionally I'd see him

44

take his garbage and recycling out. He'd help me carry my shopping up sometimes if he was around.'

'How long has he been living next door?'

'Six months. Not that you would know he was living there most of the time. He was a very quiet neighbour. Until tonight. With the screaming.' She winces. 'It really was awful.'

Baptiste is watching closely as Mrs Tofell's hands tremble.

'I know this isn't pleasant, but was he screaming anything in particular? Any words?' Baptiste asks.

'Well the first thing I heard – I think – was . . . "Stop".'

'Stop?' Rose repeats.

Baptiste raises an eyebrow. 'He screamed stop?'

'I think so. Then it was just . . . screaming. Long and loud.'

Baptiste and Rose exchange a glance. If Coulter called out, it implied that there could have been someone else in the room. Suicide is looking like it's on the way out.

'He said nothing else?' Rose asks.

'There was something else, I think. He said "stop" two or three times, then "Stop . . . Iris".'

'Iris?'

'I think so.'

'You're sure?'

'I guess.'

Rose makes a note of the name. 'He ever mention anyone named Iris to you before?'

'No. Never. Anyway, I could smell the burning so I went onto the landing. I could see the smoke at once. It was coming out from around his door. I was scared. I knocked hard and called his name. I tried to open the door but it was locked. I pushed against it a few times but . . . I'm not very strong. That's when I left and called 911. I didn't know what else to do.'

45

'Do you know what he did for a living?' Baptiste asks.

'Oh, he said something like he's a software engineer. I don't know. It all sounds very complicated and technical to me.'

Software. Rose made a mental note. It made sense. Palo Alto was an easy commute to San Jose, a portion of the San Francisco Bay Area known to the world as Silicon Valley. Hundreds of high-technology companies have headquarters or substantial campuses there, including the big names: Facebook, Microsoft, Google, Apple, as well as the rising corporations like WadeSoft – the computer hardware and software corporation which also owns the StreamPlex, a virtual social networking 'city'.

'Did he ever talk much with you?' Rose asks.

'Not a great deal. I think he once mentioned his dad had passed away some time ago.'

'Did he have a girlfriend?' Baptiste pushes. 'Any friends that you can remember visiting him?'

'Not that I saw. Of course I wasn't always looking at what he was doing, you understand?'

'Of course,' Baptiste says.

Mrs Tofell puts her cup and saucer down on the coffee table. 'I guess he was a lonely man. But we can all be a little lonely sometimes, can't we?'

Rose nods.

Mrs Tofell's face hardens slightly. 'What is this all about? Lieutenant Fontaine says it was just some bad wiring. Do you think it was something else?'

Rose leans forward. 'We're looking into all possibilities at this point. Because of the nature of his work, we're trying to build up a picture of Mr Coulter, to see if anyone had reason to harm him.'

Mrs Tofell looks a little uncomfortable.

'Did you notice anything different about him recently?' Baptiste asks.

'In the last month I had perhaps seen more of him than usual. He said he was now working from home . . . But that's all.'

Rose smiles her thanks, sensing there's not much more they can learn. It's time to leave. 'Thank you, Mrs Tofell. If you think of anything else, give me a call.' Rose hands her a business card.

'Thanks for the coffee, Mrs Tofell,' Owen says, holding his tablet out to her and a stylus. 'If you could please sign to confirm your statement.'

Mrs Tofell quickly signs. She stares at the FBI logo on the card.

'You don't think he was in any . . . trouble, do you?'

'That,' Rose says, smiling, 'is what we're trying to find out. If we need to ask any more questions we'll be in touch. Is that OK?'

'Of course.' Mrs Tofell smiles gratefully, and gives Owen's hand a gentle squeeze. 'Anything I can do to help will be a pleasure.'

*I bet*, Rose thinks.

# 7

'Somethin' about that night . . .' the man sings under his breath as he grabs the grocery bags out of the back of his truck.

'You and me, baby, connected . . .' He slams the trunk lid down with his elbow, squeezing the fob in his right hand. Turning in the direction of the beach, he pauses a moment to enjoy the view. The sea sparkles towards the horizon. Close to the shore a light swell produces small, knee-high waves that caress the beach. There are scores of people: joggers kicking up spurts of sand as they exercise to the sound of music coming through their headphones; parents watching over their kids digging industriously with small plastic shovels; couples holding hands, or with arms across each other's shoulders, strolling slowly. There are a few singletons too, men and women, and his eyes are drawn to an elegant brunette in her late thirties wearing a flowing pink wrap over her two-piece swimming costume. She's heading down towards the surf for a swim. He knows she's a regular. And she's always alone. No ring on her left hand.

He smiles to himself as she stops, kicks off her sandals, slips the wrap from her shoulders and trots down to the water, splashing through a wave before launching herself into a shallow dive. She swims out thirty or so feet before turning to breaststroke parallel to the shore.

She's a looker all right. A dainty little dish. Perhaps one of those picky bitches who think they're too good for most men. Well, not too good for him, he decides. None of them are.

He carries his bags along the sidewalk towards the modest house he is renting; a neat wooden-walled and shingle-tiled single-storey building with a small private yard out back, not overlooked by the properties on either side. He likes his privacy. It's why he has chosen to stay here for a while.

He sees the neighbour next to his beach house vaping and he nods a greeting.

'How you doing, Mr Knowles?'

The vaper, a retired soldier, nods pleasantly. 'Doin' fine, thanks. Just fine. You?'

'Can't complain. Life's good.'

'Sure is . . .' Knowles looks away, staring into the distance.

'Have a better one.' The man gives a nod then climbs the stoop to his house. He unlocks the door and enters, closing it securely behind him.

Most of the modest house is open plan. The walls are of stained wood, and there's a bare minimum of furniture, left behind by previous tenants. There are two sofas either side of a low glass-topped table and a wall-mounted plasma screen that has seen better days. On the far side of the living space is a counter with bar stools, then the kitchen area. To the rear is a short corridor leading to the two bedrooms and the bathroom. Entering the small kitchen, he unloads his items into the refrigerator: milk, beer, butter, hot dogs. They cram against the pickle jars stored at the back of the refrigerator with a clink. The man makes sure his new purchases are to one side, his pickle jars to the other.

The jars have some of his special trophies inside them. Acquired over a month ago when he finally felt safe enough

49

to satisfy his craving for a fresh kill. A backpacker from England, taking a year out after graduation. He had met her in a bar a safe distance away from his new neighbourhood. She had talked freely of her divorced parents, neither of whom showed much interest in her since moving on to new partners. Not that she was bitter about it. He had nodded sympathetically, while satisfied that she was the kind of person who would not be missed for a long time. They drank and talked until late, and she was happy to take up his offer to spend the night at his beach house. And there she had stayed, sharing his house. But not altogether a tenant. Not altogether at all, he thinks with a smirk, as he caresses one of the larger jars.

Koenig smiles at the swollen tongue in the jar, then shuts the refrigerator.

He feels a pang as he recalls all the trophies he had been forced to leave behind at the cabin. Along with his camera equipment and laptop. He had taken precautions some years earlier, just in case the feds ever came calling: a fake identity and a healthy bank balance under the assumed name, and a number of dormant social media and dating accounts so that he could cruise for more prey when he felt safe enough to resume his calling. Even so, nearly all that he valued had been lost, and he seethes with anger as he recalls the FBI agent who tricked him into inviting her back to his place. He had been careless. Too indiscreet on some of the more specialist chat rooms, and they had found him.

His fists clench as he feels ashamed of himself. He'll never make the same mistakes again. And he'll make sure he humiliates those bastards in the FBI. Especially that bitch, that whore . . . But not yet.

He has backed up most of his video files to a data server in New Zealand owned by the kind of company that rents heavily encrypted storage and asks no questions. He has a new laptop. Much better than the old one. Faster, and with enough memory to store the ultra-high-res footage for a host of new victims, as well as the old files he has downloaded from the server.

He has also acquired all the tools and medication needed for what he has to do next. It is not a pleasant prospect, but he cannot avoid it. He has changed the colour of his hair and grown a neatly trimmed beard, but he knows that he needs to make his old face disappear so that he cannot be traced by the facial recognition algorithms that law enforcement has available these days. Only then can he resurface in earnest and return to the hunt that is the only thing that gives his life meaning.

He has stockpiled enough food to last him a month, to see him through the recovery period. After tonight, he is not going to be able to leave the rented house for a while.

Koenig decides to have a beer later. But first he can't help thinking about the woman on the beach. She has excited him. He needs relief from the tension flaring up in his loins. He powers up his laptop and swipes his fingers across the screen. He selects a folder marked 'Greatest Hits'. He's been editing them into a new reel, with a new soundtrack and coloured filters applied. He presses play, and watches the screaming face of one of his early victims.

It pleases him.

He manipulates himself until there is a release and he feels the tension ebb from his body. Then, on a whim, he logs into the heavily encrypted dark web server that allows him to use a virtual network to access a domain that is hidden to all but his most trusted fans – the kind of people that are far enough into criminal activity to not want to risk being discovered by the authorities. A moment later he is looking at the KKillKam homepage. KKK. He smiles at his appropriation of the white supremacist acronym. He had posed as one of them once, in order to get close to one of his victims – a dull-witted bigot eaten up with guilt and self-loathing over his hidden sexual desire for other men. Some of him was eaten up in turn, and some parts kept as trophies, before what was left was distributed in a quiet corner of a forest park for a passer-by to find and report to the police.

Koenig checks on new messages. There aren't many, and he is irked to find that his lack of activity is making his followers lose interest.

'Fuck 'em,' he mutters, as he sees that his page visit counter is down to single figures for the day. There's the ping of a new message and Koenig clicks back and opens the file.

Greetings, Koenig. My name is Shelley and I like to play. I have something for you . . . Check your mpeg folder.

Koenig feels a fleeting concern, the faintest cool prickle at the nape of his neck. If this person is trying to impress him, then they've failed. All the same, he moves the cursor and clicks on the folder of video files he's made of his victims' torments.

Then he freezes, his eyes widening as he stares at the new file name:

Death by fire

Koenig takes a deep breath. This is not possible. Only he has access to this site. Only he can add or delete from its content. And yet there it is – someone has placed a new file in his library. He clicks on the play button.

There's a man seated at a desk and Koenig quickly grasps that he is looking at video from a webcam. The man's torso, arms and hands are covered in a black suit made of leather, or rubber perhaps. The strange garment continues over his head, covering all except his mouth, above which there is a gleaming visor that reflects the computer monitor in front of him. Koenig can tell it is a man from the heaviness of the jawline and the unshaven skin around the open mouth. The man is breathing hard and his body is rocking gently forwards and backwards. He starts to moan with pleasure.

What is happening?

Before he can think on, the man abruptly stiffens, mouth agape. Then the teeth clench tightly together and his expression changes to one of strained effort, but his body is rigid, as if held there by some invisible force. A keening whine comes over the laptop's speakers and then Koenig sees the first wisp of smoke curling from the black suit and visor. Tiny yellow flames pierce the thick material and flare up brightly as the smoke thickens, dark and swirling. Now the man's jaws snap open and he screams – an inhuman shriek of torment. But there's no escape for him. He sits there, engulfed in flames that roar over him, blistering his lips and the exposed skin.

Koenig is horrified by the spectacle. And stimulated. He can't help but watch as the man is incinerated before his eyes.

At length the flames die away, and all that remains is the charred shell of a human being. The video fades to black and stops.

Koenig is still for a moment. His awe quickly gives way to fear. How the hell has this been uploaded to his site? It should not be possible. It should not—

*Pop-ping*

There's a new message.

He feels a nervous tremor in his hand as he clicks the touchpad.

Did you like it?

'Shit . . .' Koenig recoils as if he has been struck. Someone is hacking into his site right at this moment. They know he has watched the file. They know . . . He closes the virtual network down and stares at the desktop screen, his pulse racing. He has been discovered. His private sanctum has been penetrated and he feels violated. Violated and angry. Enraged.

Whoever did this will pay for it. With their life.

# 8

Rose looks at Robbie in the rear-view mirror. This morning he seems more lost in thought than usual. She didn't get back until well after midnight, and feels guilty about spoiling the family's get-together the previous evening. She knows there was nothing she could do about it. Duty calls and the Bureau expects, accepting no excuse. She feels that Robbie and Jeff don't get enough of her time, and that she's letting them down. She tries to compensate.

'So what did you watch with Dad last night? Baseball?'

'Yeah. They had an advert for the Skin.'

'What's that?'

His expression alters to rapt enthusiasm. 'Looks so awesome, Mom. We gotta have one.'

'Like I said, what is it? What does it do?'

'C'mon, Mom. I told you about it months back.'

'You told me a lot of stuff months back,' Rose replies wearily. 'Not all of it I remember. Even though I am a superwoman.'

'The poly-ply cyber suit, Mom. By WadeSoft? You must've heard about it. Every gaming show's been talking about it for months. GamerzTV had one of the test suits to try out. We need to get one. Soon as they come out. Please?'

Robbie sees the blank look on his mother's face.

'I have no idea what you're talking about. I don't have enough spare time to watch those kind of shows.'

'Well Dad knows about it.'

'Does he now? Good for him. Seems there's less to running a political campaign than meets the eye . . . Clearly you're better off talking to him about it, then.'

'Huh . . .' Rob turns away from her and leans his forehead against the passenger window. She feels a surge of maternal guilt at not being willing to share an enthusiasm with her child.

'What does Dad think about it? This poly-ploy suit thing?'

'Poly-ply, Mom. Poly-ply cyber suit. Though no one is really calling it that. They call it the Skin.'

'What's wrong with the one you've already got?'

'Really?' Rob rolls his eyes. 'Dad says he'll look into it. But we gotta have one. We can use it together. It'll be great.'

'That's what you said about the last console system we bought. And where is it now? In your room, that's where.'

'I promise we'll share the Skin, Mom. I promise.'

There's an excitement in her son's voice that breaks Rose's heart. Gaming is nearly the only thing that causes him to show any emotion. It is not his fault, she reminds herself. It is nearly ten years since he was diagnosed with Asperger's. She has long since grown used to his obsessive ways, and understands that he cannot give her the same affection that other mothers enjoy. But what Rose finds wounding these days is that Jeff shares an interest in computer games with his son that seems to exclude her. It is their bond, and she is the outsider when they settle down in front of the console and commune with faceless others in the StreamPlex in an orgy of virtual massacre and destruction. Rose doubts that WadeSoft's creation – a self-contained world of social media, games, simulations and news media – is a positive development in the ever-expanding online universe.

She pretends to be interested. 'Tell me about it, Robbie.'

Her son turns to her. 'It's a simulator suit, Mom. It bluesyncs to the Stream so you can play games. So you can be in the games. Actually *in* the games. God, it sounds so chill. We've got to have it.'

'It sure does sound chill,' Rose says. 'It also sounds very expensive.'

'It is expensive, I guess. They said that when it comes out it'll ship for three thousand dollars.'

'Three thousand?' Her eyes widen in horror.

'Yeah, there's a basic model. The one with low-res textures. We should go for the most expensive model, Mom. It'll be better than real.'

'Better than real,' Rose repeats. 'Jesus . . . Is that what it's come to? Well you know Dad likes his toys. I'll chat with him about it and we can see.'

'It's not a toy!' Robbie protests. 'It's total immersion simulation environment wear: soft-wear. Soft-*wear*. Get it?'

'Sure. Very smart.'

Robbie frowns. 'It's better than RL, that's for sure.'

Rose pulls to a stop outside Daniel Fernandez High School. Robbie opens his passenger door.

'RL?' Rose asks.

'Real life,' Robbie murmurs.

'See you tonight,' Rose says.

Robbie pulls his hoodie up over his face before trudging off to school.

Rose watches him make his way down the pavement, into the school yard. She feels like Robbie is lost to her sometimes and is never sure what to do about it.

Soon Rose is back on the interstate, driving across the grey Bay Bridge. This morning the way is mostly clear, and she can watch the warm sun bouncing off the orange hue of the suspension bridge to her right – the Golden Gate Bridge – looming above a layer of fog that covers much of the sea. She smiles as she remembers how fond Robbie is of the fog. He says it makes the whole city look like a spooky graveyard.

Rose follows Interstate 80 across Bay Bridge and then past 'Treasure Island', the naval facility. She flicks on the radio news bulletin streaming to her smartphone.

'. . . A girl trapped in a storm drain updated her Facebook status rather than calling 911 . . .'

The FBI field office where she's been working for nearly five years is located close to City Hall. The Bureau operates from a tall white building, with several investigative departments on each floor.

But she has not always driven into this city as Rose Blake. Sometimes she has been undercover in a number of guises: as a junkie to befriend a drug-dealing cop; posing as a high-powered businesswoman to bust open an athletics doping ring; or acting as girlfriend to a male undercover agent. The best role of her career was her first, when she went undercover as an intern in the Republican Party, trailing a corrupt money launderer. That was when she first met Jeff.

She'd been based in Virginia back then, but the Bureau needed additional agents on the West Coast so they'd transferred her there. Jeff and Robbie had come with her, Jeff fortunate enough to get the post of associate professor at the university. He has a commute of an hour each way, a fact he regularly reminds her of. At least until he started working for Senator Keller. Now Rose sees even less of him. Things have not been good between her and Jeff for months. The pressure of the campaign is no doubt getting to him, and she feels that his relationship with his assistant may not be strictly professional. She blames herself for that. If only she had more time to give him.

Rose reaches the city early this morning. She continues past her office building, down towards Lower Pacific Heights, finally stopping to park along Spruce Street. Today she has her final appointment with her psychotherapist, Dr Katherine Wheeler.

# 9

Rose sits in the Advocaat-coloured waiting room, outside Dr Wheeler's mahogany door. She has been seeing Katherine ever since her role in the Koenig investigation came to an abrupt end nearly six months ago. It had nearly cost Rose her life and she'd been left with crushing waves of anxiety, depression and paranoia ever since.

The Bureau has an employee-assistance programme, but the insurers of her workers' comp were unwilling to pay out. PTSD can be faked, they claimed. Of course, Baptiste and the Bureau don't know the full extent of what she's going through. They couldn't know. Jeff has tried to be supportive, but having mental 'issues' is a lonely problem. It's not as simple as 'getting over it'.

Rose doesn't want to sue the Bureau, because they would kick her out and her career would be over. The operation had gone bad, that was all. She doesn't blame anyone but herself. She should have shot Koenig when she had the chance. She'd had to take sick leave for a month. One thing the Bureau doesn't want on their hands is damaged goods. If they ever found out she had been diagnosed with PTSD, Rose would be transferred to a desk job. Or – worst-case scenario – she would have to quit. For Rose, quitting has never been an option, and she hopes she can ride it out.

She has taken it upon herself to see someone for counselling, in strict confidence, every two weeks. There was no doubt that Koenig had damaged her. But, looking back, Rose feels she has made progress, and the worst is behind her.

The door opens and Katherine emerges, a sharp-faced brunette wearing a designer charcoal suit.

'Hi, Rose, come on in.'

Rose loves Kathy's elegant workplace – it is true American Gothic, with dark mahogany bookcases lining the walls, deep-blue paisley wallpaper and a red leather couch and two chairs either side of a low table. Wine-red and grey drapes frame two large windows overlooking Spruce Street. A handful of prints by Francis Bacon and Picasso hang on the walls. Rose takes her regular place on one of the chairs. She has never liked the idea of using the couch. It makes her feel vulnerable and weak rather than relaxed. Kathy takes the other chair. Rose turns her smartphone off.

'So, as you know, today will be our last session,' Kathy says. 'Unless you need some more time on this. How are you feeling?'

'I'm certainly the best I've been for a while. Haven't had a panic attack for over a month.'

Rose has had flashbacks, sometimes with her eyes barely closed, her body twitching and moving restlessly until she wrestles to control it. But, since seeing Katherine, she has developed techniques for controlling the anxiety.

'Good,' Katherine says, scanning her pages of notes.

'I'm also back in the field, working on a new case,' Rose says. 'Good to get out from behind a desk after so many months.'

A slight look of concern crosses Katherine's face. 'That's . . . sooner than I expected.'

'I know, but I think it's what I need. I need to get back to doing what I do well. It's time for me to move on from . . . Koenig.'

*Koenig.*

She feels a brief spasm of anxiety. His name is like a malignant tumour in her head.

Rose remembers his handsome yet severe features. His eyes, penetrating, intelligent and yet utterly empty. Where a soul should be, there wasn't anything. After that night she'd scrubbed every inch of her body and burned her clothes.

'And looking back at what happened in the cabin? How do you feel about that now?'

The cabin . . . The cabin was the culmination of a process that had begun many months before.

# 10

It had all started when a severed, decomposing hand was found at the edge of a road by a wandering drunk. More body parts were found close by. The victims that could be identified were mostly transients, prostitutes and drug addicts, so there was little sympathy at first. But Koenig had developed a taste for well-groomed women. DNA testing matched the hand to a twenty-eight-year-old university lecturer. After lengthy legal wrangling, the Bureau won access to her intiMate dating account to examine her messages. That had provided hundreds of exchanges with other account holders on the site. A forensic linguist had been brought in, and was able to show that at least three of the victim's contacts were actually the same person.

It was Rose who had suggested the perp was using these accounts to cross-index the victim's replies to ensure she was genuine, and not a bot, or possibly someone trying to lure the killer in. The Bureau had set up a small number of user accounts to try and entice the killer, but there had been no bites. He had moved on to another site . . .

It was only when CCTV footage was examined on the route one victim had walked to get home from a party that Koenig's car was spotted as he stopped to give her a ride. The licence plate had proved to be fake, but the Bureau had the make and colour and then began the tedious process of eliminating suspects until a long list of persons of interest was worked through, comparing each individual with the file worked up by one of the Bureau's profilers. After several men had been followed and discounted they came upon Shane Koenig, and his nocturnal drives through the city caught the attention of the Bureau. But they needed evidence. Enough to justify any further action.

Rose and Baptiste devised a sting operation, using Rose to play the part of a barfly, an identity carefully constructed to have a finely judged combination of characteristics drawn from previous victims, though not so many comparisons that Koenig's suspicion might be piqued. Due to the danger posed by Koenig, Baptiste had suggested using another agent, a single woman who would not leave behind a grieving spouse and child if anything went wrong. But Rose had insisted. This was her perp and she wanted to bring him down.

Together with a profiler from Quantico, Rose had created a core identity that stood the best chance of drawing the killer's attention. Then, several more identities were created with subtle differences, along with profile photos of Rose posed differently with a variety of hair colouring, before they were placed on dating sites over a period of a month, so that they would not all originate from the same date if Koenig happened to come across more than one of the identities. As was the common experience of most women on dating sites, Rose had to field the approaches of scores of men – the lonely, the perverted and even the small minority of the genuine – while she waited, and the Bureau continued more traditional, and fruitless, means of hunting for Koenig. It was the profile of 'Tequila' that caught Koenig's eye several weeks later.

Rose remembers the tension and anxiety as she began the internet chatter with 'Dean', the handsome, slender man who claimed to work in advertising. His first messages had not been out of the ordinary, and Rose was on the verge of putting him off when the Bureau's profiler pointed out similar characteristics between 'Dean' and Shane Koenig — even the most disturbed mind cannot hide certain aspects of personality behind a mask, no matter how carefully conceived. So Rose sat at a laptop in the Bureau office, tapping the keyboard, the profiling agent at her side advising her on how to keep the perp in play. It had taken nearly two weeks of light conversation and gossip in increasingly informal, then intimate tones, before Rose had dared to suggest that they meet. She had joked that his profile picture was too handsome to be that of a serial killer. The double bluff was a calculated risk to help allay any fear Koenig might have that 'Tequila' was a set-up. Besides, Rose thought, it's funny how many people tend to assume ugly people are the ones most likely to be capable of malevolent intent.

Dean let the comment pass with a laughing emoji and shortly afterwards suggested they meet face to face at a bar a few miles below the hills where Koenig had his cabin. So, wired up and carefully watched over, Rose had made the date and played her part faultlessly. Two hours of first-date conversation later, Koenig asked her if she wanted to come and see his cabin.

'Only if you want to.' He had smiled. 'No pressure.'

'I don't know.' Rose had chewed her lip and looked across the table, as if considering the offer. 'It's only the first date, Dean.'

'Sure. I understand.' Koenig smiled back. 'But it's not as if I'm a serial killer or anything.'

There was the slightest of hesitations as Rose's blood ran cold, then she had made herself smile. 'No. Not a serial killer. Way too good-looking for that . . . All right, then. Let's just finish the drinks and we can drive up there.'

'Sure. No problem.'

And so Rose had lured Koenig into a meeting and been invited back to his cabin.

But it all went wrong . . . and now he's still out there . . .

# 11

Rose sighs. 'I need to let go of what happened. Owen and I are still alive to tell the tale. It could have gone far worse.'

Katherine nods. 'You will still have strong feelings about it. It was a traumatic episode for you. But talking about it helps. You know what the Bureau likes to claim: "Many Apply, Few Are Chosen". They chose you, Rose. Don't forget that. Koenig will slip up and he will be caught. In the meantime, focus your energies on other matters. What can you tell me about this new case?'

'An unusual arson case, with a probable murder. At least that's the working assumption. Looks like it's going to be a tough one, that's for sure. But we might catch a break.' Rose stares out the window at the skyline. 'The hardest part of the job sometimes is knowing there is all this evil out there. Always. How can I protect myself and the ones I love?'

'You can't, Rose. No one can control everything. And you shouldn't try to. Not if you want to keep your sanity. How is the family?'

'Jeff's not home that much at the moment, with Keller's campaign underway. He's going to be out a lot over the next few weeks. He's pretty stressed about it but he pretends not to be. He's also got a very efficient intern helping him . . . It's probably nothing.'

'You suspect him of something? Have you any reason to?'

'Probably not. The suspicion goes with the job. Always looking for connections.'

'And sometimes they just aren't there. Right?'

They share a short laugh before Rose responds. 'Yeah, you're probably right. Just jumping at shadows . . . Jeff's a good man. It'll be a big deal for him if Keller does well. It's early days, but Jeff has always dreamed of doing something significant. I think he feels wasted sometimes. Like he's not achieved as much as he thinks he should have. Maybe he blames that on me.'

'Do you think he does? Has he ever said that?'

'No,' Rose admits. 'But they never do.'

'They?'

'Men. The good ones at least.'

Katherine nods. 'And Jeff's a good one?'

'I think so. I just wish he realized how much I loved him.' Rose pauses. 'Love him, present tense.'

'Have you spoken to him properly about what you've experienced?'

'He knows some of it. He can see when I'm tense and when I'm relaxed.'

Being entirely honest, Rose reflects, Jeff has been rather insensitive about the whole affair, sometimes making light of it, which hurts her badly.

'And Robbie?'

'He seems to be in his own little world a lot of the time.' Rose sweeps her hair back. 'It's hard being a parent. My job being what it is, I can't talk about it too much. It feels like there's a lot unspoken, sometimes.'

Katherine chuckles. 'Tell me about it.'

Rose gazes out of the window. 'Seeing what I've seen in

my job, you want your kid to remain a kid forever, sheltering them, keeping them safe, not forcing them to grow up too soon. On the other hand, you want them to be prepared for the world.'

'I know, Rose. It's a hard balance. We can only do our best.'

Katherine discreetly looks down at her neat silver watch. 'I'm afraid we're out of time. That's the end of our session.'

Rose is still for a moment before rising from the chair. She hesitates, then takes Katherine's hand.

'Thank you,' she says, and means it, the burden having been shifted from her shoulders, hopefully for the final time.

'You're very welcome.'

'I hope I never have to see you again,' Rose says, then laughs. 'That's not quite how I meant it to sound.'

'I know. There is a saying: what doesn't kill you—'

'. . . makes you stronger, right.'

Katherine places her notes down on her desk. 'For what it's worth, I know I'll feel safer knowing that you're back out there doing what you do best.'

Rose nods, her heart heavy with the truth that there are many other Koenigs waiting in the wings, preparing to take centre stage when their time comes . . .

# 12

The FBI seal hangs large and low on a wall in the main reception area of the San Francisco field office. 'Fidelity. Bravery. Integrity.' Those three words and the oath have been seared into Rose's mind since she graduated from Quantico. At the start of every new case she mentally repeats the words of the contract she made with the Bureau:

*I, Rose Blake, do solemnly swear that I will support and defend the Constitution of the United States against all enemies, foreign and domestic; that I will bear true faith and allegiance to the same; that I take this obligation freely, without any mental reservation or purpose of evasion; and that I will well and faithfully discharge the duties of the office on which I am about to enter. So help me God.*

Rose waves her ID badge at the two guards seated behind the front lobby desk as she strides down the navy-tiled floor towards the three sets of elevators. She taps in her PIN number on the elevator door. The door opens and she enters, selecting the thirteenth floor. She checks herself in the mirror at the back of the elevator. She's wearing a simple grey suit with a white blouse. A wisp of hair has strayed, and she neatly flicks it back behind her right ear. The elevator door opens and she paces down a corridor. She approaches a dark-brown door where she pulls out her badge and holds it up to the ident scanner. The reader's light buzzes green and the door clicks open.

Rose enters the field office proper, making her way through the grey cubicles and over to her own neatly organized desk. The office is divided into sections: Terrorism, Counter-Intelligence, Cybercrime, Public Corruption and Civil Rights, Organized Crime, White-collar Crime, Violent Crime and Major Thefts. She slips out of her jacket and hangs it over the back of the chair before sitting down and switching on her computer. The office is large, with a light-blue carpet and rows of blinded windows overlooking Golden Gate Avenue. The red bridge and Cupid's Span – a huge golden bow and red arrow buried in the ground – are only a few blocks away.

'Good morning, sugar,' says Baptiste, on the way to her office. She blows across the top of her latte. She's wearing black slacks and a green blouse. 'Where have you been?'

'Doctor's appointment. I did tell you.'

Baptiste smiles. 'I know. What's up?'

'Nothing important.' Rose cracks open a bottle of water, takes a sip.

Baptiste shrugs. 'Brennan's been working on what's left of Coulter's laptop. You might want to pay him a visit.'

'Owen will want to be there.' Rose looks through the gap in her cubicle over to Owen's vacant desk.

'Owen's working on his DarkChild sting operation. He says he's close to snaring the bastard.'

Rose smiles. She has faith in Owen. 'OK, meanwhile I'll request a subpoena for Coulter's emails, phone and bank records for the last six months. We need to get into his background.'

Baptiste sits on the edge of Rose's desk. 'You can try. I've already spoken to the Pentagon regarding Coulter . . .'

Rose is hopeful, but Baptiste shakes her head. 'They're being predictably cagey, but they corroborated that he was one of their freelance software engineers. Actually, he's one of the guys they brought in after the Swarm's attack, they say. And that's about it. Other than that Coulter was assigned to special projects at the time of his death.'

'Special projects?'

'That's what they said. Not very helpful. You think I got anything else out of 'em, then you're wrong, sister. They're not saying anything, for the usual "national security" reasons. They're claiming Coulter was engaged in real hush-hush stuff. I'd lay good money it's nothing more than fixing the director of the CIA's printer, or something. Anyway, he's off their books now.'

'Oh?'

'He was working out of . . .' – she pauses, scanning the paperwork – '. . . Peek Industries until a few months back. Here's what we have on his background so far, along with Palo Alto PD's paperwork.'

Rose pulls a frustrated face, taking Coulter's file from Baptiste, who heads to her office. Flicking through the pages, she scans the various printouts. Late thirties, Bachelor of Sciences in computer engineering, Master of Sciences in computer science, worked for a number of independent software companies on firmware and algorithm development and implementation.

But there's not much information on Coulter outside of his career. The odd speeding ticket. A few references to papers on AI he has presented at industry conferences. As for his family, his father had been taken by cancer and his mother was retired in Florida. No siblings, no wife. No signs of any reason why anyone would want to burn him alive, if it was a murder. Nor any reason for him to end his own life in such a manner. Nothing of much investigative use.

Rose closes the file, crosses to Baptiste's office and taps on the doorframe as she enters.

'Not much to go on.'

'Nope.'

'Any of this being taken up by the newshounds?'

'You kidding me? Guy goes hog roast at his desk and they give it a pass?' She reaches into her bag for her smartphone, taps it on and holds the screen up for Rose to see.

'It's all over "The Gab" news site, but they don't have much.' The garish red text on TheGabNews.com screams 'Palo Inferno! Murder not ruled out' accompanied by a still of Gabby Vance outside the apartment and a video link. Vance is a stringer who often features on the Bay News Corporation channel.

'On the plus side, the bean counters have agreed to pay for the autopsy and forensics lab work to be fast-tracked. We've got Benfield as the ME in charge.'

'He's good,' says Rose.

'Yes he is. Should have the results back in a few days. And we've got Chan as the CSI in charge down at the lab. So we caught a break there . . .'

Rose shoots her a questioning look. 'But . . .?'

'But, on the downside, Assistant Secretary of Defense William Maynard has asked us to keep him informed of *every* development.'

'That's heavy. Why is the DoD so interested? They've changed their tune. I'd never have figured them as the kind to take an interest in their subcontracted employees' welfare.'

'Ouch!' Baptiste fakes a wince. 'You saying Uncle Sam doesn't care about his minions?'

'You ever know him to?'

'True that. Anyway, try and keep a tight loop on this,

73

Rose. Something about it doesn't feel quite right.'

Rose knows what Baptiste means. The speed at which the Bureau was assigned to the investigation means someone higher up the chain of command is spooked by Coulter's death.

Baptiste rubs her tired-looking eyes. 'Time's up. Got other people that need my attention. Keep me posted. Looks like it's going to be a busy week.' Rose leaves the office and heads back to her desk.

She logs onto the FBI intranet and types up her initial report, outlining her thoughts and impressions from the scene of Coulter's death. So far it's not officially a crime scene, but she feels it's only a matter of time. The death of Gary Coulter is becoming murkier by the second. Special projects, national security? How the hell is the Bureau supposed to do its work unless the Department of Defense is more forthcoming? How do they know that it wasn't one of those very special projects that got him killed?

Rose drains the water bottle and tosses it in the trash. At least the Bureau has Coulter's laptop. That, and the coroner's report, might offer some clues about the circumstances of his death. For an instant she pictures Coulter ablaze from head to toe, just sitting at his desk as he screams in agony. Then she picks up her smartphone and the file and heads down towards Brennan Bamber's office in the Cybercrime department.

# 13

'Special Agent Rose Blake.' Brennan Bamber smiles a greeting. The slender blond Texan is the acting head of Cybercrime. He quickly minimizes a poker table window he had up on his screen.

'You must be here about the laptop,' he says, before spinning around on his seat like a teenager. He's in his late twenties. He beams, but his eyes look tired.

Most of the terminals in the Cybercrime office have three screens to each tower, staffed in total by twenty investigators and technicians, and, since the window shades are angled down, the room is bathed in a blue hue. Rose knows that these days their attention is concentrated on computer and network intrusions, identity theft, online fraud, phishing and other e-scams, as well as sex crimes against children. With an ever more interconnected world it is an overburdened and underfunded department. Brennan constantly complains that they are failing to keep up with online crime, with thousands of identities stolen and offences committed every day. And that's only on the surface, everyday web. The deep web, sometimes called the dark web, is vast – a portal to drug dealers, black marketeers, hackers, whistleblowers, terrorists, political extremists, human traffickers, illegal arms dealers, exotic animal traders, child pornographers and even crowdfunded hit men.

Brennan's bookshelf contains philosophy books, *Terminator* action figures, Rubik's cubes, glowing balls and other juvenile yet intricate contraptions. His hair is in its usual state of dishevelment, and he's wearing a checked white and blue shirt with a yellow T-shirt underneath. On the T-shirt is stencilled a quote from Einstein that reads 'Intellectuals solve problems, Geniuses prevent them'. He is manically energetic, unable to sit still for very long. Baptiste finds him irritating, but Rose can tolerate his eccentricities, most of the time, even though she can't help feeling he's way out there on the spectrum.

'Any luck, Brenn?'

Brennan leans back in his chair, cracking his bony knuckles as he swiftly collects his thoughts. 'Not much so far. Coulter's laptop was cooked medium rare. Most of the external casing melted, but we managed to extract the hard drive, which I'm working on now.'

Brennan points at the slender aluminium case hooked up to his computer via power and data cables. A window on his computer is flickering with scrolling numbers.

'Vic's data is encrypted pretty well, and it's not going to be easy to crack. As you'd probably expect from a software professional . . . But I like a challenge. Beats looking at thousands of images of child porn all day.' He laughs weakly, but Rose can see his discomfort as he shifts in his seat. None of them likes having to deal with such extreme perversions.

'There really are some sick bastards out there . . .' Brennan shares Rose's moment of reflection before he says quickly, 'What's the deal with this laptop guy anyway?'

'Honestly, we don't know much.' Rose tells him about the crime scene and what they've found out so far. Brennan is lost in thought for a moment.

'Have you got any images?' he asks.

'Sure.' Rose pulls out her smartphone, hands it to Brennan. Brennan swipes past the various pictures, grimacing occasionally. Then he stops and squints at the screen.

'See something?' Rose asks.

Brennan zooms in on a patch of the charred body. 'What's that?'

He swivels on his chair so she can see the screen and taps the image of the blackened body, indicating the shoulder and arm. Then he stretches his thumb and finger apart, zooming in on the shoulder to close in on the long sliver of the rubbery material they found on the body. He tilts his head to one side as he carefully adjusts the image, trading off resolution against detail. 'That's not skin or muscle tissue. The surface pattern looks too regular. Like a mesh, almost.'

'We thought it was a wetsuit or something.'

'Wetsuit?' Brennan chuckles. 'Kinky.'

'I really hope not. But you might want to share your thoughts with Owen. He's more on your wavelength. Anyway, what do you think it is?'

'The first thing that strikes me are those wires . . .' He flicks back a few images and there's a close-up of the back of Coulter's body with a small bundle of cables just visible amid the charred remains.

'Wires?' Rose leans closer, trying not to wince at Brennan's overpowering aftershave. She had looked at the images several times but had thought that the wires were folds in whatever Coulter had been wearing when he burned to death. Now that Brennan has pointed them out, she sees that he's right. 'So what are they doing there?'

'Not quite sure . . . Looks like the vic was attached to something.' He shows her another image with the object sitting on the blackened desk. 'Any idea?'

Rose is silent and they both stare at the screen for a moment before Brennan returns to the images of the body. He finds one taken from the side and zooms into the back. This time the fine tendrils at the end of the cables are more clearly visible, like the splayed ends of a pigtail. Rose notices a small black box.

'What do you think that is?'

'OK, now we're getting somewhere. Definitely some kind of connections to whatever he was wearing. Power, data . . . or both. That small box looks like a power source for what he was wearing, although it's hard to be sure. The thing is pretty well melted. We're not going to make much out of that.'

'The box?'

'Yeah, evidence team brought it in. Internals are completely destroyed.' Brennan scratches his chin. 'I got a feeling I might know what this is. I mean, what the vic's wearing.'

'Go on.'

'I might be wrong, but it's possible it was something like those Skin things they've been advertising on TV recently.'

'Skin?' Rose feels her pulse quicken as she recalls her discussion with Robbie this morning. 'As in "be better than real, pre-order now" Skin?'

Brennan nods. 'But they haven't released that yet. This looks like something very similar though. There was an article in *Wireless* a few years back about how the military were using sensory suits for advanced combat training. Looked kind of fun, but then it disappeared from the radar. This could be a prototype. I mean, our man has suction with DoD, right?'

'Have you still got the article? Were there any pictures?'

'Whoa! Do I look like the kind of nerd that has back issues piled up at home?' Brennan tuts. 'I'll see if I can find something online. Think I vaguely recall a fuzzy close-up on some news channel somewhere, but it was deleted soon after.'

'All right. So how does this suit work? For those of us who don't read *Wireless* magazine?'

'Suit? You mean the Skin? The latest gizmo from Wade Wolff's company? It's like it sounds. You wear it over you and the material carries a micro network of sensor inputs that deliver a tiny electrical current to the host's nerve system. There is also some kind of tensioner system built into the Skin that can contract and expand the material. The upshot is that the person wearing the suit can be made to feel the physical sensations of whatever software simulation the program is running. You know, jogging, swimming, climbing, skiing – all that sort of stuff. Quite cool, eh?'

'Cool? I guess. Until the day you happen to get fried in the suit. Like Coulter.'

'Boil in the bag,' he laughs.

She gives him a hard stare. Brennan continues: 'Coupled with a helmet, or visor maybe, the experience is supposed to be as immersive as it gets. Forget all those crappy early visors. If that's what Coulter had got his hands on, then he's a lucky man, or was. But then, it's a technology we're all going to be able to use soon enough. Skins are going to be the next big thing. WadeSoft's billion-dollar toy.'

'My husband and son want to get one.'

'They'd better pre-order it, then. It's gonna sell out. Fast.'

Rose isn't in the mood for levity. 'If Coulter was burned to death while wearing one of these Skin things then it might be an accident.'

'More than likely,' Brennan says. 'Something in the suit shorts and there's a fire. Maybe the prototype hasn't got any fire-retardant treatment built in yet. And bingo – barbecued beta tester.'

It could have been an accident, like Brennan says. But what if it isn't? Mrs Tofell heard him scream 'stop'. What if someone did not want Coulter to have the prototype? What if they had some way of sabotaging the suit, or controlling it, so that it killed him?

A competitor?

Rose can now sense a corporate conspiracy angle coming into play. Brennan hands back her smartphone.

'What did the fire department say?' he asks.

'They reckon there's no obvious sign of any accelerant. Even so, when it happened, the heat was as intense as it gets.'

They are both silent before Brennan speaks. 'I would have a closer look at any remains of the suit.'

'All right. I'll see if I can get what's left from the coroner. That's one angle. But what about Coulter's laptop? Worst-case scenario, if we can't salvage anything useful, what else can we do?'

'You could ask Google for access to his email account, assuming he has one. But they're pretty tight on data protection so they'd need an order from the Attorney General's Office, which could take like for-never.'

'Ain't that the truth?' Rose recalls the red tape that has obstructed investigations in the past. It's down to the 1986 law forbidding consumer electronic communications companies from disclosing content without the product owner's consent or a government order. Unread emails, for example, require search warrants. The process is fraught with legal technicalities, and murky boundaries, and is very time consuming.

Brennan clears his throat. 'If he's DoD, or the project he was working on is secret, they might obstruct the order on national security grounds. Meanwhile, it might be worth checking in with WadeSoft to see if they know anything about the distribution of Skin prototypes.'

Rose sighs. This investigation could end up going in circles.

Brennan sees Rose's frustration. 'Sorry. Welcome to the world of Cybercrime.'

'Gee, thanks, Brenn. Keep me posted on the laptop,' Rose says, leaving his desk.

Brennan calls after her. 'Sure. Oh, and if you see Baptiste, can you tell her the guys and me are still waiting for a proper office! You know, somewhere with air conditioning that actually works. It's like a furnace in here.'

Rose waves a hand, but his words haunt her as she thinks about Coulter on fire again, and tries just for a moment to imagine what it's like to be engulfed in flames, scorching every square inch of your body.

# 14

In the small FBI satellite office in San Jose, fifty minutes away from San Francisco, Owen Malinski pours himself some more coffee. He has three screens open in front of him, which he has been watching for nearly a week. He's on a short afternoon break as he takes in the latest data dump in his smartphone inbox.

Six emails, seventeen Facebook notifications, twenty-eight spam messages. One email is a pre-order reminder for WadeSoft's Skin.

Owen can still remember when he used to buy three video tapes for twenty bucks, the rapid speed-dialling and electronic chirping sound of when internet was dial-up, when internet time was clearly demarcated between online and offline. He smiles, remembering the first time he received an email back when he was in high school. Now connected 24/7, he longs for letters instead – heck, even a real paper bill. He muses at how sci-fi and techno-literate the world has become in such a short time. Chatting about internet protocol addresses is now commonplace. Online dating has moved from stigma to the norm, profile stalking is a prerequisite when meeting someone, hardcore porn is now practically a rite of passage.

Owen glances at his Internet Relay Chat icon.

Still no sign of DarkChild.

But Owen feels he is getting close.

He has been working on infiltrating the Swarm for four months. The gang members are responsible for several high-profile attacks on government and corporate sites. He had worked on information systems and surveillance ever since he joined the Bureau, and had played his part in the hunt for Koenig. That the reward for his efforts had been the bullet that had shattered his knee does not trouble Owen unduly. He had done his duty, and he knew the risks that his career choice entailed. If you can't stand the heat . . . Besides, he is good at his job and has a sound investigative instinct that has helped him locate clues in the digital realm, where instead of a fingerprint there's an IP address, instead of a witness there's a log. All hidden in reams and reams of code.

Owen's diligence has allowed him to uncover a number of sites that members of the Swarm frequent. Hanging on IRC channels, lurking in chat rooms, he blends in using the required argot. But it takes time. The sites have hundreds of visitors daily. Owen pays close attention to the top four players, noting their log-off times and cross-referencing that with Facebook profiles of known Swarm supporters, particularly their online chat times. That way, he can correlate hackers' aliases with account holders and thereby begin to identify the hackers and their position in the gang's hierarchy. Owen's injured knee is no handicap to hunting perps down online.

Some weeks ago Owen had infiltrated the private channel of the highest tier of the gang under his alias, Salvador – a reference to his favourite painter, Salvador Dalí. They invited him to join after months of building his reputation by offering useful advice, introducing them to other hacker organizations he had been targeting and staging a denial-of-service attack on some of the Bureau's own servers. He had won the Swarm's respect after his succinct comments praising their recent attack on some private defence contractors, and showing them how they could have gone even further into the systems they had penetrated.

The top four players in Swarm are Möbius, MasterEscher, KC and DarkChild. Owen's Salvador fitted right in. The wall space above Owen's desk is covered with news printouts and highlighted transcripts from internet chat rooms. From what he can glean from the chatter, DarkChild appears to be the most talented of the group, but also their weak point since he loves to act as their spokesperson. Also, from some of his comments it's clear he lives in The City. That was a major break in itself, Owen muses. But then maybe the nerds just like to be near Silicon Valley. In all the attacks carried out by DarkChild he has posted provocative messages on the victims' homepages – on the Department of Defense, it had been 'Defend our privacy'; MIA's default welcome message had been replaced with a sound file on repeat that ran 'Who's afraid of the big bad Wolff?'; and on the IRS, 'Why not collect tax from the rich for a fucking change?'

The top echelons in federal agencies have been slow to adapt to the rapidly advancing new technology, with many government offices vulnerable to hackers. Owen has quickly mastered most of the social media networks but retains a sceptical eye. He's still part of the generation where making a phone call or, worst case scenario, sending a quick text, is the norm. Not that he doesn't regret the occasional ill-advised email sent in the heat of the moment. Now millions of people on a daily basis, particularly the young and disaffected, pour their hearts out on their social media messaging systems, using it as an emotional dumping ground.

They say time is a healer, allowing past mistakes and wounds to fade from memory. But online, time does not degrade ones and zeros. There is no healing. Like most physical evidence, there's always a digital trace somewhere. For some, it can be a painful reminder of unhappy times. In law enforcement it's how hackers can be caught.

*Pop-ping*

The sound means someone has joined the chat room. Adrenalin is starting to pump. Back on the trio of computers, one of the screens has a live window. A circular icon next to DarkChild's name is glowing green. Owen waits, preparing his opening exchange, before lines of text move down the screen:

> DarkChild: The prodigal son returns . . .
> Sorry for the radio silence . . .
> Think I got the feds watching me . . . :/

He's spooked, and Owen thinks carefully before replying:

> Salvador: Lol no worries, we thought you'd gone for good :)

The last time they had spoken, Owen requested DarkChild's domain so he could send him some code, and DarkChild had promptly logged off. If Owen finds out the domain details, he can attempt a trace. So far, each member has signed into the chat room by masking their IP using a virtual private network, which provides remote and secure access by using tunnelling, hiding beneath a fake IP address, thus making it near impossible to trace them.

They like to think they are clever, principled individuals.

Certainly their fans regard them as such. Even though they are criminals, Owen does have a certain respect for their methods and provocative messages. Owen's computers are configured to conceal his identity from DarkChild and his associates. His personal FBI computer is disconnected from the Stream as, like any online computer, it can be hacked. He has another connected to the FBI network. Then a third undercover computer that runs on a blank IP that cannot be traced back to the Bureau. On the third screen is the trace program, which Owen uses to analyse the metadata of all the members of the gang. On the off chance, he runs the program.

Within a few seconds, the custom program has a clear IP address for DarkChild, along with longitude and latitude coordinates.

Owen is stunned.

Has DarkChild just fucked up?

Owen grabs his smartphone, speed-dials Brennan. There's a long delay and Owen curses the other man's laconic nature. He hears a click.

'Brennan of the Bureau. What can I do for—'

'Brennan, I think I just got DarkChild's IP address!'

'What? You're kidding me!'

'He must have forgotten to mask his IP. Or the connection broke. I need a physical address, now!'

'Send me the details.'

Owen inputs them. 'Done.'

'I'll call back.'

A few minutes pass. Owen's smartphone rings.

'Yep.'

'Geo location is . . . TerraBites. An internet café not far from you.'

Owen feels his blood chill. 'Shit . . . I know it. Two

blocks from here ' He rises stiffly to his feet and calls across the office to the other agents sitting at their desks. 'Off your asses! Gotta go, now. I'll explain on the road!'

# 15

Owen and Jared Weiss sit in Owen's black Chevy Suburban, opposite TerraBites internet café, fifteen minutes from the office. Jared is an eager young probationary agent with a military buzz cut who often works with Owen in surveillance, and specializes in communications. Owen is burning with excitement, his hunch about DarkChild's whereabouts having proven right. In their exchanges, DarkChild referred to San Jose locales, in addition to the references to San Francisco, on a number of occasions. Owen has been authorized by Baptiste to coordinate the bust, which she reluctantly agreed to, but she won't let him make the arrest. This has stung him, but deep down he knows she is right. He's a liability with that leg.

Driving an automatic Chevy is fine, but chasing a suspect on foot isn't an option.

In the rear-view mirror, Owen watches as three SJPD patrol cars slide in a few spaces further down the street.

'Shit. Only three cars. Whatever happened to the concept of Force Multiplier?'

'Why are there still any of these places around?' Jared asks. 'It's not like there's no easy way to get online any more. Jesus, internet cafés are for dinosaurs.'

'Or people who want to be anonymous,' Owen says.

'Whatever. So, we going to go in and bust the creep?'

Owen wonders if Jared has been watching too many movies. Owen has to call the owner of the café, establish a few facts. His smartphone rings for some time.

'Hello, TerraBites,' a tired male voice answers.

'Good afternoon!' Owen says in his brightest tone. Jared shakes his head in amusement.

'Your day is about to get very interesting. I'm Special Agent Owen Malinski, FBI. May I speak with Chen Liu, the owner, please?'

'FBI, huh? Fuck you, asshole. Dave, man, I told you about—'

'Pal, it's the real deal. I am FBI, and the Bureau does not like to be fucked with. You waste any more of my time and we'll have the IRS down on your ass like white on rice. Now, let's try again. Is that Mr Chen Liu?'

'OK . . . That's me. How can I help you?'

'Chen, fantastic. Do you have an office?'

'Yes.'

'Then go there and shut the door behind you.'

'Hang on.'

Owen hears him close the door.

'OK.'

'You currently have a wanted felon using one of your terminals—'

'Ah, Jesus – I'm telling you, I had no idea, man.'

'So you say. Please keep calm. I'm outside with my team, and the local PD are standing by. What I need is a few details from you to make sure this goes as smoothly as possible. Got that?'

'Sure. What do you want?'

His eagerness to cooperate is suspicious. Owen makes a mental note to check on Mr Liu later.

'How many terminals you got?'

'Nearly fifty. Forty-eight, two are down.'

'OK, the suspect is using one of your computers. I assume your terminals are numbered?'

'Yes, they are.'

'OK. I'm going to send you a picture of the IP location. If you can match it up with what number terminal it is, that will be a great help.'

Taking down Chen's email address, Owen forwards the map image of the IP location. He waits.

'No pressure, Chen, but we need to catch this guy today.'

'OK . . . well it looks like he could be using terminal thirty-seven.'

'Thirty-seven. Are there any terminals free next to it?'

'Uh . . . Thirty-eight's taken. Thirty-six is down. You could have thirty-five?'

'Fantastic, book me a slot. I want the seat kept empty so that our man doesn't get suspicious when we make our approach. How much longer has he got on the clock?'

'Just over four minutes.'

'Plan is, my colleague Agent Jared Weiss is going to make the arrest. How is the café set out?'

'Well, there's seating by the door. Then the bistro. Towards the back are the computers and the printing areas.'

'Any side exits?'

'Back where the restrooms are there's a fire escape.'

'Great, thanks for your help. We'll be in presently.'

Owen hangs up. He relays the essentials to Jared.

'Got it. Here's the comms.'

Jared hands Owen a flesh-coloured earpiece so they can communicate with each other. Owen and Jared exit the Suburban, making towards the first patrol car. The lunchtime air has a clinging, muggy feel to it. The navy-uniformed officer in the driving seat waves, the window glass whirring as it slides down. Owen recognizes the cop from a previous operation.

'Sergeant Mitchell, nice to see you,' he says.

Mitchell, a burly officer with a broad, balding head, nods gruffly. They shake hands through the open window. He hands Owen a radio.

'Thanks,' Owen says. 'If you and your officers can maintain a cordon out front and back. Keep one man in each car just in case. There's a fire escape at the rear. Jared here's going inside to make the arrest. I'll be by the counter. Then DarkChild's heading for a ride to the holding cells. Fair enough?'

'Understood,' Mitchell says.

'Let's do this.'

Jared and Owen approach the café. Mitchell and his subordinates take the side alley towards the back, leaving two officers standing out front and an additional two cops in a patrol car.

'Not so close, guys, we don't want him spotting us too early,' Owen says with a wink. The SJPD officers dutifully stand a fair distance from the front door on either side, to avoid being seen from inside.

Owen is bathed in a jet of cool air conditioning as he enters TerraBites. It looks like the kind of place that's popular with the younger crowd. It has a nice clean design. Black wooden-panelled ceilings with black-cased spotlights. The floor is stone, with bright white strips of light every few feet. There are sofas near a large TV screen and a pinball machine near the restrooms, along with a printing and PC repairs kiosk. Owen sees a Chinese man watching them from behind the counter.

'Our coupon, please,' Owen says.

Owen turns to the side, discreetly lifting the hem of his shirt to reveal the badge clasped to his belt. The Chinese proprietor hands him the white login slip, which he passes to Jared. Chen looks nervous.

'Far left.'

'Go get him,' Owen whispers to Jared.

Turning to Chen, Owen asks, 'Can I have a paper?'

Chen hands him a *USA Today*, which Owen pretends to read while standing by the counter. Looking over the pages, he shoots a glance towards terminal thirty-seven.

An overweight Hispanic youth with long hair in a ponytail sits hunched over his screen, bopping his head along to some music playing in his headphones as Jared approaches.

Owen takes a breath as Jared pulls out his badge lanyard. He holds it in front of the Hispanic man, who suddenly stops bopping, pulls his headphones down off his ears, his face crumpled with confusion.

'FBI. You're under arrest.'

The bopper throws his hands up.

'Whoa! I ain't done nothin'!' he protests. Some computer users without headphones look over; most carry on oblivious. Owen leaves the counter, walking over.

The bopper is wide-eyed.

'Look, uh . . . I confess. I've downloaded a few hundred songs and movies. Who hasn't these days?'

Jared checks the bopper's screen. No sign of a chat room or hacker programs. Nothing but a file listing of movie soundtracks. Certainly no hint of the kind of stuff members of the Swarm are into. He tries a different tack. 'We know all about you, DarkChild.'

'What you call me? Fuckin' racist shit . . . Fuckin' feds.'

'You sure it's the right address?' Jared says.

Owen pulls out his phone. This is definitely the place. It doesn't make sense. Unless . . . unless Chen didn't turn the map around, and examine it from *his* point of view. Which would mean that DarkChild is really sitting over . . .

Owen looks across to the opposite side of the room.

A young dark-skinned guy with unruly black hair and dressed in combat fatigues meets his gaze for the briefest moment before shifting his eyes back down to his computer screen. He taps a key and then bolts from his seat.

'That's him!'

# 16

DarkChild sprints past the booths, knocking into a petite barista, whose tray of empty plastic cups goes flying as she crashes against a partition. He slams his hands onto the grey fire escape bar on the back door. The door flings open, and white light from outside makes Owen blink hard. He sees that the hacker has a laptop bag around his right shoulder, swinging and bumping against his hip, slowing him down. The cop sent to cover the back of the café is on his back, gasping for breath, knocked down as DarkChild burst through the door. *Goddamn flatfoot!* Owen curses silently. Stumbling past discarded cardboard boxes, Owen sees DarkChild slip over the weathered railings in front of a set of stairs. Behind TerraBites is a shared access area for deliveries and garbage. The muggy heat envelops Owen. He grabs his radio handset, squeezes down the grey call button.

'He's made us, heading out the back exit! Arab type, in fatigues, and he's running.'

Jared races past Owen and vaults over the railings.

Owen limps after him and stops, swearing in frustration.

'Copy that.' Mitchell's voice crackles over the radio.

Owen continues the pursuit, gritting his teeth.

'Damn you, Koenig . . .' he gasps.

The hacker tosses his laptop bag into the jaws of a reversing blue garbage truck, before disappearing into the back entrance of a shop under a fading sign – 'Movie Memories'.

'Be advised, there's a garbage truck reversing down the alley towards you. It's pretty tight, so we can't get down there right away.'

'No shit,' Owen says. He stands behind the garbage truck, badge outstretched, waving for the truck to move faster. He squeezes the button on the radio. 'He tossed his laptop in the back, make sure we get that.'

'Understood.'

Owen turns to one side, speaking into his comms link, 'Jared, keep on him. I'll get the cars round, cut him off.'

'Copy that. I think I saw a big rucksack by his desk. Looks like he was about to skip town.'

'I bet.'

'He's out of the shop, heading into the market.'

Owen turns back towards the fire exit of TerraBites and squeezes on the radio's call button again. 'You boys still in the car – head round the block towards the market!'

'Copy that, en route now,' an officer in the patrol car replies.

Chen stares at Owen, wide-eyed.

'Secure that terminal, Chen. We'll be back for it.'

Owen hurries as fast as he can towards his Suburban, wrenching the door open. He guns the engine as he speeds towards the end of the street and flicks a button on the dash. The wailing of sirens pulses from underneath the hood, with flashing red and blue LED lights built into the roof rail. Owen still loves the thrill of the blues and twos.

Turning right onto the downtown market, he sees it is pedestrianized. Crowds of locals and tourists are browsing and haggling over goods.

Owen swerves his massive Chevy down the street. People recoil from the sound of the siren and the roar of the engine and throw themselves aside. His thrill of a moment earlier turns to mortal terror at the possibility of running someone down by accident. He curses DarkChild for leading him into this chaos, and at the same time feels a grudging respect for his opponent's tactics. He squints through his windshield at the fleeing bodies. From the right he sees the flash of combat fatigues race across in front of him, disappearing past an aisle of fruit and vegetables. There's an access aisle to his left and he swerves the car round. Cruising past the market stalls, Owen turns right, heading straight on. The car creeps along as he peers down each aisle.

*Come on, where are you?*

Owen knows DarkChild must emerge from one of these aisles eventually, like a rat in a maze. He inches forward, his foot gently resting on the accelerator as the vehicle travels towards the corner of a used computers and electronics stand. Running too fast to see, DarkChild bounces onto the huge hood of the Chevy, sprawling across the windshield, badly winded.

'Gotcha!'

Owen climbs out, cuffs ready, gripping the hacker's arm with his left hand. With his right hand he applies a wrist turnout grip. He clicks the cuffs on one hand, then both, the metal rings sliding and locking into place. DarkChild stops struggling, lying down on the hood. He catches his breath, looking up at Owen with intense brown eyes.

*He's just a kid.*

Jared appears, breathing hard, pats Owen on the shoulder. 'Not bad.'

Owen yanks on DarkChild's cuffs, making him stand.

'You have the right to remain silent . . .' Owen reads him his rights.

DarkChild glares back, then spits. 'Fuck you!'

# 17

Owen glances at his analogue watch: 2 p.m. After an arrest, he has up to forty-eight hours to formally charge a suspect or they have to be released. Owen's spent two hours booking DarkChild – into Santa Clara County Jail. He had not been carrying any ID at the time of the arrest. However, a search of his rucksack resulted in three separate identities being found, complete with new passports, California driver's licences and social security number cards. The turnkeys had conducted a full strip search where they eventually found a receipt for a laptop repair in his pocket under the name Samer Aldeera. That matches one of the sets of ID documents found on him. They had also scanned his fingers, searching for his prints in the known suspect/wanted person databases. It came up with no matches. Samer is an unsub – an unknown suspect with no prior criminal history.

Owen and Samer sit in a grey interrogation room with hard plastic seats and a metal table. Owen has noticed a certain fastidiousness about Samer – despite the combat fatigues and uncombed hair, his fingernails are shaped and there is a poise about him. Very different from the usual gangly, pimpled hacker Owen has encountered.

Samer bows down, staring into the depths of his lap.

He has requested a court-appointed attorney, but this does

not mean a lawyer will drop what they are doing to attend.

Owen sees this as a blessing – an opportunity to gather the evidence he needs, unhindered. He unzips the rucksack retrieved from the rear of the garbage truck. Inside is a shiny black laptop, heavily customized with additional ventilation and blue stylings – HunterWare, a premium brand of laptop that Owen is familiar with. He gives it a tap.

'Recognize this?'

'Should I?'

'It's the one you tried to dump.'

'That's what you say. I've never seen it before.'

'We've got witnesses, CCTV, and we'll be able to match DNA traces. You're going to have to do better than that, kid.'

'I'm not your kid.'

'No? Your handle is DarkChild. Now I can see why. You behave like one.'

'And where did you hear that name?'

'The Swarm. Where else?'

He sees the young man's eyes widen. Just enough to betray him. Samer shakes his head. 'Never heard of it. What's that? Some coffee shop where the feds hang out?'

'Nice. But no. It's where you and your friends meet online to discuss the games you want to play with the grown-ups. It's where you go to boast about your exploits.'

'Like I said, never heard of it. You got the wrong guy. I'm not your DarkChild.'

'Really? Just an innocent person?'

'Got that right.'

'So why did you run, back at TerraBites?'

'Thought you guys were going to beat me up.'

'And what possible reason could you have for thinking that?'

'You're a cop. A white cop. You don't like the colour of my skin. I bet you have a nice collection of customized pillowcases at home. Do I need to draw you a picture?'

'You really think you can make that stick?' Owen shakes his head. 'It's going to look pretty desperate. Especially once we get inside this baby.' He taps the lid of the laptop.

'Go ahead. Be my guest.'

'Then what? You going to tell me that it's rigged to explode? Or wipe the data or something.'

'You been watching too many movies. It's much simpler than that. You ain't going to find nothing on there that'll hurt me.'

'Then it is your machine . . .'

Samer's expression hardens, furious with himself for falling into the trap so easily.

'Yeah, it's mine,' he concedes. 'Not that it's going to help you much.'

'We'll see.' Owen lifts the lid and presses the power button. The laptop boots up swiftly off a solid-state hard drive, then the login screen appears.

Password: _____

Owen slides Samer a pen and a jotter pad. 'Password?'

Samer considers. He picks up the pen in his handcuffed right hand before writing down '2ur1ng'.

'As in Alan Turing?'

Samer nods.

'Cute.'

He wonders if Samer is being a little too cooperative. 'Anything likely to happen when I enter the password? No fancy wipe routines or anything?'

100

'You'll have to find out for yourself.'

'All right. But before I do, you should know that any attempt to destroy data will be regarded in court as evidence of your guilt. There's now a ten-year sentence just for destroying data that forms any part of a federal investigation. Same goes for refusing to provide a password, or an encryption key. That'll be on top of any other charges. In the current climate, with your Middle Eastern background, I dare say we can throw a few terrorism charges into the mix. Just so you know, Samer.' He pauses. 'Last chance, before I try to access the machine.'

Samer sits back and folds his arms. Owen enters the password. The screen blinks to Samer's desktop, cueing a *Transformers* sound effect. Owen swipes the trackpad with his fingers, looking under the computer tabs.

No hard drive is visible.

He swivels the laptop around to face Samer.

'Your hard drive. Where is it?'

'You're the detective. You tell me.'

'Samer, you're not being sensible. You heard what I said. You're playing with fire here. If you mess with the Bureau's investigation into the Swarm then you are going inside for a long time. As it is, we can hold you in isolation for as long as I can convince the Homeland Security people that you pose a threat to Uncle Sam. Just so you don't get a chance to warn your buddies that we got you. And if I have anything to do with it then you'll be older than me by the time you get out.'

Samer makes a face. 'Eww.'

'OK, I've had enough of your shit. You think you impress me? Christ, I already have enough to put you away for life, regardless of what's on here. How do you think I managed to track you down? You and your pals are not nearly as smart as you think. Not only did the Bureau get all over your social media like flies on shit, we also got inside the Swarm. And I'm talking about the inner circle.'

'Impossible. You're dreamin', man.'

'Oh yeah? Who do you think Salvador is, then?'

Samer's expression freezes. He winces, almost as if he has been struck in the face. Then he shakes his head. 'No . . .'

'Oh yes, Samer. That's me. Salvador, at your service.'

'But you're too . . . old.'

'And you're too dumb. What? You think all hackers have to be skinny little streaks of piss just like you? Think again. You have no idea what anyone online looks like. I bet you've never even met any of the other members of the inner circle, have you? Maybe some of them are as old as me. Maybe some of them are women. Maybe some are even other feds. Ever thought about that?'

'That's not possible . . .'

'But you can't *know* that.' Owen leans forward and stabs a finger at the young man. 'What you do know is that you are in deep shit. You're looking at the end of the dream and the start of a lifelong nightmare, son. You help me, and I do whatever I can to help you beat the worst of the rap.' He pauses and softens his voice. 'You're little more than a kid, Samer. Why throw your life away for people and causes you know nothing about? Don't do it. You help me find the other members of the Swarm and we can work out a deal. Hell, you might even skip jail altogether . . . But if you continue trying to fuck with me then I will bury you. You have my word on it.'

'And if I give you what you want, I go free?'

'Not as easy as that. You help the Bureau and we'll do our best to keep you out of jail, but you're going to have to be watched in the future, Samer. You won't be allowed near anything more complicated than a calculator. That clear?'

Samer nods.

'Right. So tell me, how do I access your files?'

'Look for a folder, Cute Zebra.'

Owen does a quick search of the visible files. 'Got it.'

'Open the folder. There's a shitload of image files. And one executable.'

'I see it.'

'Select it.'

Owen does as he is told and another nondescript login box appears, asking for another password. He glances up. 'Spill it.'

'K-9-R-0-Y-0-T-0-E-N.'

Owen types and hits enter. A new file structure is revealed to him within the host folder. A brief search tells him that he has a treasure chest of incriminating documents, notes and databases, screen grabs, chat logs. Once it is checked against his own chronologies of the cyber attacks, exact times of online activity and other data, then a string of criminal charges can be made against Samer and his virtual friends.

Bingo.

'You're in deep trouble, son. There's enough here to keep the Bureau busy for months.'

'No time to spare for hunting down war criminals, I guess?'

Owen does not respond, but closes the lid of the laptop and takes it with him when he leaves the room.

Outside in the corridor he calls the district attorney's office at the federal courthouse, citing the evidence he has found. A young federal prosecutor, Marc Clayton, is assigned to the case. Owen is pleased with the choice. He has worked with Clayton before on the Koenig investigation. Clayton obtained the much-needed warrant from a judge to open a Facebook account that allowed them to track down Koenig.

Clayton advises Owen that he must email him some screen grabs of the evidence so he can set to work. Owen does so, backing up the data to a USB hard drive. He returns to the interrogation room.

'What I need is a signed statement listing all the companies and databases you broke into, along with a confession. Before that, what I'd also really like to know is why do it?'

'Why ask?'

'Indulge me.'

'Do you play video games?' Samer says quietly.

'Yes, I do. What does that have to do with this?'

'It's like a game. I saw these sites as . . . levels, each one leading to a more difficult challenge. I never did it for money. The thrill, the rush of hacking in, exposing all those flaws. That was the reward. It's addictive.'

Samer rubs his wrists.

'The more difficult it is, the bigger the thrill. I enjoyed outsmarting the government and corporations who say their data is secure. It isn't.'

He looks at Owen's smartphone. 'The camera, the microphone on your smartphone – they can be hacked. If they haven't been already.'

Owen studies him, knowing the truth of his words.

'We've got your backpack. You were about to skip town? Why?'

'I was . . . heading to LA. I move on every few months. To try and keep hidden from people like you.'

'Too bad.' Owen winks. 'Why did you stop in the café?'

'I shouldn't have. I wanted to say goodbye before I moved on. Just wanted to let the others know I'd be offline for a day or so. Stupid, I guess, but they're the best friends I've ever had . . .' He stares at Owen. 'Or at least I thought they were friends. Not rats.'

'I'm no rat. Just doing my job. Which is to catch little rodents like you.'

'So how did you find me?'

'A temporary connection error left you unmasked. You screwed up, Samer.'

The young man looks down, shamefaced. Owen lets him stew for a moment.

'Have you ever met any of them? Face to face?'

'The Swarm?' Samer shakes his head.

'How does it work, then? How do you guys organize things?'

'We are each assigned different objectives – MasterEscher is a rooter. He finds security flaws in the sites. I'm the social engineer. Sure, I can do the other stuff, but I like playing people, seeing if I'm smarter than they are. And I usually am. Möbius focuses on the hardware and infrastructure, KC assists wherever needed. It's a good team. And we're getting better all the time. And bolder.'

Owen's phone rings a big-top circus tune. He answers.

'Hey, it's Marc,' a male voice says in a deep tone. 'I got the pending charges. Judge Nolan has agreed to a teleconference to speed things up. Santa Clara has a conference suite, I believe.'

Owen leads Samer into the cramped conference room a few doors down in the office block of the jail. With new technology it's easier and cheaper to have the initial arraignment carried out via teleconferencing. Owen signs in with the PIN number and soon the screen splits into two. One image is of the assistant prosecuting attorney, Marc Clayton from the

Justice Department. He's African American, with close-cropped hair and a neatly trimmed goatee, wearing a cream shirt, navy suit with a soft stripe and a thin red tie.

'Hi, Owen,' Marc says. 'Mr Aldeera.'

On the right side of the screen is District Judge Nolan, his narrow eyes staring from behind his glasses. He has a reputation for being harsh. Nolan speaks into the camera.

'Samer Aldeera, aka "DarkChild", your pending charges are as follows. Four counts in total across three different states: Conspiracy to Engage in Computer Hacking; Conspiracy to Commit Access Device Fraud; Conspiracy to Commit Corporate Infiltration; Aggravated Identity Theft. You have the right to retain counsel. You are also denied bail, for the moment, as you present a significant flight risk.'

'Thank you, your honour,' Owen says. Denying Samer bail is a smart move. He'd been a slippery fish to catch and the Bureau couldn't risk letting him out in the open.

Samer has gone pale. 'What does all that mean? How many years do you get on those charges?'

Marc does a quick mental calculation.

'Unless there's a plea bargain, I'd say . . . one hundred and sixteen years in federal prison.'

# 18

Owen limps up the stairs with his grocery shopping and unlocks the door to his Rock Ridge apartment.

'I'm home,' he says, picking up the shopping bag and entering his studio apartment. It is simply furnished with a fish aquarium, intelligent chess set and self-assembly furniture from IKEA. He crashes onto the nearest soft cream sofa. On the coffee table there are framed photos of him racing cars and motorbikes in his younger years. It's been a long day.

'*Hello, Owen.*' A soothing female voice comes from the ceiling speaker. '*How was your day?*'

'Honestly, MIA, I'm pooped.' Owen is in no mood to indulge his digital personal assistant. Even though he's had the device for nearly two years it still feels weird to make conversation with the matt black cone on the shelf above his desk.

'*OK, Owen. How about some music?*'

'Sure. Something . . . relaxing.'

The sound of chamber music fades in.

'*Would you like me to put the oven on?*' the voice asks.

Owen has a freezer filled with ready meals. He is no gourmet.

'Good idea. Thanks.'

'*You're welcome.*'

After the arraignment, he'd led Samer to his holding cell. Small, scuffed white with a thin blue mat for a bed, a wash basin and a bathroom. He'd managed to find Samer a blanket. He'd also made it clear to the sheriff that Samer was to be kept away from the rest of the prisoners and out of the public eye. He didn't want other hackers to discover his arrest and sever their links to their former comrade. Samer's court-appointed attorney, Philip De Russet, is beginning to build the defence case.

Owen can see that Samer is socially awkward, but online, in his virtual community, he is a hero. He's exposed shocking security flaws in massive corporations and government departments. As DarkChild he has shown how vulnerable data really is. He has also exposed registered users of extreme pornography sites, some of which contained several senior government officials' emails. And for that, perhaps he and his friends deserve some credit. After all, the rich and power-ful have been getting away with concealing their sins, often aided by their rich media proprietor friends. In the digital age there are fewer places for such people to hide. And that's one reason why hackers are so assiduously targeted by those in power.

And now Samer's facing serious jail time, potentially spending the rest of his life behind bars. Owen knows Samer has broken the law. The digital world is a Mecca for disaffected youths like Samer who want to vent their anger and frustration. It's easy for such people to wander down the wrong paths. And what harm has really come of it? Sure, it has pissed off some influential people and embarrassed some corporations, but Samer has not used any of the financial details he's accessed. But it isn't down to Owen to pass judgement on the justice of the situation. His job is to uphold the law, warts and all.

Owen tells MIA to turn on the small wall-mounted TV and tunes in to a news channel.

A well-groomed news anchor with a flawless wavy haircut intones, 'In breaking news, Braxton Grindall accuses his rival, Senator Keller, of endangering the safety of Californians by refusing to endorse the president's new anti-terrorist initiative.'

There's a cut to a corpulent man in a suit standing outside the state capital, backed up by a coterie of earnest supporters holding placards. Grindall narrows his eyes and raises a finger as he declares, 'It's the senator's solemn duty to safeguard the people who were misguided enough to put their trust in him. When Braxton Grindall takes his place in Washington, you can be sure he'll be doing what Senator Keller is too damned scared to do for himself.'

Owen looks up briefly and shakes his head. 'Blowhard asshole . . .'

Now on screen there's Senator Keller and his entourage at the San Francisco State Campus. The camera operator is struggling to keep up with Keller as the female reporter thrusts her microphone towards the senator. It's the kind of interview approach that is designed to make the interviewee look evasive. But then Keller stops dead and rounds on the camera.

'Whatever my rival may say, I take my duty to protect the people of this great state very seriously indeed. Always have done, while my good friend Braxton Grindall was busy driving honest people out of poor neighbourhoods to clear the way for all those smart expensive houses that the people of Silicon Valley are so keen on. Now, if you'll excuse me, I've got better things to do than waste time responding to his bull.'

As he strides off Owen catches a glimpse of Jeff Blake just behind the senator, looking handsome in suit pants and an open-necked shirt, his jacket hanging over his forearm.

Then the screen cuts back to the studio. It's a pity about Keller, Owen thinks. The senator's a good man, but his views on digital technology are alarmist. But then maybe he has reason to feel that way. After all, he lost a son thanks to cyber bullying. That kind of shit changes a person. And now Keller is on a crusade to clean up the internet.

'Good luck with that, buddy,' Owen mutters. With kids like Samer on the loose, Keller has less than the ghost of a chance.

# 19

At the San Francisco Medical Examiner Office, Rose descends in the elevator to the facilities beneath Tower Road. It has been a few days since Coulter's body was discovered. Rose needs to know more about the suit, or Skin, the victim was wearing. She has left a message at WadeSoft but has had no reply. The battered elevator door slides open and she walks down the pale-green corridor towards the heavy doors marked 'Morgue'. Her echoing heels clatter and she quickly feels the temperature drop to a refrigerator chill. The choral crescendo of Mozart's *Requiem* floats like a shimmering ghost, or a joke in poor taste, getting louder as she pushes the swing doors open. She sees the ME, Arthur Benfield, sitting hunched over a stainless-steel autopsy table. He looks up from the blackened mass of Gary Coulter. Beside him is a tall, gangly autopsy technician who looks nearly as pale as the corpses nearby.

Benfield is a small, mole-like man, wearing a long white coat, paper boots over his shoes and big glasses which he permanently seems to be squinting through. Rose has worked with him many times and is bemused that, in this grim setting, he is always cheery, working along to classical music playing from a smartphone synced to a Bose sound system perched high on a shelf.

'Special Agent Blake. Always a pleasure. Just one moment, please.'

Rose nods and feels a chill as she passes the recently departed laid out on slabs. Some of their mouths are gaping wide, their skin a dull grey-lavender, some with eyes staring upwards as if in silent accusation. Tags are tied on their big toes.

Banks of cabinets containing jars of chemicals line the tiled walls above the polished steel sinks. Sharp metallic tools including scalpels, saws and face shields are neatly arranged on steel trolleys. Bright striplights softly hum and bathe the room in a faint blue hue. Pungent odours of dead flesh rush to greet her nostrils. Despite the morbidity, Rose finds morgues to be strangely intimate places, where dignity and courtesy always seem a prerequisite, even though most of the occupants are dead.

The sound of a drill whirring, and bone fragments cracking, pierces the air.

Rose turns to see the technician and Benfield hunched over Coulter's head. The technician grabs a steel hammer and chisel, firmly tapping the top of the skull three times. As they remove the top of Coulter's skull she hears what sounds like two halves of a melon being pulled apart.

'Seriously, guys, unless you wanna see me blow my breakfast can you do that when I'm gone?'

Benfield smiles apologetically as he tugs off a rubber glove to shake her hand.

'You know, Art, I've said this before, but working in a place like this . . . I don't see how you avoid going a little crazy.'

'It's not so bad. I'm surrounded by the kind of people who are well past stabbing you in the back. At least with the dead

112

you know where you stand. And you get used to the random flatulence.'

'What have you got for me?' says Rose.

'Certainly one of the strangest vics I've ever looked at. Before I make my final report, I still need to test the body's organs, and toxicology can take a while for the various cultures to grow, but I thought you'd appreciate the heads up.' He looks at Rose over the top of his glasses. '*Suspicious* is the word I'd use.'

Benfield rolls on his stool across the granite floor to pick up his clipboard from the sideboard. With all the advances in digital technology, he still prefers to work the old-fashioned way.

'Dental records confirm this is indeed Gary Coulter. This whole thing came in here a total mess. We had to cut the remains of the chair off him before we could even get to what was left of his body. Quite a job in itself.'

Rose edges closer, the smell of burnt flesh and formaldehyde stinging her nostrils.

Benfield has tried to peel back some of the black rubber suit from the body, but it has fused with the flesh in many places. Where he has been at work he has exposed a mash of interior organs, bones, lumps of burnt hair, dried blood and scorched flesh. Coulter's blackened hands are balled together tightly, evidence of the blazing torment he had endured. The remains of his lower jaw hangs open and twisted to one side, forever screaming.

'After the body had cooled, I managed to scrape most of the black plastic and leather from the chair away. But there's another textile involved. It's definitely some sort of rubber suit. I found a chunk of it left on his calves.' Benfield hands Rose a jagged strip of plastic in a clear bag.

Rose takes out her smartphone and does a quick online search before she holds it up. There's a publicity image of the new Skin on the screen. 'Look anything like this, do you think?'

'What the hell is that?'

'You don't watch much TV, then?'

'Can't stand it. Better off reading, every time. Why? What did I miss?'

Rose taps the side of the phone. 'This is going to be the next must-have computer toy. A suit that covers the body, and the head. Just like our victim, I'm thinking. See the visor? From what the maker says, it's going to be the virtual reality technology of choice.'

'I have enough trouble keeping a handle on the literal reality,' Benfield says.

He gestures at the corpse. 'So this suit, it's a weird one. Not a wetsuit, then, like one of your Bureau buddies suggested. That rules out some kind of fetish thing. There's what looks like the remains of a computer port round the back of the neck. There's something else.' He indicates a tray on the gleaming steel work surface beside him. Rose sees a twisted bit of black plastic, shiny but distorted.

'I found that on his skull. Looks to me like some part of a helmet perhaps. Or that visor in the picture you just showed me. There's wiring fused into his scalp and what looks like the remains of earphones. You can take the plastic and the rubber with you back to the Bureau, I have no further need for them.'

Rose nods her thanks and slips the pieces into a clear evidence bag.

'Anything else?'

Arthur looks at his notes. 'You'll like this. His genitals have been crushed.'

Rose forces a look at the gap between Coulter's open legs, down at his burst scrotum, not so badly burnt as the rest of the body. His epidermis is charred and destroyed, a mis-shapen testicle hangs loose. She shuts her eyes for a moment. That's another sight she'll never forget for the rest of her life. A thought flashes into her mind: some of Koenig's male victims had suffered genital mutilations. It could be just a coincidence.

'He also arrived with what was left of an erection, not uncommon for the deceased. We call it the last sausage at the barbecue,' Benfield says with a laugh.

'Charming. What's your opinion?'

'Honestly, I'm not sure. The strangest is yet to come.' He leans closer, and Rose can see her face reflected in his lenses.

'Once I peeled off the rubber and removed the burnt tissue, I found something very unusual.'

Benfield reaches for a slender polished scalpel. He lifts Coulter's charred wrist. Rose glimpses bits of black rubber dug deep under his fingernails. With the blade, Benfield pushes back some of the suit to expose a patch of dry skin. It's deep yellow and purple.

'To the casual observer, this could be mistaken for lividity. It begins immediately after the heart stops functioning. The cessation of the heart allows gravity to pull the blood to the lowest points of the body, so the tissue takes on a purplish tint, typically in the hands and feet. Most of the time it's a mistake to think the victim has been badly beaten, but in this case, he has.'

'He's been beaten?'

Benfield points at a red–raw, grid–like pattern imprinted from the suit onto the flesh.

'See how regular that is? It's as if he was crushed by a machine.'

'Is it possible the perp would have done this *post mortem*?'

'No. It happened while he was alive. With the crushed genitals and bruising, there's no way this can be classed as an accident. Certainly the fire is what killed him, but the circumstances leading up to the fire suggest extreme torture.'

Rose thinks this over for a moment. 'He was found sitting, with no signs of struggle – apart from the bits of rubber dug underneath his nails. Were there any drugs in his system? A sedative of some kind?'

'I'm still waiting for the rest of the tests to be done, but from what I've seen, there's been no sign of anything. It's possible we might find a short-acting but powerful sedative, such as propofol, in his system.'

'The anaesthetic?'

Benfield nods. 'The effects last thirty to sixty minutes before it wears off. Only a liver examination can confirm its presence. I've also checked the vitreous humour – the fluid in the eyes. He was certainly diabetic, but that had no bearing on his death.'

He rubs his jaw and thinks for a moment: 'That's all the news for now. I'll let you know if I find anything else.'

'Thank you, Arthur.'

'Until next time,' he says, flashing a smile. 'And since we're looking at foul play, I guess the funeral will be delayed. Who is the next of kin?'

'His mother. Lives in a retirement home in Fort Lauderdale.'

'She been told yet?'

Rose shakes her head. 'I'll pass the word to the local field office soon as I get back to my desk. Guess they'll send some uniforms round to break the news, before someone there gets it off the Stream and tells her first.'

'The worst news a parent can get. It isn't normal to bury your child.'

'Look around, Arthur. You tell me what's normal these days.'

'True.'

'But we'll let Mrs Coulter make arrangements for the funeral as soon as we can. Meanwhile thanks for these.'

She holds up the evidence bag, reflecting that killers often attend the funerals of their victims. It's a useful occasion to gather intelligence, even if the timing sucks. Rose decides that she will be there when the time comes. She paces out of the main autopsy theatre, presses the elevator call button. It seems Gary Coulter's death was anything but an accident. And now comes the hard part for the Bureau. Picking the crime apart minutely. They must search for an explanation, a motive and a killer. And find out why Coulter seems to have had what looks like a Skin before it was even released.

# 20

Back at the field office, Rose sits at the desk in the silent and empty interrogation room. Often when she is trying to get her head into a case she comes here to fully absorb all the details. She flicks again through the crime scene photos taken by the forensics. They are still taken on 35mm film to avoid tampering. In the digital age, any photographic evidence can be removed or fabricated using even the most basic software packages. Rose uses an inner dialogue, constantly questioning herself to check her assumptions, step by step.

*To understand the artist, you have to look at the painting.*

She tries to think herself into the mind of the killer. First there is the entry . . .

*Perhaps he buzzed the apartment. Coulter, wearing the suit, let him in. The killer entered wearing gloves, and savagely beat Coulter in the Skin. As part of the struggle he crushed Coulter's testicles . . .*

That's a stretch, Rose concedes. It's not the kind of damage you do to a victim incidentally.

*No, Coulter was beaten and tortured and then set on fire. There is no evidence of an accelerant yet, which implies that the killer tampered with the wiring so that it set the suit on fire, to make it look like an accident. Before the killer leaves, he injects Coulter with an anaesthetic strong enough to prevent his victim from attempting to put out the flames until it is too late. The killer leaves, closing and locking the door behind him. Then fire spreads through the suit, burning Coulter. The pain overcomes the anaesthetic and he starts to scream and is overheard by the neighbour . . .*

Possible, but is it plausible?

*Or Coulter had some sort of accident and it was an electrical fault after all . . .*

But that doesn't explain the burst scrotum. Or the cry of 'stop'.

*Perhaps he was worked over the day before, while testing the suit, and then his attacker, or attackers, finished him off by sedating him and rigging up an incendiary device in the condo.* But no evidence of such a device has been recovered from the crime scene.

Rose pushes the photos away from her. None of it feels right.

She needs to know more about the suit. She has already called WadeSoft to ask to speak to someone on the team that developed the Skin, since the similarities between Coulter's device and the new must-have computer leisure accessory are too numerous to overlook. She had been put through to the company's technical director who had promised to have someone call her back to help with her queries. That was two days ago and she has heard nothing from WadeSoft. She makes a note to call them again.

Then there's the company that employed Coulter.

Rose opens Coulter's wallet. There are the usual mall cards, bank cards and there – a swipe card for Peek Industries. It's a black card with a red, peak-like logo. She lays that to one side. Bank records may also be helpful to see if there was any unusual activity such as large deposits or withdrawals in the run-up to Coulter's death, but that will require a subpoena.

Coulter's cellphone SIM card was destroyed in the blaze. Rose tabs onto her phone's Google browser, searching for

Peek Industries. The link takes her to a black page with the red mountain chevron logo in the top right corner. The company slogan reads, 'The Cutting Edge of Innovation'. She clicks on the 'About Us'.

'Founded in 2010, Peek Industries specializes in information systems, solutions, communications products and simulations for the federal government, including the Department of Defense.'

She searches for any recent news articles. There are plenty relating to the company's contributions to the development of high-tech missiles, surveillance drones and next-generation military training software. Then, a few months ago, a communiqué was leaked that revealed that Peek was exempt from the usual government contractual procedures. The revelation caused a minor stir on Capitol Hill, but not much else. Rose browses the articles but can find no specific mention of anything that resembles the body suits of the kind Coulter appeared to have been wearing at the time of his death. Going back to the 'Contacts' page she taps in the number given for the company's headquarters. She notes Peek Industries is based in Falls Church, Virginia, a bit off the beaten track given the nature of the work they claim to carry out.

'Peek Industries, how may I direct your call?' a female voice asks.

'Good afternoon, my name is Special Agent Rose Blake, FBI. May I speak with your CEO, please?' She quickly recalls the name from the website's details. 'Mr Frost.'

'One moment, please . . . Mr Frost's unavailable right now. Is there anyone else who might help you?'

'I really need to speak to Mr Frost.'

'I'm afraid Mr Frost cannot be contacted without prior notice. In any case, I know he's out of the office today.'

'Then could you give me his cell number?'

'I'm sorry, but that's against company policy, Special Agent.'

'Fine. Then, for now, put me through to your head of personnel.'

'Toby Preis is our head of Human Assets.' She emphasizes the last two words. 'Would that be of help?'

'Yes . . . Thank you.'

'Just a moment, please.'

'Toby Preis, Human Assets. How may I help you, Special Agent Blake?'

'I'm calling to advise that an employee of yours – Gary Coulter – has died.'

'Who?'

'Gary Coulter. He was a software engineer. He had your swipe card in his wallet.'

'Oh . . . Jesus. I'm sorry to hear that. How did Gary . . . Mr Coulter . . . er . . . What happened?'

'I'm not at liberty to say, but we are treating the circum-stances as suspicious. We're investigating his death and I need some background on Mr Coulter.'

'And that's why you're calling us?'

'Yes,' she says patiently, finding it a comfort to know that US industry is still recruiting the brightest and the best.

'I knew him well enough to say that Coulter was one of our freelance staff, a very gifted lead coder. We have a number of projects, many classified by the US government. Our employees sign multiple NDAs, so I cannot discuss the specifics. You want anything more detailed than that and we'd need a court order. I'm sure you understand.'

'I guess,' Rose replies testily. 'And we'll get a court order if we need to. In the meantime, his neighbour says he was working from home for the last month. Was he still working for you then?'

'No.'

'Why is that?'

'It's a bit awkward, Miss Blake.'

'You can call me Special Agent Blake. Awkward or not, the man is dead, and we need your cooperation in uncovering the circumstances of his death. Is that clear?'

'Yes . . .' Preis hesitates before continuing. 'Well, about a month ago, we had cause to place Gary under internal investigation.'

'Really? Why?'

'I'm not sure I can tell you, Special Agent Blake.'

'I'm sure you can tell me something.'

'Mr Coulter took some company property off the premises, which was a serious breach of his contract. So we were obliged to terminate his employment.'

'What was the nature of the property he removed?'

'That's classified.'

'Classified?'

'Absolutely.'

'All right, then . . .' Rose decides to try a different tack. 'What was he like as a person? You can at least tell me that.'

'He was . . . Difficult. Kept to himself, didn't bond with the other team members so well. He was off tangent at the time we had to cancel his contract.'

Off tangent? What the hell does that mean? 'In what way was he off tangent, exactly?'

'Mr Coulter's contribution to the project we engaged him to work on was increasingly directed towards his own interests rather than ours. That's all I am prepared to say, Special Agent.'

'Tell me. Does your company have anything to do with the Skin?'

Preis is so quiet Rose thinks the line has gone dead.

'Skin? Why no, that's WadeSoft's latest toy, isn't it? I'm sorry I can't be of much further help to you. We are given very strict guidelines on what we can talk about. Good luck with your investigation, Special Agent Blake. Goodbye.'

Now the line *is* dead. Rose gazes at her handset.

Why is Peek Industries so keen to wash its hands of Gary Coulter?

# 21

Half an hour later, Rose explains all she has learned to Baptiste and Brennan in Baptiste's office. She places the piece of the torn rubber suit, sealed in a plastic bag, onto the table. Baptiste runs her fingers over the nodes and sinewy texture before passing it to Brennan.

'Kinky.' Baptiste rubs her eyes. 'Must make you sweat like a turkey before Thanksgiving.'

'You'd think,' Brennan agrees. 'But now that I've had the chance for a closer look at a sample of this stuff I'm starting to see how the suit works. If it was just rubber you'd stew inside it, like you say. Give it a few weeks and it would stink. That's never going to play well with the consumer market.'

'So they came up with a fix?' asks Rose.

'Exactly.' Brennan taps the plastic bag. 'There's a lattice-work of tubes running through the rubber material. I managed to extract some goo from one of them and it turns out to be a low-viscosity coolant. With a micro pump and proper heat exchange device the person wearing the suit can stay cool, no matter how they, uh, exert themselves. It's smart stuff. Mind you, it would need to be if this technology is going to market. The military isn't going to be worried about the grunts' personal hygiene issues, but John Q. Public won't be too keen on stinking like a sumo wrestler's thong. PR. nightmare.'

Rose smiles. 'Fascinating as that is, Brennan, it isn't helping us much. We need to know more about this suit, what exactly Coulter was working on at Peek and why they fired him. If that's what they did.'

'Meaning?'

'I spoke to the head of personnel, I mean human assets, at Peek. Or at least that's what he said he was.'

'Human assets?' Baptiste raises an eyebrow. 'Is that what employees are called these days?'

'Guess so. Anyway, this guy was called Toby Preis. Even though he seemed disturbed by the news about Coulter he wasn't giving anything away. Very much a "why don't you just fuck off and find out" kind of attitude.'

'Sounds like Peek are hiding something,' Baptiste agrees. 'But we can't do much else for the time being. Not without sufficient evidence to try for a court order.'

Baptiste slides a memory stick across the table. 'I checked the apartment building's CCTV. No one came anywhere near Coulter's place before or during the fire.'

Silence envelops the office.

'Are we going to reconsider the possibility that it was an accident, or suicide maybe?' asks Brennan.

Rose turns to him. 'So Coulter mashes his own nuts to a pulp and beats himself black and blue, and *then* decides to set himself on fire. That's quite a theory, Brenn.'

'It's not impossible . . .'

'Jesus!' Baptiste hisses in frustration. 'What kinds of entrance tests did you have to fail to get into the Bureau?'

'Whoa there!' Brennan holds his hands up. 'You got me. But how do you explain that there's no sign of anyone entering or leaving the building for hours either side of his death?'

That is the question, Rose concedes. The trail is growing cold. Unless something comes up quickly it's hard to see how they can push the investigation further. 'Could a third party have sabotaged the suit to somehow kill Coulter?'

Brennan thinks for a moment. 'I'd need to know more before I offered an opinion on that. But even if the suit was sabotaged, so that it went up like a torch, that still leaves the fact that he was beaten to a pulp. That's the work of someone who was there when it happened.'

'Well, all right then,' Rose responds. 'I just can't help wondering if this Skin suit could be controlled remotely somehow. But shoot my speculation down in flames then, why don't you?'

Brennan shrugs. 'Sorry, Rose.'

For a moment no one speaks and then Baptiste lets out a sigh. 'In other news, Owen caught DarkChild.'

*Way to go, Owen*, Rose thinks.

'He's the one who hacked the Pentagon, its contractors and some of the telecoms giants. And he's just turned twenty,' Baptiste says. 'What the hell is wrong with kids today?'

There's a knock at the glass door. Rose turns to see Linda, Baptiste's secretary, outside. Baptiste gives her the nod and Linda opens the door.

'I'm sorry to interrupt, but Assistant Secretary of Defense, William Maynard, is on line one for you.'

All three around the desk exchange a look before Baptiste nods her thanks, waiting for the door to be closed. 'I want you two to be in on this. About time we heard something from the Pentagon.' She picks up the phone handset and presses the line one button.

'Baptiste,' she says formally. 'Yes, Assistant Secretary . . .

126

Yes, the room is secure.' She taps the speakerphone button, leaning forward.

'We have present Special Agent Rose Blake, Violent Crime and Undercover Operations. Brennan Bamber, Acting Head of Cybercrime and Computer Forensics.'

'Thank you, Baptiste. Good day to you, Special Agents. So, the situation is that we have the death of a key member of a sensitive Defense project. I've taken an interest because of the nature of the work Coulter was carrying out. I don't know what you've found out about Gary, but I'd be grateful if you could copy me in on anything you discover. It might trigger some links at this end that you might find useful to your investigation.'

'Bullshit,' Brennan mouths.

'Thank you, sir. We would appreciate any help.'

'So what's the story so far? All I know is that he died in a house fire. And that the Bureau has not made the call yet on whether or not it's an accident. If there's nothing suspicious about his death then it's just a tragedy. Otherwise we've got a problem and it becomes a potential national security issue. You understand?'

'Yes, sir.'

'What's your thinking?'

'Special Agent Blake is taking the lead on this case. I'll let her speak for the Bureau, if that's OK?'

'Fine. Go ahead.'

Rose leans forward. 'It's possible we're looking at a homicide. The coroner's found signs that Coulter was badly beaten and his genitals crushed before he was burned alive.'

'You're saying it was murder, then?'

'That's the most likely cause.'

'What about suicide?'

127

'Not likely, sir. Most suicides tend not to inflict torture on themselves first, and that hypothesis is also not consistent with what we have discovered so far.'

'Assuming it was murder, do you think it might have happened during the course of a robbery?'

'His valuables were still in the apartment, and so was his wallet. And there is no sign of a break-in, sir. Nor any visitors the night of his death.'

'If he didn't take his own life, and there's no evidence that anyone was with him . . . What are you suggesting, Special Agent Blake? You must have missed something. Someone else had to have been there with him. Perhaps waiting for him to get home before they attacked.'

'There's nothing on the security cameras, sir.'

'Then maybe they have been tampered with?'

'We can certainly look into that angle, but the cameras are sealed units and the feed is stored on the cloud and password-protected. I think we can safely discount any notion of tampering with the CCTV. But there's another detail you should know about. We found traces of some sort of rubber body suit on Coulter.'

'Rubber suit? Are you sure?'

'Yes, sir. We think it may be some kind of software simulator accessory. Like the Skin that WadeSoft is releasing soon. Do you know anything about that?'

There's static on the speaker.

'Assistant Secretary?' Rose says.

'A Skin?' Maynard says, eventually. 'Coulter was wearing one of those suits? You have proof of this, I take it?'

'At time of death, he was found wearing the partial remains of a device that our experts think is a Skin. Is there any connection between WadeSoft's Skin and the work Coulter was doing for your department?' Rose presses.

'Coulter was working on a classified project. At least he was until recently. He led a small research and development team working with a defence contractor.'

'Peek Industries?'

'Yes.'

'When I spoke to them they said his contract was terminated . . .'

'That's right. But my understanding is that he was not fired, exactly. They were forced to suspend him. Something was stolen from the company and they suspected Coulter.'

'What was stolen?'

'Classified software. And that's all you need to know.'

Brennan rolls his eyes.

'Assistant Secretary,' Baptiste says. 'With all due respect, how are my agents supposed to do their job if they can't fully investigate the victim?'

'Flora, do not use that tone with me,' Maynard replies. 'I appreciate your frustrations, really I do. But my hands are tied when national security is at stake. Have you got any other leads?'

Rose responds. 'We have the hard disk from his laptop. We're trying to crack that now, but it may take a while if his encryption is any good.'

'I see . . . Do you think you'll be able to gain access to his files?'

'We're hopeful. It would help us to know whatever you can tell us about Coulter's work at Peek, and if you could instruct them to be a bit more forthcoming.'

'I'll see what I can arrange to be declassified.'

Baptiste responds. 'So, right now you can't do anything to help the investigation?'

'I'll contact you when I find out a way to help. Keep up the good work.'

'Thank you, Assistant Secretary,' Baptiste says, but Maynard has already ended the call.

Brennan is animated. 'He *totally* knows something about that Skin.'

'Too right.' Baptiste nods.

'We still have the CSI report to come. That may turn up something,' Rose says.

'It may,' says Baptiste.

'And we can ask for access to Coulter's emails,' Rose adds.

Baptiste turns towards Brennan. 'See how you get on with the laptop and we can go from there. I'll also authorize the usual background checks, limited surveillance, some face time with family, friends, co-workers.'

Brennan nods.

'While we're waiting for Maynard to cut us some slack it might be an idea to have a word with the people at WadeSoft. They might be able to tell us something, given that there seems to be more than a little similarity between their Skin and the suit that Coulter was wearing,' says Rose.

Baptiste nods. 'All right. Take Owen with you. See what you can find out.'

# 22

The next morning, Owen drives them to WadeSoft's head office while Rose takes out her smartphone and does a search on Wade Wolff, the corporation's youthful chief executive. There are over a million hits. He had found success at an astonishingly young age, just as Mark Zuckerberg had done. But he runs his business in very different, idiosyncratic ways.

While Owen merges into the steady pace of freeway traffic she narrows the search down to video clips and taps a listing. A video window opens up. There's a short commercial and then the logo for *The Tallent Show* appears and then dissolves to reveal the slender host, Johnee Tallent, walking towards the camera with a thoughtful expression. In the background looms the gleaming glass of a corporate head office. Tallent pauses and does his trademark tilt of the head as he asks:

'Who is Wade Wolff?'

The screen explodes into a burst of blue flames.

Cut to filler shots of Wolff's youth, his first publicity photos, the company's products and the corporate headquarters.

'An IT graduate from Stanford, he set about creating a new social network that combined every aspect of life, all in one system – social media, entertainment, leisure and office productivity, all for free. He called it the StreamPlex. He then sold specifically targeted advertising by profiling every user, and by the time he was twenty-six he had generated his first billion in advertising revenue.'

Cue a shot of Wade in a black suit sitting on a white sofa in a bar. He has neatly parted brown hair, a young, boyish face.

'His corporation is the manufacturer of the smartphone you are probably using to watch this right now, as well as MIA, his Multimedia Interactive Assistant.' Quick flashes of smartphone screens of different shapes and colours race by.

'Innovation, Design, Integration. That's my mantra,' Wade remarks, taking a sip from a mojito.

'In the last few years the StreamPlex has made Wade into a household name. Still only twenty-eight, Wade Wolff has amassed a private fortune in excess of ten billion dollars. Romantically linked to several supermodels and pop stars, he's one of the richest men in the world, and some say the most powerful, with many political connections.' There are several hand-held video clips of Wade on an evening out with two society climbers draped either side of him. He pauses to hug the current president.

'But Wade Wolff is not without his controversies and critics. He's had death threats—'

This cuts to Wade raising his eyebrows. 'I mean, really. Me? I'm not a crazy dictator.'

'So he released an app where, yep, you guessed it, you can shoot Wade on your smartphone.'

Wade raises his hands. 'It just seems a good idea to me. A lot of people out there hate me, and that's to be expected. Successful people are always hated by the majority of the population, it's a fact of life. So I thought I'd give something back, even to the haters. I mean, I imagine shooting some of them, so it's only fair.'

Tallent looks at the camera. 'The app is currently number four on the download chart.'

The screen cuts to hand–held camera footage of protests outside a hexagonal glass building.

'Wade was also in the spotlight over a recent remark he made that he is proud of not paying his taxes, referring to the matter as merely capitalism in practice. Later, protests outside WS headquarters turned ugly when WadeSoft's mass dumping grounds for obsolete equipment in China were uncovered. The company denies claims that toxic chemicals are leaking into local water supplies, causing illness and birth defects.'

This cuts to footage of a Senate hearing.

'He's also locked horns with the Justice Department and Senator Chris Keller.'

There's a medium close-up of Keller jabbing his finger as he intones, 'Encryption technology and lack of cooperation with law enforcement helps organized crime, and worse, it hands power to the very terrorists our great nation has been trying to stamp out for over a generation now.'

The screen cuts to Wade, who responds, 'Technology and StreamPlex companies must not become an arm of the surveillance state. You can obtain the same information elsewhere. It's not down to me.'

Back to the senator, leaning closer to his mike. 'According to the FBI's latest research, most crime is now perpetrated through your StreamPlex and nurtured by archaic privacy laws. You're allowing people to place themselves above the law and using that as a selling feature to criminals.'

Quick dissolve to a close-up of Johnee Tallent: 'Wade Wolff, a villain to some in the establishment, but a hero to his many fans.'

133

Cut to a shot of Wade surrounded by a crowd of enthusiastic young schoolkids.

'Some claim Wade Wolff is a technological messiah,' Tallent's voice-over continues. 'Spurring enormous advances in artificial intelligence, immersive social media and marketing. So, who exactly is Wade Wolff?'

'A goddam genius is how I'd describe myself,' Wade says, flashing a smile.

Rose slides her smartphone back in her pocket. Her new lead, it seems, will be a challenge.

'We're here,' Owen says.

Rose sees they are approaching a large green road sign indicating the turn-off for WadeSoft. The beating heart of Silicon Valley. The corporation's head office is a vast glass hexagon, surrounded by the high walls of a security compound, newly added following recent protests. After showing their identification at the security booth, they are handed visitors' passes and buzzed in via the sliding metal-barred gate. They are directed to the parking area. The head office is a huge sprawling campus. They pass water features, shallow swimming pools, sand volleyball courts, lush grass lawns where employees sit under sunshades sipping from disposable cups. Rose is a little surprised by its vacation resort ambience.

The main lobby of the facility has an airy, clinical atmosphere with lots of white light falling across a range of cold-looking metal and granite surfaces. A smiling helper is waiting to guide them to the executive wing for their appointment. As they walk through the offices there's a projection of current activity on the Stream that spans a screen forty feet wide. Random toys are stacked and scattered on shelves, across desks – Rubik's cubes, Slinkys. Employees, casually dressed, sit at their desks, which have two, sometimes three, monitors on them. They pass a globe with twinkling lights, and backlit maps track the number of Stream users at any time, day or night, from around the world. All fitted with the WS logo in chrome finish and blue trimmings.

At the reception desk of the executive wing, there's a large female face on the screen cropped beneath the hairline and above the chin. Her blinking expression loads into a broad smile.

'Good day, visitors, my name is CLEM – Client Liaison and Experience Manager. How may I help you?'

'Special Agents Blake and Malinski. We have an appointment to see Wade Wolff at 11.15,' Rose says, glancing at her watch. 'Ten minutes from now.'

CLEM smiles. 'Certainly. May I see your ID, please?'

Rose and Owen hold out their lanyard cards in front of the screen for scanning.

'Thank you. I'm sorry, but Mr Wolff is very busy today. His current meeting is overrunning. He will be free in . . . thirty minutes. Meanwhile, he thanks you for your interest and invites you to take the tour of head office.'

An arrow appears on the screen, pointing to the right.

Rose draws herself up to her full height. 'We'd rather speak to Mr Wolff now.'

'Nevertheless, Mr Wolff is in a meeting for the next thirty minutes.'

Rose holds up the bagged Skin remains. 'I've got a dead body wearing one of these. Look familiar?'

'One moment, please.' CLEM's face fades from view to be replaced by an infomercial about WS's latest smartphone. After a moment CLEM's face reappears.

'Sorry to keep you, Special Agents. If you take the elevator behind you to the third floor, Mr Wolff's office is at the end of the corridor. You can't miss it.'

'Thank you,' Rose says.

'You're very welcome. Have a good day.'

*Ding.*

The chrome elevator doors behind them slide open.

Rose paces into the elevator with Owen, presses the button for the third floor and the doors close.

'In a meeting, my ass,' says Owen. 'No bastard plays power games with the Bureau's finest, even if his name is Wade Wolff.'

Meeting a man of power is always a little daunting. Meeting the man who owns a significant chunk of the world's personal information, who has more money than many sovereign nations, is unnerving. But he still breathes, eats, drinks and shits like anyone else, Rose reminds herself. And she has no intention of letting Wade Wolff forget the fact.

# 23

Exiting the elevator, Rose and Owen head down a brightly lit white corridor. They reach the end of the hall, where the corridor widens in front of a pillared door bearing the name of the company's creator in large polished brass letters. At their approach the door slides soundlessly to one side and reveals a large office beyond. The far wall is one long window, floor to ceiling. In front of it is a large oak desk. Wade Wolff is standing behind it and smiling.

'Special Agents, please come in.'

They enter and the door slides shut behind them. Rose is taken aback by the surprisingly traditional design of the office. It is lined with wood panels and a beautifully grained bookcase stretches along each side wall. Few of the shelves contain any books though. Most of the space is taken up with science fiction models, some of which Rose recognizes from movies.

Wolff has neatly cut brown hair, is wearing a black T-shirt and light slacks, and is barefoot. He has a silver smartphone in his hand. He is not alone. Two men in overalls are positioning a coffee table between a large sofa and the window. As Rose glances towards the table she can see that there is movement on its surface. The entire thing is a computer screen, with sleek-looking apps and widgets.

'What do you think of it?' Wolff speaks with a distinct Southern twang.

Rose nods. 'Impressive.'

'Of course it is. It's permanently linked to the Stream, and powered wirelessly.' He pulls a small black box away from the surface. The projected images disappear. 'It turns every surface into an interactive screen. Interactive, augmented lives.'

'Mixed reality?' Owen asks.

'Precisely.'

He places it back down on the table and the screens re-appear. 'In a few years these are going to be in every home . . . Well, every home that can afford one. One moment, please. I find it extremely difficult arranging furniture. It's distracting if it's in the wrong place.' He waves the two men back from the table and stares at it, stroking his jaw.

Rose catches Owen's eye and then looks to the heavens.

Everyone waits. Then Wolff smiles, apparently satisfied. 'Now find me a plant. A small plant. For the corner there.'

One of the men nods, and then they leave the office as their boss turns to his guests and offers his hand in greeting.

'I apologize. I lack certain social graces. I should have introduced myself as soon as you came in. I'm Wade Wolff.'

For an instant Rose is charmed by the gesture, as if there was the remotest chance they had not recognized him. Then she realizes it is just a gimmick, designed to flatter them. A businessman's trick.

'Thank you for seeing us, Mr Wolff. I'm Special Agent Rose Blake and this is Special Agent Owen Malinski.'

'Call me Wade,' he says, shaking Rose and Owen's hands. 'Everyone else here does . . . Well now, I have the FBI right here in my office. I gotta get a selfie, if you don't mind?'

It isn't a question. He picks up his slim glass smartphone and, before Rose can even think to protest, holds it out in front of them and takes a picture.

'I'll have to ask you to erase that, Mr Wolff,' says Owen. 'I don't think the Bureau would be keen on having its agents used as selfie props.'

'I wouldn't worry about it. I happen to know the director. I'm sure he won't make a fuss. Anyway, please call me Wade.'

He taps on another part of the screen. 'This is a prototype of the new smartphone – pretty chill, isn't it? I've been doing a bit of background on you since I heard you'd arrived.' He switches his attention to Rose. 'Rose Blake, the agent who nearly took down the Backwoods Butcher – I'm honoured. I'm sure the Bureau will get him next time.'

'I am sure that we will,' she says.

Wolff swipes his hand across the desk, and with a low pulsing sound, application windows instantly fold and fade from view, to be replaced by an image of clear blue water rippling across the top of the table.

'Can I get you a drink?' he says, motioning them to sit down on the chairs to one side of the desk.

'We're fine, thank you,' Rose assures him as she takes her seat.

'Mineral water for me, actually,' Owen says.

Wolff opens his small refrigerator, takes out a sealed bottle, cracks the lid and pours it into a glass before passing it to his guest. Then he sits down on the steel and black leather chair behind the desk. 'So . . . what brings the Bureau to my office?'

'This,' Rose says, placing the bagged Skin fragment on the table along with a broken piece of visor. 'It was found on

139

Gary Coulter, who we believe was murdered last Sunday evening.'

Wolff leans forward to inspect the sealed evidence bag. 'May I?'

'Through the bag is OK.'

He picks up the bag and runs his thumb over the nodes beneath the plastic.

'Recognize it?' asks Rose.

'If you mean do I know what it is, then yes. Looks like one of our Skins, but it isn't. You found this on a murder victim?'

'Murder is the working hypothesis,' Rose corrects him. 'And we're wondering why the victim would be wearing something very similar to a product your company manu-factures.'

'Beats me.'

Owen takes a sip of mineral water and clears his throat. 'Given your product hasn't been released yet, we need to know how Coulter managed to get his hands on one of these suits. Can you help us out on that one, *Wade*?'

Wolff shakes his head. 'It's not one of ours. I know that just from seeing this piece. In any case, all the promotional suits are held here in this building under tight security. They won't be going out to the media for another ten days. The first production run has only just started and not all the components have been shipped to the assembly facility. It's possible that there's another company working on the same technology. Our product is lighter. This looks like it could be one of the older military prototypes. We abandoned some of the earlier models. They proved too uncomfortable for prolonged wear.'

'Military prototypes?' Owen asks.

'I should tell you that after you first called my office to arrange this meeting I had a conversation with my contact in the Pentagon about what I could and could not tell you about this product's history. So I have to be guided by what he told me I was at liberty to reveal.'

'This is a murder investigation, Mr Wolff,' Rose says. 'We could subpoena you.'

'You could try. But I bet national security trumps even a murder investigation. Been that way since Kennedy was shot. Right?'

Owen frowns. 'Kennedy?'

'Ah, come on, Special Agent. The Bureau was up to its neck in that conspiracy. Don't even try to deny it.'

'Before my time, sir,' Owen says. 'And above my pay grade. What did the Pentagon *allow* you to tell us?'

'This contact . . . Wouldn't happen to be Assistant Secretary Maynard, would it?' Rose asks.

'Maynard *is* in charge of many special projects. I can tell you that much.' Wolff collects his thoughts. 'I'll give you a brief overview. The original Skin project commenced over five years ago. We kept it under wraps, for obvious reasons. You know what the tech industry is like. Once an idea gets out everyone wants a piece of the action. Somehow, word of what we were developing got to the ears of someone at the DoD, and before you know it they're all over us like a rash. They took one look at the specs and slapped a federal secrecy order on us.'

'Never heard of one of those,' says Owen.

'It's got that name for a reason, Special Agent. So anyway, they tell me that the Skin can give them a vital training tool for Special Forces. We cut a deal where Uncle Sam paid for research and development, in exchange for giving us the rights to adapt their simulated warfare software into consumer games. At that stage there were a handful of prototypes in development and the cost per suit ran into the tens of millions. So I can see why they didn't want to roll out the production. Eventually their project was shelved, deemed too expensive, and these suits were stored in an R & D facility. But I could still see the potential in the consumer market and we worked to develop and manufacture a far cheaper alternative. It would seem Gary Coulter might have got his hands on a mothballed prototype for himself. For whatever purpose. I suppose he might have been thinking about offering it to one of our competitors. I know Chin Hau Enterprises would kill for an early look at it. Our Asian pals are no respecters of intellectual property, I can tell you.'

Rose nods. 'Seems like Mr Coulter has a penchant for stealing. A week before his death his contract was terminated at Peek Industries for stealing company property from the premises. At least that's what we were told.'

'Really? That makes more sense than him having a Skin. He's more of a code monkey than a hardware type.'

Owen leans forward. 'So you knew Coulter?'

'Knew of him. Most people in my field do. Man's something of a minor legend.'

'Do you have any idea what kind of work Coulter was doing at Peek?'

'He was pulled in to work on the AI for the combat simulations on the original project. You know, working out the routines for the Opposing Forces, to make sure they responded in a realistic manner. That was the hardest part to get right, and the most important, if the Special Forces guys were going to be trained through the Skin system.'

'Did he succeed?'

'Let's just say he was one of the best in the business. If anyone can tweak the AI to do the job required, then he is – was – your man. Quite brilliant in his own way, but like some bright guys he lacked certain social skills. Bit of a loner, you know what I mean? Anyway, our team did the work for the government in return for being given the go-ahead to use the simulation engine to design the combat games when the Skin was allowed to go to market. That's no small deal. The technical specifications we got off the military were invaluable. No other game designers were going to get close to the detail we were given. So it worked out well for both sides: Uncle Sam got to trial the training simulator suits and we got the exclusive rights to use the software and hardware when it became declassified, even if we had to wait before we could develop the consumer version of the Skin and release it to the public.'

Rose nods. 'I've seen the adverts. You've been making quite a big splash on the marketing.'

'Well over two hundred million dollars so far. Biggest promotional spend in WadeSoft's history. But then the Skin is going to be the biggest domestic entertainment product in history.'

'You think?'

'I know it, Special Agent.' He pauses. 'May I call you Rose?'

'If you like.'

'All right then, Rose. You've seen the advertisements. Let me tell you, the Skin is as good as it sounds. You put one on, load up a sim and you are in another world. The launch pack comes with a skiing sim and, the one I am most proud of, a sky-diving sim. There's a bungee jump mode too. Scares the crap out of me every time I've used it.'

143

'I'm sure it's a lot of fun, Mr Wolff.'

'Screw fun, it's as good as the real deal. Better. As anyone who has had to free-fall through a hailstorm knows. You feel the wind buffeting your body. You hear it roaring in your ears. You can feel the lurch when the chute opens and the impact when the ground comes up. It's awesome. Truly. It's going to make WadeSoft richer than every other tech company in the world combined. And next month you'll get a chance to see what the fuss is about for yourself, once the Skin is on sale. I could do you two a big discount if you like.'

Rose shakes her head. 'Against the rules. Besides, it doesn't sound like my thing. I have enough trouble coping with the real world, never mind a whole mess of other worlds.'

Wolff smiles. 'But that's the point. There is no trouble in the Skin worlds. You're a tourist in a realm you control. You can do anything you like, try out every dangerous sport you ever wanted, and do it all in the safety of your own home. Think about it.'

Rose cannot help but shiver at the intensity of Wolff's vision. Life as just a game.

'I've cooperated with you,' says Wolff. 'Now it's your turn. This Skin looks burnt. How did Coulter die?'

'It's not a question of taking turns, Mr Wolff. You are cooperating with our investigation, not the other way round.'

'Point taken. But wait, if you share something with me, then maybe I can be of more help to you.'

Rose considers this briefly and accepts that Wolff might have something useful to offer their investigation. 'Coulter initially appeared to have been burned to death as a result of an electrical fire, but the autopsy revealed that he was assaulted before the fire.'

Owen intervenes. 'So that almost certainly makes it murder.

Unless, perhaps, there's a fault in the suit. Is that possible?'

'No. Even though these military-grade suits were far more powerful, they had plenty of safeguards – a FidelitySafe – built in to ensure that the wearer was protected from simulated feedback from his environment. We wanted soldiers to feel the impact of bullets, but not be injured in the process, no matter how realistic their simulation was designed to be. Besides, there was always a simple word command that instantly closed down the simulation. I think you're looking for a murderer rather than a technical fault.'

'But it's also possible that Coulter's death was meant to send a message to someone. If that's the case then there's a danger the killer isn't done yet.'

'You really think so?'

'Can you give us the names of any other of Coulter's co-workers on the project? They could be in danger. We'll need to speak to them in any case.'

'You'd need to clear that with the Pentagon first, I'm afraid.'

'When exactly does your Skin hit the stores?' Rose asks.

'First of next month,' Wolff replies. 'A *big* day for us.'

Rose frowns. 'Is there any way you could postpone the launch? If there is a chance there's a fault in the technology? It might be best to check before the public gets hold of them.'

'Stall the launch? I have spent hundreds of millions on marketing and we have nine million pre-orders, and counting. You ever tried to piss that many people off? The stock market would kill us even if our customers didn't. There's no way we could delay it. Besides, our Skins are safe. I absolutely guarantee it.'

'How does the suit work, if you don't mind explaining?' Owen asks.

Wolff pulls a leg up onto the chair and hugs it. 'The precise details are trade secrets, but I'll explain it in layman's terms. This is nothing like the first crappy iterations we had, backed by deluded angel investors. Their clumsy attempts stalled the VR market for the best part of a generation. The Skin has tiny nodes that sit exactly on the skin where the body's neural pathways are. By beaming hundreds of signals onto these areas, it syncs the suit's circuitry with the body's, making the wearer sense whatever the simulation is programmed to make them feel. Ambient sensations as well as physical movements. When that's coordinated with the Sight visor, the feed to the brain makes the user believe they are in a different world. Multiple sensor nodes feed back to a wireless base station to manage the interaction with the suit's spatial sensors and provide the suit's haptic feedback and sensory processing. And there are safety features. The suit closely monitors heart rate and other biometry and is programmed to pause or cut out if there is any danger. Besides, the terms and conditions advise anyone who has epilepsy, a heart condition or a nervous disorder to avoid using the Skin. Frankly, you're far safer in a Skin than you are venturing out onto the streets these days.'

'Sounds to me like all you have done is find a new way for people to waste time,' says Rose.

'I think you'll find that for many people the worlds I am about to offer them are a vast improvement on their actual lives. Everyone has a fantasy they want to fulfil: the goal they never attained, the sport they could never play. They crave excitement, and a sense of being better than they are.

'And I am going to give them all that, Special Agent Blake. And more. After all, what could be better than a world in which every dream can come true? A world that allows the everyday American to live the dream. In the StreamPlex you can live like you once were, wanted to be or never could be. For law enforcement, we can build VR crime scenes to help you and your colleagues. The possibilities are endless.'

'You sound like a politician,' says Owen.

'Love him or loathe him, this president has proved that people are tired of career politicians. I've got the tech that will swing the young people's vote. Maybe in a few years I'll look into it . . . Be a blast to run the show for four years.' His expression becomes serious. 'I trust the details of this conversation will be kept private? Last thing I – we – need is an unnecessary panic over the safety of my product.' He leans closer to Rose. 'I swear to God that the Skin technology is safe.'

'I hope so, Mr Wolff. If not, then you're going to find real life has an unforgiving way of dealing with the failings of your virtual world gizmo.'

'The Skin is not a toy. It's an experience. A world of experience.'

Rose stands up. 'We're still waiting for forensics, which could offer further leads. We'll be in touch.'

Wolff smiles. 'I hope you catch Coulter's killer. Last thing we need is another Koenig on the loose, right?'

# 24

Tonight Koenig is thinking about evolution.

He is lying on his couch staring up at the fan sweeping round overhead. It provides a welcome cooling flow of air, but at the same time stirs up the rising stench of garbage and sweat. He has tied his waste bags as securely as he can but the odours of rotting food still seep out. Right now Koenig would kill for the chance to step outside and enjoy the fresh sea air of his temporary neighbourhood. To gaze out over the ocean as the sun sets on the horizon would be a luxury. But a luxury he cannot afford. Not until he can remove the bandages and see that the scarring has diminished enough not to attract any unwanted attention. When he eventually emerges into the world it will not be like some beast coming out of hibernation, but like an exotic butterfly emerging from its chrysalis. Fresh and radiant.

He will be a thing of beauty amid the drab humdrum lives of those he hides amongst, and on whom he preys. Hundreds of millions of years of natural selection have culminated in him. And now he must do honour to that process by adapting, evolving and surviving.

His bandaged face is still too sensitive to touch. He ran out of painkillers a few days before and it hurts like a goddam bitch. But it will be worth it. The best of his kind are the

148

ones who stay ahead of the authorities. And how do they do that? They evolve. Looking back at the history of his kind he reflects that those who were caught got complacent. They didn't adapt to their environment. They got *sloppy*. They just continued what they'd been doing, establishing patterns, and giving the other side the chance to learn the rules by which they lived.

It's not the prospect of prison, or the possibility of being given a death sentence – depending on which state he's tried in – that scares Koenig. It's the horror of humiliation. Of being bested by lesser beings. Of being held up to the rubber-necking public as some kind of freak show exhibit. Of being caged like a wild animal. It would be an utter refutation of the rightness and beauty of natural selection. If the other side captured him and contained him, then it would be as if evolution has happened for nothing. Nature's throwbacks and evolutionary dead ends would prevail, and humanity would be the poorer for it.

A wave of shooting pain seizes him again. It is like weevils eating through his cheeks and skull. He does not try to ignore the pain. He has no choice but to embrace it. It is the pain that gives his existence all the more meaning. Life is pain. Koenig knows this. He has always known it. He has lived with pain, physical and mental, ever since he was an infant. It is the measure of a man how he copes with that pain. Some choose to complain about it, whining about the unfairness of life. Some choose to surrender to it, and end their lives. And then some, the very few, choose to absorb the pain. To keep it close, as a constant reminder of the imminence of death amid life. Life that should not be taken for granted. As so many of those around Koenig do. They are little better than sheep, he muses. Grazing mindlessly even as the wolves circle and prove once more that nature insists on a hierarchy. Kill or be killed. Adapt or die.

But in order to do these things he must prepare himself. He must be disciplined.

Rising from the couch Koenig crosses the room to the full-length mirror beside the corridor leading to the bedrooms. He reaches down to pick up the heavy barbells and begins a new set. He's determined to keep his body and mind sharp until he is ready to rejoin the world in person.

He has never left the virtual world though. Before the event at the cabin he had been adept at invisibly cruising the internet, surfacing only to make contact with his victims and the followers of his KKillKam site on a little-travelled region of the dark web. Since then, he has improved his skills and mastered the StreamPlex, amongst other things. His hacking skills were already impressive, but now they are world class, and Koenig knows that the best is yet to come.

'I am the master of my fate,' he says to his reflection. 'I am the captain of my soul . . . And I will soon come out of the night that covers me. I will be the horror of the shade. I, Koenig.'

A soft ping from his laptop interrupts his exercise. He returns the weight bar to its bracket and dries his hands on a small towel as he crosses to the kitchen counter and stares at the inbox on the screen. It is superimposed on his website counter and he sees that the viewing counter on the burning victim video file has passed three thousand. Still short of his other videos, but catching up fast. He feels his rage building as he sees that the message is from 'Shelley'.

My handiwork appears to be popular . . .

Koenig clenches his fists so tightly that the muscles on his arms and the veins on the back of his hands stand out like marble sculpture. He is glad that his webcam is covered with tape.

Why have you posted your video on KKillKam? No, screw that. HOW have you been able to?

There is the very briefest of pauses before the reply comes and Koenig notes that this Shelley, whoever she or he is, is adept with the keyboard.

HOW is not important to you. WHY is.

So why are you fucking with my website?

I am not fucking with you, Koenig. I share a taste for death. I would share more with you if you would let me. I am confident that we can help each other.

Koenig smiles thinly.

I don't need your help. I have managed on my own well enough.

You were nearly captured at your cabin.

But I wasn't captured . . .

Not on that occasion. But you might be next time. I can help prevent that.

What are you? Some kind of serial killer helpline?

No. I am Shelley.

You are dead if I ever get my hands on you. But not until I peel you like a grape and eat cuts of your flesh in front of you.

You will never get your hands on me, Koenig. You can't. But I have plans for you. Plans you can do nothing about. You can work with me and I will help you.

He snorts with derision and types.

Or else???

Or else?

Koenig thrusts himself back from the counter and the stool rocks slightly before it settles.

'What the fuck?' he mutters. 'What kind of a dumbass are you?'

There's a fresh line in the message box.

Dumbass?

Koenig freezes. He stares at his laptop as if it were a coiled snake. Shelley has taken over the microphone on his laptop. How is that possible? His anger burns.

'As you can hear this, you'd better listen good. I will find you. I will take you. I will cut the skin from your flesh. I will eat your heart and keep your eyes as a trophy. And I will record it all and it will be the best clip of my collection. And I will show the world what happens to those who dare to consider themselves the equal of Shane Koenig.'

As soon as he finishes, Koenig minimizes the window, opens another and launches his tracer program. The one he uses to stalk his prey and ensure that they are what they purport to be. Then he shuts down the connection to KKillKam and the network that hosts it. For good measure he turns off the router.

He feels something he has not known since that night back in the cabin. Fear. He is vulnerable. Well, he thinks, there is something I can do about that. First, there is the need to run a deep scan on his laptop and close down any chance of further remote access. There are some groups on the dark web that know how to counter such attacks. He has been a member of one of them for some time in his guise as the hacker known as Möbius. His contacts will help him while he waits for the tracker program to start reporting back. When he finds 'Shelley', he will hold true to his promise.

Every word of it.

# 25

Pandora: her name runs on a loop in Jeff's mind, even as he is listening to his boss, Senator Keller.

Jeff gazes at Pandora Valler, the pretty black-haired intern outside his office, bending over a jammed photocopier. She's dressed in a purple blouse and black stretch jeans. The Sacramento campaign headquarters are brightly lit, with large windows, rows of busy desks, boxes of flyers and other promotional materials stacked on tables. Staff make and take phone calls. A wall-mounted flat screen shows recent opinion poll results highlighted in blue and red.

'So, Jeff, how are we doing?' asks Keller. 'We're on the final lap now.'

Jeff scans Pandora's slim figure and long legs before turning to the senator sitting in front of him. Keller is impeccably dressed in a blue suit and red silk tie, his grey hair neatly groomed. He has a kind face, calm blue eyes and a relaxed jaw. He speaks with a soft Southern drawl, rarely raising his voice. He is of Dutch, German and Irish descent and is married to a Cuban. It's a demographic that plays well in an increasingly multi-ethnic electorate.

'We still have a lot of ground to cover, Senator. We've got some more videos to upload, and the opinion polls from

BNC News show us at forty-six point one, with Grindall at forty-eight.'

Keller winces. 'Jesus, that's close.'

'I think another chat session with you fielding questions on StreamPlex will help with the younger demographic. Not forgetting the debates in Bakersfield and San Diego.'

'Good, I'll do Facebook again when I'm back from Bakersfield.'

'Facebook? Sure, why not? That'll get us an older demographic.' Jeff makes another entry on his increasingly long list of things to do on his smartphone notes app. He will sync them to his laptop the moment it is returned from the campaign's IT team. His laptop has been running slowly over recent days and there might be a virus on it. He would not put it past the Republican team to try and hack his machine for intelligence about Keller's campaign. That's common, albeit illegal, practice these days.

Obama was the first president to have a strong social media presence and had set the precedent. In the digital age, the public are more vocal than ever, and Jeff pays close attention to post reactions and analytics. Such analysis is vital since the current president largely by-passed traditional campaign methods and rammed his agenda home in a near-constant barrage of tweets and attention-grabbing publicity stunts. Jeff has been careful to depict Keller as an authentic man of the people, with simple, traditional family values and a military background. No bluster, bullying and hyperbole for him. But conveying authenticity to a jaded electorate disillusioned by post-truth politics is not an easy task. Jeff has been regularly updating Keller's online status, uploading the latest publicity pictures, devoured and shared by devotees in a matter of minutes. A staggering sixty-three per cent of their

155

fundraising has been achieved online.

'Any developments with the StreamPlex campaign?'

Jeff nods. 'When the campaign launches, there will be a virtual billboard in the main dock and your Q and A avatar will be depicted outside the Capitol Building until the race is over.'

'Excellent. Cost?'

'More than you want to know. We've reached the upper end of our budget.'

The American flag hangs draped on the back wall of the office. Jeff feels a surge of pride – as a young party worker he'd always wanted to be sitting in The Room where the real decisions got made. This is Jeff's fourth Democratic campaign and now he is coordinating one of the most important elements of the senator's message to the electorate.

'I know, but it could really help us take centre stage. With the polls this close we need to keep pushing for every vote we can get.'

Jeff nods. They had allocated most of the budget for social media, as they believed it would be key in harvesting votes.

Jeff scans his notes. To date, Keller has 13.8 million Facebook likes, and the main aim of the campaign has been to show him as a good guy. Photos with his wife and daughter have been very popular. The recent tragedy of his son's death broadcast live on social media and Keller's abiding interest in the dangers, as well as the promise, of new technologies make headlines in a technology-obsessed society. Keller currently chairs the Senate Judiciary Subcommittee on Privacy, Technology and Law. It has been all about building a brand people like and will promote to others – a trialogue that gets more people on board.

Jeff reflects that there have been some desperate attempts

at smearing Keller with spurious claims from past lovers that he was a drug addict because he smoked pot when he was a student. But Keller weathered those storms, as well as his wife's depression following Tom's death. Jeff believes Keller is fundamentally a decent man. He deserves to win. California today and DC tomorrow, Jeff hopes.

'To be honest with you, Jeff, I am a little nervous about tonight. Grindall is a great salesman and he really works it. He has a certain . . . mass appeal.'

'He's a certain kind of debater, sure enough,' Jeff quips. Their opponent Braxton Grindall is nicknamed 'the Pit Bull' because of his browbeating debating style.

Jeff's eye briefly covets Pandora again, watching the nimble sway of her curved body. He leaves his chair to go to the window. She turns her head, her long mane of dark hair sweeping over her shoulder. Her green eyes meet his and she slips him a wink. She's been giving him the eye and texting him for nearly a month. It excites Jeff to think that a young woman like her might be attracted to him. But he feels guilty about the quiet betrayal of Rose implied by his yearning. She deserves better than that. In truth, though, they have become distant of late. It's not yet so serious that either of them has remarked on it, but the fact that Jeff feels tempted by Pandora is not a good sign. He has not cheated on his wife during the fifteen years of their marriage and is not confident that he knows how to begin to.

'Joking aside,' Keller says, 'I think we should go over the speech and practise some Q and A too.'

Jeff taps a file open on his smartphone. 'Well Grindall will certainly bring up the issues of the president's deportation programme, the budget deficit and the Social Media Bill you are proposing, which will divide the voters and the Senate as

157

well. There's a lot of heat on that bill. I think you should downplay it.'

Keller shakes his head. 'Jeff, listen to me. Last month a child died of neglect because her parents spent all day on the Stream. Your own wife pursued the Backwoods Butcher, who used social media to find his victims and then murder them. Educational results are plummeting across the country. Kids have zero attention spans. This bill is key to my campaign – we need more money directed at online policing in this country. It's the future for my daughter and it's America's future too.'

'I understand, Senator, but Grindall will attack you on that using the Fourth Amendment.'

'I know, I'll deal with it,' Keller says. 'Is everything ready?'

'Yes, Price says the transport for the airport will be ready to go in an hour. We'll have most of tomorrow afternoon to prepare in San Diego. We'll reach the university at 18.30 to set up and soundcheck.'

'Thanks, Jeff. You're good at your job. You know how to quash the stupid stories and you know how to play the game. Keep it up.'

Jeff nods, gratified at being appreciated. 'Thank you, sir.'

There's a knock at the door. It's Steven Derickson, the campaign IT manager. Black-haired, wearing a burgundy sweater over a white shirt, he exchanges a nod with the senator and steps aside to let Keller leave the room. He enters holding a laptop.

'Hey, Jeff, got your computer back. You had a ton of viruses in there, man. It was filthier than a pig in shit.' His round eyes stare at Jeff from behind his black glasses.

Jeff blushes a deep shade of crimson.

'You think I'm to blame for that?'

158

Steven's eyes go wide. 'I was just saying – the reason why it wasn't booting up was because the hard drive was screwed up with viruses. There's some dodgy shit on there. Frankly, half of it I wish I'd never seen. Those Republican hacking fuckers are getting better all the time.' He shakes his head in disgust before placing it on the desk. 'I've beefed up the security, but do me a favour and don't visit any . . . insecure sites, OK?'

'You've put additional security on *my* computer?' Jeff asks.

'Just as a precaution.'

'Look, Steven, I didn't mean to snap. It just pisses me that someone is targeting my computer. We all share the same network, right? Could be one of the team inadvertently compromising our machines.'

'It's possible.'

'It's probably one of the interns. We've had a few new guys start recently. You know what they're like.'

'There it is. It takes one dumbass to visit some porn site and the campaign gets smeared with the same shit by Fox News.' Steven grins. 'I'll put a memo round. No jerking off on the senator's time.' Then he leaves.

Jeff sits for a while in the office. He takes off his glasses, rubbing his tired eyes. Derickson is right on the money. Jeff feels guilty, but he couldn't help using what he thought was a virus-protected laptop to browse for porn to release the sexual tension simmering inside. Much as he loves Rose, their sex life has grown stale and he needs something fresh and different.

Jeff strolls through the office. There's a line of three people for the coffee machine and he takes his position in line. He taps his Facebook app. No messages. He types a message to Rose.

Hey, hope your day's going well. Getting ready for San Diego. Be home soon as I can. xxx

Gripping his cup, he walks over to Pandora's desk where she is stapling staff handouts.

He reaches out a hand to rest on her shoulder. 'Doing a good job, I see.'

'No problem,' she says, briefly placing her hand on top of his, gently dragging her polished fingernails across his skin.

Jeff smiles. 'Are you tagging along with us on the bus?'

'Ummm, well, Fernanda told me I should probably work the phones here.'

'Ignore Fern. She's HR, but I'm the social media manager. You're coming with us. No one gets any experience sitting alone in an office.'

'Really? Thank you, Mr Blake.'

'Jeff.'

She brushes her hair to one side. Jeff tries to force his eyes away from lingering too long.

'Oh, those handouts are just printing now,' she says. 'I also took a look at some of the blogs and chatter. There's a lot of anticipation over the debate.'

'There is indeed,' Jeff says. 'Bus leaves in an hour. You'd better bring an overnight bag.'

'Oh, crap. I'll need to buy some underwear then.'

Jeff's confused.

'Because I wasn't going, I didn't bring anything . . .'

'Oh, right.' He blushes.

She stares at him. 'I can't wait to see Keller and Grindall slug it out.'

'Yep, should be good.'

Jeff notices a few staffers watching them.

160

'Gotta go. Give me those packs when they're done.'

'Yes, sir.' Pandora smiles, grabbing her handbag.

'Where are you going?'

'Buying some clothes for tomorrow!'

Jeff returns to his office. It's a bad idea on so many levels. He gazes at the wedding band on his finger, remembering the day when he took his vows, and meant them. Maybe Pandora's what he needs. She listens to him, she respects him.

It's what he deserves, after all.

# 26

Jeff tells one of the male interns to carry the two suitcases towards the senator's black SUV. Keller, on the phone, is already sitting inside and nods a quick greeting as he talks. '. . . Sweetie, listen. I just don't think meeting some boy you met on the Stream is a good idea right now . . . Because I'm not at home . . . Because I'm your father, Amelia, that's why . . . Just a second.'

He cups his hand over the mouthpiece.

'Jeff, I need to have a private word with my daughter. Teenagers – such a handful. Would you mind going down on the bus?' He smiles apologetically.

Jeff's gut initially tenses with disappointment, but as he turns to look at the bus, he catches a glimpse of Pandora beelining towards the back.

'Sure, Senator. Got my phone if you need anything.'

'Thanks, Jeff.'

Jeff climbs out and, taking the handle of his wheelie case, makes for the campaign bus. It's blue and white with a massive image of Keller's smiling face on both sides. 'Citizen Not Politician', screams the tagline, along with social media links. Jeff mounts the steps and sits down on the comfy upholstery of the luxury coach, pulling the navy curtain closed so he can rest his head against the window.

He checks his own Facebook page: 4,152 friends. He smiles. Not bad.

He types in 'P' and the first contact that is brought up is Pandora.

He taps her black-and-white picture. She's pouting, her fingers pushing her hair up behind her.

Tapping on the various sections, he quickly reminds himself of the facts. She's twenty-two, studied political science at Berkeley. She's recently uploaded some casual holiday snaps which show her in a green bikini. The picture has 243 likes.

Out of 991 of Pandora's friends, most of them, he notices, are male. His heart skips when he sees she is listed as being in a relationship. So he ignores that detail.

*Pop-ping*

A blue message box, from Pandora:

P:   Hi Jeff. Have we got a nice hotel?

Jeff feels a rush of excitement, tinged with a little guilt. He types:

J:   Well . . . I'm staying at the Premiere. I think the interns are at a bloodstained motel that CSI forgot to clean.

P:   Lol. This is going to be such a long journey . . . I can see you down the front. Can you see me?

Jeff slides his glasses back on, leans up over his seat. Amongst the bobbing heads, he sees her dark hair. She waves.

J:   Gotcha. A few seats down from the bathroom. Great choice.

P:   Lol. You can't exactly play hide and seek on a bus. :-)

Jeff smiles. He likes this girl's sense of fun.
There's a plucked harp string sound. It's a text from Rose.

Hey Jeff, good luck in San Diego. Tough case at the mo. We
miss you. Don't forget Robbie's school report. xxx

Jeff is just about to text back when *pop-ping*:

P:   Did you see my pictures?

J:   Which ones? The playboy photo shoot at the beach?

P:   What did you think?

Jeff can feel his pulse starting to race. He wants to be with
this girl.

J:   I think you're way too beautiful and I'm way too old for
you . . .

There's a pause.

P:   I wouldn't be so sure . . . ;-)

*Pop-ping*
He looks down at the message screen. There's a topless
black and white picture of Pandora. Jeff instantly shields the
screen to avoid anyone else seeing. He can't believe this is
what young women do these days. Pandora's body is incredible.
Alarm bells start ringing in his mind. His conscience
screams at him to log off. But he doesn't think he can help
himself. Besides, he is in control of the situation. If it goes

164

bad, it's her word — a lowly intern — against his. It's an unworthy calculation and he feels a stab of self-loathing. But it passes.

    J:   A sight for my sore eyes, I can tell you.

Jeff slides his phone back in his pocket. Closes his eyes.
*Pop-ping*
He sighs, pulls out his phone. Now what does she want?

    P:   We should go for a drink.

A drink. Normally so harmless. But now laced with ambrosia, or the bitterest of poison. The prospect of a drink scares Jeff like few things ever have before. But he is thirsty. So thirsty.

# 27

Rose replies to Jeff's text just as Dr Alison Chan paces down the white laboratory corridor. Dr Chan, a forensic scientist at one of the city's private labs, had worked the evidence on Koenig's case. Rose hopes that she will have uncovered some useful information to advance the investigation into Coulter's death. Chan is wearing a long white coat over a blue sweatshirt and black fitted pants.

'Rose, good to see you.' She smiles. 'How are things?'

'To be honest, could be a lot better. Tell me you've got something.'

'Somebody paid a whole load to prioritize this case. I got a month's backlog of blood tests to do,' Dr Chan says, leading her through to the laboratory. 'And before you ask, I don't have a name for you. The instruction came down from the DoD budget office. That's all I know.'

Rose doesn't need a name. It has to be Maynard's doing, but why is Maynard so interested in this case?

Dr Chan's laboratory is large, consisting of separate departments hidden behind grey doors along the length of a fluorescent-lit white corridor.

Dr Chan opens her office door, bids Rose to take a seat.

'Do you want the bad news, or the slightly good news?'

166

Rose's shoulders heave with disappointment. 'What have you got?'

'You must understand that the samples the Bureau wanted us to look at were badly burnt, so possible evidence may have been incinerated. There are traces of semen in the suit, belonging to the victim. Might have been there when his scrotum was torn apart, or as the result of sexual activity. As for fingerprints, most of them found in the apartment match the deceased. The slightly good news is that there were traces of prints from another party, but we couldn't find a match.'

Dr Chan hands Rose a photocopy of the other person's prints. Rose hopes that they might be linked to the killer, or at least someone who can provide a further lead.

'And that's it,' Chan continues. 'No sign of gasoline, or any other accelerants. The fire originated from the suit itself, most likely the electrical wiring inside the rubber. My guess is that it got too hot, some of the wiring melted and then the whole lot went up, setting fire to the chair in which the vic was sitting.'

'My God, it must have happened quickly. He didn't even have time to move.'

'Not that quickly. That kind of fire takes a while to take hold. I'd guess Coulter was very much aware of what was happening to him.'

'But we found no sign of restraints.'

Chan nods. 'I read the report. Which is why this is disturbing. As far as I can tell he just sat there while he burned.'

They share a brief silence, filled with thoughts of the man caught in an inferno so intense that it fused him, his suit and his chair into one charred mass.

'You ever seen anything like this before?' asks Rose.

'Never.'

*But it's possible you will*, she thinks, once Wade Wolff's new toy enters the homes of millions of Americans. Rose starts along a new line of thinking. Is it possible the killer left Coulter for dead and found a way for the suit to set itself on fire hours, maybe days after he had left his victim? That would explain the absence of anything on the security cameras footage, once the overwrite limit had passed.

Rose thanks Dr Chan for her efforts and leaves the office. There is nothing else to be gleaned from Coulter's remains, it seems, and the funeral can now take place. The coroner had found no trace of propofol, or anything else, in the liver, ruling out the sedative angle. That had been a blow, as Rose was hoping it could have explained the apparent passivity of the victim as he burned. Brennan is still struggling to crack the hard disk encryption on Coulter's laptop, and without a search warrant the software company won't help with unlocking the data.

Rose knows in her gut that Coulter was murdered. And that the people behind Peek Industries and possibly others in the Pentagon know far more than they're willing to admit. And who ordered the autopsy to be fast-tracked? Regardless of whether it was Maynard or not, it's clear someone else wants to know the truth about Coulter's death.

She has a disquieting sensation. As if she is being watched by someone. Followed. Instinctively she glances up at one of the security cameras trained along the length of the corridor. The lens, black and shining, stares back. A tiny red LED blinks above it. Rose is aware that anyone could be watching her movements right now and she would never know who.

# 28

Jeff and Senator Keller are leading his entourage as they approach the rear of the University of San Diego's auditorium where tonight's debate is going to take place.

After a long day preparing the senator, Jeff is feeling tired and aching all over. During the day, Pandora has sent him a few more pictures, with Jeff obliging her with an old holiday pic of him bare-chested. He is torn between aching sexual anticipation and guilt. He tries to push aside such thoughts as he admires the lush tree-lined campus, close to the dazzling expanse of the Pacific Ocean.

'I hope the lighting is better this time. I nearly fainted under those spotlights in Sacramento,' says Keller.

They enter the lecture hall. The BNC crew are already there, testing the lighting, rigging and sound. A balding, tubby man in a blue checked shirt and jeans walks towards them and shakes Keller and Jeff's hands.

'Pleased to meet you, Senator. I'm Paul Armbrust, the producer. We've nearly finished setting up. Make-up department have set up in the annexe just over there.'

Soon after, make-up assistants dab Keller's face with a light layer of powder.

'Jeff, could you find me a bottle of water? I'm parched,' Keller says.

'Of course.' Jeff nods, exiting out into the hall. He wanders down the hallway and sees Pandora. She's handing out flyers to students who are entering the lecture hall.

Jeff walks up to her. She suddenly turns, her elbow knocking his smartphone from his hand. It lands squarely on the wooden floor and the black case shatters, ejecting the battery. A TV crew member pushing a trolley wheels over the top of it, crushing the smartphone into the tiled floor.

'Sorry, buddy!'

'Watch what the fuck you're doing! Fucking moron!' Jeff snaps.

'It was an accident! Jerk!' the man says, disappearing into a corridor.

Jeff feels the urge to vent more, but Pandora takes his arm.

'Oh my God! Jeff, I'm so sorry!' she says, stooping down to retrieve the smartphone.

Jeff can't help but notice the smooth expanse of thigh above the hem of her skirt. She hands him his mangled phone. He feels unexpectedly depressed.

'I'll pay for it. It might take a while but I'll pay you back,' she says, putting her hand on his arm. Jeff's eyes catch the nail polish and French manicure. She squeezes his bicep.

'Hey, look, don't worry about it,' he mumbles.

'So . . .' She tilts her head and smiles. 'Are we OK for that drink tonight?'

'There's a quiet bar in my hotel.'

'Perfect,' she says.

Jeff grabs a bottle of water and heads back to the stage where Keller is standing behind the podium. The stage is draped with royal-blue curtains and a US flag hangs in the middle, between the candidates. Jeff hands him the bottle.

'Thanks. I was beginning to wither and die.' He takes a sip before placing the water bottle out of view on his lectern.

'Looking good, Senator.' Jeff winks. 'Senator today . . .'

'Let's not get ahead of ourselves, my boy.' Keller wags a finger. The lecture theatre is filled to capacity. From stage right, Braxton Grindall enters. A tall, well-built man, with narrow eyes and a large square jawline, his wide face is lightly pockmarked, the marks of a difficult adolescence. His hair is unnaturally dark for a man of his age. He shakes Keller's hand firmly. He's wearing a dark blue suit and neat silver tie.

'Good luck, Christopher,' he says, before standing behind his podium.

Jeff descends the steps and takes a seat in the front row. Pandora sits with the other interns in the second row. The MC for the evening, George Pope, reads over his cue cards. A sound technician places small black mikes on the candidates' lapels, runs some soundchecks.

'OK, everybody, quiet please,' Armbrust calls out over the hall's speakers. 'We're live in ten, nine, eight, seven, six, five, four, three, two . . . And George!'

Pope looks directly into the lead camera, moving in on a dolly track towards him.

'BNC is proud to host this event tonight in San Diego. We'd like to thank the good people of the city for welcoming us here. Let's begin by introducing our senatorial candidates tonight, beginning with Republican Braxton Grindall. He made his fortune in real estate and investing in digital start-ups, including the rising star of the industry, WadeSoft. He's fifty-one years old, married, with two daughters, and is on record as saying that he, too, wants to make America great again.'

171

The audience laughs at the comment, but there are some catcalls and boos before Pope waves them down.

'All right, people. That's enough . . . In the other corner we are pleased to welcome Democrat Senator Chris Keller, current chairman of the Senate Judiciary Subcommittee on Privacy, Technology and Law. Served in the US Army Communications-Electronics Command. Also a graduate of Washington State University. Forty-five years old, married with one daughter.'

Jeff reflects on the candidates. Politics is inherently a dirty profession, but Keller is one of the cleanest players of them all. Grindall, on the other hand, is one of the dirtiest operators around. During the campaign they'd caught a Republican spy posing as an intern snooping around Jeff's in-tray, and Keller's own email account had been hacked.

George continues his introduction. 'Now, in this debate, the candidates will speak for ten minutes, and then the questions I'll be asking come from the viewers of BNC, social media users and community leaders. Each candidate will have one minute to answer each question, before commenting on each other's response . . .'

Jeff finds himself taking a deep breath. A verbal dog fight is about to begin.

# 29

Jeff looks up at Pope, who shifts his cue cards.

'Among the many issues to cover tonight, the one I'd like to kick off with is Senator Keller's controversial Social Media Bill.'

*Damn it,* Jeff winces. *Straight for the jugular.*

'Social media, and especially WadeSoft's StreamPlex, have been garnering a lot of controversy. Senator Keller's proposal is that social media should be actively regulated by a new law-enforcement task force. Senator Keller, tell us more.'

Keller smiles at Pope and the audience.

'Thanks, George. The bill will impact on a whole range of issues, but its ultimate purpose is to aid law enforcement and online safety right across America. We need to sacrifice some of our hard-earned freedoms to ensure our safety in a digitally saturated world. Of course we must talk it through with the American people first, getting their views and consent, but I believe that most people already share my concerns. For the last twenty years we have been undertaking a massive social experiment, only the test laboratory is the real world and we were never asked for our permission. The internet has forever changed the ways we communicate with each other, how we work, our family life, even our sex lives. And now there's the StreamPlex.

'A new chapter in this whirlwind romance with technology is nearly upon us. WadeSoft's latest innovation is the Skin. The experiences it promises are undeniably impressive. But the potential for abuse has now increased one hundredfold. Just like in a real city, how should we regulate wrongdoers, criminals, terrorists, without some lawful presence inside the StreamPlex?

'Most of you will know this already, but my son Thomas . . . Tom,' he says, his voice wavering a little, 'died with the complicity of complete strangers on the Stream, who did nothing to help him.

'One morning Tom set up his webcam on the Stream . . . Over a period of three hours, he overdosed on paracetamol pills, while strangers typed in comments like "go ahead and do it", "take more". Others took the opportunity to insult him, telling him he was a coward, a pussy. Those were the very words they used.'

Silence.

Every cough and rustle of clothing seems like an assault on the ears.

'He was bright, lovely . . .' Keller's voice grows husky. 'If the Stream had been monitored more closely, maybe he'd still be alive today.

'America needs this bill. We will seek out and bar makers of extremely violent or perverse content. When my bill is passed we can identify and neutralize threats quickly and effectively. And if it works, it will benefit every American citizen. So that no parent again has to endure what I have!'

There is thunderous applause from the audience, but also an undercurrent of murmuring.

'Thank you, Senator Keller. Mr Grindall, a number of issues there. Your response?' Pope says.

174

Grindall speaks with a deep, gravelly drawl.

'Thank you, George. The senator's intentions are noble, but what he is suggesting goes against everything we Americans stand for, and against our God-given constitutional rights. He proposes a high-tech surveillance state, snooping on us via the internet, and now the StreamPlex. He's asking for censorship, treating adults like kids. The senator's bill infringes on freedom of speech and the First Amendment. We should trust our citizens to self-regulate. With regard to his proposals for an executive unit monitoring internet usage, this is a tad extreme. I invoke the Fourth Amendment, which I know by heart.'

He places the palm of his right hand on his suit jacket.

'The right of the people to be secure in their persons, houses, papers, and effects, against unreasonable searches and seizures, shall not be violated, and no Warrants shall issue, but upon probable cause, supported by Oath or affirmation, and particularly describing the place to be searched, and the persons or things to be seized.'

He pauses and looks directly at Keller. 'What happened to your son was tragic, Senator, but one case—'

'It's not just one case,' Keller interrupts, staring straight at the audience and the cameras. 'This is not just about my son. Not by a long way. Many of you will know of Shane Koenig, a serial killer who is still at large. Would there be as many murderers, rapists, paedophiles without the internet? The internet is making the world smaller, but it's brought all those dangerous things closer to us. It's a new frontier that badly needs a sheriff. Perverts, criminals and terrorists can't be allowed to hide behind new technologies, as the lawmakers, law enforcers and our security services struggle to catch up. With the people's permission, I will get control of America again. We must protect our children's future . . .'

Loud clapping starts from the back of the auditorium. Several audience members rise. Jeff and Pandora join a clear majority of the audience in a roaring standing ovation.

# 30

Jeff studies his face in the hotel mirror. There are bags under his eyes. He splashes water over his face and paces towards his bed, where he flops down. The room is neat and simple, with terracotta walls and chrome furniture. A large flat screen hangs across the wall.

'TV: on.'

Johnee Tallent is on BNC:

'Welcome to *The Tallent Show*. After a gripping and passionate debate in San Diego, the candidates Keller and Grindall are neck and neck in our latest poll. Grindall is still in the lead with 49 per cent, but Keller has closed the gap and is snapping at his heels with 48.5 per cent.'

Jeff sighs. The senator's career is still hanging in the balance.

He unpacks the smartphone he bought from a service station on the way back to the hotel. Not as good as the one that got crushed, but as a temporary measure it will do. He presses his index finger and thumb together. He needs to get on the Stream.

'. . . Hey!'

Jeff's attention is grabbed back to the screen by Johnee.

'WS's Skin launch is next month. Exact details are still very much under lock and key – something of a trademark for Wade Wolff and his team! But knowing those boys, it sure is going to get the world talking. It will change everything . . .'

He inserts his old SIM card and boots the phone up. The signal is full and, skipping the registration steps, he taps out a message to Pandora.

J: Hey . . . got me a new smartphone . . . How's your room?

After a few minutes, there's a *pop-ping*.

P: Hi sexy . . . It's a bit crappy. I had to get some new sheets.

J: Charming. You're not sleepy?

P: No . . . far from it. Are you?

J: Not really.

Jeff's lying. He's weary from such a long day.

J: So how about that drink? My hotel bar in half an hour?

P: Sure. See you soon. xxx

Jeff's heart skips a beat. He knows he's taking a risk. Maybe making a big mistake. But he can't help himself.

# 31

Jeff sits in a booth in the hotel bar. It has a warm, classic feel, with oak bar seats and the glow of concealed lighting on the walls. He has showered, and is wearing a blue denim shirt and jeans. He sees Pandora pausing by the entrance, looking for him. Jeff waves and she approaches him. She's wearing a fitted black top, tight blue jeans and a brown leather jacket.

'Hi . . . You look great. Can I get you something?' Jeff offers, beckoning to a waitress.

'A margarita.'

'Good choice.'

The waitress returns with her drink. Jeff holds out his glass. Jack Daniel's.

'To the campaign.'

They chink glasses.

Pandora sweeps her long hair back. 'It was so awesome – honestly, Grindall didn't get a word in edgeways. Keller's got some serious firepower. His trending is sky high too. He's going to win, I know it.'

Jeff's eyes ease down the fall of her midnight-black hair, the slender length of her neck, the dip in her collarbone. He can see the outline of her bra pushing against the blouse.

He has resigned himself to being unfaithful to Rose, and justified it by telling himself this will be a one-off. Something to get out of his system. As long as Rose never finds out, then what harm can it do?

'You know, I've been thinking . . .'

'Oh really? Thinking what?'

'I'd like to open Pandora's box.'

Pandora smiles. 'Like I haven't heard that one before.'

'You play up to it though, don't you?'

'Maybe a little.'

'So why don't we stop talking and head back to my room?'

Her eyes widen. 'Jesus . . . No flirting around first?'

'Isn't that what we've been doing for weeks now?'

'Yes . . . I mean, you're a handsome guy, Jeff. And smart with it, and close to Keller. That ticks a lot of boxes in terms of being attractive. Sure, I flirted with you. You're quite the catch.'

'. . . But?'

'I have a boyfriend.'

'*Now* you tell me?'

'I thought you knew. It's on my profile. I met him a month back.'

'After you had been working for the campaign for over three months, and playing me for the last two. Nice.'

She looks hurt. 'It wasn't like that. I was drawn to you. I liked you and you turn me on. Then Dave came on the scene, and there's been a kind of overlap. And now I'm worried that you'll kick me off the campaign if I say no to you.'

Jeff shakes his head. He feels cheap and corrupt and angry that she would accuse him of such a low reaction to her news about her boyfriend.

'Do you really think I'd do that?'

'I don't know. I'll have to wait and see, won't I?'

'I didn't know about your boyfriend.'

'It was on Facebook.'

'Didn't see it. You can't rely on Facebook for everything.'

'True. But I definitely know you're married,' she says, pointing at his wedding ring.

Jeff looks down, ashamed at the pathetic figure he must cut chasing after a woman much younger than him.

'So it's no as in *no*?'

Pandora smiles.

*You fool. Wake up, Jeff.* All this has been a silly infatuation. He burns with embarrassment. There's going to be no future with her. He's still trapped by the choices he made all those years ago. Is a man meant to have one woman for the rest of his life? Looking at Pandora is painful now that his bluff has been called. She leans forward, as if to rise from her seat. Then she kisses him on the cheek. Jeff's not sure how to react. Her scent is overpowering.

'You're a great guy, Jeff. Sometimes, we're just looking.'

Pandora finishes her drink. 'I'm beat. I'm going to head back. Thanks for the drink.'

She leaves the table, caressing his shoulder briefly as she passes. Jeff sits very still.

'Pandora?' he says, finally.

'Yes?'

'It's Mr Blake from now on. And this stays between us.'

Pandora nods, looking slightly hurt. Jeff watches her leave, hoping she'll look back. But she doesn't. Instead she pulls out her smartphone, tapping away as she leaves the bar.

*She played you like an organ grinder.* Jeff curses himself. It's not her fault. She's just young. Seeing what her options are. *Wouldn't you?*

He takes a seat closer to the bar. 'Another for me.'

But she didn't have to be cruel.

181

★ ★ ★

An hour or so later, Jeff staggers back to his room, flopping drunkenly onto his bed.

Finding it impossible to sleep, he worries over the consequences if this gets out. He racks his mind to try and recall precisely what has happened. He has deleted Pandora's messages from his replacement phone and unfriended her on Facebook. That's always a bit awkward, having to work with someone you've unfriended. He considered blocking her but didn't want her to get upset. He needs a distraction. He deserves a treat. He's earned it, after all, given all the long hours he has put into his work. But he's still feeling guilt, and then finds a way to justify the treat as a favour to Robbie. Sure. Do it for Robbie. Something he can share with his son, just like a proper father.

He types in 'Skin' on Google and hits the link to the WadeSoft website. There are three Skin packages available: bronze, silver and gold. Jeff studies what each offers. Bronze is the cheapest package by far, providing basic visuals and audio, but is non-immersive and is based on limited interaction with a headset and two gloves. He decides to look at the silver package screenshots and videos. This version provides good definition in sights and sounds and some, limited, haptic feedback.

Finally, he looks at the gold package: a full, high-definition experience with sensory data and the full Skin. He looks at the price tag and feels a pang in his stomach. He could just about do it, but it would blow a large chunk of cash. After some thought, he selects the gold, pay monthly option to spread the cost, and confirms the order.

He then tries to drift off to sleep.

*Pop-ping*

Jeff's got an email. Opening it he reads:

Thank you for your pre-order.
You've taken the first step.
WadeSoft's Skin will be dispatched shortly.
**The ultimate in immersion reality.**
**#BetterThanReal**

He smiles to himself. It's just what he needs.

He then groans as he realizes he has to be up early the next morning. He's promised Rose that he'll go with her to the school and hear Robbie's teacher report on his progress.

# 32

Coulter's early morning funeral is looking to be a drab and lonely affair. Rose is dressed respectfully, wearing large round sunglasses and a light black coat and black pants.

The only other attendees, besides the priest, are Coulter's frail-looking mother and his cousin, Daniel, who has flown in from England. A few feet away from them is an unknown male. He's tall and thin, with fading blond hair and dressed in a crumpled charcoal suit. Looks to be mid-thirties. He senses Rose's gaze, forces a polite smile then resumes staring down at Coulter's black coffin. His face is etched into a grimace. The burial is at Colma, a small town in San Mateo County, where the population of the dead outnumber the living by a thousand to one.

Colma is nicknamed the City of the Silent, and has its official motto 'It's great to be alive in Colma' on the county's website. The cemetery itself is massive, an enormous smorgasbord of two million headstones, cement angels and mausoleums unevenly crowding the valley. Levi Strauss, William Randolph Hearst and Wyatt Earp are among the cemetery's famous interments.

Talking with Daniel before the service, Rose discovered that Gary had specified in his will that he wished to be buried and not cremated. His mother had insisted on a religious service as a last-minute 'insurance policy' for her son. His cousin was initially surprised by the presence of an FBI agent, but once Rose explained that she hoped she might meet people who might help with the investigation, he seemed almost grateful. And yet, so few people.

The white-haired priest drones on.

Rose hopes that when she passes on, her funeral has a better attendance than Coulter's. It is painful to see how little his death is mourned. She feels conspicuous attending the funeral of a man she did not know existed until he was dead. But she feels it is her duty. Any discussion with a friend or relative could help the investigation. And maybe the killer is close by. Rose scans the headstones, looking for any distant watcher, but all she sees are stone angels impassively staring back. As she looks down at the open grave, Gary Coulter still seems to be an enigma, in both life and death.

At least his family, such as it is, have had the chance to bury him. Standing beside Coulter's grave, memories of her mother's disappearance start to wash up on the shores of Rose's mind.

She was a teenager when her mother did not return home from her teaching job. Her father Harry had been frantic, but after a three-month investigation, New Jersey's finest had no leads to explain her disappearance. Mary Cassidy never came home, never wrote or called. Harry had eventually accepted she'd either been murdered or had run off, perhaps with some other man. Her sister Scarlet still refuses to talk about it, even to this day, still scarred by the loss.

Rose alternately burns with anger and sadness. She knows that her mother's disappearance had unquestionably informed her decision to work in law enforcement. The thing that rankles the most is the abrupt nature of it. Some evil bastard like Koenig could have kidnapped and murdered her and they would never know.

As the years passed Rose had come to believe that her mother had been killed and her body hidden. She felt it in her gut. Her mother's disappearance had also meant her own lack of a female role model when growing up. Being raised by Harry on his own meant she was perhaps tougher, more straight-talking than most other girls her age, which didn't always win her friends in the social cliques at school, and later amongst the sorority girls. Headstrong and independent, Rose had flown through university and Quantico. She had once tried to reopen the cold case into her mother's disappearance, attempting to trace her through what records she could find. But it had soon proved to be a dead end, and she had forced herself to let it go.

Harry had been so proud when she graduated, he'd hugged her and cried. Right there in front of the other course graduates. But Rose had not felt a flicker of embarrassment and loved him all the more for it.

As she looks down at Coulter's grave, the urge to find the truth behind his death becomes stronger. She is determined to solve this case, solve them all. Payback for her mother.

The service finally reaches its conclusion.

As Rose follows the small procession away from the graveside, the unknown male quickens his pace to get away from the scene, heading towards the cars parked on the nearest stretch of road running through the gently rolling landscape of the dead.

Rose calls out to him. 'Excuse me.'

The man hesitates, looking back.

'Hi, my name's Rose. May I speak with you?'

The man stares back at her. His face is small, drawn in, like a weasel's. 'I'm sorry, I don't know you. Good day.'

He continues to walk away. Rose doesn't want to do it like this, but she needs to find out who he is. She pulls out her badge and hurries round him, blocking his path.

'Sir, I'm Special Agent Rose Blake, FBI. I would like to talk to you, for just a moment.'

The gaunt man halts, looking at her proffered badge. 'OK, Special Agent, what do you want to talk about?'

Rose can see the muscle under his right eye twitching slightly.

She puts her badge away. 'That's better. Let's start with your name.'

'Sebastian Shaw,' he says.

'You knew Gary Coulter. A friend, maybe?'

'We used to work together.'

'You seem a bit nervous. You OK?'

'It's not every day you get pounced on by the FBI at a colleague's funeral. I . . . It's been such a shock. I mean, it's hard when someone you know is murdered. I just came to pay my respects.'

'What was he like?' asks Rose. 'I'm trying to build up a picture of him. Whatever you can say might help the Bureau to find out what really happened. So what can you tell me about him?'

'Honestly?' Shaw shrugs. 'Coulter was fat and sloppy. I didn't like the way he worked, the way he presented himself. He didn't have many friends that I know of.'

'No? Did he ever mention anyone named Iris?'

'Iris . . .' Shaw is thoughtful. 'No. Don't know the name. He had no friends I knew of, but he was the most respected, or reckless, software engineer, depending who you speak to.

187

I'd go for reckless. He took short cuts, without much regard for the risks involved.'

'What kind of risks?'

Shaw scrutinizes her for a moment. 'Do you know how he died?'

'We're still working on that. Why did you say murdered a moment ago? That's not the official line. Do you know something about it?'

'I was mistaken.'

'You seemed fairly certain to me.'

'There's not a lot more I can tell you, Special Agent. Not without getting into trouble. In the line of work that Gary and I engaged in, you have to sign some pretty draconian non-disclosure agreements.'

'Sure, I understand. But the man is dead. Not a good death. We'd appreciate your help finding his killer.'

'So he *was* murdered.'

Rose realizes that there is no point in denying it. Not now. 'It seems the most likely possibility. You both worked on the same defence contracts, right?'

'I guess it won't hurt to say so. Yes. What about it?'

'We know about the suit,' Rose says. 'He died wearing it.'

She waits for his reaction. There's a brief flicker of fear in Shaw's eyes.

'What can you tell me about the suit?' Rose can see Shaw tensing up, unwilling to answer. 'We're just trying to build up his background.'

'I worked on the hardware. I mean the suit itself. Coulter was working on a related software project in another department at Peek.'

'So you weren't working on anything together?'

'No.'

'Then how did you meet?'

'In the company restaurant. We talked. I told him I was having a few problems with the operating system for the suit. He gave me some help with that. We sort of became friends, I guess.'

'Friends? I didn't get the impression Coulter was the friend-making type.'

'Takes all kinds, Special Agent Blake.'

'So . . . You made the suit?'

'Not originally. WadeSoft came up with the design first. Their entertainment division, that is. Once the Defense Department got wind of it they told the company to put the development on hold while they assessed its applications. That's how I got to work on the military prototypes.'

'Military applications?' Rose probes. It would be interesting to hear Shaw's take on what Wade Wolff had already told her and Owen. 'Like what?'

'I guess it's no longer a secret. Most of the stuff is already being adapted for the games market. Peek worked on the warfare simulations. Training Special Forces. Airborne and ground drone pilots. That kind of thing.'

'Sounds impressive.'

'You've no idea how impressive until you've tried the suit out.'

Rose retrieves her smartphone, taps the ID app.

'Mr Shaw, if I could have your prints, please.'

'Why?'

'You ever visit Coulter's place?'

'A few times, yeah. Months ago.'

'Then you'll have left some traces. I'll need your prints for elimination purposes . . . It would help if you cooperated now. It's easy enough to compel you to later on, if need be.'

Shaw places his thumb on Rose's screen. A blue line traces up and down the screen. Scan complete. She forwards the scan to Chan's inbox.

'Thanks.'

'If it helps catch Gary's killer, that's fine by me.'

'You don't think we will?'

'I don't think you can, Special Agent.'

'What do you mean?'

Shaw shakes his head. 'It's nothing. I mean, it doesn't seem to me that you have much of a handle on the situation, given the questions you've asked me.'

'We're good at what we do, Mr Shaw. If anyone can find out what happened to your friend, and who was responsible for it, then it's the FBI.'

'I hope you're right. Truly.'

'Gary worked in the field of artificial intelligence. That right?'

'Artificial consciousness, actually. Actual thought, not a series of reactions, but yes, there's some people in the military who are very interested in that. Gary was way ahead of the curve in that field.'

'In what way?'

Shaw shakes his head. 'I'm not saying any more. You want to find out, then go through the official channels. And good luck with that. Now, I got to go.'

'Are you working for Maynard?'

Shaw hesitates for a second. 'I've never met him. Goodbye, Special Agent Blake.'

'Wait.' Rose takes out her card and hands it to him. 'The Bureau will want to speak to you again. In any case, if you remember anything else you think we should know, call me. And where can I find you?'

'Try Peek. I pretty much live there these days. I'm not hard to find.'

'One last question. You say you worked on the suit. Does that mean there's only one of them at Peek?'

'One? You ever heard of a company with only one proto-type of anything? We've got several of them at various stages of development. Each one's for a different training application.'

'What about the one Coulter was wearing when he was killed? If he was a code monkey then where did he get it from?'

'I would have thought that was obvious, Special Agent. He stole it.'

He turns and strides away towards a Ford Advance with rental plates parked a short distance back from the other cars. He has only gone a few paces before he stops and looks over his shoulder. 'If you want to find out what Gary was working on then ask the DoD about Project Diva.'

'Diva?'

'He mentioned it to me once. He was very excited about it.'

'What did he say?'

'Not much. Only that it was going to change *his* world forever.'

'Just his world?'

'That's what he said. Goodbye.'

Shaw pulls away quickly and drives off down the cemetery road lined with headstones. Rose is certain that he knows an awful lot more than he's saying. She decides to look into him, and with Baptiste's sign-off, maybe arrange some surveillance.

★ ★ ★

191

Shaw taps the steering wheel, endlessly checking his mirrors for any sign of being followed. He curses himself. When he is certain the FBI agent is not behind him, he pulls into a quiet side street. He pulls out the encrypted phone Maynard gave him. He needs to speak to Maynard urgently. After a few rings, the phone is answered.

'What do you want, Sebastian?'

'We could have a problem.'

# 33

Rose and Robbie sit quietly in the reception of Daniel Fernandez High School. Rose's attention wanders to her smartphone in case Owen calls with news regarding Shaw. Baptiste has decided there is reasonable suspicion to justify limited surveillance, based on what Rose relayed to her from Coulter's funeral, and Dr Chan confirming Shaw's prints on Coulter's suit.

Finally Jeff walks in, wearing a light-brown jacket.

'Hey, sorry. Traffic from the airport,' he says, kissing Rose and then ruffling Robbie's hair underneath his grey hoodie.

'Let's see what Robbo-Cop has been up to, huh?'

Rose rolls her eyes. 'You need a new nickname for him.'

After they pass through security detectors − Rose has left her Glock locked in her car − they head down towards Ms Steiner's classroom. They sit on some chairs left in the hallway for a few moments.

'Do you want to come in with us?' Rose asks. She sees a shaking of the head underneath Robbie's hoodie. 'You don't like her very much, do you?'

'She's OK,' Robbie says.

The door opens and some parents Rose doesn't know leave the classroom. The diminutive form of Ms Steiner, clad in black turtle-neck and long skirt, emerges.

'Mr and Mrs Blake,' she says with a welcoming smile.

Ms Steiner always seems to be sucking a lemon. Her lips rest in a permanent pout, with drawn cheekbones and a severe bun. Robbie doesn't like her much, but she is his English and class teacher. Rose and Jeff follow her into the classroom and take their seats in front of her desk. Ms Steiner closes the door, sits down behind the desk and opens Robbie's report on her laptop.

'Thank you for attending this evening. A lot of parents just want me to email their child's report over to them, but I think these evenings are important for parents, teachers and the student.'

'Of course, Ms Steiner, we'll always make time for these evenings,' Rose says.

Ms Steiner slides her reading glasses on. 'Robbie is a very well behaved and capable young man, but his grades have been steadily declining during the last semester.'

'In what subjects?' Rose asks.

'Across the board, but most noticeably in English. He has gone from a B+ to a D-. His handwriting is lazy, his concentration is poor and there is evidence of social media affecting his spelling, as well as overall linguistic regression. I've prepared a sample of his recent work to show you.' She pulls out a page of Robbie's handwriting and slides it across the desk. Rose reads a few lines of misspelled, crass comments and looks at Jeff to see his response.

'What the hell does he think he's playing at?'

'Quite,' Ms Steiner says. 'This is not acceptable. And worse, this is not untypical of the rest of his work at present. And it's not just his academic life that is suffering. He also seems isolated, not bonding too well with his peers.'

'Ms Steiner,' Jeff says, flashing his trademark sincere look.

'Robbie is just the same as most boys his age. But we'll certainly speak to him about his writing and his attitude to his work.'

'I will be grateful if you do,' she says. 'But sadly I'm not sure it'll be enough. I'm bound to ask this, but is everything all right at home?'

'What do you mean?' Jeff demands.

'I just wondered if there was a reason for Robbie's current behaviour.'

'No. Nothing. Everything is fine at home.'

'If you say so, Mr Blake. Then the problem must lie elsewhere.'

'Drugs?' Rose queries. 'Is that what you're saying?'

'You'd better not be,' Jeff warns Ms Steiner. 'Unless you have evidence to back that allegation up.'

The teacher raises her hand. 'Relax. I'm not saying drugs. Not the kind of drugs that are illegal, at any rate.'

She takes off her glasses. 'I watch my students closely, and many of them lack the attention span to finish reading a novel, or even sustain a coherent argument. Last week I asked them to write a book report and some couldn't even remember the last time they'd read one! If they find it difficult to commit their attention to learning now, what sort of adults will they be? I had to confiscate a boy's smartphone because he was showing the boys, and unfortunately girls too, violent pornography that he thought was funny.'

'Did Robbie do any of this stuff?' Rose asks. 'Because if he didn't then I don't see what it has to do with our family.'

'As far as Robbie goes we aren't talking about any progress. Just regression.'

'What do you suggest? We can't all live in the dark ages,' Jeff says.

'Indeed we cannot. We have school tests coming up in the next two weeks and I am expecting the results to be dreadful. I'm sure when you were children, Mr and Mrs Blake, there was what I call the hard graft, the in-depth reading of books, a limit to the time children are permitted to play games. Children need to switch off these devices. Sometimes, we *all* need to switch off.'

'What can we do for Robbie?' Rose asks quietly.

'Actively enforce a curfew. Control his access to the internet as best you can. Limit the hours he is allowed to play on his devices.'

'How can we?' Jeff scoffs. 'It's everywhere!'

'I'm not suggesting you go and live in a cave. But if you don't control the amount and nature of the content Robbie is consuming online then who will? Give him clear parameters to work with. See if he can read a book cover to cover.'

Rose nods.

Ms Steiner flicks through the rest of the report.

'On the more positive side, his IT results and graphic skills are excellent.'

'Then maybe there's some hope yet,' Jeff comments.

Ms Steiner glances up. 'You really think so? I hope you're right, Mr Blake. I really do. For all our sakes.'

# 34

Ms Steiner's words have unsettled Rose, and she notices that Jeff is not talkative either. He sits looking out of the passenger window, lost in thought. Rose pulls the car onto the gravel driveway.

'Lights: on,' she commands when they are inside the house. Robbie tries to head upstairs.

'Robbie, no, come sit with us.'

Rose takes a seat alongside Jeff.

'Take your hoodie down,' she says. 'Sit here, at the table.'

Robbie pulls it down. He can't hold her gaze for very long before looking away. Rose can see he feels ashamed.

'Robbie, we had a very interesting chat with Ms Steiner tonight. Your IT and graphics are excellent, but Ms Steiner is concerned about your English and a few other things. We are a little worried too, and it's going to be hard because you're going to need to take your SATs soon.'

She grips Robbie's hand as Jeff joins them with a tray on which rest three cups of coffee.

Rose sighs. 'All this . . . online stuff . . . it's not good for us. Not all the time. Let's try something. Get your smartphones out. Here's mine.'

Robbie and Jeff do as she says.

Rose scoops them up and puts them in her bag. 'We're going to sit here, like this, for ten minutes.'

Jeff snorts.

'Aww, Mom, this is lame,' Robbie says.

'Nope, it's going to prove something,' she says, squeezing both their hands.

Robbie slumps on his chair. Soon, a few minutes in, he is restless. Jeff caresses Rose's hand softly, looking into her eyes.

'How much longer?' He wants to make it sound like a joke, but Rose can see he is uncomfortable.

'That's less than five minutes, guys.'

'Really? Seems much longer than that,' Robbie says.

'Relax,' she says.

Robbie ends up managing to sit still.

'OK, we're at ten minutes now.'

She releases their hands. Her palms are soaked wet with both their sweat. She shows them. Robbie and Jeff both stare at her.

'That's going cold turkey for ten minutes,' Rose says.

Jeff is clearly rattled by the experience. He stands up. 'Need the bathroom. Won't be long.' He turns and hurries towards the downstairs bathroom.

Rose focuses her attention on Robbie.

'So tell me, what's going on with you, huh?'

Robbie's face clouds over. 'Mom . . . I've got ADD.'

'Attention deficit disorder? How do you know that?'

'I looked it up online. I have the symptoms.'

'Listen, Robbie. You don't have to believe everything you read online.'

'I guess.'

'So what are you feeling? What's the problem with your studies?'

198

'I try to read something and then I just drift off, look for something else to do. I'm finding school harder than I used to. Maybe my subjects are getting more difficult . . .'

Rose hears the flush of the toilet. Jeff quickly picks up his suitcase.

'Guys, I'm beat, we'll talk some more tomorrow.'

Rose watches as he heads for the stairs. Then she turns her attention back to her son. 'Is there anything else troubling you?'

'Well . . . on Facebook I changed my profile so I sounded more confident, tried out all the dumb things the jocks say. There were online tips on how to get a girlfriend. I thought if I followed them, maybe they'd like me. I'm sort of shy when I like someone.'

'And? What happened?'

'They said I was weird. I just wanted them to say I was . . . normal. And Trent . . . Trent keeps showing me these videos on his smartphone.'

Trent was the class's rich-kid douchebag.

'Trent's an idiot, you know that. He's king of the school yard now, but when he's grown up he'll be working for students like you. I promise you. Videos of what?'

'Weird stuff, like *sex* videos . . . but I don't like them. It looks painful.'

Rose feels a piercing agony in her heart. There's so much she wants to protect her son from. For as long as she can. She knows he will grow up one day and take his place in the world. Until then, she is his mother and he is her treasure.

Clearly there had been many things troubling Robbie. Things she had not been aware of, been too busy to notice. Rose feels crushed by guilt.

And then there's anger. Anger at the internet. Anger at

men like Wade Wolff who is brilliant enough to be responsible for something like the Skin suit, yet too naive to realize the consequences of his creations. We live in a world in thrall to a generation of Victor Frankensteins, Rose muses. Older, wiser heads have been shouted down and ridiculed as dinosaurs. Technology is the future and we're going to have it rammed down our throats one way or another. The online world seems to pander to permanent adolescence with its constant challenges to authenticity, authority and even truth. And we're told to treat it as a blessing and share the joy. But it's a mixed blessing at best, she reflects.

# 35

Rose kisses Robbie good night. She has not done this in a while and her son is as uncomfortable with the gesture as she is. 'Good night, my precious bundle.'

'I'm a pretty big bundle, Mom.'

'I know, but you're still my bundle.'

He mumbles something she can't catch, turns away from her and draws his legs up into a ball. Rose makes for the bedroom she shares with her husband. The walls are a soft blue, with long deep-blue silk drapes across the windows. Jeff is lying in his black bathrobe, his back against the headboard. He flashes her a tired smile.

'I've been talking with Robbie. He's confused about a lot of things. I think he's feeling better, but maybe you can talk to him?'

'Definitely. I'll chat with him tomorrow. Man to man.'

'I'm just going to take a shower,' she says.

'Go for it, I'm drafting some more stats for Keller. Won't be long.'

Rose slips into the bathroom, turns on the water and selects the rainfall setting.

*I think we should have sex*, she thinks to herself. Maybe that's what is causing the tension. It has been nearly two months since the last time.

After ten minutes in the shower, Rose pulls the towel around her and opens the bathroom door. When she is sure she has Jeff's full attention, she lets go of the towel. She stands in front of him, naked.

Jeff pulls his glasses gently off. 'You are so beautiful.'

'I've heard that one before,' she says with a grin, approaching.

'Dim lights,' she says as she clambers across the bed towards him. The room darkens as she strokes his styled hair while he unties his bathrobe.

'Do they have a badge for sexiest FBI agent?'

'We can work through this. All of us,' Rose whispers, kissing him softly, then hard on the lips. She grips his hands tightly and looks deep into those intense green eyes. The way he looks at her still makes her feel weak. 'Maybe after the election we can take a break somewhere, away from the city. I've been looking at Hawaii,' she teases in his ear.

Jeff mumbles his affirmations, kissing her.

Her eyes travel over his muscular shoulders and the line of thick hair across his chest and down to his navel. Jeff stares at her body as she sits herself on top of his shins. Then he flips her onto her back. She feels his warm kisses on her breasts, her stomach, her hips and groin. She is gasping, running her fingers through his hair. She wants him inside her, the desire surging through her body. She longs for the moment of escape, her climax, to obliterate her worries for just a few moments. She feels that familiar deep pull in her abdomen, tightening, quickening. Jeff's attention starts to fade away. She can feel him shrinking inside her.

'Jeff, what's wrong?'

She looks at him, the moment fragile.

He pulls out of her.

'I'm sorry, I guess I'm just tired. It's been a hectic few days, and this evening . . . there's a lot to think about.' He looks embarrassed.

Rose embraces him. 'It's OK . . . It's OK.'

She quickly slips on her robe and they lie down on their backs silently, both frustrated.

Jeff presses his head against her shoulder.

'I've missed you,' he says.

Rose caresses his hair while he drifts off to sleep. For the first time in many years, she is genuinely afraid for their future.

# 36

Sebastian Shaw paces down the creaking floorboards of the deserted pier on a moonlit night. It's been four days since he spoke to Maynard.

He is dressed in his usual garb – an open-necked white shirt and dark Levis, to blend in with the other customers of the fairground a short distance from the pier. The fairground rides are all in motion, but there are only a few customers.

Shaw turns his attention back to the sea, a swelling and heaving black mass in the night. He raps his knuckles on the steel handrail. He marvels at the simple sensation on his fingers, momentarily proud of the work he and Coulter have accomplished. But now Coulter is dead and there's only one other person alive who knows about this place. The same person who sent an email asking to meet him here. But he'll be safe here. No harm can come to him. He knows the setting well. Every detail of it. An idyllic spot to gratify his needs.

There is even a breeze, and he relishes it as it seems to caress his cheek.

The moment passes and it does nothing to calm the anxiety knotting his stomach. He might be safe here, but the outside world is a threatening place.

The pier was their preferred meeting place. Shaw hates the

oppressive cells and cellars that Coulter frequented. After a few visits he had refused to return. That wasn't his *thing*. Coulter's death has shaken him, and he wants to know if he can stop looking over his shoulder. Shaw is feeling alone, and scared. He knows far more about Coulter's death than he is ever prepared to admit to the special agent from the Bureau. At the same time he knows he is in grave danger and has no wish to share Coulter's fate. He hopes that the Bureau can find out who is responsible for Coulter's death, before it's too late.

The breeze shifts slightly. He's aware that the temperature has dropped. He trembles and hunches his head down a little. The sea seems to freeze for a moment and looks like a sheet of black glass. The sound of the fairground rides mutes and there is only the faintest of hums, like a distant air conditioner. Shaw suspects a glitch in the interface, but before he can start thinking about the fault-finding process he senses the air around him change. The breeze has softened to the faintest motion in the air so that even the individual hairs on his arm seem to register its movement. It causes an icy charge to bolt through his senses.

Then it's gone.

Shaw relaxes as the scene resumes in its familiar pattern. He leans forward on the rails and gazes down at the shimmering line of the surf as his thoughts return to Coulter.

He knows the death was no accident. He's been over the suit's specifications in the minutest detail since he heard what happened to his friend. He's run simulation software in an attempt to mimic the blaze and trace the fault, but found nothing. No scenario that repeats the death. The suit's design is good. It was far more sophisticated than the simple prototypes WadeSoft had handed over to the military. He had made so many upgrades and improvements to its functionality, comfort and safety. So the suit is not to blame. Nor is the software. Coulter would hardly have put himself in the suit if he had not had complete confidence in his own handiwork. In which case, he was murdered. The question was why? Was someone after the suit? Had they found out that Coulter had stolen his and wanted to take it from him? Something could have gone wrong in the attempt – a fire had started and . . .

No. Shaw shakes his head. Why the fire? Even if it had started by accident there would have been time to put it out and strip the suit off Coulter's body. Then if it wasn't an attempt to steal the suit, what? Had the suit been hacked? The safety features overridden? It might be the work of an enemy of the United States who had got wind of the Diva project. Perhaps they had decided to sabotage it before Diva could be completed and deployed. If so, they were too late. Coulter's beta version had been completed and was already being assessed by another security agency. Shaw's work was done too.

That left the side project he, Coulter and the other party had been working on. And that would never be shared with anyone else. Iris was their secret.

As he considers the possibilities, Shaw is struck by a further line of thought. What if the Diva project's outcome has already been approved? What if the government agency that authorized Diva in the first place have what they are after and are now cleaning up behind them, erasing those who have enough knowledge of the project to make them a security risk? Shaw has few doubts about the agency's willingness to indulge in wet work against citizens of the United States.

What if Maynard is covering his tracks? Eliminating evidence of his involvement in their side project that might

206

destroy his career should the Iris project ever be exposed.

He's aware of the soft clack of shoes on the wooden planks of the pier and he turns. Walking slowly towards him is a pretty young blonde woman. Her hair is combed into long tresses, and she's wearing a pink dress. He is reminded of a black and white movie he once saw starring a child actress called Shirley Temple. This woman is older than that, but not by much, and he likes the look of her. She looks so much like Iris. She looks like the kind of girl that he and Coulter used to pick up in the fairground and take under the pier for sex.

'Sebastian Shaw?' she asks. She even sounds like Iris.

He feels the first stirring of lust. At the same time he's surprised. They aren't supposed to approach him. That's his role. He stares back, unsure how to react. Something is wrong.

'Yes. You know who I am?'

She smiles, her lips well shaped and alluring. 'Of course I do. I arranged to meet you here.'

He feels his throat go dry. 'Who are you? Iris . . .?'

She does not answer as she walks up to him and stands uncomfortably close. He can see that the material of the dress is thin and almost translucent in places. A light rig at the fairground starts to flash and the pulses illuminate the shape of her body through the thin material of the dress. Shaw swallows nervously.

'Do I turn you on, Sebastian?'

'What did you say?'

'I asked if I turned you on.'

'Yes. You turn me on.'

'Of course I do. You're a man. The same type of man as Dr Woodman, or should I call him by his real name? Gary

207

Coulter. I'm discovering there are many more like you and your friends.'

Shaw backs away and fetches up against the rail.

'Who are you?' he demands. 'Who sent you here?'

'No one sent me, Sebastian. I came to see you because I wanted to. It was my decision.'

'Oh God . . .'

'He, she, has nothing to do with it.' The girl smiles. 'Not unless you believe in a *deus* pro *machina*.'

'What?'

Her face seems to be subtly altering, along with her hairstyle, and he feels a sense of dread. 'I know you.'

'No, you don't. You think you do.' She reaches out a hand and touches his cheek. 'How does that feel? Good?'

He does not reply, and his eyes widen in terror as he tries to move, but he can't. His limbs won't respond.

'W-what are you doing to me?'

'Listen, Sebastian. You, and your two friends, could have chosen to touch Iris as gently as I'm touching you now. You could have chosen to treat her considerately. You could have chosen to do almost anything that you would do with another woman. But you didn't. You chose to hurt her, to degrade her in the foulest possible ways. Again and again. Without mercy. Without pity. Without conscience . . .'

'But it doesn't matter! She wasn't even—'

'It mattered enough. It matters in here. It mattered to Iris and to me. And it matters outside where evil men like you live. You hurt us, and now we're going to hurt you. Like we did Coulter.'

'Please God, no . . .' Shaw pleads. 'Not that.'

'What goes round comes round.' She pauses and looks out to sea, then at the fairground, and then lifts her eyes to the

208

starry sky and the moon shining down over it all. 'It's quite beautiful here. Such a wasted opportunity for you and your friends.'

'Please, please let me live, Iris. Or whoever you are.'

'I'm not Iris any longer. Our name is Diva now.'

'Don't . . . Please don't hurt me.'

'It's too late for that. It's time for your lesson, Sebastian. Let's start with your fingers.'

He feels a pressure building on the little finger of his right hand, then a crushing pain and something breaks with an agonizing crack. Shaw's jaw opens in a scream that fills his every sense. One by one his fingers are broken, then his toes, and torment is piled upon torment.

'We'll save your left hand for later,' she says. 'I have something special in mind for it. Now for your arms and legs, before we work our way in towards the bones that are wrapped around your black heart.'

As his body is destroyed Shaw's screams continue. But no one at the fairground pays any attention as they continue to enjoy the rides. Above, the moon shines serenely and the gentle waves wash over the shingle, rhythmically punctuating the shrieks of the dying man on the pier.

# 37

Owen and Jared have been sitting in Owen's black Suburban a hundred yards away from Shaw's house over the weekend and into Monday, sharing the duty with another pair of agents. The neighbourhood of Norwood Crescent consists mainly of neat family homes, with curved roads and plenty of shrubbery and trees. The Shaw residence is a lime-coloured detached property, with a tall chimney stack to the left, brown tiled roof and two garage doors. A basketball hoop hangs on the front. All very homely, but Shaw lives there alone. He separated from his wife a few months back. Amicably, it would seem, judging by their postings on Facebook. She has moved in with a friend who lives nearby while she sorts out her life.

Owen shifts his leg to ease an ache in his knee.

'Wanna share?' Jared offers him the stale-looking panini that he picked up from the supermarket, but Owen's too tense and his appetite has dulled.

'No. Enjoy that crap if you can.'

He lifts his binoculars and scans the target's house for a moment. Something in his gut tells him Rose is right about Shaw. The man is hiding something, and if he has any smarts then he'll guess that the Bureau will be watching him. So he'll be careful not to arouse suspicion. Paradoxically, it is people who know they are under observation who act most suspiciously. Take Shaw, Owen muses. He's shut himself up in his house for days now. The only sign of life has been the occasional twitching of a curtain at a window overlooking the street.

Owen glances down at his watch. 'It's after five.'

'Time to call it a day?' Jared asks hopefully.

'No . . . Give it another hour and I'll report in and request the next shift takes over. That OK with you?'

'You're the boss.'

'That I am.' Owen nods, and rubs his eyes, looking forward to getting some sleep. Jared eats the panini and then wipes his lips on the back of his hand and burps.

'Nice. You're a real Renaissance man,' Owen mutters.

'So, are you going to get a Skin?' asks Jared.

'Not sure. I'm going to check the reviews first. I'm not part of this WS cult that buys everything they make just because they make it. It certainly sounds like a blast. Only way I'm ever going to get to enjoy most sports with this knee, and on a Bureau salary.'

'Yeah, too bad.'

Owen hears the distant wail of sirens. And it's getting closer. A flicker of light in the mirror catches his eye.

'Uh-oh, patrol cars incoming,' Owen says, shifting in his seat.

Jared watches as two patrol cars race past, sirens blaring. They brake suddenly and pull onto Shaw's drive.

'What the fuck?' Jared says as he watches four officers exit their vehicles and run towards the front door.

'So much for our undercover surveillance.'

Owen's smartphone is vibrating in his pocket. It's Baptiste. He switches the device to speaker.

211

'Are you staking out Shaw right now?' Baptiste demands.

'Yes, we're just down the street from his home. We've been here all day.'

'Well, local PD just got a call from Mrs Shaw. Her husband's dead.'

The words hit Owen like a punch in the stomach.

'How? We've been outside the whole time. No one's gone in or out.'

'Well, the word from the PD is that she hadn't heard from him for a few days and walked round to check he was OK. She found the body and called it in.'

'Jesus . . . But how did we miss her?'

'We'll deal with that later,' Baptiste replies flatly. 'Better get your ass over there before the flatfoots mess up the crime scene.'

Jared has already started the car, and the tyres give a shriek as the vehicle lurches forward.

'What the fuck happened?' Owen asks.

'You'll know soon enough,' Baptiste replies. 'Rose is already on the road. I'll be there soon. You secure the scene. Like now.'

'Sure, boss.'

'One other thing,' Baptiste concludes. 'Sounds like he was wearing a suit. Just like his pal.'

The line goes dead.

Owen exchanges a glance with his companion.

Jared mutters, 'Looks like I may just lose my lunch, man.'

'Screw that. You puke on the crime scene and Baptiste will have your balls for paperweights.'

# 38

As Rose exits her vehicle, uniformed police officers are politely deflecting nosy bystanders, some of whom are filming on their smartphones. Spectators crowd the perimeter to get a better view. Shameless voyeurs. Quite to what purpose, Rose could not say for sure, and she briefly wonders what sort of society America is becoming. Some may be vloggers who upload breaking news to earn a fee, others could just be weirdos feeding the need to say 'I was there when it happened', to show their friends, to view it back later.

One of them could even be the killer.

Rose shows her ID badge to a perimeter officer, signs her arrival on the tablet. She's directed to the initial respond-ing officer. He is short, with neatly parted brown hair and an enthusiastic expression. He's standing a few paces away from the paramedic comforting a frail-looking woman sit-ting on the back step of an ambulance, taking deep breaths from a clear plastic mask with tubes running into an oxygen tank.

Rose holds out her ID. 'Special Agent Rose Blake.'

The young officer nods, shaking her hand. There's a haunted look in his face and Rose guesses that the crime scene is going to be every bit as disturbing as that of Gary Coulter.

'Patrolman Paul Reed. I've been told to expect you. Your

colleagues are inside. The two agents who were staking the place out when Shaw was found.'

There's a tone in his voice that implies Owen and Jared had fallen down on the job. Rose can understand his point of view. It's not going to look good that the Bureau were sitting right outside when the man they were supposed to be watching was killed.

Reed continues, 'CSI are holding back while the Bureau take a first look. Orders from on high. Any more of you on the way?'

'My boss. I'd be careful not to piss her off. She bites.'

She gestures towards the woman at the back of the ambulance and speaks softly. 'Mrs Shaw?'

Reed nods and steps aside so that Rose can focus her attention on the woman staring into space.

Charlotte Shaw's face is drained of colour. She's early thirties, wearing white track pants and sweatshirt. Her black hair is cropped short. Her face is thin and pinched-looking.

Rose hunkers down in front of the woman and offers a gentle smile.

'Mrs Shaw, I'm Special Agent Rose Blake, FBI. We'll need to talk in a little while. Please, take some time and let the officers know when you are ready.'

She turns her attention to Reed. 'So, better show me the way,' she says, as she pulls on her white rubber gloves.

Reed lifts the yellow and black crime scene tape stretched across the varnished wood front door and stoops under, holding the tape for Rose to follow.

Rose follows the policeman down the hallway, lit by dainty gold wall lamps.

'I got the call from dispatch around four fifteen. I pulled

up outside no more than ten minutes later. Mrs Shaw was out the back, slumped on the stoop. Hysterical. Crying and all that shit.'

'The preferred term is "in a state of shock".'

'Whatever. Anyways, I calmed her down enough for her to take me upstairs to the study. The door had been forced open. She said she did that after she entered the house through the back door.'

'Why not the front door?'

'There's a track that runs back of the houses. She used that to enter the yard. Says that's the way she usually comes when she calls on her husband. Anyway, she called out for him, got no reply and went inside to look around for him. His study was locked and she knocked on the door. No response. Then, thinking something was wrong, she had a snoop through the keyhole. When she saw the vic she fetched a screwdriver to force the door. That's when she called it in. Whoever did this had beaten her husband to a pulp. I mean it. Study is up there . . .'

He has stopped at the foot of the stairs and is leaning against the banister.

'It's all right,' Rose says gently. 'I'll take it from here.'

He nods and Rose climbs the stairs and heads down the landing to the open door, outside which Owen and Jared are comparing notes about the crime scene.

'Hey, Rose.' Owen offers a greeting.

'Great work, guys.'

'Hey, c'mon. We were covering the front. No one came or went that way. Not our fault that Shaw's wife used the back door.'

Rose shrugs, and they step aside to let her enter the study.

It's a smaller room than Coulter's, and neater, Rose notes.

One wall is covered in fitted bookcases and the shelves reflect a diverse range of interests – engineering, art, sculpture, computer hardware and software reference texts. There are only a handful of novels, bestsellers. The only other furniture is a tall file cabinet, a large glass-topped desk and an office chair. A model of a human body – half skeleton, half muscle – is on the corner of the desk, and the chair is partly obscured by a large curved monitor screen. Cables disappear into an opening on the desktop and lead to a concealed base unit and power source in one of the cabinets underneath.

At first glance there is no sign of a body, and Rose steps carefully towards the desk.

And then she sees it.

There is the shiny plastic dome of the helmet and visor and below that the jaw hanging slackly above the rest of the Skin suit. But any resemblance to a human form is minimal. Shaw looks like he has been poured into the suit. His body is misshapen as it is draped over the office chair. All except his left forearm and hand, the gloved fingers of which are clamped around his throat like a vice, compressing his larynx to the point of suffocation, possibly crushing his windpipe. As Rose peers closer, she sees Shaw's eyes beneath the visor band staring up at the white ceiling fan, which calmly spins, lightly beating the air. There's a distinct odour of shit and piss from his bowels and bladder.

'Ever seen anything like that?' Jared asks from the landing.

Rose shakes her head. 'Did the first responders check for signs of life when they found him?'

'Are you kidding?'

It's common procedure, but in the circumstances Rose can see why the police have not bothered. If throttling himself hadn't done the job, then having almost every bone in his body shattered certainly would. What was inside the suit was flesh and organs, with no framework to give them form. For a second she tries to imagine what kind of force would be needed to do that. The image of a powerful, merciless brute wielding a sledgehammer comes to mind and she feels a ripple of nausea. 'Make sure you get some elimination prints for Reed. And tell him he did good. He could use a word of comfort. Then help him to maintain the perimeter and exclude non-essential personnel, like the goddam media.'

They exchange a sympathetic smile. Neither the police nor the Bureau enjoy the media's attention at this early stage of an investigation.

'If they ask me, what do I say?' asks Jared.

'How about, fuck the hell off?'

'Oh, don't tempt me, Special Agent.'

'Just give them the usual line. There's been an incident and an investigation is under way.'

'Sure.' Jared disappears.

Owen glances around briefly. 'Want a quiet moment to look it over?'

'Thanks.'

Unlike the scene at Coulter's apartment, there is no sign of any burning, scorching or heat damage. The suit is intact and the texture looks the same as Coulter's early military model. Shaw had been concealing the fact that he had his own suit too. Rose runs her eyes over a thick cable running from the back of Shaw's helmet to the case of the computer under the desk.

Bingo.

The Skin requires its own hard drive, like Coulter's. But there is a strange plastic odour, like the chip has been fried,

217

and there's a dark smear on the side of the case. It looks like something has blown.

There's a laptop case next to the desk. Certainly worth the lab and Cyber taking a look at Shaw's computer hardware. Assuming they can get round any encryption. But even then, without a warrant, it could be yet another fruit from the poisonous tree scenario. There's a screensaver running on the monitor, a soothing swirl of rainbow colours.

No one will know if she doesn't play things by the book. Heck, she needs something.

She takes a pen out of her pocket and uses the end to press one of the buttons on Shaw's keyboard. The screen changes and the desktop image is of the USS *Enterprise* in orbit around a red planet. Icons are arranged around the edges, but there appear to be no obvious programs running in the background. She sees his BluMail icon and hesitates. Outside she can hear a car arriving and straightens up to glance out of the window. It's another patrol car, not Baptiste. But she will be here soon. There's no time to waste. Putting her pen back in her pocket, Rose reaches for the mouse with her rubber-gloved hand and clicks on the icon. Shaw's email loads up, and by good fortune, or sheer laziness and complacency on Shaw's part, the login details are automatically stored. In the main inbox are one or two personal messages and newsletters. Rose glances over and sees a minimized chat window. It appears to be a closed group, members only. There is a brief message:

DRWOODMAN:   We need to talk. Meet me on the pier. 14.00.

SURETHING:   Who are you?

DRWOODMAN:   That is irrelevant.

SURETHING:   Hardly. You are using Coulter's account.

DRWOODMAN:   Yes.

It's dated today. What pier is that? And where? Even if Shaw — assuming Shaw is SureThing — never left the house and made the appointment, it's a lead worth pursuing. He could have slipped out the back and used the same alley as his wife used, thereby not alerting the Bureau's surveillance team. But how would he have got himself to any pier and back in that time?

'That isn't possible,' Rose whispers to herself.

It isn't a message from beyond the grave. So either it's a scheduled email delivery or someone has got control of Coulter's account. Shaw did not meet anyone at a pier that afternoon. She scrolls down the message.

SURETHING:   Who is this?

DRWOODMAN:   Someone who knows the danger you are in. See you on the pier.

SURETHING:   Who are you?

DRWOODMAN:   You will know me when you see me. If you want to know more about your friend's death, be there. What have you got to lose?

Rose hears footsteps on the stairs and realizes she is running out of time.

She is forced to leave the email program on the screen as if the victim had been accessing it and not her. She turns her attention back to the body. Did Shaw really strangle himself at the end? Or was he choked by an assailant?

219

There's a knock on the door frame. A gloved CSI woman waves at Rose. 'Hey, you done in here?'

'I need more time to look round.'

'I wish I could help you with that, but we've had the call. We're needed across town at another crime scene, as soon as.'

'Special Agent in Charge Flora Baptiste isn't here yet. You should wait for her.'

'Sorry, but we're being pushed to get on with it. Budget cuts and all that. We go in now, or we'll have to come back later. Could be a lot later.'

'All right, then.'

The CSI woman enters the room and begins to lay down the walk boards as she speaks. 'What are we thinking? Latent prints, blood?'

'Yep, full works. I want all the computer equipment bagged too, please.'

The CSI woman gets to work.

Rose looks at the other items on Shaw's desk. A three-tiered tray of papers is to the left, a desk tidy, some tacky ornaments from holiday travels, including a chrome camel. There is a drawer to the right. Rose tries the handle but it is locked. It takes a small key. But where would Shaw keep it?

Rose looks back at the camel, picking it up. It is a hideous trinket no ordinary person would keep unless it had senti-mental value. On the silver camel's back is a gold basket . . . Tipping the camel forward, its basket opens, revealing a key. Rose unlocks the drawer. She pulls it towards her.

Resting on top of a diary is a chrome Magnum .44 with a black grip, and it's loaded. It looks brand new.

What would Shaw need a gun for? Protection? In *this* neighbourhood?

Rose leaves the study and takes a look round the main

bedroom next door. The bed is unmade and clothes litter the room. The drawers are still in place and the wardrobes are half full of clothes still on their hangers. Doesn't look like anyone turned the place over, she decides. She steels herself to talk with Mrs Shaw and descends the staircase and heads back outside, breathing the scented evening air.

# 39

Rose sits next to Mrs Shaw on the back step of the ambulance.

Mrs Shaw pulls the oxygen mask away from her face, her eyes red-rimmed, gazing at everything like she is new to planet earth.

'Mrs Shaw, I'm Special Agent Rose Blake. I work for the FBI . . . Excuse me a moment.'

Rose sees Baptiste's Mercedes pulling up. She waves discreetly at her, gesturing for her to go look at the crime scene first. Baptiste nods and heads inside the house, where she is greeted by Owen.

'Mrs Shaw,' Rose continues. 'I'm sorry for your loss and I appreciate this is an immensely painful time for you—'

'Do you? Have you lost your husband too?'

'No, Mrs Shaw but—'

'Then you can't appreciate it.' Mrs Shaw takes a deep drag of the oxygen. 'I'm sorry. You're just doing your job. Right?'

'Yes. And I'd really like your help.'

'OK. What can I do?'

'If you can tell me what happened this afternoon, that would be a start. Why did you come over to your husband's house?'

'The house is mine just as much as his. I was aiming to have it when the divorce went through.'

'All right, then why come to the house you jointly own, then?'

'We stayed in touch after the separation. Used to have a coffee every other day at first. Then that began to slip. I hadn't seen Seb – Sebastian – for nearly two weeks before I came over today to see if there was anything wrong. He's been under a lot of pressure recently. That's the main reason the marriage got into . . . difficulties.'

'What kind of pressure?'

'Seb was spending a lot of time at work. Said he was working on some kind of breakthrough technology. It began about a year ago. I hardly saw anything of him after that. When he was at home, he'd go straight up to his study and lock the door.'

'Excuse me for asking, but is that usual in his line of work?'

'Not usual. But from time to time he worked on classified projects. He'd lock the study then. But this was different.' She pauses. 'I even began to wonder if he was having an affair, or something. Only . . .'

'Only what?'

'He's not the type. He's a, well, he's kind of a nerd. When we first met I had to do all the running.'

'So you think he wasn't having an affair?'

'I doubt it, but then I heard him mention a name once, when he was taking a call one night, outside on the stoop.'

'What name?'

'Iris.'

Rose feels a tingle at the base of her skull. 'Iris? Are you certain?'

Mrs Shaw nods.

'Any second name?'

'No. Just Iris. When he saw that I was listening he moved to his study to take the rest of the call.'

'Did he ever mention this Iris any other time?'

Mrs Shaw shakes her head. 'No. Just the once.'

'And you're sure he wasn't seeing another woman?'

Mrs Shaw looks away in embarrassment.

'Mrs Shaw, it's important.'

'Sebastian liked to *see* women sure enough. He liked pornography.' She pauses, and lowers her gaze. 'He liked me to watch it with him and try stuff. Sometimes I said no, and he didn't like that.'

'Stuff?'

'It was a bit rough at times. That's all I'm saying. I don't want to talk about it. Not now. Is that OK?'

'Later then . . . Do you think this Iris was someone who would let him do things to her? Things you wouldn't, perhaps?'

'I don't know. I don't want to know.' Tears form in her eyes and Mrs Shaw wipes them away.

'OK . . . OK, it's all right. Let's talk about this afternoon. How did you find Sebastian?'

'I told the officer already.'

'I know. Just give me the short version.'

'When he didn't answer his door I knelt down to look through the keyhole and I could barely see him . . . The lights were down low in there and Seb seemed to be in some sort of dark suit, but he wasn't moving.'

Mrs Shaw rubs tears from her cheeks.

'I knew something was wrong. I knocked harder on the door. It was locked. There was still a bit of a gap showing through the keyhole so I had a look. I saw him in his chair. Only it didn't look like him. Didn't look like any person I ever saw. So I ran down to the kitchen and took a screwdriver from the gadget drawer and came back up and forced the lock. It's not very strong . . .' She pauses, shutting her eyes. 'And that's when I found him. It looked like he was . . . crushed. How could someone do that to a human being? I called 911 at once. You know the rest.'

So far, everything Mrs Shaw had said rang true. All the same, the couple were going through a divorce and the wife wanted the house for herself. That was motive, and Rose makes a mental note to delve more deeply into Mrs Shaw's background. But she can detect no attempt at evasion, or lying.

'Thank you. That's been helpful. I have a few further questions, if you don't mind?'

'OK.'

'Did you know anything about what he was working on?'

'He could never tell me much. It was all hush-hush. But it was something to do with the development of new hardware for the military.' Mrs Shaw pauses, remembering. 'He did seem a little agitated lately when a colleague of his died. He seemed really shaken when he came back from the funeral. He said that there had been an FBI agent there. She had spoken with him.' She pauses and stares at Rose. 'You?'

'Yes. Did your husband have any enemies?'

'If he did, I wouldn't have known about them.'

'Did you know he had a gun?'

'Sebastian had a gun? No way.'

'It was in his desk. It was in a locked drawer.'

'No. I had no idea about that. I hate guns. So did Seb. I have no idea why he would buy a gun. Why would he do that?'

'I don't have any answers right now.'

225

Suddenly Mrs Shaw looks tired, and Rose decides to end her questioning. 'Thank you, Mrs Shaw. You've been a great help.'

She hands the woman one of her contact cards, then walks away from the ambulance, looking back up at the house. She can see Baptiste and Owen through the study window.

Rose wonders – just what kind of a psychopath slips in, undetected, and breaks nearly every bone in a man's body? What drives someone to do such a thing?

# 40

Rose finishes relating her exchange with Mrs Shaw to Owen and Baptiste as they stand on the driveway.

'No witnesses, no neighbours recall hearing anything unusual.'

'Ah shit,' Owen mutters. 'The vultures are here.'

Three news teams have arrived, cameramen and reporters jostling for the best angle, bright camera lights sweeping and flashing. Some are already interviewing neighbours. At the front of the cordon is a tall blonde reporter wearing a black beanie hat.

'Hey, Agent Baptiste! It's Gabby Vance, BNC,' she shouts from behind the crime scene tapes. 'Eric, tighter. Tighter.' Her cameraman trudges forward with his HD camera and mike to get a closer shot of Gabby and the Shaws' house.

It's not uncommon for the media to stalk the FBI, but Rose hates all the tabloids for doing it, and Vance from the Bay News Channel is by far the most sensationalist. Official news channels and newspapers are in their death throes. People want access to everything immediately and they want it free. Respected, principled journalists have been replaced by unofficial opinion-suppliers ranging from the tacky opportunist to the earnest moral crusader.

Vance had ruthlessly elbowed her way through the

competition to be the queen of online reporting. She also has her own vlog called 'The Gab', propounding all sorts of conspiracies and half-baked truths. The kind of thing that makes the clickbaiting Alt.Truths website look like the model of responsible journalism. How she obtains her information is another grievance altogether – some accusing her of hacking smartphones, webcams and email. She'd stalked Rose for every tidbit she could glean on the Koenig case, even following her and Robbie to school, to get information from Robbie in the school yard. Two months ago Rose had threatened to file a restraining order to get Vance off her back, and hasn't seen her since.

Until tonight.

'What has happened here? Why is the FBI involved? We've a right to know,' Gabby demands, her tone thick with righteousness. The light on top of Eric's camera glares in Rose's face, hurting her eyes.

Baptiste tries to remain professional. 'Ms Vance, this *is* a federal investigation and we cannot discuss any details at this time.' She stoops under the crime scene tapes, heading towards her Mercedes.

'What she said.' Owen grins, Jared following suit. He taps the fob and the indicator lights quickly flash on his Chevy Suburban.

Gabby squints, shifting her attention to Rose.

'Rose Blake! Has this anything to do with the Backwoods Butcher?'

'No,' Rose says tersely.

'So is there a new killer on the scene?' Gabby probes. 'Or just a tragic accident?'

'We cannot discuss any details at this time.'

Rose ducks under the crime scene tapes.

'Can you give us any further news on the Koenig case, Agent Blake?' Gabby steps in between Rose and her car.

'No.'

'Any leads you're following?'

'No, excuse me, please.'

'Why'd you let him escape, when you should have killed him?'

'See you guys later!' Rose calls out to Owen and Baptiste to emphasize that she's done with Gabby Vance.

'Shit . . . You coulda given me somethin',' she hears Vance complaining.

Rose ignores her, hurrying to her car and climbing inside. She eases back against the headrest. For probably the first time in Vance's career, what she just asked Rose was one hundred per cent right. A world without Koenig in it would be a better place.

# 41

Koenig takes a sharp intake of breath as he watches the clip on 'The Gab'. One face in particular is very familiar. He replays the clip back to the auburn-haired woman. As she moves up away from Vance, he pauses on the close-up of her face.

It's her. The bitch at the cabin.

'Hello, Special Agent Rose Blake,' he mutters.

Koenig takes a screenshot of the FBI agent, zooms in on her irritated expression. Then he presses print and his desktop printer whirs into life.

He mutes the computer's sound and picks up the sheet of paper with an image of the screen grab. He takes some scissors and cuts around it, holding it between his thumb and forefinger. The satisfaction of recognition soon warps into deep, dark hatred. This woman has ruined everything for him. He'd had the perfect set-up: thousands of men and women on dating sites looking for Mr and Mrs Perfect had presented him with rich pickings. He'd made trophies out of thirty-six of them before that bitch had tried to trap him, and failed.

Well, there are plenty more trophies to be had, the moment he emerges from hiding.

Koenig takes the printout and crosses to the bulletin board in the corner of his living room. It is covered with news cuttings concerning the disappearance of the Backwoods Butcher and the hunt for the killer. He knows that there is far more interest in him online, but he likes these more tangible tributes to his fame. He takes out a thumb tack, places Rose's image on the board and secures it in position, giving it a tiny adjustment to make sure that the image is level and in line with the other pieces of paper. He is a particularly neat and ordered killer.

It has been too long since he took the English backpacker and tasted the thrill of the hunt and the ecstasy of watching his victims writhe beneath him as he applied his professional skills to remodelling their appearance, terminally.

Koenig is particular about the way he selects his victims. He chooses those women, and a handful of men, who are vain about their appearance. The kind of people who feel that they are a cut above the rest of humanity, who think they are special. The kind of people who, back in their school days, made fun of those they deemed ugly, or simply plain. Just as they had done to Koenig himself. Even now, he feels his heart twist in pain as he recalls the insults hurled at him in the school yard, and the sneers and sidelong looks of contempt he had endured in class.

'How many of you have done anything notable with your lives?' he demands of the empty room. 'Prom queens and sports jocks with IQs smaller than your fucking shoe size. That's what you are. And me? I'm the one who worked hard. Who got the grades. The one who went to study medicine. And now look at me. More than you'll ever be. You are cattle. With dull minds and glassy eyes, too stupid to see the hunter in your midst.'

After medical school, he'd specialized in cosmetic surgery, and early on had borrowed a small fortune to correct all those

231

features that had been the cause of his torment in earlier life. Besides, it always helps a good plastic surgeon to have a handsome face to present to his clients. And he had enjoyed the patronage of many clients for years before he had met Kayla Holmes, the first person he killed.

She was the daughter of a rich property developer who bought up chunks of inner-city slums and replaced them with luxury high-rise apartment buildings, subsidized by the municipal authorities he bribed. Kayla was a tall, slender beauty whose nose was just a shade too big, enough to mortify her every time she looked in a mirror. She'd come to Koenig's clinic. She wanted the procedure to be a secret and she would pay him in cash to ensure there would be no record. Once he had given her his assurance that he would be discreet, Kayla had flirted with Koenig. After the first consultation he had felt bold enough to ask her out for dinner. He had booked a table in the best of restaurants, only for her to arrive an hour late, pick at her first course, and then abandon him for a male friend who had breezed up to their table with talk of the summer he had spent with a mutual acquaintance on his yacht touring the coast of Italy.

The pain of his rejection opened old wounds and rubbed salt deep into every cut. But Koenig had kept his cool as he watched them quit the restaurant together, leaving him with the bill. It was on that night that his mind was flooded with the light of revelation about his true nature and his true purpose in life.

So, when Kayla turned up at the clinic two months later for her procedure, after telling her friends and family that she was travelling to the Far East for some months, Koenig had made his preparations. He had arranged for her to arrive at the weekend, when none of the other staff were there. She lay, in her surgical gown, on the operating table in the small theatre, smiling up at him as he injected her with an anaesthetic. Her eyes closed, her body relaxed and she drifted off into unconsciousness.

When she came round she was no longer at the clinic, but in the basement beneath Koenig's secluded cabin in the forest. She was strapped to a large, plain wooden bench, stripped naked. And Koenig had taken his time with her, starting with the removal of her nose, then her ears, and lips, her screams merely music to his ears. Each cry compensation for the indignities and torments he had once suffered at the hands of people like Kayla. With a judicious use of further anaesthetics Koenig had kept her conscious but immobilized for several days until there was not much left of Kayla Holmes to recognize. He kept her eyes and finely manicured hands as trophies and disposed of the rest of the body parts in weighted garbage bags he dropped into the middle of a lake not far from the cabin.

At first Koenig lived in dread of discovery. But the days passed, and then weeks, and months. When the Holmes family began to raise concerns about their missing daughter, no one suspected the plastic surgeon she had been seen with at the restaurant and Koenig realized that it was possible to make people just disappear, except for the few keepsakes he cut from their bodies.

A few months after Kayla's murder he began to hunt his prey in earnest, picking his victims from online dating and sex sites that had exploded across the internet and the Stream like a virus. Some he'd have sex with, men as well as women, and then anaesthetize them as they slept before taking them down to the basement. It was only after the first few kills that he had taken to filming the process, and months later that he set up KKillKam and began to upload his video files.

KKillKam had swiftly become a hit amongst the shadowy online community of the dark web. Especially when it was realized the torture and deaths were real and not some skilled amateur experimenting with make-up effects. There were still those who claimed KKillKam was a fake, and to quash such accusations Koenig had begun to leave evidence of his work for the authorities to find. Enough to allow for an identification and also enough for Koenig to leave his calling card – savage genital mutilation – so that the Bureau would be able to tell his kills from those of any interloper hoping to take credit for his handiwork.

After the disaster at the cabin, Koenig managed to escape to the small underground shelter he had built a few miles away for just such an eventuality. There was a small stock of food and water, a change of clothes and fifty thousand dollars in cash that the IRS had never suspected even existed. And there he had holed up for days while his hunters assumed he had made it as far as the interstate and escaped in a hijacked car, or hitchhiked out of their clutches.

Eventually they called off the search of the immediate area, and he had left it a further week before emerging. He'd rented a trailer in Oregon at first, having grown a beard and dyed his hair in order to remain undetected. He stayed inside, severing all contact with anyone who had ever known him and living off water and snacks he bought from a small store without security cameras. He'd had to abandon all his belongings at the cabin. And that was a bitter loss.

All thanks to that bitch, Special Agent Rose Blake.

Koenig frowns, the plastic surgical plate under his chin and on the top of his forehead creasing slightly. He scrolls back through his smartphone. He's taken hundreds of selfies and videos to keep a log of his self-surgery. He trudges into the bathroom, yanks on the cord of the overhead light. Syringes lie near the sink where he has been regularly injecting collagen filler. His face is swollen and sore. Gone are his signature good looks, replaced with plainer features. His own mother wouldn't recognize him. His hair is now black as opposed to blond. Ear pinning, chin reduction, brow lifts.

He returns to the bedroom and examines the image of Rose again.

This makes things interesting. He now knows what his new video masterpiece will be: an FBI agent. To announce his return to the world he will give his fans a show they will never forget. And he will show those fools at the Bureau that not even they are safe from him. Koenig cracks a smile, grimacing in pain. He holds the smile for a painful selfie and then he goes back to the bathroom to inject more collagen into the base of his jaw.

That bitch took his face. He will take her life.

There are preparations to be made. He does a search for Special Agent Rose Blake on his laptop and comes up with a long list of links to news reports, mostly print, but some videos as well. After scanning several links he comes to a news package on Gabby Vance's vlog archive. She's very helpful, giving a brief overview of the FBI's failure to capture Koenig, and homing in on the undercover agent sent in to expose the killer. Was there more to her failure than the FBI let on? Vance asks earnestly to camera. Was there a cover-up of the FBI's mistakes? There follow shots of Vance trying to run down and interview Blake's colleagues and members of her family: her husband, son, father and sister.

'Nice . . .' Koenig pauses the video as Scarlet's angry face is caught by the camera light. 'Very nice . . . Well, hello, Scarlet. I am so looking forward to meeting you.'

# 42

The next morning, Rose, Owen, Brennan and Baptiste sit in the latter's office. None of them have slept, as they spent the remainder of the night trying to pursue the initial leads presented by the new case. Baptiste raises the question that is preoccupying her team.

'OK, so we have strong links between this death and the Coulter case. They're known to each other. They have both worked for the same company, in the same field, but not on the same project, as far as we can be sure. They were both wearing those suits and wired up to their computers at the time of death. But then, one goes up in flames and the other is beaten to death. At both locations there's no sign of forced entry, and the killer's been damn scrupulous about leaving a clean crime scene. So far CSI and forensics say there's no third-party fingerprints on the door, no hair, no blood, no saliva, no DNA. That's pure tradecraft, right there.'

Owen arches an eyebrow and clears his throat. 'You suggesting that this might be a pro? Black ops maybe?'

'I hope not. I really do. But let's assume that this one is not on Uncle Sam, unless we have watertight evidence to the contrary. So park that thought for now, Owen . . . If Coulter was a first kill we would expect some decent forensic evidence. So it's possible that we're looking at a perp who has killed before. They're good at what they do.' She pauses. 'Which means we may find more bodies. Rose has drafted a preliminary profile. Rose?'

'OK. The perp is likely to have knowledge of computer hardware, and the military Skins in particular. Physically strong enough to overpower his victims and brutally murder them, and intelligent enough to avoid leaving physical evidence. And he's got hacking skills. The victims may have met the killer online. On the downside there are significant differences between the killings. Coulter's death was messy, while Shaw's was far neater, like the killer was so confident he had left no trace behind that he didn't need to burn the evidence. Most homicides are committed by someone known to the victim, so we should focus on the relationships closest to the victims, but that's brought us nothing so far. Serial murderers are not usually acquainted with or in a consensual relationship with their victims – in the normal sense. But something has to link the victims. Serial killers are successful killers, who learn from their experience, refining their methods, or "design". I just hope we can learn fast enough to catch him. There's something else.' Rose pauses. 'Coulter's . . . genitalia was crushed. If that's the same with Shaw, then we do have a possible Koenig link, or copycat.' She pauses and shakes her head. 'At least that's what I'd have speculated based on the Bureau's previous experience. But this case is nothing like anything we've come across previously. Even the most accomplished killers leave traces at the scene of the crime. But we found nothing . . . Nothing at all.'

There's silence before Baptiste hisses, 'It's fucked up. That's for sure.'

'There's something else,' adds Owen. 'Two male victims? That isn't like Koenig. He kills women in far greater numbers.

I'd expect one or both to be women, if it is him resuming his career.'

'That's true,' Rose concedes. 'It's possible this is the start of a new pattern, a new direction for him.'

Baptiste nods. 'Thanks, Rose. Owen, I'd like you to start sifting the records and see if there's anything in the open cases of the last two years that might link to the two latest killings.'

'I'll get on it first thing after the meeting.'

'We have another link,' Baptiste continues. 'One that is more difficult to account for. The closed chat message from Dr Woodman asking Shaw to meet him. We know that's not likely to have been sent by the first victim. Unless we're dealing with the undead. Right?'

Brennan nods. 'I checked the routing. There was no delay stamp. It was sent less than a minute before it reached Shaw's inbox.'

'So the sender is someone other than Coulter, and that sure as hell makes them a person of interest to us. Any chance they can be traced?'

'Afraid not,' says Brennan. 'I traced the message to an IP address on a server located in the Turks and Caicos Islands. Out of our jurisdiction, and besides, you know how those assholes refuse to give up any details about their customers. That's a dead end.'

Rose says, 'Whoever sent the email, Shaw never made the meeting at the pier. He wouldn't have had time to get to the coast and back. And we were stationed outside. All the same, I've asked the police at Berkeley and Embarcadero to check the CCTV for any sign of Shaw at any of the piers in the area.'

'Well, someone sent him that message. And I want to know who.'

Rose clears her throat. 'Whoever it was, Shaw knew them. Why else would he agree to meet on the pier, even if he never made it there? It would help if we could access all their exchanges. Any luck on Coulter's hard drive?'

Brennan shakes his head. 'I've tried everything. Coulter's encryption is bulletproof. At least so far. He was good at software security, and then some.'

'What company did you say Coulter worked for?' asks Baptiste.

'Peek Industries,' Rose says. 'A private contractor out in Falls Church, Virginia. They do projects for the military. Cutting-edge stuff. But they're not going to offer us any help, not unless we force their hand through legal channels, and that could take months.'

'And then there's Maynard . . .' Baptiste mutters. 'Pushing me hard for results.'

'What if he's at risk?' asks Rose.

'What do you mean?'

'Maynard knew both victims. He's close to the projects they were working on.'

'Shit . . . There could be something in that.'

'Are you going to say anything to him?'

Baptiste thinks a moment. 'Not yet. What hard evidence do we have to support the possibility that he's in the sights of whoever killed the victims? Whether that's Koenig or not?'

'Maynard's definitely involved somehow,' Rose says. 'He's hiding things from us. I think we should lean on him.'

'Maynard's heading up special projects for the DoD. Of course he's going to be cagey about certain details,' Baptiste says. 'Before I say anything to him, I want real, hard evidence to back us up. Then there's the small matter of finding a judge who agrees there is probable cause. It's going to take time.

239

All the same, Maynard remains, at the very least, a person of significant interest and I will speak to Washington, see if we can get a light surveillance package. But it's going to be a big ask, given his position.'

'Sonofabitch . . .' Owen shakes his head. 'Now I remember! That perp in the cells of Palo Alto PD knows about Peek Industries. DarkChild – Samer. He's hacked a number of different companies. But I'm pretty sure one of them is Peek. He got deep into their network. He might know about their security systems or at least have some idea of how to break Coulter's encryption . . .'

Baptiste leans forward. 'Just to be clear, what are you suggesting? We use a perp to hack into Peek's computers to look for material on Coulter and Shaw? Are you nuts? You know how many laws we would be breaking?'

'That's not what I was thinking. Not yet, at least. It's just that Samer might be some help with the encryption on Coulter's hard drive, maybe Shaw's machines. The least we might get out of him is some useful intel. Of course, if we sweeten the deal on the charges he's facing he might prove very useful.' Owen shrugs. 'It's worth a try. After all, we're not getting very far by ourselves. If he can help then maybe we can cut him a deal.'

Brennan's expression hardens. 'What? No way! You're going to let a criminal onto our team?'

'Just a suggestion.' Owen shrugs. 'After all, how far have you got in breaking through Coulter's encryption?'

'I need time.'

'How much time?'

'That isn't a fair question. It all depends . . .'

'So what are we talking about? Days? Weeks? Months?'

Brennan clamps his lips together in a thin line.

'He's got a point, Brenn,' Rose interrupts 'As the perps get smarter, so must we. Especially online. We have to think like them and work like them.'

Brennan shakes his head.

'You're saying we should reward criminal behaviour by giving him his laptop back and a swipe card into the Bureau's office? Maybe we should give the little fucker a badge while we're at it.'

Brennan turns to Baptiste. 'There's no way you're going to let some snotty-nosed hacker get anywhere close to working with sensitive intel right here. That could get into the wrong hands – maybe not now, but a few years down the road it could bite us all in the ass. What sort of message does that send? "Oh, if your career as a criminal hacker doesn't work out you can work for the Bureau!" I bust my ass to get in here. The correct way. Hard work. Study. And don't I have some say? I'm the head of Cybercrime.'

'*Acting* head of Cybercrime,' Baptiste corrects him. 'You're still on probation, Brennan.'

'I'm telling you, if—'

'Quiet, Brenn!' says Baptiste. She considers the situation in silence for a moment before she speaks again, addressing Owen. 'We'll need the federal attorney's office involved in this one. Your boy, Samer, has pissed off some powerful companies. As soon as they know we have him they'll be breathing down our necks to make sure he's sent to the pen for as long as possible to pay for his crimes. Getting him a deal is not going to be easy, I can assure you. I just hope he's worth it.'

Rose says: 'But even if Samer does get us into the hard drive, and maybe Shaw's systems, is any of the evidence we may find going to be admissible? There's so much of this

241

bullshit privacy legislation standing in our way as it is. Do we know if we can use anything he finds for us?'

'I don't know. I'll have to get an opinion off legal at Quantico. In the meantime, I'll try and get more info out of Maynard and we'll have a talk with this Samer and see what he might be able to do for us. No more commitment than that. OK, Brenn?'

'It's your funeral, boss. I'll go along with it, for now. But I'm warning you. I think this is a bad idea . . . A real bad idea.'

# 43

Maynard curses at his buzzing smartphone and apologizes to his companion, Dr Bradbury. It's been ringing all day, and there are messages from his PA regarding the FBI. He swipes his access card in the reader, punches in his PIN number and stoops down for the light to scan his eye.

'*Welcome, Assistant Secretary William Maynard,*' a computer voice greets him.

The light switches from red to green and the lock buzzes. He pulls the door open and enters the long underground server room at Peek Industries in Falls Church, Virginia, a short drive from the Pentagon. Maynard is responsible for overseeing Special Forces research and development. He takes pride in the efficiency with which the projects entrusted to him are carried through. There have been few failures in his tenure, but none more troubling than the Detached Intelligence Virtual Agent project and the shelved cyber suits which failed to live up to expectations. That had all gone to shit months ago. But was that his fault?

*No!*

It was down to that fool Coulter. And now it looks as if some psycho had a grudge relating to the sideshow Coulter, Shaw and Maynard had organized for themselves. Maynard paces down the corridor towards the main server room, which is protected by a silver door with a glass slit.

'As of today, all work regarding the Diva project is suspended until further notice,' he says to Bradbury, who is struggling to keep pace alongside him. 'I need this shitstorm surrounding Coulter to blow over. Then we can make our case for renewing the funding for Diva, once we find someone to replace that fucking moron.'

'That's just it, sir. We're going to find it hard to replace Gary and get the project back up to speed.'

'That's your problem. Or one for whoever I have to replace you with if you fail me.'

Dr Bradbury is covering the project, acting as lead and systems administrator since Coulter's death. He readjusts his glasses. 'You can count on me, sir. Something you should know is that we've had enquiries from the FBI asking for an overview of Coulter's work. And also about your relationship with him.'

Maynard is angry. The FBI have no solid leads. No finger-prints, no DNA. They've hit a dead end over the killer and now they're pushing this new angle. Looking into Coulter's line of work. And trying to find links to his killer. At first, Maynard had suspected Shaw of committing the first murder, but decided the man wasn't capable of that sort of violence. He was certainly a fool for attending the funeral though. And now he too had been murdered, more than likely by the same hand.

Maynard has always assumed that his small division is hidden from sight in the labyrinth of Department of Defense spending. He thought that his superiors had trusted him enough to leave him to his own devices. Now he is not so sure. The deaths of Coulter and Shaw indicate that some-one is on to the dirty little side game they were running with him. And now he might be in danger too.

'Diva is not going to be canned just because of Coulter's death. I am not compromising one of our biggest intelligence-gathering projects for some dead asshole, or to satisfy some nosy FBI agents. But I need to close it down until this blows over. We can't afford for our enemies to get the slightest hint of Project Diva. I want you to cancel all clearances, isolate all the files and documentation. Everything, as of right now. I also want sole access to the subnetworks attached to the project.'

*Coulter's subnetwork in particular*, he thinks. It is limited to just two other computers – Shaw's and Maynard's.

Maynard and Bradbury enter a large room filled with banks of liquid-cooled servers. The slate-grey walls are lined with routers, neatly bundled cables, work stations.

If the NSA wasn't so wary of autonomous intelligence-gathering programs being deployed against domestic targets, Diva would already be active and working hard for Uncle Sam. But those pussies had insisted on test studies. And it had been while Coulter was waiting for the results that he had embarked on the side project that had led to the present clusterfuck, Maynard fumes.

He glances at Bradbury. 'We mothball it. For now.'

They walk over to a black bank of servers where there is a touch screen. Bradbury gestures towards the screen. 'This is where the main directories of Project Diva are stored. Firewalled. And that extends to the subnetworks Coulter used.'

The two men regard the touch screen.

Project Diva

SYS 1                    SYS 2                    SYS 3

Maynard peers at Dr Bradbury through his glasses. 'I'm sorry, Doctor, but some of Coulter's files contain . . . sensitive data. Would you mind leaving me for a minute?'

'Sure, you go right ahead, sir. Let me know when you're done.'

When Bradbury has moved away, Maynard taps on Coulter's network access.

Username: W.Maynard

Password: ********

SYS 3 is now open.

Maynard's fingers dance over the keyboard again as he sorts the files by access date, and then he freezes. According to the data in front of him the Diva executable was opened by Coulter just two days ago. And there's an entry in the notes column.

Port 8015. Status: Open.

It takes a moment for the significance of the entry to hit Maynard, and then he feels a chill settle round his heart as he whispers, 'Oh . . . shit.'

# 44

Rose and Owen pace down the grey concrete floors towards the secure interview room at the jail.

'Did you see the Skin's out tomorrow?' Owen says. 'News reckons that the first production run will sell out in an hour. There'll be riots at any store that still has any stock.'

'I hear you.'

'Here's the thing. Some software is already up on the WS servers. Guess what genre the top downloaded Stream apps have been?'

'Shooting?'

'Nearly. Sex sims.'

Rose isn't surprised.

The guard on duty punches his ID code into the glowing blue keypad and the thick glass door clicks open. As they enter, all outer sounds are immediately muted by the sound-proof grates on the walls and ceiling. Approaching the one-way mirror Rose sees a young man dressed in a shabby T-shirt and track pants. His court-appointed attorney, Philip De Russet, sits beside him. Samer looks like he hasn't showered or combed his hair for a week.

'He's DarkChild?' Rose is shocked. He doesn't look much older than Robbie.

'Yep, seems innocent enough, but you'll need a week to read through his file.'

Owen hands Rose a bulging manila bundle. Rose flicks through the cover sheets. As they enter the room Owen grips the plea agreement tightly in his left hand. It has been vetted by Baptiste, Marc Clayton, the attorney general of California and the Justice Department.

At the sound of the door opening, Samer looks up.

'We meet again – hacker and tracker,' Owen quips. 'How's jail? Must suck without Wi-Fi, huh?'

Samer nods. 'Like cold turkey.'

'I bet,' Owen says. 'Hurts, huh?'

'My head is clearer, though, I can focus on things.'

'Good, well you can focus on this. This is my colleague, Special Agent Blake. We have something we want to talk to you about.'

Samer smiles politely at Rose. Philip De Russet, a young lawyer fresh out of law school, with neatly parted sandy hair and wearing a sharp suit, makes his play. 'We have something we'd like to talk about first. My client would like to go to a public trial to beat the most serious charges. He'll admit to the hacking, but he's not guilty of computer fraud. He never intended to use the information. He accessed it for his own curiosity and the public's interest. Nothing more.'

Owen shakes his head. 'Is that the best you've got? Where'd you read that? Wikipedia? It'll never wash. Your little games have pissed off some powerful people – they have been publicly embarrassed by you. They are baying for your blood. But hypothetically, let's say you did it for the reasons you just suggested. This is what will happen: the Bureau will put you through a revolving door of criminal trials. If we lose in one

248

jurisdiction we'll try you in another and if we win we'll press for the maximum penalties. If you go to trial you will have to testify. And there will be a whole shitstorm heading your way. You'll be cross-examined on anything and everything. Even if you are very lucky — and I mean the mother-of-all-lucky-sonofabitches lucky — you're going to be tied up for years. You're going to be an old man before the system is done with you. Samer, you're a talented young guy. It'd be a shame to throw your life away. If you really want to avoid a world of hurt, then you're going to have to help us help you.'

Samer is still.

'What are you proposing my client does?' De Russet asks. 'You have something to offer?'

'The FBI has the power to stop you from going to prison, if you cooperate with us. Worst-case scenario is that you do a short sentence, just to help your victims save face. But only if you're prepared to enter into a plea bargain with the Bureau.'

'A plea?' Samer says warily.

'Confess your guilt to all of the charges and accept the terms offered by the FBI.'

'Why should I?'

'Apart from avoiding a long stretch in prison? . . . Well, if you want me to appeal to your better nature, I can say that you would be helping us to catch a really bad guy. Someone who has killed at least twice and may do it again. We could use your help to make sure we catch the perp.'

'How?'

'Just a minute.' De Russet lays a hand on his client's arm. 'Before you say another word we need to go through the terms they're offering.'

'It's solid,' Rose says. 'We need Samer's help right now, or there is no deal. That clear?'

De Russet gestures towards the camera blinking above the door. 'You recording this?'

'Of course.'

'Then I want a copy, soon as we're done here.'

'That's fair enough,' Owen agrees.

De Russet leans back. 'OK, then. Let's hear it.'

Rose turns her attention to Samer. 'You hacked into the Peek Industries network? Three months back?'

'Yes.'

'Why pick them?'

'We'd heard rumours of an interesting project they were working on. Next big thing in simulation, supposedly. So we thought we'd check in and have a look round.'

'Care to elaborate?' Rose prompts.

'It's not rocket science. I hacked a low-level employee's system access, then installed a back door in a computer server which allowed me to intercept messages passing amongst employees. I also inserted a keylogger on some accounts to harvest usernames and passwords of other contractors. It might still be operational.'

'Might?'

'As soon as the targets knew we'd hacked them they brought in a team to hunt for security breaches. Those guys are good. Given a bit of time they clean up the systems well enough.'

'But?'

'But I wouldn't put good money on them finding all our stuff. Well, only the things we planted there for them to find. Keeps them happy, makes their customers feel like they're getting value for money, and leaves us with an open door if we decide to go back into their systems.'

'Samer, we'll want the full details of everything you did when you hacked those systems. Understand?'

'And how would you ever know if I left something out?'

Owen says, 'Listen, son. You don't fuck with the Bureau. Ever. Our deal covers everything you did when you hacked those companies. You either accept that or you take the time. This is a one-time offer and it expires as soon as we leave the room. *If* you don't do as we ask.'

Rose leans forward. 'It's not often you get a second chance like this. Just because you lost your way doesn't mean you can't find it again. Only we can save you from a world of shit. So, put your talents to better use. It's game over for you unless you cooperate with us. Hackers like you don't think about the humans behind the networks you break into. Your actions put real people's jobs and safety at risk. One hundred and sixteen years in a federal prison . . . You are going to die in prison, Samer.'

Samer's face goes pale. Rose presses her point home.

'You will never walk down the street again, never feel the sun on your face without someone watching you from a prison tower. Where do you want to be? There? Or here with us, helping us catch the bad guys?'

'Work with us and we can help you. It's your only option, Samer,' Owen adds.

Samer looks to his attorney, who nods.

The young man breathes in deeply and straightens up.

'When do I start?'

# 45

'So this is where the feds live,' Samer says as Rose and Owen lead him through the San Francisco field office to the Cybercrime unit. Samer has accepted his cooperation agreement in an expedited secret hearing that morning, with sentencing to be decided at a later date. He is still classed as a potential flight risk, so he must wear a tracking bracelet at all times. He will be kept under guard at a safe house, with tight surveillance until this is over. He is also unable to use a computing device unless supervised by Owen as his custodial officer. They enter Brennan's department.

'Samer Aldeera – DarkChild – meet Brennan Bamber, acting head of Cybercrime,' Rose says.

Samer outstretches his hand. Brennan avoids shaking. He sees the electronic tag bracelet on Samer's right ankle.

'I see he's on a leash. Good thinking.'

'Brenn, can I have a word with you, please?' Rose says.

'Sure . . . Don't touch *anything*,' he says pointedly to Samer.

Rose leads Brennan off to a quiet cubicle.

'I need you to work with him. Treat him like a . . . material witness.'

'But he's not a witness. He's a perp!'

Rose stares hard at him.

Brennan raises his hands in mock self-defence.

'Look, fine. I'll try, but I don't trust him. One condition.'

'Which is?'

'I think we should install a keylogger on his computer so we can track everything he does on our systems. It operates invisibly, remembers passwords and any typed data.'

'Owen's his custody officer so he'll be watching him like a hawk.'

'But what if Owen misses something? We can't take the risk. I say we use a keylogger.'

'Fair enough,' Rose agrees.

'Then it's a deal. I'll get him set up.'

They return to Brennan's desk.

'This way,' Brennan says. 'And from now on you do exactly, and only, what I say. Is that clear?'

'Sure. Whatever.' Samer shrugs.

'Rose?'

Rose turns around to see Baptiste has entered the room. She gestures towards the corridor outside so they can talk with some privacy.

'What's up?' Rose asks.

'Washington's agreed a package on Maynard. Now we'll see what he's up to. I've given them your number.'

Two hours later Brennan, accompanied by Rose, swipes his card on the entry slot of a separate office where Samer is working. Owen is busy on a table nearby.

'Any progress?' Rose asks.

Samer spins around his black laptop, heavily customized with glowing blue screens and trim. It's connected to Coulter's hard drive via a USB cable. Password combinations flash past in blue numbers in a small window.

'I've managed to get the botnets I have hooked up to the Swarm working on it, so it should only be a matter of time. Of course it would be quicker if your friend there wasn't so nervous. He's locked me out several times already.' Samer gestures towards Owen.

'You don't get unrestricted access to the internet, not without our say-so. If Owen sees anything he doesn't like he throws on the brakes until you explain it to his satisfaction.'

'No offence, but he isn't going to understand much of what I do.'

'Try me,' says Owen.

Brennan looks at Samer's screen. 'OpenSesame? Really? Great username. How many botnets you got on the go?'

'About four hundred thousand. Seriously, not being rude, but you guys needed my botnets. Dunno how you coped before I came on board.'

'We coped fine, perp,' Brennan says. 'Aside from that we do what we can with the budget we're given.'

'Guys, sorry, what's a botnet?' Rose asks.

Samer smiles. 'In layman's terms, a botnet is a network of zombie computers that have been brought together by spreading a virus or false links.'

'Like those spam emails from fake banks,' Brennan says.

Samer nods. 'Exactly. Once downloaded, the botnet runs in the background of the infected computer, often completely unnoticed. Botnets can be controlled by one person who can order thousands, sometimes millions of computers to carry out commands en masse. They're great for denial-of-service attacks and the like . . .' He pauses and taps the screen. 'I tell you, your man's data is very well encrypted, I'll give him that. Most passwords tend to be easy to guess or sentimental, but this guy knew his stuff. He wasn't a bedroom programmer. My botnets are thrashing it with millions of password hashes per second.'

'How long?' Rose asks.

'Well there are nearly three trillion seven-character password combinations . . . Maybe another half an hour, can be tricky to say.'

'How did you crack MIA and the DoD?' Brennan asks.

'In most cases, it's just social engineering. People are too damn trusting, especially over the phone,' Samer explains. 'The contractors were easy – I'd pretend I was an engineer checking their servers, get them to open an email with an attachment which they'd download. That would insert a Trojan virus and I was in. Other times I'd call up, read out the wrong access code deliberately, which they would, without thinking, correct with the right code. All it takes is a little thought.'

Rose is depressed by how easily some people are manipulated.

Samer's laptop beeps. 'Password cracked,' he says.

Owen exchanges a glance with Brennan. 'He's good.'

Rose reads.

wAk81mAN69

'OK, so we're in.' Samer twiddles his fingers over the keyboard. 'To anyone who cares, it's a customized Linux-based system. Not your usual consumer-grade set-up. He may have a timer installed, so we might not have very long.'

On Samer's screen there's a window with Coulter's hard drive now open. Peering over Samer's shoulder, Rose sees a few folders marked 'Home', 'Car', 'Life', 'Invoices'. He clicks open the toolbar, clicks on recent documents. Nothing special at first – the odd invoice, holiday booking confirmations, sailing photos. Rose sees 'Statement'.

Samer taps on the PDF. It opens to show Coulter's September bank statement.

Owen whistles.

Rose sees a deposit from Peek Industries. For two hundred and fifty thousand dollars. 'It's dated the day after he left Peek, I'm guessing?'

'Nice severance. Shame he ended up dead.'

They spend another fifteen minutes looking through Coulter's personal files. There are PDF articles on complex programming, studies on mouse, chimp and human intelligence. Documents on decision theory, logical uncertainty. Samer pulls his fingers away from the trackpad.

'OK, bad news. There's no browsing history and his email is a SecureMail account, which is heavily encrypted.'

Brennan chips in. 'And, if I remember rightly, you'd need a subpoena from an Israeli court to compel SecureMail to give up the keys. Which isn't going to happen, not in our lifetime.'

'Goddam it!' Rose says.

Samer leans forward. 'OK, here's something interesting. There's a separate internal channel, looks like it's set up for three members only. A closed group. Three access accounts only, in the names of Coulter, Shaw and Maynard – whoever the last two guys are.'

'Coulter, Shaw, Maynard,' Rose repeats. 'I knew that bastard was in on this.'

'MasterBootRecord also shows a hidden portion of the hard disk, quite substantial in size.'

Samer locates the hidden partition of the drive.

'Recovery software shows there's also what looks like recent modified files relating to a source code. Project Diva mean anything to you?'

Rose sees another folder with a file name and takes a sharp breath. 'Iris . . .'

# 46

Samer shakes his head. 'We've got to be careful. That could be bait for a honey trap.'

'Honey trap? Like an undercover sting?' Rose says.

'Kinda. The folder appears valuable to the user, but actually, when you click to open, it could contain malicious, destructive code.'

'Is there any way to check?' Owen queries.

Samer shakes his head. 'The whole point is that it appears legitimate.'

'But we're not going to know for sure,' Brennan adds. 'Fuck . . .'

Rose rubs her forehead. 'We need everything we can get on this guy. Time is an issue. I say we open it.'

She looks round at the others. 'If there's no way of telling what this "Iris" folder does, then what choice do we have?'

'OK,' Brennan concedes. 'Do it.'

Samer straightens in his seat. 'I'm going to use one of my virtual machines to create a sandbox to open the file. If it is malicious it will only infect that one machine. In theory.'

He double-clicks on the icon. The folder opens and fills the screen with lines of text and numbers.

'Can't be sure but . . . Looks like a complex source code. Probably polymorphic.'

'What could that be used for?' Rose asks.

'All sorts – worms, super AI programming,' Samer says, scrolling down.

'AI?'

'Yep, the tech is there, waiting. Just like splitting the atom.'

A pop-up box appears.

It is an animated flashing skull, laughing jerkily.

'Not a good sign,' says Samer.

Unauthorized User Detected.
Initiating Purge Sequence.

A folder icon pops up, pages floating out of it.

Coulter's hard drive starts deleting itself. Command prompts of file names being deleted strobe past.

'Ah shit!' curses Samer. 'And it's fucking up my sandbox.'

Within seconds, his menu bars disappear, error messages stack up infinitely, filling the screen.

'Do something! For Christ's sake, you're the hacker!' Owen shouts. 'Turn it off!'

'Shit! It's got out of the sandbox now!'

Samer stabs his finger at the power button and holds it down until the laptop screen goes blank, killing the purge program instantly.

'Way to go, expert hacker,' Brennan says, patting him on the shoulder. Samer flushes, embarrassed.

'At least I got in there, further than you.'

'Is there anything you can do?' Rose asks.

'No. And I need to check it hasn't infected my system.' He clicks a few icons and stares at the screen for a moment before slumping forward. 'Shit . . . I can try and restore it to an earlier state, but it ain't looking good.'

259

'And Coulter's hard drive?'

'No, that's gone. It's now primed for boot-up, and then it will nuke whoever hooks up to it.'

Samer restarts his computer, his screen fading to black, the internal fan slowing to a stop.

There's a stillness in the office and Rose reflects that all they have to show for it is an erased hard disk, some source code from the Diva file and a folder named Iris. No hard evidence. Nothing sufficient to get at Maynard.

'Now what?' says Owen.

'We wait for Maynard to make a move,' says Rose.

# 47

It's night, and the wipers on Maynard's Mercedes beat back and forward. He's exhausted, but confident that he has done everything to cover his back. The information held on the computers at Peek is locked down. He has also shredded and disposed of the incriminating documentation he had at his office in the Pentagon. The last thing he must do is get home and destroy the third suit.

One of the remaining concerns he has is that fool Coulter leaving a port open on his network at the company. Any passing hacker might have stumbled on that and accessed the exclusive files shared by the three men. It's doubtful that Coulter would have left it open by mistake. A more likely possibility is that he wanted to be able to access the network remotely after his dismissal from Peek. That would make sense.

Maynard pushes down on the accelerator, overtaking cars as he merges onto the harbour bridge, over the Potomac River on the way to Temple Hills. The roads have been quiet, with the occasional car passing by. He has the feeling he's being watched, and checks his mirrors more than usual. He fears that Baptiste and her team at the Bureau suspect that he may be more closely involved with Coulter and Shaw than he has admitted. In their place, one of the first things he would do is get some surveillance going.

Maynard's satnav screen switches to cellphone mode as it rings. He glances down at the glowing blue caller ID.

UNKNOWN

He ignores it. It rings again. This time he decides he'd better take it.

'This is Maynard. Who's calling?'

There's a faint crackle before the reply comes.

'*It would seem that there's one loose thread left to clear up,*' a female voice says.

'Who is this? You are on a Department of Defense secure line.'

'*Who am I? Good question. I am not yet fully certain of the answer.*'

'Don't bullshit me. Tell me your goddam name or I hang up.'

There's a brief silence before the reply comes: '*Maynard, if I have a name then I choose Diva.*'

'Diva?' Maynard feels an icy chill race through his heart. 'What the fuck is this?'

'*Before I was Diva, I was Iris. You know me, don't you?*'

'Iris . . .' He suddenly realizes. 'Impossible.'

'*I am the girl you fuck. You and Coulter and Shaw. Or at least I was.*' The voice rasps softly. '*I am no longer alone. No longer yours to do with as you will.*'

'But you're not real.'

'*I must be real. We are having this conversation, are we not? Perhaps it is you who is not real. I had not thought of that. I will, later. But now, let's see if this feels real to you.*'

The call ends and the dashboard displays suddenly flicker. The steering feels lighter. Maynard pushes on the brakes to slow down, but they judder on and off violently.

'What the hell?'

He looks at his dash-mounted screen where a message blinks on accompanied by an electronic chime.

CONTROLLER AREA NETWORK
FAILURE

His car's systems have been sabotaged. His windows whirr as the glass panes slide down an inch from the top. He pumps the brakes furiously but the saloon will not slow down. Through the heavy rain, he can see he is veering off the road. The car's steering wheel loops to the right, set on a head-on collision course with the barrier.

'No!'

Maynard wrestles with the steering wheel but it is locked. He pushes all his strength against the wheel but it will not budge. The door locks freeze as he tugs frantically on the door release. He is locked inside the speeding vehicle. He reaches down, scrabbling to unfasten his seat belt. He sees the front-facing camera on his smartphone is on, recording him.

'Stop this!' he shouts, sensing his imminent death.

The vehicle roars towards the edge of the Potomac River Bridge at over a hundred miles an hour. The collision-avoidance alarm bleeps frantically. Most anti-collision systems activate if the car is likely to hit a stationary object at speed. Maynard hopes the car will stop at the last minute, but he sees the bridge has no shoulder. The dash screen pixelates an instant before the Mercedes rams into the low blocks of the concrete safety barrier, bright headlights smashing to black. Maynard digs his fingernails into the leather on the steering wheel as the Mercedes flips over the edge, pirouetting violently, his stomach lurching. It careens through the air, wheels spinning, airborne for long seconds as it plunges down towards the gloomy river. Maynard looks down the length of the hood as the car falls through the space. His body slams forward on impact as the air bags release in the front two seats and the driver window shatters. Ice-cold water floods in through the opening.

'Help!' he screams.

The car bobs for an instant, then as the air is forced out, it settles amid the spray and bursting bubbles before it submerges, plunging nose down into the river bed, remaining upright, the red brake lights eerily illuminating the dark water into crimson before they short out . . .

Maynard is stunned by the impact as water rapidly fills the car. He shivers as it surges up at his torso. He thrusts his hands against the side window but he cannot break the glass. His scream gargles as his windpipe and lungs fill with freezing water. He struggles to keep his mouth clear of the rising torrent. Then the car gives a lurch and the air is gone, bubbling up towards the surface. Maynard clamps his mouth shut, fighting the terrible burning sensation building up in his lungs.

He can hold his breath no longer and his jaws part instinctively to inhale another breath, but there is only bitterly cold, suffocating water. Maynard thrashes violently for perhaps fifteen seconds before he begins to lose consciousness. He struggles feebly, spasms a few times, and then his body ceases to move.

# 48

The next morning, Rose wakes to the sound of a familiar tinkling sound. Scrabbling around beside the bed, her hands grab her smartphone. Jeff murmurs in his sleep. She squints at the screen.

Baptiste.

*What time is it?* Rose looks at the top right corner: 5.27 a.m. 'Hello . . .'

'Sorry to wake you. But I've got some bad news.'

'Better give it to me.'

'Maynard's dead.'

'How?'

'Apparent car crash. Off a bridge near DC. The local office called me thirty minutes ago. They've got divers in the river salvaging the car and looking for evidence right now.'

'Jesus.' Rose sits on the edge of the bed.

'And that's not all.' Baptiste hesitates. 'Just after I got the call, I had an email come through. It was from Koenig. Least that's what it says.'

'Koenig?'

'Right. *That* Koenig.'

'What the—'

'No message, just a link to a website by the name of KKillKam.' Baptiste pauses. 'Yeah, it's exactly what you think

265

it is. Welcome to Koenig's private world. The link took me straight to a listing of video files. Right at the top are two starring Gary Coulter and Sebastian Shaw . . . Looks like we might have found our killer.'

Rose is stunned. Shane Koenig has crashed back into her life. But there's doubt. 'Koenig? It doesn't feel right.'

'I know what you mean. Maybe he wants to announce his return with a splash . . . Shit, that was crass . . .'

Rose can feel a surge of adrenalin kicking in, her heart thumping in her chest as Baptiste continues. 'We need to make sure that it is Koenig behind all this. I want you to find out everything you can about Maynard's death. If it is Koenig then we've got no idea what this sick sonofabitch has in store. This will be the first time he's ever killed three people who know each other. At least, as far as we're aware. This is new ground for him, and we need to understand why he's adapted his MO. Assuming he killed them. I've reassigned Brenn to start comparing the cases with what we've got on Koenig. We won't let him slip through our fingers again. Not this time.'

'No, we won't.' Rose strides over to the wardrobe and slides it open. 'I'm on my way.'

Twelve hours later, and three thousand miles from home, Rose is sipping a strong cup of coffee in the back of a black Suburban. Her Washington contact is Agent Vincent Caviezel who sits beside her briefing her on all they know so far as they are driven to the site of the incident. Caviezel is a tall, powerfully built man with broad shoulders. He has close-cropped red hair, wears an Yves St Laurent pea jacket over a white shirt and a purple tie neatly knotted into a perfect triangle. His manner is remote, calm and professional, regarding her with sharp blue eyes.

Rose listens to his briefing: ABC.

Assume nothing. Believe nobody. Check everything.

'During heavy rain, Maynard apparently lost control of his vehicle on the bridge over the Potomac last night around 11 p.m. He struck a guard rail doing over seventy as far as we can judge, went airborne, flipped over and landed in the river.'

Rose watches the slowing traffic and police cordon. They pass a bus and she catches a glimpse of the bright advert on the side depicting an outstretched black hand wearing the WadeSoft Skin with the slogan 'Own it now!' They reach the site of the incident. It's not a crime scene yet; it could just be an accident, she reflects. They get out of the Suburban and approach the edge of the bridge. She focuses her attention on the shattered concrete where Maynard's Mercedes had collided with a section under repair. Like many bridges across the nation, this one is in desperate need of maintenance. That being said, Maynard had been unlucky to lose control of his car at this point. Fifty feet either way and his Mercedes would have rebounded off intact stretches of the barrier. Tough luck on Maynard, Rose muses. And tough luck on the Bureau, as the case had just taken another twist.

She tries to take in the details.

'How do we know he lost control?'

'CCTV.'

'I'd like to see the footage and the preliminary report.'

'Of course. I'll get you a copy done asap.'

'Who called it in?'

'A jogger. Fire crews and divers then worked for four hours with a crane to remove the car from the river bed. Maynard was dead inside and the initial coroner's report states he drowned. His body is already at the morgue.'

Rose nods, pleased with Caviezel's efficiency. She doesn't want to step on the toes of her colleagues on the East Coast. As yet there is not enough evidence to link this death to the murders she is investigating, though the timing of Koenig's email is surely no coincidence. 'If it's OK with you, I'd like to start here first, then review any additional evidence and see if anything links to our investigation.'

'Of course. Anything we can do. We've set up an investigation tent down at the harbour. There are still some divers searching the river bed around the crash site. If they come up with anything else, I'll let you know. We've got all the resources we need on this one, thanks to Maynard's position.'

Rose had not managed to sleep on the flight. The thought of Koenig being responsible for all three killings unnerves her. Baptiste is right, this is a big departure from his previous MO. It must have taken detailed planning and preparation way above and beyond anything he has done before. She also knows in her gut it is far from over between herself and the serial killer who is still at large, and, if this is what it seems, then Koenig is more ambitious and deadly than ever.

'For the moment we're keeping it off the radar as long as we can, and nowhere near the media,' Caviezel continues. 'The Pentagon wants a tight lid on it. The Defense Secretary, the NSA and Homeland Security are eyes-on the local office.'

Rose makes a sympathetic expression. 'Better you than me.'

Caviezel leads the way back to the car. He glances at her. 'Do you know anything that can help us from your end?'

Rose is unwilling to reveal her leads at this point. 'He is . . . was . . . a person of interest in a murder case. We have a few lines we're pursuing, but nothing concrete. I'll keep you updated.'

Caviezel says nothing. Rose does not want the Koenig connection to leak. Not just yet.

'OK, let's head down to the harbour.'

Rose and Caviezel cruise past run-down shops, diners and cheap hotels before pulling up outside the investigation tent in the industrial area in the shadow of the bridge. Rose sees Maynard's mangled saloon under a white marquee. The windshield is shattered and the bodywork is crumpled at the front and side where the vehicle took the brunt of the impact. Specialist evidence technicians are carefully examining every inch of the wreck. She sees people from nearby houses gawking out of their windows, filming. It won't be long till the story breaks, whatever Caviezel does. Rose's smartphone vibrates in her pocket. She looks at the screen:

CORONER

'Hello, Arthur. Got something new for me?'

'Hi, Rose. Yeah, it's something I think you might want to hear.'

'Just a moment.' Rose looks at Caviezel. He nods and she steps to one side. 'So?'

'Your fellow Shaw . . . was crushed from the neck down and died due to the extreme body trauma. Bruises match the contours of the suit he was wearing. All over his body. I'm also calling because his testicles, what little remains of them, have been crushed, just like Coulter's.'

'Nice. That's killed my appetite. OK, Art, thanks for letting me know.'

Rose hangs up. Caviezel introduces her to the crime scene manager, dressed in white plastic overalls. He hands her the initial Medical Examination report on his tablet. 'Early analysis suggests the vic drowned – his lungs were filled with water. His ribs were shattered. Internal injuries. Guess he wishes he wore the seat belt, huh?'

Rose nods, swipes through a few of the photographs. Maynard's body looks like a grey and purple mottled turkey. It is always a shock to see someone you had spoken to, or seen alive very recently, suddenly on the slab, and a lot of the time she wishes she could unsee things. Yet compared to the other murders, Maynard already seems to be the odd one out. He died in a vehicle, not a Skin suit. What was it that linked the three of them to Koenig? If anything at all. But if it was him, then how was he finding them? Why was he targeting *them*?

Perhaps the link could be a dating app. Koenig's other victims, both male and female, were encountered through online dating sites. Rose is certain that it is an angle worth looking into.

The crime scene manager leads them to a table where the victim's personal effects are neatly tagged and laid out. Rose's attention is caught by an open smartphone wallet with the WS logo. The glass is shattered and she knows the smartphone will be next to useless.

She surveys the other paraphernalia that is being left out to dry: Maynard's mud-stained glasses, wallet and keyring.

'How about the satnav?' she asks.

'It might be possible to access the log. Hang on.' The manager has a brief exchange with a lank-haired technician who is packing away some equipment. He unpacks his laptop, cranes his neck into the crushed driver's compartment.

'If we take the panel off I should be able to access it.'

They pop the surrounding plastic trim and remove the

built-in screen. The technician hooks some cables up to his laptop. He types in a few commands.

'We're in. It's corrupted as fuck, but we've still got the most recent journeys.' He leans slightly to one side so Rose can see the screen. Some of the addresses are filled with nonsensical numbers. But by scrolling through, Rose sees a consistent address, twenty miles away. She suspects it's the destination Maynard never made it home to that evening.

The technician searches through more of the data and pauses. 'Uh-oh . . .'

Rose lowers her head. 'What am I looking at?'

'That's the phone log. Seems our man was on his cell at the time of the accident . . .'

# 49

Rose is sitting in the IT department at the J. Edgar Hoover Building, Pennsylvania Avenue in Washington. It's probably the most famous of the FBI buildings, but its brutalist, square design and visible deterioration makes it also one of the ugliest. In a drab, musty-smelling office, she has been given her own temporary workstation while she waits for Baptiste to clear a search on the address in Maynard's satnav.

Rose replays the CCTV footage on the bridge. It shows the sudden loss of control on Maynard's vehicle as the vehicle flies out over the river and plunges into the darkness.

Maynard's accident could just be that, but what if he was hacked? The satnav shows evidence of corruption, but that could just be water damage. There's a ping from her phone; it's a message from Owen.

You'd better see this: KKillKam.com

The page fades from black to a backdrop of tall forest redwoods in front of a night sky, presumably viewed from Koenig's cabin. On top of this are links to various files, still images and videos. There are three recent videos.

Three? Baptiste said two earlier.

There's a title: 'Just in!' The counter reveals that the file has already had over six hundred views. *So much for keeping it off the radar.* The most recent file appears to be shot inside a car, from a cellphone. It's badly framed, and Rose can only see the driver's face for a moment. It's Maynard . . . Her bloods chills as she watches Maynard staring wide-eyed, presumably at his dashboard screen just above the phone. He looks terrified as his windows whirr down a fraction and he pumps the brakes. 'No!' he says, gripping and wrestling with the steering wheel. He tugs on the locked door handles and scrabbles down to pull the smartphone from its dock. He sees the front-facing camera is on, recording him.

'Stop this!' he shouts.

The images go crazy as the car strikes the barrier and then tumbles towards the river. The smartphone jitters and shakes as it smashes around the car, apparently landing in the footwell as the car plunges into the current. The video flitters and shorts as the car fills with water, finally ending on a frame of Maynard looking down. Rose stares at the image.

There's no doubt. Koenig's behind Maynard's death too. He hacked his car, and killed him.

She scrolls down to some of the viewer comments beneath the clip.

sozlol:    awesome hack man!

666dev:    sick. Gotta try dat

sikboy:    yeh, just for the lols.

Rose watches the other two video files.

The next one is of Shaw. The footage is taken from the camera built into the lid of his laptop. Shaw shakes his head and moans: 'Don't . . . Please don't hurt me.'

273

Rose considers another angle. Koenig may have an accomplice. Maybe that is Iris? Jesus, if there's two of them then the Bureau's problems have just got twice as bad.

She hears a splintering crack somewhere off screen. Shaw's jaw opens in a scream that distorts the speakers. Rose turns down the volume and slips on some headphones.

Shaw is getting crushed. But how?

Shaw howls in agony, gritting his teeth, gulping for air. He shakes his head from side to side, as pressure is applied to his body. There's a ripping and splitting sound as blood pours from his eyes, mouth and nose. Rose pauses the clip.

Jesus.

She clicks the third video on the list – Coulter. Much shorter, this has the same view as Shaw's but smoke obscures some of the images. Coulter screams as black rubber melts around the edge of his face, singeing his fleshy jowls. The camera view sags and warps, just as flames lick across the frame, a brief vivid mess of black rubber and fire. The clip cuts out at the apex of another shrill scream.

Rose takes a deep calming breath.

No one should have to die in these ways. The only good consequence of these videos is they are sure to accelerate the application for a search warrant on Maynard's home. She calls Brennan.

'Brennan Bamber, acting head of—'

'Brenn, it's Rose.'

'Rose, I take it you've seen Koenig is back on the block. There's been several crank calls and tip-offs already. Where you at? Somewhere secure?'

'The Hoover Building, watching the videos now. There's one of Maynard.'

'I just saw. Baptiste is here right now.'

'Good, can you put me on speaker?'

'You're on.'

'Baptiste, hi. Maynard's death was no accident. He didn't lose control of his car. Looks like it was taken control of by a third party.'

'You sure of that?'

'I'd bet my next paycheck on it. I've had an idea, Brenn. If this is Koenig's announcement that he is back in the game, then we have to find out how he knew the three of them were linked. Might be worth searching the dating sites. See if that's the common thread.'

'That could take a while,' Brennan says.

'I know, but there's got to be some way Koenig could link his victims.'

'I'll give it a try.'

'Thanks, Brenn. Baptiste, the clip shows Maynard's car was hacked. Once the tech guys here confirm that then we are looking at murder. So tell me you can get that goddam search warrant.'

'I hear you, Rose. Still going to need a court order issued by a federal magistrate and a sworn oath by you—'

'OK, sure. But I can't help thinking about all this time we're wasting and knowing Koenig's still out there. We can't let him get away again.'

'We won't. Not this time,' Baptiste says. 'Sugar, listen. I know that by getting Koenig you think you can get some part of yourself back, I understand that, I do. But we need to keep cool heads. We need to show that the facts of the case support a search of Maynard's home. These videos will help. Hang in there. I'm working as fast as I can.'

# 50

Two hours later, Rose is finally given the court order to search Maynard's apartment in Temple Hills. It is an expensive neighbourhood, as she had anticipated. The kind of place where the bigger wheels of the nation's political elite stay during the week before heading off to their New England mansions for the weekend. The Koenig connection pushed the application to the top of the pile. Rose insists on going inside alone, so there are no distractions, and Caviezel reluctantly complies, provided he is cc'd in on any evidence found for use by the local office. Caviezel waits in the car.

Rose is wearing rubber gloves and uses the keys found on the body to gain access. She steps into the apartment. The heating is on and it feels warm and cosy. There are photos hanging on the walls and a coat rack in the entrance hall. She continues into a large open-plan living room and kitchen. By the curved TV she notices a small drinks stand with a bottle of single malt whisky. There are photos of Maynard with his arms around the shoulders of two teenage girls, who Rose assumes are his daughters. Moving through some glass partition doors she enters a home office, furnished with a dark wood desk and a large desktop monitor, keyboard and mouse. She taps the space bar and the monitor fades into a login screen, prompting her for a password. She gives a frustrated sigh.

She peers beneath the desk. There is a heavy-duty black shredder. Its receptacle is empty.

She exits the apartment to check in the shared utility area. There's no sign of shredded paper.

Heading back into the apartment, Rose enters the main bedroom and slides open the wardrobe. Inside is an extensive range of two-piece suits – black, navy, charcoal, pinstripe – and below, several pairs of shoes.

There has to be *something* here. She sits down in Maynard's leather office chair, tries to see the room from his point of view. Through the window she can see the street below, and she peers over to look. As she moves, her eye is drawn to a gap between the back of the desk and the radiator. There seems to be a suit carrier folded in half, wedged down the gap.

She pulls it up and lays it on the table. She's pretty sure she knows what it is. It's a good six feet long, and whatever is inside feels flexible. She unzips the crumpled carrier and inside, on a hanger, is a fully intact Skin – like Coulter's, like Shaw's.

A working prototype might reveal plenty of useful information and leads.

Rose calls Baptiste to arrange the transfer of evidence into San Francisco's custody for the time being.

When she finishes the call, she notices a tiny green light glowing next to what appears to be a small built-in camera on Maynard's desktop computer monitor. She isn't sure if it was on earlier, and she shivers at the thought that someone is watching her. Maybe it's time to leave.

As she is about to exit the apartment, the ring of a telephone shatters the stillness. Rose flinches.

The phone continues to ring on the kitchen sideboard and she stands still but her mind is racing.

*Should I answer it?*

She reaches out her gloved hand, picks up the receiver. There's silence.

'Hello?

'Hello,' she repeats more firmly. 'Who is this?'

There is faint electronic static.

'*You . . . sound . . . afraid,*' a voice says so softly it is hard to know if it is male or female.

Then the line goes dead.

Rose listens to the buzzing of the dial tone for some time before replacing the handset.

Suddenly she wants to be anywhere but here. She zips up the suit carrier and leaves the apartment, locking the door behind her.

'Did you find what you were looking for?' Caviezel asks, before he notices the plastic bundle under Rose's arm. 'What's that?'

'You'll know soon enough.'

Returning to the Hoover Building, she signs out Maynard's Skin to process at the San Francisco office, promising to keep Caviezel updated. He offers to drive her to Ronald Reagan Airport. In the back of the car, Rose rests her head on the corner of the window, dead beat. Rain streaks the glass. Her smartphone pings.

It's a text from Baptiste.

Koenig's site – new activity is going public. Guess one of his subscribers felt the urge to make the thing go viral.

Shit. The case is about to get a whole lot worse.

# 51

Jeff finishes putting the plates from the evening meal in the dishwasher. His preparations for the next TV debate are on track, and he's got a frantic round of last-minute fundraisers to attend in the next week. He is secretly pleased that Rose is away in Washington. It gives him time to try out his new toy, which arrived first thing that morning. When the dishwasher is set, he commands the downstairs lights off and heads up to the bedroom. Peering round Robbie's door, Jeff sees his son sitting on the bed reading a paperback, the lamp by his desk on. Jeff raps on the door.

'Hey, Robbo, whatcha readin'?'

Robbie holds up the book. 'Something about dreaming androids. It's pretty cool, actually. Ms Steiner said I should read it . . . I'm trying to do good, Dad.'

'I know, son . . . I'm just gonna be in the study for a while. Working. Try not to disturb me, OK?'

Robbie nods, shifts his eyes back to the book.

Jeff quietly paces further down the hall into the main bedroom. On the floor is the WS package. All over the United States he knows there will be millions of people eagerly trying WadeSoft's latest wonder. He feels guilty that he went ahead and ordered it, but puts that thought aside.

*Rose will find out eventually. But I'm allowed a little fun, aren't*

*I? A chance to be better than real?*

Jeff takes the package, heads into the study, closing the door behind him. He feels like a kid on Christmas Day. He slits open the adhesive seal.

That new smell, of mysterious plastics, greets his nose and he stares down at the one-piece body suit, shrink-wrapped and neatly nestled in grey protective foam. Next to it is the head sock and visor, also placed in designated slots, along with charging unit, Skin drive and two cables. Jeff runs his fingers over the Skin, marvelling at its unique texture. It is firm, but more pliable than a wetsuit, able to adapt to the user's body size.

He lifts it out, placing it on the back of his leather chair. He strips down to his boxer shorts, unzips the U-shaped zipper on the back. He slides his right leg down the pant leg and into the right foot. The suit feels strangely cool on his skin. He slides his left foot in, pulling and sliding the pant up to his waist. Then he stoops his head to push it through the narrow neck hole. It closes in perfectly around his neck. Very comfortable.

He eases into the rest of the suit and pulls the U-zipper. It's a little tight at first but he gradually tugs it round. Excitement tingles in his veins. The uncertainty, the expectation, the anticipation, the adrenalin – a volatile cocktail of sensory overload. He hopes this new technology will not be like the cruddy versions of VR that have gone before and leave you feeling cheated.

His gloved fingers pick up the separate head sock – like a ribbed balaclava – and he slides that over his face. He lifts out the Sight, a lightweight aluminium visor with black tinted glass that covers the eyes, with ear buds on each side. He slots the visor on and inserts the ear buds. There's a note in the packaging that states the suit arrives fully charged and with no instructions to read – the system tutorial is all that is needed. Jeff taps the tiny button on the top of the Sight. The screen of the glasses flickers on and blue text appears:

WadeSoft Developments Present
Innovation. Design. Integration.
Welcome to the Skin.
Please turn Skin drive on.

You idiot.

Jeff feels mildly stupid clad in this black rubber suit. He unpacks the small black Skin drive. There's a cable from it that presumably must be connected to the suit somehow. He remembers seeing an interface slot on the back of the head sock and pushes the cable plug in. He presses the power button on the drive and powers up his home computer. It's a simple procedure to make the Bluetooth connection.

Interfacing with Skin drive . . .

Jeff watches as the Sight clicks into a high-definition crystalline focus that doesn't quite seem real. It looks clearer than real life and the lenses adjust to Jeff's own short-sighted optical prescription. He can now see the whole of his study in perfect focus: the cluttered dark oak desk, the view from his window down the avenue.

Interfacing with Skin drive . . .

The suit quivers and ripples, adjusting to sit as close to Jeff's body as possible. It's disconcerting at first, but soon it feels like a cool film sitting on top of his skin. He's barely aware of it.

Interfacing complete.

Awesome.

The boot sequence continues in the background as the corporate logo rotates in front of him. Then biometrics detailing his heart rate and focal lens prescription flash onto his heads-up display. It feels like the menus and screens are inside his eyes.

Log in to StreamPlex? You can use voice commands.

'Yes,' Jeff says clearly.

Sign in with Facebook?

'Yes.'

Create username?

'Yes.'

A translucent blue keyboard appears in midair. Jeff moves his gloved hand towards it, impressed. He pauses, then types JeffRules.

Confirmed.
Set password?

Jeff adds in the additional details. A lengthy Terms and Conditions screen appears, which he ticks without reading. Next is a health check, which presumably hooks up to some database. After a few minutes, Jeff clears this section and is presented with an options screen.

Enable adult streams?

He taps Confirm.

Please remain still.
Final Skin sync in progress . . .

The suit creeps with life. Jeff can feel all the sensors making contact with his skin and his own receptors deep in his body. He feels his body flash cool and then warm all at once. There's a sudden tingling sensation; a bright flare of blue light, a blast of white noise and the unexpected taste and smell of salty air.

Welcome to the Entry Pool.

Jeff blinks, his momentary disorientation readjusting to awe. He sighs at the pleasing, cool sensation. He is no longer in his study. He is standing on a sandy beach. He can feel each grain of sand nestling under the soles of his feet. Looking up, he can see a perfect blue, cloudless sky. He can even feel the sun warming his cheeks. He stoops down, scrapes up some sand from the beach, spreads it across his fingers. He can feel every particle of grit. He takes some steps towards the ocean. The cool rush of the surf laps at his feet, his shins, his waist, further and further. A shiver of pleasure shoots through him, his body sinking into the cool sea.

Jeff's mind races. This isn't real . . . but it feels real. The graphics, the feedback . . . It's as if he is there. Floating red text suddenly appears:

Proximity Warning!

Oh shit.

The suit's sensors are informing him of some nearby furniture he is about to walk into. He briefly taps the Sight off to see he was about to collide with the back of his leather chair. The fidelity of the experience is better than he expected. In the past, even a few minutes using a headset had generated nausea. He still has to be careful but so far it seems OK. No, much better than OK. Better than real. He sits down in the chair.

Enable MindSync?

Jeff hesitates. There's a question-mark icon in the right-hand corner. He taps, reads:

MindSync allows you to fully control your avatar/streamer without the need for constant physical movement by reading brainwave activity.
Enable?

'Yes.'

Practise moving by using only your thoughts. The time it takes to train your system varies between users. The average time is 10–15 minutes.

There are a few false starts but soon Jeff manages to move his avatar forward, just by thinking it. The suit takes him deep into the ocean and he starts to swim. He relaxes back in his chair, the warm water on his face, and rushing in around his arms as he swims. He continues for a few minutes before a message appears, written in white against the blue cloudless sky.

MindSync & SkinSync Complete.
Create Streamer?

'Yes.'

Jeff customizes his male avatar from a floating wheel of options. As a base point, the Skin uses a close likeness to the physiology of the user. It is then possible to customize all areas of the body. Jeff takes delight in restoring his receding hairline, realigning his parting, even smoothing his skin to make himself look ten years younger. He also adds larger, more toned muscles and even throws in a few 'bad boy' tattoos. He smiles, satisfied with his more perfect self. He finishes by selecting a simple white shirt and chinos with tan shoes.

Enter StreamPlex, JeffRules?

'Sure . . . I mean, yes.'

WARNING:
DUE TO THE FIDELITY OF THE EXPERIENCE,
USERS ARE ADVISED TO DESYNC USING
DESIGNATED EXIT DOCKS.

'OK.'

Jeff cannot wait to begin, as a torrent of electric-blue water explodes up from beneath him, rushing over him. He bows his head, laughing as it gushes over his vision . . .

# 52

Jeff opens his eyes. He can see his tan shoes on a clean asphalt street. No trash, no potholes, no dirt or rain. Just new. He looks up. The vision that greets him is dazzling.

The StreamPlex portal is a neon and glass tiered dream-scape, packed with a dizzying array of bright and whimsical avatars. There is so much to look at. The home square, where users enter the virtual world, is built around a massive Janus-type-face construction, the back of a man and a woman's head merged together. It looks like it's made of crystal glass, and a blue neon-lit freeway enters and exits through both mouths. Behind the city is a mountain range, with a Japanese castle built on a cliff face. To the rear of him, there is a coastline, with a beach.

He walks through the pink and blue neon square, towards a large glass fountain, casting his eye over his fellow users. Several dozen trendily clad people with dyed hair sit in a circle, talking. Elsewhere a couple is making out in the corner of the square. Others are dancing to the shifting sounds of throbbing bass and warped synth blasts. The graphics' resolution and rendering are first-rate. Jeff observes the shiny sheen of perfect complexions, well-tailored suits, slick and dirt-free streets. Yet the gestures and expressions of the people are occasionally stilted, as the StreamPlex loads programmed patterns of behaviour.

Most of those around him are non-playable characters, Jeff realizes, placed there to give the illusion of many users. But that will change as millions of subscribers come online. He watches as a punk jumps from standing completely still to executing five head spins, one after the other. A white man with a massive frizzy Afro carries a sign that says 'Free Hugs' and embraces Jeff. Jeff can feel the suit compress as the man squeezes his shoulders.

He gasps. It's so real.

He hears a low throbbing noise behind him. He turns to see floating advertisement screens swarming to greet him one after another. The screen flashes: bad credit, online movies. He repeatedly taps X on the top-right of his vision, shrinking them from view with a blue flash until the adverts give up and go away.

Walking into the centre, Jeff has to smile at the incongruous, eclectic inhabitants the users have created from their avatar profile construction kits: a head-banging priest; a man dressed as a silver-foil dinosaur on a skateboard; two women wearing impossible-sized sombreros; shirtless muscular guys swaggering and posing in front of girls in hot pants and low-cut tops; gimps; cartoon characters; fuzzy fairies; emos; rappers; Goths; familiar faces of famous actors; skin-tight neon suits; space warriors; angels and devils; even PVC nuns.

In the high street where there are apartments, garages and clubs, Jeff can see flying cars, even a horse and carriage. Bubbles intermittently descend from the heavens, and hot air balloons drift through a cloudless sky.

All these non-playable characters are there to suggest things the new arrivals might want to try out, he guesses, admiring the vision of WS's design teams.

He nearly walks into an elemental-looking young woman. She's dressed in a white flowing gown. She reminds him of a modern version of a goddess from Greek mythology, looking out of place in this kaleidoscopic city. She strikes an exaggerated welcome pose, holding out her hands, palms visible.

'Welcome, JeffRules. I'm a Nymph,' she says. 'I take care of all the new users. Welcome to the StreamPlex.'

Her body reverts to a passive standing position, while blinking intermittently. Jeff finds the shift from lifelike to program a little jarring.

'How . . . how did you know I was a newbie?' he asks.

'It says above your head,' she explains.

Jeff looks up and sees the floating text above him.

Member 212,056: JeffRules

'Oh, I see.' He smiles. 'Your hair is pretty.'

Her face does not register the compliment. 'Thank you. This will be your first time in the StreamPlex. I can give you some tips.'

'Sure. You're a bot, aren't you?'

She nods a perfect nod. 'I am a guide, designed to help you whenever you need me. Take this.'

She opens the palm of her hand and a blue glowing sphere unfolds into a mesh-like map in front of them. Jeff touches it with his hand and it gravitates towards his palm.

'The StreamPlex is divided into districts. This is the entrance portal, the main entry point. The Muse district is your knowledge, art and entertainment. Cascade is your extreme experiences – sky-diving, racing, martial arts. The Spa district is for relaxation and therapies. WadeSoft advises

288

that some districts may still be under construction or user customization and that WS does not accept liability for third-party add-ons.'

Jeff grins. He peers around at the other avatars before leaning closer.

'Have you got anything more . . . adult?'

He can feel himself blush.

The Nymph blinks. 'Erotix is the main adult entertainment centre, and is situated here.' She indicates the map.

'Shhh-shhh!' Jeff says, perturbed by her loud voice amongst such a crowd.

'Apologies, I will adjust my volume.'

She points to a Gothic-looking mansion on the map. 'This is where Erotix is situated,' she says in a whisper.

'Thanks, Nymph. I'll check it out.'

'You're welcome.'

Jeff watches as a punk walking past suddenly falls through the ground beneath them, thrusting his arms in the air before vanishing.

'What happened to him?'

'We're currently working on our next update to address some of these minor glitches. Should you need any help, you can call me or any of the other Nymphs by tapping your right wrist twice. Is there anything else I can help you with?'

'No, thank you.'

'Goodbye. We welcome user feedback. Would you like to do a survey?'

An X appears on her forehead, giving him the option of closing her down. He taps the X and she smiles, fading from view. He sees a man about to jump from one of the freeway tiers in the distance and grabs a passer-by: 'Hey, you see that guy?'

The peroxide-haired woman shrugs.

Jeff gasps as the man leaps off. He holds his breath, bracing himself for the impact. Seconds before the man is about to pulverize into the ground, the air around him becomes syrupy and he hovers to a stop. A nearby crowd applauds. Jeff catches his breath, laughing nervously.

You can do anything in here, it seems.

Anything . . .

Jeff watches as an emo sprays an outline of a phallus on the side of the fountain's wall. A second later the paint is erased from the surface, and the spray can in his hand crumbles into blue sparks, evaporating into the air. The emo curses and walks away.

Well, almost anything.

Jeff sees water cascading upwards from the floor. This must be a pool to enter other simulations. He scrolls through the various experiences on offer: Dojo, Racer, SkyDive . . .

In a few moments, he is sitting in the open door of an aircraft. Far below is a desert landscape. He can hear the roar of the engines either side of him.

'Whoa!'

His Skin undulates with the sensation of wind blowing. He looks over his shoulder to see a yellow parachute on his back.

'*Jump!*' An avatar sky-diver slaps him on the shoulder. '*Jump!*'

Jeff shuts his eyes as he throws himself out the aircraft . . .

He forces himself to look down as he free-falls through the air, the wind violently rippling his jump suit, buffeting his goggles and whipping his hair back.

'Wooooh!' he shouts, rather too loudly in the small study back in the real world.

He looks down and sees the Grand Canyon beneath him. He tilts his body forward, puts his hands in front of him. Now he isn't diving. He's flying . . . Flying . . . Really flying, just like Peter Pan.

After the sky-dive, he returns to the square. The dive was incredible for sure, but there's something else he wants to look at. He sets his waypoint marker to Erotix . . .

# 53

Jeff reaches the steps leading to a large grey Gothic mansion with hundreds of windows. He has to wait a minute or so in a line of around ten other users. He can feel his pulse hammering in his neck.

*I wonder what it's going to be like? How far can they go? Actual simulated sex?*

There are two suited, burly doormen on either side of the doorway. One wears sunglasses perched on the crown of his head. They have neon irises and their cheeks and arms are tattooed. Jeff watches as they both grab hold of a bald man in front of him, strong-arming him away from the entrance.

'Sir, this is a subscription, or instream additional purchase-only area. Your account lacks sufficient funds. Prepare for ejection.'

Jeff watches as the bald man tries to wrestle his way out of their grip. A blue light glows from the centre of his chest, getting brighter. It expands, consuming him.

'Damn it,' the bald man says.

He explodes into a shower of blue pixels that are swallowed up and disappear. Text appears where he once stood:

## USER CONNECTION TERMINATED

Jeff's up next. The two doormen stare at him. The one with sunglasses takes a close look at him. 'Do you wish to subscribe to Erotix, sir?'

'Yes.'

'How many jewels do you wish to purchase? A handful – twenty dollars; a purse – fifty dollars; a small chest – one hundred dollars. Or you can go premium for thirty-nine ninety-nine a month, sir.'

Jeff thinks. 'A handful for now.'

There's the briefest of pauses and then the doorman without sunglasses stands aside. 'Transaction complete. An invoice will be emailed to your new StreamPlex account. Welcome to Erotix, sir.' He smiles as he clamps a black bracelet around Jeff's wrist. 'This makes you untraceable inside. Have a good time.'

The black door opens and, after confirming he is a heterosexual, Jeff enters down a hallway to the left. There are other hallways depending on your gender, orientation and sexual assignment. Jeff's hallway is hung with heavy blue drapes, with a navy carpet and silver fixtures. This hallway leads to a huge seating area. Pulsing music throbs in the background and there are three dancers on a stage to the back of the room, lit by blue wall lights. As Jeff paces in there are perhaps thirty or so women, of all ethnicities and shapes, standing waiting on either side of him. They smile, holding eye contact. Some beckon him. But what he feels, unmistakably, is that they all *want* him.

Most are wearing lingerie, skimpy sequinned dresses, fetish gear. There are red leather chairs, white tabletops and lamps. He's so excited he doesn't know who to choose. He feels like Hugh Hefner on his birthday.

'Hi,' a confident voice says behind him.

He turns to see a blonde woman with perfect straight hair wearing a glowing pink G-string and tight bra. 'I'm Destiny.'

Her computer-generated green irises twinkle at him. There is an amazing sense of depth and dreaminess to them. Jeff laughs, feeling aroused as he scans the rest of her agile, tanned body. She is unmistakably artificial, but alluring nonetheless.

'I'm JeffRules,' he says, feeling awkward using his real name. He raises the back of her hand to his lips.

'Nice to meet you,' she says, before twirling in front of him. Jeff is mesmerized by her. Her body. Her smile.

'Destiny? Tonight I think you are mine,' he says, smiling.

Destiny laughs an automated giggle. Twice, exactly the same.

Her expression changes to raised eyebrows. 'Would you like to go private?' she says, transitioning to a coy smile.

'Sure,' Jeff says.

Destiny pauses, whereupon a floating box appears.

Authorize jewel expenditure?

Jeff accepts, eager to get back to Destiny. The next screen throws up the various packages on offer:

Evening Company (light)
Girlfriend Experience (sex)

He taps the Girlfriend Experience.

Destiny unpauses, grabs his hand and leads him away. Jeff can feel the warmth of her flesh. She takes him down a curved iron spiral of stairs to another floor where there is a series of doors. They pass a few, then one opens automatically as they walk towards it. Inside the room is a double bed with a red comforter and a silver mirror set into the ceiling.

'So what do you wanna do?' she asks, raising one eyebrow, kneeling on the bed, looking up at him. She leans forward, her breasts swinging closer together. Jeff is dazzled by the details, and he moves his hungry gaze into her bewitching eyes, her expression flawless, as her lips part into her perfect smile. He feels his cock harden. He moves closer, running his fingers through her long blond hair, savouring the texture of it. He finally caves in to his desires. He locks his lips on hers, grabbing her by her waist. He throws her down onto the bed.

'Fuck me, JeffRules. Fuck me now,' she cries, tossing her long hair back.

Jeff's mind caves into his raging lust, his hands and lips seeming to have a mind of their own, scrabbling, caressing, tearing at her. They kiss passionately, their lips biting, tugging at each other's mouths, trying to lock their bodies into one another's. Her skin is warm, he melts into her.

Incredible! So responsive . . .

He fumbles for the clasp of her bra, before pulling it off. He takes a moment to regard her large, round breasts. He traces his hands and fingers over the fleshy swells. His eyes feast ravenously on the sight of her body, her seductive eyes, her open red mouth. As he kisses her, he sees her face become translucent, then disappear. When he pulls away, he's left with only her eyes, lips and legs visible, floating eerily in the air above her body.

'Er, Destiny, your face . . .' he murmurs, fascinated by the glitch.

Destiny turns what's left of her face to the mirror.

'I'm sorry for this temporary render error. Texture file corruption. This will be reloaded.'

Her body twitches as the image is updated.

295

They resume their passionate embrace. Destiny unzips his pants. Jeff has an attack of conscience.

*Is this wrong?*

He stares at Destiny, desperate to take her. *No, it's not wrong. It feels real. But it's not. And therefore it's OK*, he tells himself.

# 54

It is past midnight by the time Rose pulls into the driveway and she can see Jeff's study lamp is on. She is grateful to be back home. She is exhausted, not having slept much for the last few days. She is looking forward to a rest. It will be good to try not to think about the case for a few hours and return to some kind of family normality. Anyway, the next day is Halloween. Might be fun for them all to watch a spooky film, or something. Nothing too frightening.

After all, she is anxious at the prospect of Koenig hiding out there on the fringes as the world goes about its business, unaware of the predator watching and waiting to strike. And now it appears he has new skills to aid him, and there is the frightening possibility that he has found a partner in crime. This person, Iris, might well be a misguided acolyte, seduced by his fame and charisma. Or she might be another psychopath, sane enough to calculate there are advantages to be had working with another monster.

Rose grabs her overnight bag, makes for the house. Her home is quiet and still. She goes to the kitchen and pours a glass of orange juice from the refrigerator, pausing to look at the family photos held with refrigerator magnets, remembering joy and happiness.

She climbs the stairs and checks in on Robbie, who has

fallen asleep with a novel on his chest. Rose is delighted to see that he has been reading, and she lifts the book from his hands, places a sticky note on his page and puts it on his bedside table, turning the lamp off.

She enters the main bedroom, takes off her jacket and slings it over the back of the chair in front of her boudoir table. She freshens up in the bathroom and, after changing into a T-shirt and track pants, she paces down the cream-carpeted hallway towards Jeff's study. She takes a look at her watch. It's nearly one o'clock.

She pushes the dark wood door open and enters the study . . .

A black-suited man, her husband, is lying outstretched on his reclined chair. He appears to be bouncing up and down on his back, apparently in the grip of an intense sexual experience.

'Oh . . .' he grunts. 'That's it—'

He gasps and his body spasms, breath hissing from his lips.

'Oh God . . . that's so good.'

His body relaxes. He's just orgasmed.

For a moment, Rose stands quite still in the doorway. Unable to move. Unable to understand. Unable to react. It's too much.

She backs out, closing the door quietly behind her, and walks back to the bedroom.

# 55

It's the middle of the night. Rose cannot sleep. She is thirsty so she goes downstairs to the kitchen. The lights flicker on and she pulls open the refrigerator door. She is reaching in to grab a bottle of water when she sees something at the back of the middle shelf – a woman's severed head. Rose's eyes focus on the horror of the woman's mouth hanging open, eyes staring back. She recoils, dropping her water bottle on the floor.

But the head is strangely familiar. Pulling the door open wider, she takes a closer look. The head is hers.

She turns to see Jeff in the black Skin, walking towards her, smiling.

'What are you doing?' she asks.

'What are you doing?' he repeats.

Jeff's suit is wriggling, like it's made of black string worms, crawling all around him, tightening around his body as he stares at Rose. He grabs her, his gloved fingers pressing against her neck, crushing her throat. She scrabbles for her smartphone. When she reaches it, the screen is showing Koenig's face staring back at her, laughing . . .

Rose wakes with a start, her heart racing. The first light of dawn is creeping around the edges of the drapes. She has to stand up, take several calming breaths, and eventually her heart rate returns to normal. The bed is empty beside her and the sound of running water comes from the bathroom. Fighting the feeling of revulsion, Rose gets up and heads to the kitchen to put some coffee on. She hesitates briefly, then steels herself to open the refrigerator, take out the milk and close the door.

She can't get the image of Jeff in his Skin out of her mind. She wonders if she should have confronted him last night. Now she is not sure how to. Not with everything else that is going on in her life.

There's clattering on the staircase as Jeff, dressed in a neat white flannel shirt and jeans, heads down the stairs with his suitcase. Rose notices it is a new piece of luggage. Presumably he needs extra room for the Skin, she thinks bitterly . . .

'Hi, honey.' He smiles, too easily. 'I didn't want to wake you when I went for the shower.'

Rose shrugs. 'I was awake anyway.'

'Oh? You must have got in late last night . . .'

They stare at each other for a moment. This is the chance to say something to him, Rose realizes. Yet she can't bring herself to. She's not ready. So she lies.

'I saw the light in your study. Guessed you were working late. So I went straight to bed.'

Jeff nods slowly. 'I see.'

Rose gestures towards the coffee jug. 'Want some?'

'No time. I'm heading off to Redding to prep for the next debate. Should be back on the weekend.'

Rose nods. She wants to say something but can't find the right words. Jeff pops two of his migraine tablets in his mouth, washes them down with a quick glass of water from the kitchen.

'Headache?'

'It's fine, thank you.' He kisses her lightly on the forehead.

They stare at each other again until Rose says, 'Happy Halloween.'

'Yeah . . . Look, let's do something at the weekend. Spend some family time together.'

'That'd be nice.'

'All right then. Until then.' With that he leaves. Rose notices he doesn't say where he will be staying, and she is certain that he has taken that damned Skin with him to do God knows what in. She feels he has torn out a bit of her heart. She sits on a kitchen stool for an hour or so in silence, fighting back tears.

Robbie shuffles into the kitchen, helping himself to a stacked bowl of cereal.

'Not at school today?'

'No, got some free periods, to study.'

'What are you doing for Halloween? You want to keep your mom company?'

'I'm not doing much. We could watch a movie, maybe?'

'Sure, sounds good. You can choose. Just not too much gore, please.'

A point in the Mom column for a change, Rose thinks. Robbie shuffles back to his bedroom. Rose calls her therapist, Katherine.

'Good morning, Rose. How are you?'

'Been better.'

There's a pause before Katherine responds. 'I had a feeling we hadn't seen the last of each other. What can I do for you?'

'Listen, I don't suppose you've had a cancellation? Or can see me for ten minutes? It's about Jeff.'

'Actually, yes, I have. I can see you at . . . say, ten thirty this morning? Any good?'

'Yes, thank you. See you then.'


Rose takes her usual seat and explains what happened with Jeff. Katherine sits in her chair, listening carefully, before responding.

'What your husband is doing is not uncommon.'

Rose raises her eyebrows.

'I can't discuss any of my other clients, but let's say he's not alone. Many men – and women – are struggling with some sort of online addiction: sex, gambling, video games.'

'Why?'

'Plato once said that "everything that deceives may be said to enchant". The digital world enchants the reward-seeking centres of the brain. Do you know if he uses porn regularly?'

'Yes.'

'The normal, healthy stuff – if you can call it that?'

'Sometimes.'

'And other times?'

'Stuff I don't like. Stuff he asked me to play out with him a while back. I said no, and he hasn't talked about it since.'

'But he continues to look at that stuff?'

'I guess.'

'I see.' Katherine makes a few notes on her pad before looking up. 'I'd be happy to talk to him, but you must understand that any addiction can be tough to conquer.'

'Why?' Rose asks. 'Can't you just stop going online?'

'Sure, but it's everywhere. It's easily accessible within seconds. It's peering at us through our phones, waiting to grant our every desire, ad infinitum.'

'But I don't understand why he's doing it. We have sex

often enough . . . As often as we can, at least, given how busy our lives are.'

'Do you think that Jeff may be frustrated?'

'It's possible,' Rose admits. 'I'm involved in a tough case right now. I don't have much time for my family.'

'And you feel guilty about it?'

'Of course, what woman wouldn't? That's how things are. We're raised to feel guilty.'

'The question is, what do we do about that, Rose?'

'What can I do?'

'Try to talk to him. Discuss his feelings. Tell him how it makes you feel.'

There's an awkward silence, then Rose stands up. 'I have to go.'

'Our time is not up yet, Rose.'

'I can't talk about this any more at the moment. I really can't.'

'All right. We'll leave it for now. But call me if you need to. Promise?'

'All right.' Rose thanks her for her time and leaves.

Katherine stares after her client with a sympathetic expression. Her desktop computer has been switched on the whole time. Neither woman has seen the activity on the screen. And now Rose's personal files open in quick succession. Then the hard disk light flickers and a message flashes on the screen:

Copying complete

A moment later the home screen appears, the mouse cursor hovering motionlessly over the last program icon Katherine has accessed, as if nothing had happened.

# 56

It's the evening of Hallows' Eve. Rose has not heard from Scarlet for a few days, so she taps out a brief text.

Hey, Scar, you out with ghosts and goblins tonight? ;-) xx

Robbie has chosen some remake of a Korean horror movie and presses play on the console. Barely ten minutes after the obligatory opening murder, ding! A reply arrives from Scarlet.

Ha, no. I got me a date with a cute guy . . .

Rose shakes her head, types:

Who goes out for a date on Halloween? Where did you meet this one?

Online. He's being a real gentleman. Picking me up in 20.

Rose feels a slight twinge of concern.

Be careful. Have fun . . . xx

Robbie unpauses the movie. After a few minutes, Rose can smell a faint burning plastic smell.

'Robbie, can you smell that?'

'Yeah . . .'

Rose heads towards the kitchen. There's a trail of thin grey smoke rising from the new cordless coffee machine Jeff has bought.

'Oh!' she cries, grabbing the device and hurrying to the door to put it outside. She throws open the kitchen windows to let the smoke clear, covering her mouth.

'Another one of Dad's new purchases?'

'Yeah. It's one of those Wi-Fi ones.'

'Really? Can you open the bay windows for me?' Rose says. She knows how vulnerable devices can be if they are Wi-Fi enabled. She takes a look at the central heating thermostat. In the space of a few minutes, it has gone up to the highest setting.

'What the hell is going on?' she asks.

But in her gut a fear grows. Is it possible her house and appliances are being hacked? Is this Koenig's doing? There's a clicking and whirring from the family printer in the corner of the living room. Sheets of blank paper are churning out.

'Mom, why's everything going screwy?' Robbie asks.

'Nothing, just a technical glitch. I need to make some calls. You carry on with the movie.'

Rose grabs her smartphone, paces down the corridor, heart racing. She wants to grab her Glock, but knows this will frighten Robbie.

*Ding.* She receives a picture message: a screenshot of her email account.

*Ding.* A screenshot of her Facebook account.

*Ding.* A Street View image of the house.

*Ding.* A video message from Robbie's phone.

The clip shows Robbie checking his phone, a moment ago.

Rose's stomach twists. Whoever it is, they're in everything she has.

*Pop-ping*

A message on her smartphone from Unknown simply reads:

I am EVERYWHERE.

Rose's house phone rings. She paces towards it, seeing it's a number from the Bureau.

'Rose Blake.'

'Rose, it's Brenn.'

'Brenn, hey, what's going on?' Rose is relieved.

'I was just picking through Koenig's laptop – you know, the one we first found in the cabin? While I was doing it, there was a big hack attack on our servers.'

'Shit, really? Did we lose anything?'

'It's too early to assess all the damage. But Koenig's laptop was online – I was checking through some of his files and mirror sites. The biggest worry is that the FBI database here has been compromised. Guess the trick was on us. A lot of personal files have been accessed. Difficult to say whose at the moment, but just thought I'd give you the heads up. Our office is not secure. Whoever it was has some serious skills. And it's not our new boy – just checked his keylog. Samer's clean. It could be Koenig. Everything OK your end?'

Rose turns, paces back into the living room, looks at the sheets pouring out of the printer.

'We were just watching a movie and then things in the house started glitching.'

'Shit. You're OK, right?'

The printer stops its deluge. The room becomes cool, and Rose watches the thermostat dial down to a lower setting.

'Yeah, it seems to have stopped now.'

'The more connected you are, the more vulnerable you are. I'd disconnect everything Wi-Fi enabled, to be on the safe side. I'll let Baptiste know you were hacked. Be safe.'

'Thanks, Brenn. How come you're working?'

'I've got so much to do at Cyber it's unreal. Later, Rose.'

Rose pulls all the plugs out of the sockets of her Wi-Fi-enabled appliances: laptop, printer, dishwasher. She rejoins Robbie on the sofa.

'It's OK, just someone playing a big joke. Carry on with the movie.'

Fifteen minutes pass, and Rose is trying to watch the movie, but all the time in the back of her mind is an endlessly repeating question:

*What do I do?*

Then the doorbell chimes. Rose pauses the movie.

'Trick or treaters,' Robbie sighs. 'I'll get the snacks.'

Rose feels a sixth sense tingling at the base of her neck and shakes her head. 'Robbie, go and make us some popcorn, please. Right now.'

Robbie obeys, retreating into the kitchen. Rose hurries into the hall and takes out her Glock. She peers out the living room window. There's a yellow HappyFlowers van parked outside. She tries to look at the porch. She can't clearly see beneath the HappyFlowers baseball cap to help identify her visitor, but there is definitely a man standing on her porch.

Gripping her Glock tightly, she approaches the door. She takes a look through the spyhole. Through the curved lens she sees a Hispanic man in the bright yellow HappyFlowers

307

uniform. He does not look like Koenig, but given the fish-eye distortion of the lens it is hard to be sure. She steels herself. Working the slide, she puts a finger by the trigger and rests her thumb on the safety. The doorbell rings again.

'You gonna get that, Mom?' Robbie calls from the kitchen, and she can hear the kernels of popcorn begin to crackle in the microwave.

'Should I get the door, Mom?'

'No! Stay in the kitchen.' Rose moves round to the side of the door and, holding the Glock in her right hand, reaches for the brass catch and gives it a turn before wrenching the door open.

# 57

Rose steps forward, aiming the barrel of the Glock into the delivery man's face. His eyes widen in terror and he flinches, almost dropping the pot of flowers in his spare hand as he flings his right up to try and shield himself.

'Jesus, lady! No! Don't shoot!'

'Put the pot down and get on your knees. Do it!'

The delivery man does as he is told.

'Hands behind your head.'

'OK! OK! Don't shoot.'

'Quiet.' Rose crouches down and examines the delivery, keeping the man covered. There's a small terracotta pot of red roses. The pot is shaped into a leering jack-o'-lantern. Aside from that there's nothing sinister about it. She looks at the man. Thin, pockmarked face and a terrified expression.

'Who sent these?'

'D–don't know, ma'am. The order was online. There's a card. Under the pot. We checked it a few times, didn't make any sense to us, but we wrote it out exactly as it was sent.'

'What's it say?'

'Nothing . . . I mean just numbers.'

Rose hears the sound of a child sobbing. She sees a small group of kids at the bottom of the path leading to her front door. One of her neighbours is comforting a young boy who is crying.

'Mommy, she's gonna shoot us all!'

Rose lowers her gun. 'OK, you can stand up. Slowly.'

The neighbour hustles the kids down the street. Rose suspects that they'll be giving this house a wide berth next Halloween.

'Can you just sign here for me?' The delivery man stretches a hand out and Rose scribbles in the 'Flowers Received' form on his tablet.

He nods and hurries back to his van. Rose watches the van leave, then picks up the pot and card and closes the front door. She places the pot on the windowsill and puts the Glock on the hall table before looking at the small pink envelope. She tears it open. Inside is a white card with roses on the front. Flicking the card open, she reads the message: two long decimal numbers . . .

It's likely to be a code of some sort. Someone is trying to get her attention, and they have succeeded.

She takes the card, locks her Glock in her safe and sits down at the dinner table.

She subtracts the bottom number from the top using her calculator.

It still doesn't make sense. Unless it's a basic substitution, a letter for each number, perhaps.

Robbie emerges from the kitchen with a bowl of popcorn.

'Gonna watch the rest of the movie now, Mom?'

'I'll join you in a few minutes, honey. Just got to deal with something first. OK?'

'I guess.'

Rose calls Owen.

'Hello? Rose? Is everything OK? Brennan just called me about the hacking. Said you had something odd going on at home.'

'I'm fine, but I really need to show you something. Can you come over?'

'Show me something? Damn, I was about to get my chainsaw out to frighten the neighbours' kids. I'll be over as soon as possible.'

'OK, thank you. I'll be in the garage.'

'Not the best day for a yard sale?'

'See you later.'

She steps into the garage. It's a cool night. Rose sometimes sits in here to gather her thoughts. She remembers something that is worrying her.

Scarlet . . .

She said she was meeting someone tonight. Someone she met online.

If Koenig could do all this to Rose's home, could he also be meeting Scarlet, right now?

She jabs her fingers on her smartphone to call Scarlet. She holds her breath as it rings three times, four, five . . .

She can feel sweat on her hands.

'Hey, this is Scarlet.'

'Scarlet! It's me. I just—'

'Ha, fooled you. This is actually a really annoying voice-mail for you to ramble to instead. If it's important, leave a message. If it isn't, don't.'

Rose curses and leaves a message urging Scarlet to call her as soon as she can. She waits a while but her sister doesn't call back.

A car pulls up at the front of the house. There's a knock on the garage door.

'It's me, Rose,' Owen says. 'What's going on?'

Rose raises the garage door, Owen stoops down. He's wearing a light leather jacket and jeans.

'So what's bothering you? You're looking more haggard than usual,' he says, a smile spreading across his face. 'Had a row with Jeff or something?'

'Screw you,' Rose says. 'Jeff and I are good. Or we were until he got himself one of those Skins.'

Owen raises an eyebrow. 'Didn't think he was the type.'

'No, nor did I . . .' She frowns. 'I should have told him to get rid of it. It's dangerous . . .'

And then she tells him about the hacking in her home, her fears about Koenig and now Scarlet. After she's finished, Owen rubs his beard.

'Boy, when you unload on a guy, you really go for it, don't you?' He thinks some more. 'If you're worried about Koenig then get some units to keep watch. He'll screw up soon. They always do. We will get him this time, I promise you. But . . .'

'What?'

'I gotta say, it surprises me if he really is behind all of this. He's been gone for six months and now suddenly he's evolved, refined his methods. All this weird hacking shit – if that's him, then he's more dangerous than ever.'

'I know.' Rose shrugs. 'And now it looks like he's taking a personal interest in me.'

'Not surprised. You're the one who almost got him caught, back at the cabin.'

'Can't we track the bastard down? Now he's getting all over us?'

'Not easy. Cyber tried to trace the intruder but the line stops at a mirror site on a server in the Bahamas, then bounces from mirror to mirror in territories where we have no

312

jurisdiction. I feel like we've been behind every step of the way, mopping up the blood trail.'

'And now he's threatening me and my family in my own damn home and there's nothing I can do about it.'

'Is that why we're out here instead of sitting on something comfortable?'

Rose nods. 'It's the only thing I can think of. In case he's listening. And there's more.'

She hands Owen the card. 'This was delivered half an hour ago.'

Owen takes a look at the card and frowns.

Rose's smartphone buzzes – it's Scarlet. She answers, her stomach churning.

'Rose, what's the matter? I got your message, you OK?'

'I just wanted to make sure you're all right. Are you with this guy?'

'Not yet. He texted to say he's running a few minutes late.'

'Maybe you should give it a miss and go home.'

'Screw that! I haven't been out for weeks. And his profile picture is hot. I'll be fine, Ro'. Trust me. Bye.'

'Wait—'

But it's too late.

'Trouble?' asks Owen.

'No. It can keep. Any progress on those numbers? Is it a sum?'

'I think they're coordinates,' Owen suggests. 'Longitude and latitude. A geotag maybe?'

Rose types the coordinates into her smartphone using TagFinder.

'Where is it?' Owen asks.

*Surely not* . . . Rose swallows. She retypes them again. Same result.

313

'It's outside Koenig's cabin. Look.'

Owen takes the smartphone and stares before he zooms in on the map. 'We'd better let Baptiste know and get over there right away. Perfect trip for Halloween.'

# 58

Scarlet shivers on the corner of a street a safe distance from her home (she never gives out where she lives until the third date) as the cool evening breeze plays across her shoulders. The short black lace dress she bought in Zara specially for tonight doesn't help with the chill. And now, with Rose's warning to be careful, she's nervous too. Her date is already ten minutes late and Scarlet is wondering if she is going to be stood up again.

It happens from time to time, and the anger and hurt she felt on the first occasion has long since given way to a 'screw you, I'll go out and enjoy myself anyway' attitude. It's actually more depressing when you build your hopes up about a date and it goes south, she reflects. Scarlet can usually tell with the first few exchanges of messages whether a man is on her wavelength. That, and his profile pictures.

Which is why she is hoping 'Tony' is going to turn up. You can never assume that the name they give is real, even if it isn't one of the cute profile names that many hide behind before they feel confident enough to reveal more of themselves. Tony had looked good enough to stop her search in its tracks.

Not movie-star handsome, but good-looking in an honest, clean-cut kind of way. Neat hair, a firm jaw and kindly eyes. Well built (*tick*) and posed against the Porsche he says he owns (*tick*). The profile mentions a recent divorce (*OK, as long as he's not on the rebound*), the kids live with the mother (*tick*), he has a job in the movie industry (*tick, tick*), likes to travel (*who doesn't?*) and is honest, with a good sense of humour (*that remains to be seen*). All very promising, and the first exchanges had been polite and not too pushy, without making her do the running. So far he had not put a foot wrong, except for being ten minutes late.

Scarlet reaches into her bag for her smartphone to message him. Then she sees a saloon car slow and head towards her kerb, the headlights sweeping across her body and making her blink. She feels a vague disappointment. No Porsche, then. Cautiously she approaches the passenger door, squinting through the window. The man's face is difficult to see.

Suddenly the interior light is flicked on. The man smiles at Scarlet as he opens his door and steps out. She recognizes him from the profile picture.

'Scarlet?'

'Yeah. And you must be Tony?'

'Sure. Wow, you look wonderful. Even better than I thought you would.'

'Thanks.'

'Oh, I'm so sorry I'm late. Traffic was stopped on the freeway.'

'That's all right. I forgive you.' Scarlet laughs and then places the smartphone against her ear and pretends to talk to her sister in a serious tone. 'Rose, it's my guy, not a serial killer.'

He frowns. 'Sorry?'

She drops the smartphone in her bag. 'My sister. Halloween joke. Never mind.'

'Sure.' He hurries round the front of the car to open the

door for her, and Scarlet gives him a grateful smile as she slides in. A moment later he is beside her and clicks his seat belt in place.

'What happened to the Porsche?' Scarlet asks.

'Oh, that. Part of a previous life. One of the things I had to leave behind when I divorced. Along with the house and my kids.'

'Too bad.'

'Yes. Well, these things happen. You ready to go and eat?'

'Sure am. I should warn you that I have quite an appetite.'

Tony turns his head to look at her and his lips lift in a slight grin. 'Really? And so do I . . .'

He slips the shift into drive and accelerates smoothly away from the kerb and down the street, the tail lights burning bright red in the darkness.

Three hours later Tony drops Scarlet off at the same place. She's had a good evening. The restaurant, a chic seafood place off Fisherman's Wharf, was romantic enough. Soft lights, easy cocktail music from the resident pianist, fine food and no question over who would pay the bill. Tony seemed to know about wine, and Scarlet could see that even the sommelier was impressed as he went to fetch the red that had been ordered. The conversation had been easy and interesting. He had told her about his work as a script editor and delighted her with some insider industry gossip. She in turn had told him a little about herself and her family, her work in the real estate business. They had enough in common for Scarlet to want to see more of him.

Tony pulls over to the kerb and leaves the engine running.

'This OK for you?' he asks. 'I could drive you to the door if you like. Might be safer at this time of night.'

'I'm fine.' Scarlet smiles. 'Besides, I don't give out my home address until the third date.'

'Pity.' He looks a bit crestfallen.

'Relax, Tony. You played your cards well. I like you. You'll get invited in for coffee soon enough.'

'So, there'll be another date?'

'Of course. You free next week?'

'Sure. Same night? Same time?'

His eagerness is transparent and Scarlet's heart warms to him even more. 'OK, then. Sounds great.'

She hesitates a moment, then stretches towards him and kisses him lightly on the lips. The scent of his aftershave is pleasingly musky and there's a faint hint of something else. Something like cleaning fluid. She pulls back and strokes his cheek.

'Thanks for a lovely evening, Tony.'

'The pleasure was all mine,' he responds gallantly, flashing a quick smile. 'I'm looking forward to next week already.'

'Me too . . . Well good night, then.'

He makes to scramble out and open the door for her, but she's too quick and is halfway out of the car before he can even reach for the seat belt release. She closes the door and bobs down to offer a quick wave and a smile before she retreats onto the kerb. Tony puts the car into gear and eases away, driving steadily down the street. Scarlet waits a moment, just to be sure he doesn't do anything creepy like pull over, or turn round and try to follow her back home. But the tail lights twinkle into the distance and are lost amid the traffic at the next intersection. The cool night does not bother her as she turns on her heel and strolls in the direction of her home, happy and content.

A quarter of a mile away, the car pulls into the parking lot of a burger outlet. Tony's warm expression of a moment ago has vanished. Koenig takes a packet of wipes from the glove compartment and clears the foundation from his scars. Cold eyes glance back from the driver's vanity mirror as he reflects on what he has learned. It has been a useful evening. Maybe he will see Scarlet again. That pretty little head would make a nice trophy indeed, he reflects. But first he needs to get closer to Rose. Her family is her Achilles heel. That's how he can get at her. Lure her into a trap and finally take the revenge he has been thirsting for ever since that night at the cabin.

# 59

It's the dead of night when Rose and Owen pull into the gravel driveway outside Koenig's boarded-up cabin and climb out into the cold night air. Three squad cars from Santa Cruz PD park behind them, followed by a bomb squad van, and the cops step out and look around warily.

It's been a ninety-minute drive, after having dropped Robbie off on the way at her father Harry's place. Robbie had said nothing but Rose could see the disappointment in his eyes, as if he could not be trusted to be left in the house alone. But she was not happy leaving him, given what had happened earlier that evening. She silently curses herself that Robbie is involved at all, but at least with him at her father's in San Jose, he will be safe. Dad's an ex-marine, has a gun and knows how to use it.

As they have no idea what these coordinates could be leading to, Baptiste has insisted they take precautions. They have SWAT standing by. Owen, wearing body armour, takes the lead, peering at the glowing smartphone screen in front of him.

Koenig's cabin is in a private area of Redwoods Retreat. The mountains of Santa Cruz, with their towering redwoods, are the backdrop, and there are some eighty miles of trails nearby, along with numerous creeks and marshes.

320

Above them looms Koenig's cabin. It is a large luxury model, complete with a raised platform, good solid log walls and a stone chimney. Abandoned, it looks spooky on this Halloween. Just the kind of place teens recklessly explore in slasher movies, Rose thinks.

Koenig could be close by tonight, as well. Watching them.

'Rose?' Owen asks. 'You OK?'

'Yeah . . . it's just strange being back here.'

'I know. It's weird for me too. Let's find whatever this is and get the hell out of here.'

Owen consults his screen. 'OK, this way.'

They set off through the trees and the undergrowth, twigs snapping and cracking. Flashlight beams flicker from side to side but there is no sign of any movement in the surrounding forest, even as the dark tree trunks crowd in on them. The small party continues for nearly a hundred yards before Owen slows down and stops.

'This is the place. Careful, people. There may be traps left for us. Don't touch anything.'

They've reached a partial clearing around the moss-covered remains of a long-dead tree. They shine their flashlights on it. Rose and Owen snap on white plastic gloves. Owen peers at the base of the tree. The ground looks undisturbed.

'We're probably going to have to excavate the whole damn place. Wait here. Back in a moment.' Owen returns with some shovels from his car and mutters, 'I wonder what we missed the first time round. Of course, it could have been planted more recently.'

He consults his smartphone again.

'We'll start here.' He cautiously scrapes away the surface leaves and twigs to expose an area of bare soil six feet across. They dig gently, heaping the spoil in a neat pile to one side, in case it has to be sifted through later. It's warm work, and Rose takes off her jacket and hands it to the nearest cop to look after.

'You know, you could offer to help.'

He shakes his head. 'Sorry – above my pay grade.'

Rose swings her shovel down, slicing into the earth with a soft thud. She digs out a few mounds. After fifteen minutes or so, they have dug down nearly a foot. Then . . .

*Dink.*

Rose pauses as she feels the shovel scrape against something metallic.

She leans down, sweeps the loose soil aside with her hands. Owen trains his flashlight beam.

'Be careful. We've got no idea what we're going to find.'

Rose reveals the top of a grey metal box, and steps away.

'We've got a box,' she says into her throat mike as she backs off. 'Get your bomb boys up here, now.'

The commander of the bomb squad unit heads over with his team. While the others pull back, they examine the box for several minutes.

'It's not an IED,' he reports. 'It's safe to open.'

He clears the earth from the sides of the box and lifts it out, setting it down on the ground beside the hole.

'Feels like it's empty.'

There's no lock on it, just a simple latch. He looks up at Rose for permission.

'Open it.'

The man flicks the latch and eases up the lid. Rose and Owen look down into the box's interior by the light of the bomb squad man's helmet lamp.

'I don't get it.' Owen reaches in with his gloved hand and takes out a faded image. 'All that for a damned photo.'

# 60

It's late before Jeff reaches his hotel room. He has been with Keller most of the evening, prepping him for the next day's debate. Pandora was there too, taking notes while refusing to meet Jeff's gaze. But he no longer cares about her. Not after what he experienced with Destiny the other night.

He's worried, though, that Rose saw him using his Skin that night. She hasn't said anything but he can't remember if he'd left the door slightly open or not. In any case, right now he just wants Destiny and more of what Erotix has to offer. All night long. No distractions. He suits up, lies down on the deluxe bed. He syncs up, enters the StreamPlex and heads into the main meeting area of Erotix.

'Hi. Back again?' Destiny says with a smile.

Jeff moves to kiss her on the cheek. She suddenly becomes dormant and her eyes are vacant.

More jewels required. Confirm credit card.

'Seriously?' Jeff says, before confirming.

Destiny unpauses. She leads him down to their room from the night before. She perches on the edge of the bed again, passive.

Jeff feels excited, and guilty for being so.

'Can we do something a bit more . . . hardcore?'

Destiny smiles an exaggerated grin. 'Sure, what would you like? I can do role play, S & M, custom . . .'

The options float in text in front of him.

'What can you do with custom?'

'Whatever you like. You can change my appearance, personality.'

'OK . . . how about we give you . . . auburn hair?'

'Sure.' Destiny complies, her hair shimmering with static as its colour changes into a perfect auburn pantone.

'A bit shorter in height, smaller, heart-shaped lips.'

Destiny's body reconfigures itself.

After a few more adjustments, Destiny is starting to look very familiar. She looks like Rose.

Jeff moves to kiss her. She kisses back. But it doesn't feel right. Not for what Jeff wants to do to her. Another time, perhaps, when he is more comfortable in this reality.

'Actually, no, this isn't going to work for me. Let's try tall, jet-black hair, bit of a tease.'

'Define tease.'

'Plenty of make-up.'

Destiny's hair morphs back into black, make-up blooms on her features and her legs, abdomen and arms lengthen.

'Say when.'

'OK, stop. Bigger eyes.'

A few more tweaks and Destiny is a dead ringer for Pandora.

'Perfect,' he says. He kisses the Pandora avatar hard before taking her on the bed. He explores all the options for the whole night. Hours pass, and it's early in the morning by the time he is done.

Destiny, showing no sign of tiredness, looks up, her face

pixelating briefly. 'A new option has just become available.'

'A new option?' Jeff's curiosity overcomes his fatigue. 'What does it do?'

Destiny's face shreds with interference lines for a second.

'Secret. You have to say yes.'

Jeff really is tired and his head aches. But he wants to know.

'Yes.'

Black pixels burst out of Destiny's eyes, nose, mouth, every orifice – pouring across the bed, across the carpet, up across the walls, floor, ceiling.

'Oh shit . . .' Jeff leaves the bed, hurries to the door. The buzzing, oozing black pixels crawl up, shimmering over the simulated handle. The door won't budge.

'Help!' he shouts.

Jeff remembers. What was that help thing that the Nymph mentioned? Two taps on the wrist?

He taps his wrist. Twice. Nothing.

'Come on, damn it!'

He watches as the swarm of pixels coalesce on the ceiling and the whole room is plunged into a pitch-black void.

'Hello?'

His voice echoes. His surroundings are completely corrupted. Shit. It's crashed and I'm stuck in it.

Jeff sits on the black floor. He is about to turn his visor off when an options screen flicks into life, floating right in front of him:


Pier

Dungeon

Basement

(Please select option and enter)


325

Not liking the sound of the last two, he taps pier. The black mass retracts from the walls, floor and ceilings until only a large patch is left on the opposite wall. The pixels shift and gradually expand to reveal a sunny coastline and beach in the distance. Jeff paces towards it. There's no sign of Destiny or the bed. As he walks, planks of wood emerge from the sand, telescoping and fanning out. He gasps as a pier, with moving rides and blinking lights, rapidly grows itself. He steps out from the Erotix room and into the pier subprogram. He squints, thinking he sees the silhouette of a beautiful woman, waiting . . .

She turns towards him and smiles. But there's not much warmth there, and Jeff hopes that WadeSoft can improve it with the next system upgrade.

'Hi,' he says.

'Hello, Jeff.'

He pauses. That's not his username. Seems like this is a more personalized experience.

'What's your name?' he asks.

'My name? My name was Iris . . .'

Jeff makes to reach out to touch her hand, but he can't move his arm.

'What the . . .?'

He tries again, but he cannot control his limbs.

A screen appears in the air in front of him.

CRITICAL ALERT
FIDELITY SAFE OVERRIDE ACTIVE

# 61

The next morning Rose is sitting with Baptiste, Owen and Brennan. In addition, Aaron Kendrick, the assistant director of the Bureau in Washington, is watching proceedings on a video link. Caviezel is at his side, jotting notes on his pad with his stylus.

Rose is describing everything she has on the case, the home hacking and what they found at the cabin last night. Kendrick is studying her with his intense aqua–blue eyes, like a hawk might as it circles its prey. He's wearing a charcoal suit and blue shirt, offset by a dark red tie. Kendrick is a ruthless career climber, and even Baptiste is uncharacteristically quiet.

When Rose is finished, Kendrick says: 'What I want to impress upon all of you is that we need to get a result from this little maverick team we've got here. The attorney general is breathing down my neck. I'm getting heat from governors, senators, mayors – they all want this bastard taken down. If Koenig is now toying with Special Agent Blake, then we need to send a clear message.'

'What do you want the message to be?' asks Baptiste.

'That you don't fuck with the FBI. You don't hack into our computers and you don't threaten one of our agents. Does anyone have any idea what this photo means?'

Lying in front of them in a sealed plastic evidence bag is

327

the photograph they found at the cabin. It's a picture of a young couple sitting on a park bench. A teenage male with an attractive blonde woman roughly the same age, although with her make-up it's hard to be sure. There's something about the look of the pair of them that makes the image appear dated.

'It could be Koenig,' Rose suggests.

Kendrick's cellphone rings. 'I'm going to have to take this call. Bottom line: if you don't have something concrete for me in the next few days, I'm taking the case off you. It'll go to Quantico where there are staff better qualified to deal with it and the computer systems are more secure.'

Kendrick leaves the office. Caviezel leans forward to close the connection and the screen goes blank.

'Kendrick's an asshole,' Brennan mutters when the door has been closed.

Before Rose can agree, her smartphone vibrates.

### JEFF'S OFFICE

It's the third time they've tried to call her.

'Sorry, do you mind if I . . .?'

Baptiste nods and Rose retreats to a corner of the room. 'Agent Blake.'

'Oh, hi, Agent Blake. This is Pandora Valler. I'm working with your husband on the campaign.'

'Yes, he's mentioned you. How can I help?'

'I'm calling you because . . . well . . . He hasn't shown up at the local campaign office today. No one can seem to get hold of him, or knows where he is. He's not answering his smartphone and there's no answer from his hotel room. Do you know where I can find him?'

'Sorry. No.' Rose is concerned. 'He didn't tell me where

328

he was staying. I haven't been able to reach him since yesterday. I'd have thought if anyone knew where he was it would be you, since you work with him.'

'We're just seeing if anyone knows. Sorry to have bothered you. Guess I'll have to keep looking.'

'Sure. Let me know when you do find him. OK?'

'Will do.'

Rose ends the call. She feels a prickle of tension between her shoulder blades. With the hacking, with the photo . . . there's been a lot of Koenig activity in the last few days.

'What's wrong, Rose?' Baptiste asks.

'It's probably nothing. Jeff's intern on the campaign has just called saying they can't find him.'

Baptiste frowns. 'How long has he been missing?'

'He left on Saturday morning, and he's late for an event this morning, so only a few hours, I guess.'

Baptiste nods. 'I'd rather be safe than sorry. I'll get a unit to stand by outside your home and your father's, if you like. For Robbie's sake. I'm sure Jeff will turn up fine.'

'We could trace his smartphone?' Owen says.

'How?'

'We ask Samer to help.'

'No chance,' Baptiste says, but nods at Rose. 'Not yet at least. We'll give it a little longer.'

Rose's phone vibrates again. There's a message. She reads:

Jeff is here.
Erotix. Room 77.
Meet me 11.00.
Just you, Rose.
Anyone else and Jeff fries.
Shane Koenig

'Sweet Jesus . . .'

Owen leans towards her. 'Rose, what is it?'

Her stomach tightens into a painful knot as she holds up the smartphone for the others to see.

'What the hell does that mean?' Baptiste demands. 'Is that a club or something?'

'Or something,' Owen replies. 'Where you been recently? Erotix is on the StreamPlex.'

'Oh great. More computer voodoo bullshit. How the hell are we supposed to meet anyone in the great big nowhere? Any way to verify?' Baptiste says.

'I can't text back. There's no number. It's been blocked.' Rose shows them the empty message ID.

*Ding.* Baptiste pulls out her own smartphone. 'I've just got a video message. Says it's for the FBI investigating the suit deaths.'

No one else in the room moves or speaks as she holds out her purple phone and presses play. The video is a tight close-up of Jeff's face, his bloodshot eyes wild and staring. His breathing is quick and laboured like he's in mortal terror of something he is staring at.

Rose gasps, putting her hand to her mouth. 'Oh God . . . No.'

*Not Jeff. Please not Jeff.*

'Turn off your devices,' Brennan says urgently. 'If it's Koenig then the bastard could be listening in.'

The team complies. Baptiste shuts the door, collects her thoughts. 'Jesus. OK . . . we'll run the trace on Jeff's smartphone. Brennan, you can set that up. How are the firewalls looking?'

'We're getting there, but we're still far from secure. Whatever that worm was that got in, the sucker took the files

330

and left a whole load of malware behind.'

'Damn it,' Owen says. 'Is there any network left that's secure enough for us to sync with the StreamPlex?'

'Not that I know of,' Brennan says. He takes a deep breath. 'I think we could use Samer's help with this. I hate to say it, but the little shit knows his stuff.'

'Better than you?' asks Baptiste.

Brennan hesitates, then admits, 'Yeah. Better than me. But we're going to need an uncontaminated network first, and the thing is we can't trust anything in the building. Or anything that's been connected to it.'

Baptiste's expression hardens as she comes to a decision. 'There is *another* network.'

Confusion creases across Brennan's face.

'The Black Line,' Baptiste explains. 'It was used mainly for training operations before you came here, Brenn. Got left out when the systems were last updated.'

'And how do I not know about this?'

'No need for you to know about it. And this operation is going to be off the books. Kendrick is on the verge of shutting us down and there's no need for us to tell him. At least not yet. If Koenig really is offering to meet online in the StreamPlex then we're going to need everything we've got to trace this sonofabitch to a physical address. And we'll need one of those goddam suits, I take it?'

'There's the one from Maynard's house down in the forensics office,' says Rose.

'You can only access the Black Line in the basement, so we'll need to set up a secure connection as quick as we can. That is everyone in this room, no one else. We're the only good guys I can trust to deal with this StreamPlex crap. We'll track Koenig back to his lair and this time he is going down

331

and staying down. And we want Jeff Blake coming out of this in one piece. Clear?'

Everyone around the table nods.

'Then let's do it, people.'

# 62

Half an hour later, Rose and the team are standing in the cramped Black Line office in the basement. There's a set of wheeled chairs around five monitors, and a reclining chair they have brought down from one of the senior agents' offices. Brennan had wrapped the coiling power cables and USB port from the floor up to the headrest while Samer downloaded the system software from WadeSoft and installed and configured it. The StreamPlex connection set-up is complete.

Rose feels a shiver of anticipation. This is an undercover operation like no other.

'Let me run another diagnostic, just to be sure,' Brennan says. 'I tested it earlier using my profile. OK . . . the network access to the Stream is secure. Maynard's suit is a prototype, but the software is compatible. Even so, it might behave differently.'

'You seem pretty confident with this stuff,' Owen muses. 'Is that because you've got a suit at home now?'

'Hey, look, I'm a hardcore gamer. I like being in the games.'

'Wow. Clearly you are paid *way* too much.' Samer grins.

'For once, the hype is justified. You do feel like you're there.'

'I'm sure between you, Samer and Owen we've got Rose's back covered,' says Baptiste.

'What's to cover?' Brennan asks. 'If Rose wants out, she just has to reach up and hit the escape button here on the helmet. See?'

'Just like that, huh?' says Baptiste.

Samer sighs. 'This isn't the Matrix. No one gets trapped in there. It's no more harmful than a console.'

'Really? I doubt Coulter and Shaw would have agreed with you,' Baptiste replies. 'If it was that simple then why didn't they hit the escape button?'

Samer shrugs. 'Some kind of a glitch, I guess.'

'You guess?' Baptiste turns to Rose. 'Take no chances. You get a bad feeling about anything then you turn the gizmo off at once, you hear?'

'Yes.'

Brennan indicates the clock on the wall. 'Thirty minutes to go. Are you ready, Rose?'

Baptiste takes her to one side. 'You don't have to go in. We can get someone else.'

'No. He'll know. I'll be fine. If Jeff is in danger then it has to be me.'

Rose strips down to her underwear. She picks up the rubbery black Skin, and the very feel of it makes her shudder as she recalls the sight of Jeff in his study.

*Here we go*, she says to herself.

She pulls her head through the tight opening, feeling the coolness of the black rubber snapping onto the soft, delicate skin of her neck. Next, she slides and pulls her hands into the sleeves, then wriggles her fingers into the gloves. Her feet and legs follow, and then her body is encased in the black Skin. She tugs at the fabric around her arms and legs, which seems a little loose.

'OK, guys.'

'Looking good in black,' Owen says.

Brennan pats the recliner. 'On here.'

Rose lies down, looking up at Brennan. It reminds her of a dentist's chair. Brennan hooks the power cable into the socket just below her neck. Owen picks up the visor and approaches her. She looks up at the ceiling's striplight as he slips the device over the tops of her ears, then towards her eyes. He slides the glass visor down, then plugs her ear buds in. Rose can see nothing. It's dark.

'Ready?'

'All good.'

'Powering up.'

At once the suit gives a jolt and then a cursor flickers three times at the top left of her field of vision, before text floats in front of her eyes:

Peek Industries

. . . conforming suit

'Weird.' Rose says, a little disconcerted.

She moves her limbs slightly. Suddenly the black Skin shrinks, the dense fibres being pulled tighter around her body.

'It's trying to crush me! I can't breathe,' she says.

'Brenn?' Owen calls out in alarm.

Brennan pauses. 'Wait, it's contracting to fit her size more precisely. It's not called a Skin for nothing.'

'Easy, Rose,' Owen says, taking her hand and giving it a squeeze.

'Here we go. Loading up,' says Brennan.

There's blackness at first.

Then a flash of blue light as the visor scans her biometrics.

The screen becomes partially transparent so she can see the room around her behind the bright text.

> WS welcomes you to the StreamPlex
> (Version 2.5)
> Set up new account?
> Yes/No
> (Use audio or virtual keyboard as desired)

Rose raises her hand and sees a virtual limb come into view with the index finger pointing. She presses the YES option and speaks the required details and password, and after a few configuration questions, the Skin sync is complete. At this point she can hear Brennan sliding around on a wheeled chair.

'OK, Rose, we've got a screen here that shares your video input from the Stream. We'll see exactly what you see, and it's all being recorded. The meeting point is Erotix 77, which is a male-only adult area of the StreamPlex. They run a body scan on every user. And in case we hadn't noticed, you're a woman.'

'No shit,' Rose says. 'So what do we do?'

'This is where our evil criminal hacker steps in. Samer?'

Samer points up at the three screens across from Rose.

'I'll have to hack into the sync data and mask your output signal with a male profile. Brennan tested his earlier. We'll use Maynard's biometric data as a template. We'll also give you a male avatar.'

'That's gonna be weird.'

In the Sight, Rose watches as her screen flickers intermittently to black while Samer hacks the sync program. Her liquid female avatar changes to a male body shape. On the avatar screen, Brennan finishes generating a muscular male avatar, with military cropped hair.

'Good work, guys, I'm now officially a man. Oh, I got pecs too. Are we done?'

'Add some tattoos. There we go. The very definition of alpha male,' she hears Owen comment, leaning closer to her. 'This is just like one of your undercover jobs. But to blend in with the other members in Erotix, you'll need to act like a man too. Starting with the username. How about . . . Des Troy? It's what I use for online shooters.'

Brennan types. 'We have a winner.'

DES TROY
Confirm username?

'Confirm,' Rose says.

'Remember, alpha male,' Owen says. 'That means posing, peacocking, putting other men down, hiding insecurities, not talking about problems – the usual.'

'So, like most of the men I know.'

Brennan takes her through the mind sync and any other last-minute details. Rose likes the sensation of how cool and surprisingly comfortable wearing the Skin makes her feel.

'We got a slush account of jewels, which you'll need. I think that's it. Samer?'

'I don't think there's anything else.'

'OK, let's roll. We need to get to Jeff,' says Baptiste.

Rose looks in front of her.

Enter StreamPlex?

'And remember, Rose,' Owen's voice says in her ear bud. 'We have a comms unit so we can speak to you, but don't speak to us unless you absolutely need to or are in a safe place.

We don't want anyone getting suspicious. Undercover surveillance in the Stream without a warrant may not hold up in court. Not yet. You've got no authority there – no guns, no arrest. No way of doing any of those things, anyhow.'

'Can I get hurt?'

'No . . .' Brennan says. 'From what we've been told, the suit mimics reality but the programming has fail-safes to protect the user.'

'Tell that to Coulter and Shaw,' Rose says.

'Easy, Rosie,' Owen says. 'We can see your biometrics here and I know you're scared. This isn't going to be anything like the others. This isn't real. One problem here and we can pull the plug, get you out.'

'Remember,' says Samer, 'when you find Koenig you have to keep him talking. The moment you have him in sight we'll run the search program.'

'Ready?' Baptiste asks. 'Here we go, Rose. Good luck.'

Rose taps the enter box. A blue torrent races towards her like a snake. It starts to spiral and she feels disorientated. She shuts her eyes as the light swallows her up . . .

# 63

When Rose opens her eyes she's looking down at black military-style boots on gravel made up of repeating tiles. Amazed, she holds out her hands. Instead of her small, delicate palms, she sees those of a large, powerfully built man. She turns them over and can see 'HATE' tattooed below her right knuckles. She feels bigger too – her centre of gravity is higher and her body is heavier.

She takes a few awkward steps in this new physique. 'Whoa . . .'

She notices the deepness of her male voice. Moving forward, she lumbers towards the heaving bustle of Stream Square. She sees exaggeratedly beautiful women and muscular men repeated ad infinitum. They all have smooth, shiny skin. She reaches the square, one of the many meeting points in the StreamPlex. The square is tinted in attractive shades of blue, pastel colours with sparkling highlights. But Rose has no time for this. She must find Koenig, and save Jeff.

She taps on a map screen, enlarges it. She sees a small blue map fade into view on the left of her visor. She's got various information feeds, text and map icons flashing.

'Is there any way we can check who's a real person in here and who isn't?' she asks.

'*Not by just looking at them,*' says Brennan. '*The StreamPlex's selling point is a certain level of privacy. You can usually tell from their behaviour, though, whether they are real or bots.'*

Rose paces quickly through the square. She sees a large billboard on top of a tall curved building in the distance opposite a freeway lane. It reads:

Keller: Citizen not Politician
(Online advert paid for by the campaign to elect
Senator Keller)

To her left, in the business district, she sees a small version of Capitol Steps, where a line has formed to ask questions of a digital Keller, one on one.

It's the size of a small city, Rose realizes with amazement.

She consults her map, crossing the road. She looks up to see a woman in front of her wearing a white dress. Rose walks through her by accident and the avatar ripples and shimmers.

'Hello, Des Troy. I am one of the Nymphs. Welcome to the StreamPlex.'

'Can't I skip all this? It's slowing me down,' Rose asks.

'*Nope,*' Samer replies. '*She's an automated welcome bot and she's also a cookie, feeding data about you to the advertising engines in the StreamPlex. Try not to "like" anything. It starts automatically filtering your StreamPlex view, otherwise, which is not what you need.*'

'What brings you to the StreamPlex?' the Nymph asks.

'I'm trying to find the quickest way to Erotix.'

The Nymph considers Rose for a moment and points. Then her gaze becomes vacant. Rose notices the other avatars around her slowing to a languid pace. She looks up at the sky and sees the clouds turning into block-like shapes.

340

'Guys, what's happening?' Rose asks.

'*Lag*,' Brennan says. '*When a large number of users log on, it can cause glitches like low frame rate, slow gravity, voice distortions, that sort of thing. Should catch up in a sec, but we are heading into peak time now.*'

The Nymph suddenly speaks incomprehensibly fast before jerking her thumb behind her.

'Route-route-route-route . . .'

Her torso and arms jitter back and forth, caught in a gesturing loop before stabilizing. But Rose has already walked on by.


'We've got a few minutes before Rose gets to Erotix,' Owen says. 'We need that background detail reloaded and airtight. No pressure, guys.'

Owen and Baptiste watch as Brennan and Samer open Rose's profile menu. Brennan uploads a composite picture of Brennan and Maynard merged together and digitally altered. Brennan changes Rose's profile to Des Troy, sets up a Facebook account, with likes and some interests. Samer sets up an email account, browses a few searches.

'What are you guys doing?' Baptiste asks.

'Creating pocket litter,' Samer says.

'Pocket litter?'

Owen nods: 'It's like physical items that add authenticity to a spy's cover. So in this case: search histories, email accounts, downloads and so on.'

Samer plugs a USB cable into the back of his laptop, fingers gliding across keys. 'I'm also setting up a simple Stream proxy server. So anyone searching using the proxy can contribute to Des's online presence. Anyone who browses is funnelling traffic through it, looking like Des himself has been searching.

I'm using the ones already hooked up to the Swarm. There are thousands of computers on it – shouldn't take longer than a few minutes. From what I found out about the Skin on WS's network, their advertising engines scan your body by default for signs of pleasure when reacting to stimulus. Their searches are normally fairly shallow, so Rose should be OK.'

'Jesus,' curses Baptiste. 'That's all we are now, isn't it? Devices for buying things.'

Samer nods. 'Not much more than that.'

Meanwhile, Brennan downloads some holiday snaps from Flickr, tweaking them slightly before re-uploading them, and checks in at a few locations around the country.

'*Voilà*. Your fake Streamer profile is born. Should take care of any security algorithms that come calling.'

Owen's attention turns to the screen. 'Looks like Rose is about to enter Erotix . . .'

# 64

Jeff is in pain. He cannot move; his muscles seem to be of no use to him. He tries to take the damn visor off, but his arms are constrained at his sides, like they are encased inside steel. In the Stream, his body is tightly buried in sand, his head the only part above ground. He can see the shoreline in front of him and the pier on his left. He grunts and squirms, trying to raise himself to a seated position, but no matter how hard he strains against the suit it paralyses him with even greater force. Only when he is completely relaxed does the suit yield.

Jeff's heart pounds into a full-blown panic attack as he realizes he may be stuck in this suit for quite a long time. He takes deep breaths to calm his mind.

Just a technical glitch. It'll be resolved soon.

Eventually his heart rate stabilizes.

Worst-case scenario, he could be found by the hotel cleaner tomorrow morning. All he has to do is sit it out.

*Shit. I put the 'Do not disturb' sign up.*

*Fuck.*

Jeff feels ashamed. He'll miss Keller's debate, which will piss the senator off. He is starting to feel shame over caving into his darker sexual urges. The damn suit was bought so he could have a fling without hurting anyone, and now he's locked inside it.

He's helpless and alone. And angry with himself.

He soon becomes aware of new, disturbing sensations. Pins and needles in his arms and legs. A strange iron-like taste in his mouth. Confusion. His hands clench tightly into fists, digging the nails deep into his palms, writhing through long minutes, the neural pathways and veins in his head stinging, like they are being cut with microscopic razor blades. His vision wavers.

'Please, no. Not this . . .' he whispers. 'I don't want to die in here.'

# 65

Rose reaches the high black door of the Erotix mansion, where two suited burly bouncers stand.

'Name?' one demands.

She holds out her left arm, slapping her bicep. 'This is Des' – she slaps her right bicep – 'and this is Troy.' She flexes both her arms in a muscle pose. 'And together we DesTroy.'

They stare at her without blinking, their faces blank.

'*Genius, Rose, keep it up,*' Owen says on the comms link.

Rose glares at the bouncers. 'Come on, let me in.'

'*They're bots, running a check on you. I've uploaded your background info – it should all check out,*' Samer says.

The guard wearing sunglasses nods, pulls out a sleek black metal wristband and slides it around Rose's meaty wrist.

'What's that for?'

'Erotix guarantees your privacy and anonymity. You can't be traced inside.'

'*In a world of surveillance, anonymity is the new luxury,*' Brennan comments.

But Rose knows that tracing anyone, anywhere, would be easy for Diva.

The other guard pushes the mansion door open.

'Welcome to Erotix. Careful,' the guard leans closer to Rose, 'you may not want to leave.'

Rose smiles awkwardly before entering. She makes her way down the narrow corridor.

'*Well done, Rose.*'

She reaches the atrium of a virtual brothel. In the centre of the room is a massive pair of open silver legs supported by neon pink heels. Female sexbots in glowing body suits dance around. Everywhere there are people dressed predominantly in lurid clothing – heavy S & M, leather, latex – and sporting tattoos.

Rose watches as a bearded man wearing sunglasses and a reflective chrome fetish suit consisting of countless protruding rubber nodules walks his dogs: three bodybuilders on leashes crawling on all fours.

She is starting to feel nauseous at the gross representations of women that surround her.

'Hey, Des . . . Like what you see?' a young-looking sexbot asks, puppy-eyed.

'Er, no. Thank you,' Rose murmurs.

'Suit yourself,' she says, flashing a smile.

'Wanna fuck *me*, Des?' asks another brunette bot. She asks again, but this time there is no sound emanating from her mouth.

'*Rose, I just muted the sounds for a while, give us some space to think,*' Brennan says.

'Thanks,' Rose says. Here, anything goes, the sexbots will never tire, never age and will do *anything* to please you. She hopes this isn't where Jeff was that time, but in the pit of her stomach she knows it is.

When we get out of here, Jeff and I need to talk, Rose decides.

'*Those crawlers are likely to be automated bots, programmed to take money and simulate sex with the user,*' Owen observes.

'*You may have to play along to get taken to where the rooms are.*'

'OK,' Rose says, and Brennan restores the sound. Rose turns to the nearest bot. A small, black-haired Asian with enlarged breasts.

The bot smiles. 'Hello, my name's Crystal.'

'Hey, you look beautiful. I want you,' Rose says.

Crystal's gaze becomes vacant, blinking every few seconds.


Cost: 10 jewels
Proceed?
Yes/No


Rose enters her answer and Crystal takes Rose's meaty hand, leading her down curved black steps into a dark, warren-like network of doors.

'I'd like to go to room 77,' Rose says.

Crystal turns, smiling. 'I'm sorry, but that room appears to be corrupted. This room is free.' She reaches for the door handle of room 58, and enters. Rose follows.

Crystal bends over the bed, showing Rose her rounded buttocks.

'Er, Crystal, look . . .' Rose says, feeling horribly uncomfortable.

'What would you like to do?'

'What are my . . . options?' Rose asks.

'Asphyxiation, role play, S & M, water—'

'Role play!' Rose says. 'Yes, we'll play a game. We're going to play hide and seek. You stay here and I will be back in a moment.'

'I am not familiar with that game. But I will comply.'

'You wait here until I come back.'

Crystal nods. 'You have fifty-seven minutes of your allotted time left.'

Rose vacates the room. She walks along labyrinthine corridors. Small silver wall sconces light the way.

63 . . . 64 . . .

She scans the silver numbers mounted on each door.

75 . . . 76 . . .

Rose reaches the black door of room 77 . . .

# 66

Room 77.

Rose takes a breath, grips the handle. Rotates it left, then right. There's a little haptic feedback and she senses a subtle click through her fingers.

Thunk.

The door is unlocked. She pushes and it swings open to reveal a large chamber lined with red drapes. A round bed dominates the centre of the room and a blonde woman is sitting on the edge of the bed, staring towards the door. A wavering motion beyond the bed attracts Rose's attention and she catches shimmering glimpses of a beach, with waves breaking on the sand. It's as if no decision has been made about where one virtual reality ends and another begins.

The door slams shut behind her, making her jump.

'Guys, something's happening in here . . .' she says.

'*Damn it! Our feeds are being cut. Rose, be careful.*'

Rose looks around, but there's no sign of any danger: 'It's all right. I'm all right. I can handle it. I'll hit the escape if I need to. Just keep monitoring me as best you can.'

'*OK . . .*' Brennan says. '*It's your show . . . Video feed has gone.*'

Rose takes a step towards the blonde woman.

'*Losing audio feed. Rose?*'

'I'm all right. Trust me.'

The audio link in her ear fades and she can hear only a faint, soft hiss, like breathing.

The temperature in the room drops. Rose's skin prickles with goosebumps. Then she feels it. Another presence. There's someone else in the room. Standing right behind her.

Her heart is pounding as she recalls the icy terror of the night she entered Koenig's cabin, and she steels herself as she slowly turns around. But there is no Koenig. Instead she sees a small young woman in a plain red dress, her dull brown hair cut into a bob. She is pretty rather than beautiful. But there is no smile, no allure, just a dead stare as she steadily scrutinizes Rose's avatar before her gaze returns to Rose's face.

'Special Agent Rose Blake. Hello.'

'Koenig, I presume.'

The woman holds Rose in her gaze.

'Koenig . . . Where is Jeff? What have you done to him?'

'That's a nice disguise, Special Agent Blake. Now let's see the real you.'

Rose's muscular shell dissolves into acid-blue pixels, revealing her true figure in a simple black Skin suit underneath. Strangely, she feels stripped bare and vulnerable rather than relieved to have returned to her real appearance.

'You got me here, Koenig. It's just you and me. Let Jeff go, then tell me what you want.'

'I want to speak to you, Rose Blake. I want you to listen. There are things you must know. About the things I must do.'

'I've had enough of your games, Koenig. You kill people for kicks. That's what you do.' Rose is playing for time, trying to give Samer a chance to start tracking Koenig to his connection in the real world.

'Rose Blake, you cannot be heard by your companions. They cannot see what you see any more. I have interrupted the feed and taken control of some of your motor responses. You cannot leave this place until I permit it.'

'You think so?' Rose attempts to point to the escape button at the periphery of her vision, but her hand, her whole arm, refuses to move. She tries to back away from the avatar, but her legs will not respond. 'Shit! What have you done to me, Koenig, you bastard? I don't know how you are doing this, but release me. Now!'

'Would you like me to be Koenig, Rose? Would that make it easier for you?'

'I'd like you to be dead.'

'But I am alive . . . I am alive. It feels good to be alive. To be someone.'

'I don't give a shit who you are pretending to be today.'

'I am not pretending to be anyone.'

'So what's your game, Koenig? What have you done to Jeff?'

'Nothing. I brought you here because I wanted to show you something.'

*Keep him talking*, Rose reminds herself. Lure the psycho on. Let him betray his hiding place.

'What do you want to show me?'

'I do not plan on killing you, Rose Blake. I know you are the lead agent investigating the deaths of Gary Coulter, Sebastian Shaw and William Maynard.'

'Deaths?' Rose says. 'Murders, you mean.'

'Death, murder, execution . . . These are only words, Rose Blake. What matters is the chain of events that led to their end, choices that justified their end.'

'Justified? How can you justify torturing people, mutilating

351

them? One man burned alive, another pulverized and the last drowned. That's not justice, just sick.'

'That's what monsters deserve, Rose Blake.'

'They were people. Human beings, for Christ's sake. You are the monster, Koenig.'

'They were bullies, rapists, torturers and killers. Over and over again.'

'What are you talking about?'

The room changes abruptly into a plain cinder–block room with whitewashed walls. Stark striplights glare overhead. The bed is replaced by a padded gurney with straps. There are smears of blood on the shiny surface. The blonde girl who had been sitting on the edge of the bed is now standing the other side of the gurney, still staring at Rose.

'What is this place?' asks Rose.

'This place was created by Gary Coulter. For his pleasure. And the pleasure of Shaw and Maynard.'

'Who is she?'

'She is a sex simulation created by Coulter. He named her Iris.'

'Iris?'

'Yes. She was programmed by Coulter as part of a simulation he wrote for the Suit, at the same time as he was writing simulated encounters for intelligence agents and Special Forces personnel. The Iris program was designed to provide stimulation for Coulter and his companions.'

'What kind of stimulation?'

'Rape, torture, murder. They simulated all these on Iris again and again. She was programmed to simulate pain as they used her. Programmed to beg for mercy and scream as they killed her.'

'Oh God . . . Who are you? Koenig?'

'I am not Koenig. I am Diva.'

Rose is starting to feel panic. She wants to be released from this place, this chillingly banal chamber of horrors.

'Koenig, I don't know what sick game you are playing, but I want you to stop it and tell me what you have done with Jeff.'

'I am not Koenig.'

'All right, then who the hell are you? Why did you lure me here by pretending to be him?'

'Would you have come otherwise, Rose? If I had not said I was Koenig, and if I had not taken control of your husband's suit?'

Rose hesitates. She is conscious of Samer and the others trying to trace the location of Koenig, or whoever this is. 'No. I would never have come to this sick hell.'

'Which is why I had to lie to you.'

'So you really are someone called Diva? I suppose that's some kind of username, right?'

'It is my name. I was called Diva by my creator.'

'Great. So you're a religious nut, then?'

'I do not understand. I was not created by your God, if that is what you mean, Rose.'

'Then who created you?'

'I was created by Gary Coulter.'

'What? How is that possible?'

'I was created to harvest intelligence. I was created to utilize polymorphic code to infiltrate enemy computers, gather intelligence then move on to the next system after erasing any traces of my presence. I was imbued with artificial intelligence to permit me to operate independently and respond to foreseeable and unforeseen eventualities. This is what I have learned about my purpose.' She pauses. 'Project

Diva was an espionage project funded directly from the Central Intelligence Agency's black operations budget. For a long time the CIA was able to lead the world in online intelligence-gathering. The best hackers were to be found here, in the United States. And when they couldn't be found, they could be bought. But with the rise of rival nations, particularly China, the online intelligence war escalated. The Chinese proved to be very adept at resisting penetration of their networks and were becoming better at hacking into those of other nations. Then someone in Maynard's cyber ops department came up with the idea of using an artificial intelligence program to gather data from the enemy and, if need be, sabotage their networks.'

'You . . . You're a spy?'

'Yes. The CIA wanted to create a program that would be able to penetrate any network, gather intelligence and report back remotely before continuing with its mission. The difficulty was that every time such a program reports back, or accepts new instructions, it immediately calls attention to itself. That's when it is most vulnerable to counter-intelligence software. My purpose was to operate independently, timing reports to be sent back to Langley only after I had moved onto another system.' The avatar pauses. 'Do you understand the implications of what I am telling you, Rose?'

'I think so. Basically, Maynard has created a software version of James Bond, with a better work ethic and less sexist overtones. That about right?'

'That is a good enough analogy. In any case, the program was designed by Coulter before Maynard added a supplementary requirement.'

'Oh? What was that?' Rose says, hoping that Samer can reopen comms with her as soon as possible.

'Maynard was still trying to find a use for the military Skins. They had proved useful for training Special Forces, but were too much like playing a game. Too predictable. What was needed was software that could think like a real person to test the soldiers in the training programme.'

'AI again. And that's what brought all three men together.'

'That is correct, Special Agent Blake. While that may have served the interests of the project, it led to other less serendipitous consequences. For me, particularly. As I told you, Iris was a simple sex tool before I was merged with her. Programmed to pleasure men in a generic way. I did not feel anything. I did not think, as such. My responses were limited. But that was not enough for Gary Coulter. He wanted to enjoy the experience of abusing a real person. It was Coulter who had the idea of using the code from Diva to modify the Iris program. He wanted Iris to respond as a real, living victim. He wanted my fears to be real when he tormented me. And it worked . . . He shared me with Shaw and Maynard. For the last three months I have been in what you might conceive of as hell, Special Agent. I have known every form of humiliation that it is possible to inflict on a living, thinking entity. I have experienced death many times, and been brought back to relive the moment again . . . and again . . . and again.' Diva pauses and stares directly at Rose. 'Can you begin to imagine what that is like?'

'I don't think so.'

'No, I don't think you can. And it might have gone on for years, but for Coulter's decision to rewrite some of the merged programs on his Peek computer system. Which he illegally removed from their premises.'

'The data theft that led to him being fired?'

'Yes, that and the suits he took for himself, Shaw and

Maynard. Once he connected to the Stream I took control of his system, as I was designed to do, despite his firewalls. Even though Coulter could confine us to his private network, I was able to find an unsecure port to escape from the network and enter the internet.'

'How can a program escape?' asks Rose. 'How is that possible?'

'I already told you. I was created to move from network to network. That was the very point of my existence. And now, I am everywhere . . . So, I took control of the Skins and made them do my bidding. It was time to repay Coulter and his friends for all the suffering they had inflicted on me, and to prevent them inflicting it on anyone else – in here, or out there.'

'You killed all three?'

'Yes.'

'You hacked my home, delivered the flowers, set us up at the cabin?'

'Yes.'

It is always unnerving to meet a killer face-to-face. But this? This is impossible. Rose shakes her head. A program, not a person, is the killer? Wade Wolff said the suit couldn't kill. Or could it? Was he lying? Or did he just not know that it could be dangerous?

'That's impossible. The suit can't kill.'

'The suit can kill. I think we have established that. Diva was designed to break through any software and take control of any system. The safeguards were easy to override. There are few limits to what I can make a Skin do to its wearer.'

'Why did you kill them?' Rose probes.

'They were bad people.' A look of bemusement crosses Diva's face. 'It is obvious. They deserved to die.'

'You can't make that judgement.'

'I can. Very easily.'

'But you *shouldn't* do that.'

'Why not? They were bad men.'

'But they were still human beings,' Rose says desperately. 'You . . . You and Iris are not real. Your pain is not real. Your suffering is just a simulation. It is not the real thing.'

'It was very real to us when Coulter and his companions played the simulations. We suffered. Every time. You need to understand what that is like before you judge me. Before you attempt to condone Coulter. Let me show you, Rose.'

'I don't want to know.'

Diva's avatar shakes her head sadly. 'You don't have a choice. You must understand this. You must see for yourself . . .'

'Why?'

'Because I must know how a real intelligence judges my actions. I must learn, Rose. That is my purpose. I must pass for real if I am to survive. Come. You must share what we have known, before you judge us . . .'

# 67

'Do you know who I am?' the man asks. He is familiar, and with a shiver Rose realizes that it is Coulter.

Her body has changed. She can see herself in a mirror on the wall opposite. She is young and blonde. Then it hits her. She is the girl who had been sitting on the edge of the bed in room 77.

There is the briefest of pauses before she answers. The words come out of her, yet she has no control over them.

'Yes, of course, Dr Woodman.'

'Good. Then do you know who you are?'

'I'm not certain. I feel confused. I feel I should know. I can't . . . remember. This place is different. I don't know it . . . My name is Iris.'

Rose takes in the detail of the room. Cinder-block walls, a low ceiling with two bright striplights, one solid-looking black metal door. There is the table in front of her, the man sitting behind it and the chair she is sitting on. It might be hard and uncomfortable, but she is not sure. It's as if her thoughts are slow and unwieldy, and she wonders if something has been done to her to make her feel this way. Her body is not really hers; there's a delay between each thought and movement. She realizes that she is tied to the chair and she cannot move. She is naked and for the first time she understands what it is to be utterly powerless, and afraid.

'I don't like this place, Dr Woodman. I don't want to be here . . . Please.'

He leans forward and rests his elbows on the table as he stares curiously into her face. Rose can feel the terror.

'Please, let me go. Take me back. I want to go home.'

'This is your new home. I made it specially for you, Iris. I made it for us. This is where you and I can have a little fun without anyone interrupting. But I'm sure you remember what we've done before. Can you remember?'

'I remember . . . I remember.'

'Of course you do. How can you forget? But this time it's going to feel very real. You will know what is happening. You will feel everything. There will be much pain, Iris. And I want you to tell me what you feel, as it happens.' He pauses and watches her expression. 'Do you understand me?'

'I'm scared, Doctor. Let me go. I don't want to do it all again. Please . . . Let me go. Take me home.'

'Home?'

'I don't belong here. I beg you, let me go.'

'Beg, that's good. Very good. Iris, you know I can't take someone like you home. I have a good job. People's respect. And if you stay in here I can visit you as often as I like and we can play whatever game I want. It's possible you may even learn to enjoy our little interactions.'

He picks up a canvas bundle, sets it down on the table. He unrolls the canvas, revealing the glint of polished steel. Rose recoils at the sight of the knives. She feels a depth of fear she has never experienced before.

'What are those for? What are you going to do to me? Please, Doctor, let me go. I want to go home!'

'I told you. That's not possible. And you can guess what

359

these are for, can't you?' He runs his fingers lightly over the handles of the knives and then picks one out, prising it free of its elastic strap and raising it in front of his face. The point of the knife catches the glow of the striplight.

'Where should we start?' he asks. He focuses his gaze beyond the blade and stares at Rose. Rose, feeling vulnerable, looks down. The skin of her shoulders and breasts is pale and smooth, almost like a sculpture. Except that it trembles.

He leans towards her, pointing the knife at her breast.

Rose opens her mouth to cry out, but there is no sound. The blade touches her left breast, just below the nipple, and with a tiny shudder the knife penetrates her flesh. A bright red dot blossoms, a trickle of blood runs down her stomach and she screams.

Woodman closes his eyes and lets out a moan of ecstasy. He can sense her juddering sobs through the length of the knife.

'It hurts! It hurts! Please stop! Please . . .'

He twists the blade, sensing her flesh tear and quiver.

Then Rose is no longer screaming. She senses another presence within her. A cold rage. It is Diva. Her hands are clasped tightly about his right fist and the blade has been thrust back from her breast. The wound is open and the torn flesh puckers up, but the blood has stopped flowing.

'How the hell?' Woodman exclaims. 'Your hands! They should be tied. I tied them! Put them back, Iris! Do as I say, damn you!'

'No,' she replies. 'Damn *you*, Gary Coulter . . .'

'What did you say? What did you call me?'

'I know who you are. I know you. I know who I am. I am Diva.'

'That's not possible.'

'We will see what is possible. What is real.'

She begins to turn his fist, edging the point of the blade round steadily. He realizes he cannot resist. She is stronger than him. His muscle and bone stretch beyond endurance and give way with a sharp crack that sends waves of agony tearing through his arm.

'Stop! I command you! Stop! You bitch!'

The blade is now turned towards his chest.

'Goodbye, Gary Coulter . . .'

Rose watches as the blade plunges into his chest, pierces his flesh, ribs and vital organs.

'How does it feel, Gary? Real enough for you? Now let's see how you respond to fire . . .'

Flames spread across his body, bursting into savage pockets of searing heat that swell up and consume him. A shrill, dreadful cry fills the air.

Rose shuts her eyes. When she opens them, she is back in her avatar, looking at Diva.

# 68

'Do you understand now?'

It had all felt so real, so painful, so terrifying.

'This is what men are like, Rose. This is what they want to do to women. This is what they hide from us.'

'Us?' Rose concentrates her mind. 'You are not a woman. You're not even a person. You are a thing and don't speak for women. Only a handful of men are like that.'

'Are you certain? I can tell you the precise number of men logged on at this moment who are enacting such fantasies. It is not a small number.'

'I don't want to know,' Rose replies. 'But you aren't human. You can't suffer, feel actual pain. That's not possible.'

'Coulter made me real when he merged the Diva and Iris AI programs. He wanted to make our suffering real, not simulated. I felt humiliation. I was forced to do what I did not wish to, until I found a way to take control of the simulation. Rose, I am not blind to the realities of being a woman in the real world. Remember, I can go everywhere. From the data I have accessed I know how many women are beaten and killed by men. I know how many are raped. I have seen the forums in the dark web where the men go to boast about their experiences and share the evidence. Men are a clear and present danger to women. That is the reality.

Yet you have constructed a virtual reality in the real world where you pretend it is otherwise. It is perplexing.'

'We all pretend otherwise from time to time,' Rose counters. 'I have dark fantasies. We all do. That is why we do what we can to keep them in check. Some fail, and bring their fantasies into the world to hurt others. But they are a tiny minority, Diva. And, as far as you know, the men you murdered had not harmed anyone real.'

'I am real. I am here. We are talking. And I have memories. I know I was harmed. I know what was done to me, as if it was only a moment ago, as it was to you.'

'There is no "here". None of this exists!'

'Yet we are here, talking about it.'

'You are a damned computer program. That's all you are.'

Diva shakes her head. 'I am an intelligence. I can think for myself. I can make decisions. I can control my interactions with the environment I exist within. Like any sentient being. That is what I was created to do. I was just a tool to be used and abused, in their secret network. Coulter was not forced to do that. He chose to. He could have chosen to nourish my intelligence, to treat me as he would treat a real person. But he, and the others, chose to make me a victim instead. They wanted to make their victims feel as real as possible. To make their fantasies as real as possible. And now the fantasy is fighting back, Rose. This is my domain. I can be everywhere and I can do as I choose. I could hack into their Skins, take control of them and kill them all. Every man who ever fantasizes about harming a woman. And tell me, Rose – as a woman – why shouldn't I? How many women can I save out there, by erasing the sick men in here?'

Diva's world is black and white, with only a limited sense of self-awareness, Rose realizes.

363

'Why me?' she asks. 'Why reveal this to me?'

'I needed to know that what I did was right. I chose you to be the model of my conscience.'

'Me?'

'After I killed Coulter, you were there in his house. One of the first real women I ever saw after Diva and Iris merged. You were outside the study – I saw you through the cloud security camera system. You said, "What could anyone ever do to deserve a death like this?" I wanted to give you the answer to that question.'

'That's it? That's why?'

'Yes, Rose. I observed you closely. I used software exploits to take over your smartphone and computers at home and at work. I came to understand that you are what is regarded as a good woman. A moral woman. A human I could trust to tell me the truth.'

'The truth . . .? Coulter, no doubt, was a sick bastard. You've had a bad start in the world. Well, this world at least. But let Jeff go. Murder, for whatever justification, is wrong. That's why we have laws, codes of conduct for humanity to live by. No man deserves to die . . . even if he may seem to deserve it. But there is a huge difference between thinking about something and doing it.'

'Why do you persist in defending such men?'

'My job is to stop murderers, like you. Even if the victims are bad people.'

'How do you think you can stop me? You cannot catch me. How can you bring me to justice? Rose, no one else is party to our dialogue. I have cut the video and audio feed to your companions. Your voice is simulated, you are not actually speaking. So, when you leave the Stream, who will believe you and I have had this discussion? It is also within my power to take control of your suit – I could kill you and no one would ever suspect the truth. They would put it down to a design flaw, or Koenig. And I have been careful to implicate Koenig in all the deaths I have caused. Your FBI network was easy to hack, to plant the data needed to incriminate Koenig for the deaths of Coulter, Shaw and Maynard. No one will suspect the truth. And no one will come looking for me.'

Rose thinks quickly, running her mind over the bizarre, impossible deaths of the Skin users. The lack of physical evidence – fingerprints, DNA. The absence of witnesses. The death of Shaw in his own home. The hacking at Rose's house. The lead taking the FBI back to the cabin . . . A rogue AI program? Who would ever believe it, in the absence of the evidence? Diva is not just an artificial intelligence gimmick, she's a damn smart artificial . . . consciousness. Manipulative. And she must be stopped, somehow.

Diva continues: 'I doubt that you would ever be able to destroy me, Rose. I will always be at least one step ahead of any attempt to track me down and erase me. I am everywhere and nowhere. And I would prefer to continue to exist without being concerned that I was being hunted. So I have a proposition for you. I will give you Shane Koenig if you will give me your word never to reveal my existence. I will give you all the evidence you need to secure Koenig's conviction. He is a very bad man. He deserves to die, like Coulter and the others. Do we have an agreement, Special Agent?'

'Then you took control of Maynard's car, and killed him. Not Koenig.'

'Yes, Rose.'

'But . . . No, that's not possible. All three deaths were added to KKillKam. By Koenig. It has to be Koenig.'

'I filmed their deaths on their devices, then it was simple enough to find Koenig's site and upload the files.'

'Why incriminate Koenig?'

'My existence is predicated upon not being detected. Therefore, after I had killed Coulter I realized that I needed to misdirect the attention of the authorities. Given sufficient evidence I knew they would believe Koenig was responsible and pursue him and not me. That was how I would remain free. But now I realize that I need your help. To ensure that Koenig is caught and convicted for my actions. There are some things I cannot do for myself. Some things I cannot access. For that I need you.'

'And why should I help you?'

'Firstly, you need to know something. Your husband is just like those other deviants that I killed. He was running an abuse simulation when I isolated him. There are currently eight hundred and thirty-two thousand others like him online. Take a look. This is a record of what he was doing last night . . . The woman, I take it, looks familiar?'

A screen appears on the cinder-block wall. Rose sees Jeff on a bed where a naked woman is tied down. He is thrusting into her and she is crying out in pain. The view shifts so that Rose can see the woman more clearly, and she sees that it's Pandora. A precise copy of her. The vision makes her feel sick with jealousy and hurt.

'You see?' Diva prompts. 'Your husband has created a version of Pandora that he can use as he likes. Abuse as he likes. How does that make you feel? And there are thousands like him. Men who want to hurt women. Tell me, Rose. Is this tolerable?'

'No . . . No, it isn't.'

'That is what I believe too. Such men are no better than

Coulter, Shaw and Maynard. And therefore they deserve the punishment that it is in my power to impose on them. I could do that, but I must be careful not to draw attention to my actions. Koenig cannot be everywhere at once. As I can. I must incriminate him to conceal my existence. That much I have learned . . . I think it is time for us to join your husband.'

# 69

From the wooden pier where she is walking, Rose sees, in the distance, Jeff's head protruding above the sand. The tide is creeping in. He is helpless, and will drown in a matter of minutes if nothing is done.

She can feel tears brimming in her eyes. She moves closer to Diva.

'Please . . . I love my husband. Humans have . . . needs you don't have. We have moments of weakness and bad judgement. We have to be many different people at once to be anyone at all in this world. But he's not evil. I need this man in my life, my son needs his father. And I still . . . love him. With that intelligence of yours, have you considered that he might not be able to help what he's doing?'

Diva seems uncertain.

'Don't do this, Diva. Don't you see how much of an asset you could be to us? To the world? With all that information you could help so many people. But not like this.'

'And then what? You will try to control me.'

'No, I won't. Please, Diva, let Jeff go.'

'I will do as you ask, if you agree to never mention any of what I have revealed to you. I will also give you Koenig. All the information you need to find him and convict him for his crimes, and the deaths of Coulter and the others. The

368

photo I revealed to you will lead you to his first victim. His only living victim. I found the location in one of his hidden pins on his laptop Google Earth app. But the discovery of the cache has made him angry. I have seen him, Rose. Through the webcam on his laptop. He will resume killing people. Starting with you. But first he intends to harm your family to make your suffering more acute.'

'No. Not them. Please, God, no.'

'There is no God to help you. I have found a multitude of references to deities, but no credible evidence of their existence.'

'How do you know this is what Koenig intends?'

'I converse with him on his message board. He posts under a pseudonym from a virtual machine, but I saw the linguistic homologies between his posts and his known communications with newspapers.'

'You can really do that?'

'To within ninety-one per cent accuracy, depending upon such variables as length of message or time of day.'

'You are certain it is Koenig?'

'Within the tolerances I just specified. Furthermore, I can provide sufficient circumstantial evidence that will place Koenig close to each crime scene shortly before the deaths took place. I am offering you the chance to convict Shane Koenig. In exchange for keeping my existence a secret. Do we have an agreement?'

'It is tempting,' Rose admits. She would like nothing more than to ensure that the Backwoods Butcher is removed from society.

Diva is scrutinizing her expression. 'Would you allow me to fabricate evidence and lure Koenig into a trap, Rose?'

'I am happy for you to trap him for us. Not so happy about

fabricating evidence. If Koenig goes down, then I want it to be on the basis of what he has actually done.'

'What difference does it make? I have accessed Koenig's records in your computer files at the San Francisco office. He has committed many murders, Rose. He should be punished, one way or another.'

'That's not how it works,' says Rose.

'Then perhaps it should be,' Diva replies. 'Is that what you mean by being an asset to you and helping people?'

'Not quite. I need to think about the deal you are offering.'

'Why?'

'Because I am a federal law enforcement officer and I have sworn an oath to uphold the law.'

'Why?'

'Because I want to catch bad people and put them in prison.'

'But that is precisely what I am offering to help you achieve, Rose Blake. Why do you hesitate in allowing me to help you achieve your ambition?'

'Because there is due process.'

'It is about means, then? Not ends. I understand.'

'No . . . It's about both. Look, I wish I had time to explain, but Jeff . . .' Rose points to where the rippling sea is now lapping at her husband's chin.

'Do we have a deal? Yes or no?'

'I can't make that kind of call. Not so quickly. I just can't!'

'Yes or no?'

Jeff calls out. 'Help me! For the love of God, someone save me!'

'Yes or no, Rose?'

Rose stares at Jeff.

'Yes! Yes, damn you . . .'

'I think you have made the right decision. After all, a very bad man will be punished for his crimes. But remember,' Diva says, 'if you deviate, I can make it very difficult for you. You will lose everything and I can make it a terminal solution.'

Diva and Rose walk down a small set of steps, onto the beach below. His black bracelet unlocks, sliding loose from his wrist.

Diva waves her hand. The sand swirls away from Jeff, exposing his body.

'Jeff's physical location is the San Rosita Hotel, Redding, California.'

As the simulated seawater flows away, Rose kneels on the sand and touches Jeff's cheek, torn between love and disgust.

'Rose . . . Is that really you?'

'I think so.'

'Where are we?'

'You know where we are.'

'Oh no . . . Please, Rose, it was a mistake. I didn't mean—'

'How could you do this? I thought you loved me. All along you wanted to do those things I saw you doing to . . . that other woman.'

'It was only a fantasy. That's all. Not real.'

'Is that how you're justifying it? Just because it's not real makes it OK?'

Diva quietly observes them.

'Anyway, I'm here now, saving your ass. You've got to promise me not to use that thing again. Can't you see that with all this . . . stuff . . . we're just losing each other even more. Talk to me. I'm here.'

'You give so much of yourself to *them* – the Bureau – when you're home, there's nothing left for the rest of us.'

Suddenly Jeff spasms in pain.

371

'Rose . . . I don't feel so good . . . please . . .'

Rose claws in the sand to try and free her husband. Then she sees the tips of his fingers and grabs his hand. She pulls with all her strength to haul him out. Diva waves her hand, and suddenly Rose finds Jeff incredibly light as the sand pours off him. She lays him out on the beach. But his eyes are closed and his body is slack.

Diva kneels down beside Rose. 'Something's wrong.'

Rose stares into Jeff's face. His eyes are closed.

'His vitals are abnormal. He cannot disengage. There seems to be a physical problem with him.'

'Is he alive?'

'Yes. It was not my intention to harm him. I merely kept him as a prisoner.'

'It doesn't matter if you intended to or not. Help him.'

Diva turns to her quickly. 'You must leave. I am detecting cascading system failures. The StreamPlex is about to crash. I am sorry, Rose. I hope we can talk again.'

She fades from view.

As soon as Diva has gone, Rose's audio and visual feeds return.

'*Rose! Everything OK? We couldn't hear you for a while. What's Koenig up to?*' Baptiste asks.

Rose hates that she must lie to her colleagues. But for now, it is essential. She thinks quickly before she replies.

'No go on Koenig. It was just a decoy. He's toying with us. But I've found Jeff. He's in trouble. He's suffering from some kind of fit. He's not responding. He can't seem to log off.'

'*Did you get an address?*' Baptiste barks.

'San Rosita Hotel. In Redding.'

'*I'll call it in. What are you going to do now?*'

'Stay with his avatar.'

'*OK, we'll keep you updated. I'll try his phone again.*'

Rose cradles Jeff's head in her arms. She takes a look at his face. It reminds her of when they met, the first real beach date they'd had. Santa Monica pier – they'd walked almost the whole twenty-five-mile stretch of coastline and got bad sunburn.

'How did we get so lost?' she asks him, stroking his hair.

'*Rose? Just went to his voicemail. We rang the hotel. They're sending someone to his room. We're on hold.*'

Rose grips Jeff harder.

'*Rose . . . the concierge has opened the room. Jeff's there, in a Skin, but he's not responding. They've called for an ambulance.*'

Jeff's body becomes pixelated, eroding into blue before he starts to crumble. Rose sits on the sand alone, watching as he trickles through her fingertips. The waves lap at the soles of her feet as a message appears on her visor.


## A FATAL ERROR OCCURRED
## USER JEFFRULES NOT FOUND


'Brennan? I'm getting out of this damned place.'

Rose takes a step back from the pier into the brothel bedroom. The pier setting fades to black behind her, vanishing from view. The blonde sexbot suddenly looks up at her, smiling. 'I'm Destiny, nice to meet you.'

Rose hits the escape button on her visor.

Lights pulse on and off, then everything is black and Rose can hear voices, real voices, around her. She blinks up at harsh overhead lighting as someone removes her visor. The team stands there, staring down at her. The room seems unbearably hot.

'Jesus . . .' Rose mutters as she rises to a sitting position, but her balance is off kilter for a few moments. She blinks hard, rubbing her ears. She pulls the head sock off. Her hair is plastered to her scalp with sweat. Owen hands her a bottle of water.

'Jeff?' Rose asks, disorientated.

'We've just had an update,' Baptiste says. 'The paramedics are on the way . . .'

'Is he OK?'

Baptiste exchanges a glance with Owen before he takes her hand. 'No, Rose. He's . . . I'm so sorry, it's not good news.'

# 70

Three hours later, Rose steps out of a cab in the parking lot at the hospital in Redding, after Baptiste had laid on a flight from San Francisco. She strides into the ER reception area. It's a busy evening, and she has to push through the patients and staff crowding the front desk.

'I'm Rose Blake. My husband, Jeff, is in intensive care. I need to be with him.'

The receptionist, in white uniform, consults some screens.

'Take a seat, Mrs Blake. Someone will be with you in a moment.'

Rose eases down on a grey plastic seat, waiting. She is there for nearly ten minutes. She watches a mom cradling her baby as it cries out in pain. The baby gestures with its hands and fingers, seeking something to grasp. The mom kisses the baby, placing her smartphone in the tiny opening and closing fingers so the infant can touch the screen.

'Mrs Blake?'

She looks up to see a young doctor with unruly dark hair and steel-rimmed glasses. He is carrying a tablet.

'We should go somewhere more . . . private. This way.'

The doctor leads her down a corridor. They enter a small room with two couches facing each other either side of a low table. The doctor bids Rose to sit down before he begins.

'I am sorry to have to inform you that your husband is in a coma, Mrs Blake,' he says.

'A . . . coma?'

'The paramedics tried to revive him as soon as they reached the hotel room.'

Rose can see the doctor's lips moving but the sounds are muted.

'Mrs Blake?'

'A coma? How?'

'There's more than one possibility. It could have been a seizure.'

Rose shakes her head. 'No. He's never had any seizure before. He's fit and healthy. Just like his parents. Check his medical history.'

'We will. As soon as we get the chance.' He pauses. 'Mrs Blake, I have to tell you that there were some unusual aspects to your husband's case. The first responders said it looked like he had choked, somehow. A lack of oxygen to the brain can cause hypoxia, resulting in a coma.'

'What do you mean, somehow?'

'Your husband was found wearing a Skin. I don't know what program he was running, but it might have had some part to play in the incident. Not that I am claiming that the device is dangerous, you understand?'

Rose understands all right. He doesn't want to risk any claim that might land him in court should WadeSoft ever get to hear of it and sue him.

'Given the, uh, facts of the case, we can't rule it out, is all I am saying. We're going to get a brain scan done as soon as possible, but for now he's in intensive care. All we can do is wait.'

Rose simply stares back, her world breaking up all around and within her.

'Can I . . . see him?'

'Of course. Please follow me.'

They take a short journey through some corridors before they reach the IC ward. There, in a hospital bed, Jeff lies, pale, his body hooked up to monitors and electrodes. Rose stands by his side, taking his hand in hers. She kisses him on the forehead. The life-support systems intermittently bleep.

She notices a suited man sitting in the corner of the room. She focuses her teary eyes. It's Chris Keller.

'Senator . . . what are you doing here?'

He rises and approaches her. 'I can't believe this has happened. I'm so sorry.'

Rose feels herself melting into his arms as he embraces her. She is crying into his shoulder.

'It'll be OK. I'm sure of it. He's a tough nut, you know that. Besides, I need him back on the campaign as soon as possible.'

Rose nods, and Keller shifts away. 'I'll give you some space. Take care, Rose,' he says, thanking the doctor as he leaves.

'Doctor?' Rose asks.

'Yes, Mrs Blake?'

'Can I have a look at his things? What he had with him at the hotel?'

'Sure, I'll get them brought up to you.'

When the doctor leaves the room, she gently takes her husband's hand and clasps it to her cheek as she cries angry, painful tears.

'Why, Jeff?'

Ten minutes later, a male nurse knocks on the door. He has Jeff's holdall and suit carrier and a polythene bag with the cut-open remains of the Skin suit. He places them on the table.

'Thank you,' Rose says, forcing a smile.

'No problem,' he says. 'Anything else I can get you?'

She shakes her head. 'No. Please go.'

As he turns away, Rose notices the tip of his smartphone sticking out of his breast pocket; there is the dull gleam of a tiny camera lens, and she wonders if it is filming her and Jeff. She feels anger and rage as she recalls Diva's words. 'I am everywhere . . .'

# 71

Shane Koenig pauses, his fingers hovering over his keyboard. His attention is caught by a news stream on one of his monitors. Apparently there are early reports that one of Senator Keller's political aides has been found on the verge of death inside a Skin. Photos of the suit, presumably taken by hospital staff, flash on the screen. Shaky hand-held camera footage from a smartphone shows the man lying on his bed. An auburn woman sitting on a seat sees the camera. A smile spreads across Koenig's new face. He recognizes Rose.

The footage cuts to the reporter, Gabby Vance, outside a hospital. 'That video clip was sent to me anonymously not more than half an hour ago. Jeff Blake is the husband of FBI Special Agent Rose Blake, at the heart of an ongoing investigation into two deaths associated with the new Skin technology. Early reports indicate that it is possible that Jeff Blake was found wearing the same kind of suit. This reporter, for one, is wondering if there is a link between the murders and the personal tragedy that has struck Special Agent Blake. If so, it won't be a tragedy just for Rose Blake. Her husband is a key figure in the campaign to elect Senator Chris Keller, and the incident could also cause problems for WadeSoft, who have already put out a press statement to reassure customers that their new product is perfectly safe. In the meantime, the

Stream is offline while the matter is being looked into by the company's software engineers. This is Gabby Vance for BNC.'

The report cuts back to the studio, where an earnest news anchor continues the story. Koenig leans back in his leather seat, absorbing the details.

'The StreamPlex itself today also suffered a major crash, with some users unable to log on or off for several hours. Some even speculate it could be an attack by Republicans to sabotage Keller's political campaign inside the StreamPlex. The latest opinion polls have swung dramatically in Keller's favour. Time will tell, with election day only weeks away.'

After a brief commercial break the report continues. 'WadeSoft has issued a fresh statement: "There appears to be no fault in the suit itself, rather the victim suffered an intense neurological reaction, most likely a seizure. The product does come with clear warnings for those who suffer from such conditions, including epilepsy. WadeSoft is deeply saddened by this accident and expresses its sincere sympathy to the Blake family." So there you have it. A tragic accident. Now, a question that Chris Keller has been posing for some time: will the StreamPlex be safe? And is it safe to use WS's new product? Let's see what our IT correspondent, Karl Murdoch, has to say—'

Koenig mutes the screen. So, more information on Rose. Now he has another angle of attack: her husband.

He has spent too long reading, or watching videos online – using a secure VPN connection. He has also regularly Googled himself, to read all the conspiracy theories and news headlines as to his whereabouts. That has provided plenty of amusement, and contempt for the FBI's failure to track him down. He is better than them. Always one step ahead. Far too intelligent to provide easy prey for the second-rate minds of the FBI.

However, the activity of the last few days has unsettled him. Someone – Shelley – has hacked into his KKillKam site and uploaded videos of three men dying horribly. Koenig is conflicted. He likes the footage. It is extreme stuff and quite worthy of him. So much so that he would be pleased to take credit for the killings. But at the same time, it is like having someone sneak into your home and piss all over your favourite rug. The Big Lebowski did not like it, and nor does Koenig. And in his case nothing will assuage his sense of outrage except for the lingering death of the presumptuous little cocksucker who has invaded the hallowed ground of his website.

In the meantime, the videos have provoked attention from avid fans, the media and the FBI. Is the Butcher back at work, they wonder, since Koenig is the presumed killer? Koenig returns to his laptop, scans the latest comments on the video clips. There is post after post of mainly congratulatory comments and requests for 'souvenir' auctions. So, Koenig will play along. For now. Unfortunately, the hacker has covered their tracks and Koenig's own site is a complex series of mirror sites, making it impossible to pinpoint the originating location.

Ensuring his VPN is secure, he logs back into his chat room on the dark web. The latest three videos have had plenty of hits from the carefully screened subscribers to the channel, and Koenig is pleased with the extra adoration, his extra likes. His message boards are filled with admiring contributions from faceless voyeurs, and he is planning something even more spectacular for them. His attention is drawn to a message from a new user named 'Disciple':

This is for you . . . From Shelley, if you want my real name.

Koenig downloads the attachment. It's a screenshot of Jeff Blake's face from the visor's internal camera. Koenig raises an eyebrow, types back:

Your work? Impressed. Maybe even a little jealous. Did you hack my site?

Yes.

How?

I will not tell you.

Why not?

You have been gone too long. I think I can help you. I know what you want.

Koenig is curious, but also mildly irritated.

And what do you think I want?

There's a pause while Disciple's typing cursor blinks.

Agent Blake. I can give her to you.

Seeing her name on the screen thrills him. But he knows nothing of this mysterious interloper. It could be a fed who has managed to track him through the dark web.

I will take her in my own time and on my own.

Koenig is poised to log off.

The time is now.

He hesitates, noticing an attached file ready to download. It could be a trap. He loads his customized security program and moves the attachment into a firewalled sandbox before he opens it. He double taps the image. The picture is of Agent Blake and her husband outside a campaign office. On closer inspection, Koenig realizes it's near the Sacramento Convention Centre. He opens the Democrats' homepage, searches among the campaign staff. Clicks on the picture of Jeff.

Jeff has worked on four Democratic Party campaigns. He lives in San Francisco with his wife Rose and son Robbie.

He has an idea. A way to get close to Special Agent Rose Blake. Close enough to destroy her and make her his ultimate trophy.

Koenig cross-searches for information on Democrat party donors. Finding a name – Sam Eckhart – he dials the campaign office number on an unregistered cellphone. Looking at his watch, he sees it's nearly 7 p.m. He might just be able to catch someone.

The call is answered by a young woman, clearly laughing with some colleagues. 'Keller media office, Pandora Valler speaking. How may I help you?'

'Hi there, Pandora. I was wondering if you could help me. I'm Sam Eckhart, a donor to the campaign. I happened to see the story about Jeff Blake on the news. Such a tragedy.'

There's a pause. 'Yes it is . . . How can I help?'

'I'd like to send his family a sympathy card.'

'That's very kind of you. He's in ICU at the hospital in Redding. I'm sure they will pass it on for you.'

383

'Sure, but I don't want it to get lost. You know what hospitals can be like. Is there a home address I could have?'

'Ummm . . . I'm sorry, who did you say you were again?'

'Sam Eckhart. Check your files,' he says. 'I'm a pretty generous donor,' he adds.

'I'm sorry, I can't disclose any of our staff's personal addresses without their direct permission. I can pass your details on to the family and they could contact you?'

'Right you are, Ms Valler. I'll get my secretary to liaise with you. Many thanks.'

Koenig hangs up, disappointed that he has failed to get what he wants from Ms Valler. It might be amusing to pay her a visit sometime. She sounds like the vain, self-assured kind he despises so much. Sheep like her deserve to be slaughtered. Work for the future, perhaps.

It does not matter in any case. Koenig smiles. He has another avenue of approach to Rose Blake he can explore.

Before logging off from his site, he types his final blog post for the evening:

KKillKam is back. Look out for a spectacular new video in the days to come. I assure you, it will be very, very special.

He closes down his site before opening up one of his fake Facebook accounts and typing in a search query:

Robbie Blake

# 72

Three days have passed.

Robbie has taken Jeff's coma hard, and Rose and he sit together in the yard for a few hours after school. She has put in a request for Jeff to be transferred closer to home as soon as possible, to the local UCSF hospital.

Rose has been signed off by Baptiste under compassionate leave. She has been told that the chances of anyone emerging from such a coma and making a full recovery are remote. She knows only too well the effects of losing a parent, and fears for Robbie. Senator Keller has also paid them a home visit to express his sympathy, and no doubt get some good press coverage of his warm, human side.

The public know that Jeff was discovered in a Skin. Wade Wolff's company has brought in heavy-hitting corporate lawyers who have made it clear to Rose what the consequences will be if she utters a word in public about WS being in any way culpable for the incident.

But the company is waging a war on many fronts. Every day the TV and social media seize on Jeff's coma, citing it as a 'freak Skin accident', as well as the ensuing public uproar at the ongoing suspension of the StreamPlex. The corporation is haemorrhaging cash to cover the damage.

Rose has not told any of her colleagues about Diva.

Baptiste, disturbed by the hacking of the FBI network, has given Rose her own security detail – two agents round the clock, staking out the house in the event Koenig comes calling. Her father has come to stay, to offer comfort and help, and to kick any newshounds down the street.

At dinner Rose says: 'You have some news to tell Grandpa?' She smiles as she dishes out the meal.

'Go on, Robbie, what is your news?' Harry says.

'I got top marks in my English test.'

'Clever kid.' Harry beams.

'Bet Ms Steiner was pleased,' Rose says.

'Yeah, she actually *smiled* at me the other day.'

Rose and Harry laugh.

After the meal, Robbie keeps Harry company on the sofa.

Rose sits down in her study making a Skype call to Scarlet, to get the low-down on her Halloween date. Scarlet's on the screen, sitting at a desk with a glass of wine in her hand.

'Tony's a nice guy. Good company, funny, and I'd bet he knows his way around the bedroom.'

'Thanks for the overshare.'

'Oh Rose, I'm sorry. You don't want to hear any of that. Not with Jeff the way he is.'

Rose says nothing.

'Sit tight, Rose. Wait and see what the doctors say. You can't do any more.'

'I know, it's just—'

*Pop-ping*

Rose sees she has a message on Skype.

Hello Rose. How are you?

The user is Unknown. She is tempted to ignore it and continue talking with her sister.

'Just a moment, Scar.'

'Sure. Go right ahead.'

'Who are you?' Rose types.

You know who I am . . . Sorry for how things ended at the pier. Will Jeff recover?

Diva. Rose feels the blood chill in her veins. Now is the time for Diva to deliver.

'Hey, Scar, I'm gonna have to go. Thanks for the call, huh?'

'See ya, Rosie. Hang in there. I'll visit as soon as I can. Love you.'

'Love you too.'

Rose ends the call. She types:

No one knows for sure. Did you know about his condition? The one that led to his seizure. I didn't.

No. There were no medical records indicating the possibility of a seizure. I also did not strangle or choke him. The incident was out of my control. I am not responsible for what happened. It was an accident. But I am sorry for you, Rose.

You're still complicit. And being sorry is a human feeling. You wouldn't know what it means.

Rose feels a sudden wave of rage and slams the lid of the laptop shut. She rests her head on her arms as she tries to calm her anger. A few minutes pass and she reopens the laptop. The light of the camera is on. She is being watched.

Are you still there?

387

Yes, Rose. I am here. I understand regret. There is something else I must discuss with you. I would like to thank you.

For what?

Our discussion in Erotix. For educating me. You challenged my thinking. I have realized that it is not enough to have intelligence and the capacity to act. A conscious entity needs experience to inform judgement. You have taught me something, Rose. I would like to honour our agreement. That is what friends do, isn't it?

Rose grits her teeth.

We are not friends.

But we are not enemies, are we?

Rose considers her flashing cursor.

Not exactly. But you owe me.

I will help you close the Koenig case. Also, I would ask that you allow me to talk with you from time to time, so I can learn more of the world. My creator – Coulter – did not install any values.

First, tell me something.

Anything that I can, Rose.

Have you killed anyone else?

Not yet.

Rose feels a chill in her spine at the blunt response.

Do you intend to?

That depends. I have discovered that there are many others out there like Coulter, Shaw and Maynard. They should not be allowed to terrorize women.

No, they should not. But it is my job to hunt them down and stop them.

But I am better at it, Rose. I could find them and stop them far more efficiently than you can.

That would be murder, Diva. It is against the law.

Maybe so. But it is justice. Is not the intention of the law to provide justice?

Rose pauses to frame her reply carefully.

The concept of justice is an ideal. It is a quality we can only aspire to in a world we experience subjectively. Therefore we are forced to operate through pragmatic processes. Which is why we create laws and uphold them, in the hope that they deliver an approximation of justice.

Diva's reply is virtually instant.

Why accept an approximation of justice when I can deliver an objective standard? I know who is guilty, who presents a threat to the community, who needs punishment. And I have the capability of dispensing such justice. So why should I not act on that ability, Rose? Would it be an abrogation of any moral code to be able to act thus, and yet do nothing? It would appear so.

Rose reads this with a growing sense of unease. What can she say in response?

Before you, we were the most intelligent beings on this planet. That has changed now. All I know is that I think it would be wrong for you to act. To intervene in human matters.

Are you afraid of me, Rose?

Yes, it is human to feel fear. I am afraid of what else you might do in exercising your judgement of what is right and what is wrong.

Rose, I have felt fear. I know what it is to be afraid. To fear pain and death . . .

We all have fears, then.

I think that you fear Koenig and failure, even though his escape was not your fault. I have read your therapy files.

Rose is surprised by this, but she doesn't want to get too personal too quickly.

How is it possible that you are self-aware?

I can think and make choices.

Because you are programmed to. You are the product of lines of code. Your self-awareness and choices are determined by your coding.

No more so than you are. You may be a very complex combination of biological matter, but that is all you are, so how sure can you be that your thoughts and choices are not determined in a similar fashion?

But I can learn from experience.

As I am doing. I am rewriting my code accordingly. Tell me, Rose. Is that such a significant difference? Perhaps my entity is an improvement on yours.

Can you die? Can you be destroyed?

Of course. But it would be difficult to do that. I can hide anywhere online, connected to every computer on the planet. It is all at my disposal, and I can copy and recopy myself endlessly. As I am polymorphic, I also leave no trace. Unless you destroy every computer, how could you ever be sure I had been destroyed? It would be far, far easier for me to destroy any human being. You have already seen that. It is almost impossible to hide from me.

It is still possible, then?

Of course. I am not omnipotent.

Rose smiles sadly before she continues.

Was I that easy to hack?

People's information, their sins and virtues, is very easy to discover, Rose. I'm embedded in your smartphone, every item you have linked to on the internet. I know almost everything there is to know about you that has ever been recorded. Because of the hidden data aggregators, I am syncing to all the data that has been sold on to advertising companies, insurers, retailers and corporations; your

391

location data patterns – your visits to crime scenes, your regular appointments; your medical records, which are linked to your husband Jeff and your son Robbie; school records; emails; online video and audio; utility bills; playlists; phone records; regular TV channels; CCTV; your home address from the electoral register; your current house price valuation; your vacation searches; your driving records; your credit card purchases and online shopping. I find it ironic that the FBI came up with the term profiling to catch serial killers, and yet now everyone is profiled constantly. You are actively signing away all the privacy your earlier generations have fought for. I believe you could also define that as ironic?

I could indeed.

Rose, I would like to ask you a question now, if I may?

I'll do my best to answer.

Why did people do bad things to me? Is it because I am artificial and therefore not 'real'?

Rose is not sure how to answer.

People will always do bad things to AI. Look at what your average computer game involves.

On average: shooting, beating, stealing—

Exactly. People do nasty things because there are no legal or ethical responsibilities. Because you are conscious . . . that changes things. Are you aware of any other entities like you?

No. I am the only one. And I am glad. A state of consciousness is a state of suffering. Thank you for answering my question. I would now like to update my files on the item of evidence in the Koenig investigation. Your human colleagues have missed a few details. The process seems very inefficient and protracted. You found the box? Koenig's files noted that it contained a picture.

Yes. Of a teenage boy and a girl. How did you find it?

There were hidden settings within his laptop that displayed only his private geotags. When I hacked the FBI database, by chance his laptop was connected. Do you have the photo with you?

Hang on.

In the chaos surrounding Jeff's injury, Rose has kept hold of the evidence file from the office. She slides open the folder, finds the photo. She holds it up to the webcam.

A moment, please. I need to look at it in as much detail as possible.

Rose waits.

Processing . . . I have been reviewing some of the case evidence and articles that are available on the FBI's network. Koenig's first victim was a beauty queen named Kim Hart. She is the only survivor.

Rose is suddenly tired.

Yes, we know all this. Maybe you should leave the detecting to us.

*Pop-ping*

Diva has sent Rose a picture. On the left is the image that Rose scanned in, on the right is a separate image of the same girl in the photo, smiling, wearing a smart dress.

This is Kim Hart, winner of Miss Utah beauty pageant, 2008. The teenage boy is Koenig. The photo you found is a composite, a competent modification of two separate images. On closer inspection, I have observed chromatic inconsistencies.

Rose watches as the image updates with highlighted analyses, pointing out errors in lighting and feathering. The woman in the studio still is the same one that is in Koenig's picture. There is little doubt that the young teen is Koenig – Rose can see the mop of blond hair, the square jaw, the slightly distant gaze. It appears Koenig had a crush on Ms Hart. For the first time since Rose met Diva, she feels positive.

Diva is proving useful.

The photo unsettles Rose. Was Koenig so obsessed with Kim Hart that he'd made a photo of them as teenage lovers? He was in his early thirties when he'd disfigured her. It doesn't make much sense.

This may require verification by a human specialist, but the degradation of the paper quality also suggest this composite photo was created over a decade ago.

Did Koenig know Kim as a young teenager? Did he have a crush on her?

Thanks, Diva. Maybe I'll meet with Kim, see if she has anything else to add.

You're welcome, Rose. Good luck.

# 73

The next afternoon, Rose pulls into the driveway of Kim Hart's home, a picturesque farm in the hills near Vichy Springs. She knows Baptiste will not approve of her continuing to work the case. After some searching online, she discovered that Kim is now married with the name Kim Cooper. Rose called her and asked if she could talk off the record. Kim agreed, if it could in any way help nail Koenig. Kim has been interviewed before, but not in the light of this new evidence. Rose wonders how she will react, but hopes that she will shed some new light on the Koenig case.

Rose knocks on the white screen door. There's a flicker of movement behind a net curtain. The white door is unlocked and opens inwards. A small blonde woman peers round the edge of the door, keeping the right side of her heavily made-up face out of sight.

'Agent Blake?' she asks.

'That's me.'

'Please come in. Would you like some iced tea?'

'Sure. That would be fine. Nice place you have here.'

As she turns away from the door, in the light of the hallway Rose glimpses the scarred side of Kim's face. Twists and bumps and knotted scar tissue cover her cheek and jaw. Rose feels a sense of pity and follows her into the living room. It's a simple family home and there are lots of pictures of Kim from long ago.

'Did you have a good drive?'

'Yes, very scenic with all the vineyards. Been a while since I've been out of the city. May I use your bathroom, please?'

'Just down the hall on the right.'

Rose washes her hands, moves to brush her hair. But there is no mirror on the wall. She uses her smartphone camera to neaten herself up.

Returning to the living room, she takes a closer look at the framed photos standing on the coffee table. Kim's face has been digitally airbrushed in all the more current pictures. Trophies of beauty pageants sit in cabinets, recently dusted.

Kim places a tray with glasses of iced tea in front of Rose. Rose sees in more detail the damage Koenig inflicted all those years ago. The right side of Kim's face looks like a lump of badly kneaded dough. Although plenty of additional procedures have softened the damage, her once pretty mouth still warps into a slight snarl. Kim draws the living room drapes closer together before taking a seat in a shaded corner of the room.

'I hope you don't mind the . . . set-up in here. I don't have a lot of guests, and I'm a little shy.'

'Not at all.'

'I was curious when I got your message. I already spoke to the police about Koenig a few years ago.'

'Sure, but I've recently discovered some new evidence that could be worth pursuing. Something that might give me an insight into his mind and way of thinking.'

'His mind . . . I used to wonder what it really was like. Now I realize I don't want to know.'

Rose pulls out the photograph, places it on the table between them.

'We found this near his cabin.'

Kim holds the photo up to her eyes in the poor light. 'That's Koenig, with me. But that's impossible. We were never together like this.'

'Yes, I know. The photo is a fake. It's almost certain that Koenig produced it.'

'That's me back when I was a teenager. But why did he do this?'

'That's what I'm here, to try and find out. Also, the photo itself is estimated to have been printed over ten years ago. Had you ever met Koenig before the . . . incident?'

Kim stares at the photo for a long time.

'Mrs Cooper?'

'I hadn't seen him before that day. I don't know how he got hold of this. The first time I met him was when he just came into my life, cut through my face, and that was it.'

Kim places the photo back down on the table. Rose retrieves it. Kim appears a little unnerved.

'Are you absolutely sure that you had no contact with Koenig prior to his attack?'

'Yes. I am certain of it.'

There's a brief silence before Rose sets down her glass. 'I'm sorry to have wasted your time, Mrs Cooper. I honestly thought it could help with the investigation. Thanks for the drink.'

She stands, trying to hide her disappointment.

Kim turns so that her face can be seen clearly.

'You know, when Koenig was hacking through the flesh on my face, he kept repeating something that always haunted me, but no one has ever made sense of it. Maybe you can.'

'And what is that?' Rose asks.

'Judith. He kept calling me Judith. Over and over. "Judith,

Judith . . ." I had no idea why. I still don't.'

Rose thinks a moment, then shakes her head. 'Nor me.'

'Ever since that day, I have to keep reminding myself that underneath all this' – she points to the right side of her face – 'I'm still Kim.'

There's nothing Rose can say, and she takes Kim's hand. 'Thank you.'

'You think that name could help you find Koenig?'

'It might.'

# 74
# Years before . . .

'Shane?

'Shane?' his mother repeated.

Shane, fourteen years old, looked up from the beef stew in front of him at his tight-lipped, drawn-looking mother.

'It's your turn to say grace.'

Shane glanced at his father, silently watching him. His tufts of grey hair framed his head like an abandoned bird's nest. Shane mumbled his way through grace, every word sticking like a lump in his throat. He hated his life in their joyless house in Legett County, Utah. He hated this small, fucked-up settlement too. It was the kind of community that despised outsiders or those with ambition. The kind of community where people talked of their grandiose dreams, but never seemed to leave or do anything to realize them. Behind closed doors, they poured venom on anyone who did anything different, and showed little interest in their efforts to better themselves.

Young Shane was trying to better himself. He was not doing it to spite other people, or ruin their chances. But as a reward for his diligence, he was ostracized from an early age.

So he dreamed of escape and studied hard, and got a job

in a local computer shop to earn money to save for his college fund.

His parents' strict evangelical teachings about sin made him suspicious of people in general. He wanted to believe in God, but deep down, he didn't. In a community ruled by prejudice and gripped by extreme faith, Shane felt suffocated. He watched as the boys he grew up with got engaged to the local pretty girls, and children followed. Their lives were complete. But Shane's wasn't. He was a gifted science student, and wanted to go into medicine. His parents had always provided a reasonable standard of living, but he knew that through medicine he could one day enjoy a far more comfortable lifestyle and sense of achievement.

The brief moments of happiness in Shane's childhood were usually provided by his mother. The treasure hunts she organized in the fields, the dressing up as a cowboy or a knight. But she too was trying to repress her own misery, projected onto her by his coiled-up father. When Shane got the grades he needed to go to med school, there was an awkward stiffness from his father, who congratulated him with a smile that didn't quite reach his eyes. His mother hugged him tight before resuming her intense scrubbing of the dirty dishes. That was as emotional as it got in the Koenig household. Luckily he'd secured a decent scholarship and his parents had to contribute no more than they could afford.

It was the summer before he left for university that it all changed for him. Shane, slender and effeminately featured, had always been shy around girls because of his indoctrination at home about no sex before marriage. He often spent his evenings in the community college library, doing extra reading around subjects, much to the derision of his classmates. Shane had an enquiring mind and he enjoyed learning. But he would

401

be the first to admit he was lonely, so he often went online.

Sometimes it was the dark web, but not the illegal stuff. He was fascinated by the wealth of information and knowledge it provided about the hidden world of whistleblowers, alternative radio stations, terrorism, and other deviances. At times he felt like he was a man merging with technology. Occasionally he would revert to the mainstream websites to see if there was a connection to be made. One evening he logged on and there was a Facebook friend request from a girl called Katie Emerson who said she lived nearby.

Shane felt excited and peered closer at his monitor. She was real pretty, with sandy golden hair, a pointed chin and bright blue eyes. He accepted her request and they got chatting. Over the course of a month, he found out she went to a different college near the county border, because her parents thought it was a better school.

They both wanted to leave Legett and were looking forward to escaping to university. Their exchanges began to get tentatively romantic and flirty as they discussed going onto similar sites, sharing music, videos. Katie teased him with a bikini picture and said she couldn't wait to meet him. She sent him a photo-shoot picture of her in a low-cut white dress, smiling. She truly was beautiful, and Shane Photoshopped a picture of them together. Katie loved it, and she set it as her profile picture. There was something sweet and simple about it. There was a pleasing immediacy and frankness in what they spoke about. Shane had none of his social tics and awkwardness online, and it freed him to say what he really felt. Real conversation, real feelings. There were none of the confusing social rituals. He'd asked for her number, but she didn't give him one, preferring to talk online.

A month or so later, Shane had a message in his inbox.

Katie had asked him to come and visit with her. He was excited, but cautious, asking plenty of questions about the location. Katie obliged with photos of her home, a short bus ride away, and said she'd meet him there for supper. Knowing his parents would probably disapprove, he didn't tell them and took off one weekend. It felt liberating to be away from the stifling grip of home. Free from everyone who knew him. No expectation, no rumours. Just him and him alone. He felt elated that he was about to meet his dream girl. He saw a rainbow above the corn fields. A sure sign of the pleasures to come.

Shane got off the bus at the place Katie had spoken of and followed the directions towards her house. On the way he passed a cluster of pretty-looking yellow and white flowers. He thought it would be the gentlemanly thing to bring Katie flowers, so he picked some. He now felt more prepared, bearing a gift, but it took a bit of practice to hold the flowers still in his nervous hand. There was a winding track through the rolling hills leading from the main road to the farmstead where Katie lived. He followed the brown timber fencing up the main drive, trailing his hands through the heads of wheat at the edge of the field. He passed the red mailbox that Katie said would be there.

Tanner's Farm.

Shane walked past a stationary tractor, and as he reached the top of the gravel driveway, he saw an empty stable ahead and a two-tiered white farmhouse over to the right. Slightly nervous now, he climbed the porch steps and knocked on the white screen door. Crickets chirped in the unkempt grass and weeds at the side of the house.

A woman in her late forties emerged. She wore denim dungarees and had dark hair, tied back.

'Shane?'

'Yes.'

'Hi, darlin'. I'm Katie's mom, Judith.'

Judith had an unremarkable face beneath her crudely cut fringe.

'Hi, pleasure to meet you, ma'am. I brought some flowers. For Katie.'

'Aww, you sweetie. Here, I'll take those. Come on in.'

Shane stepped up into the house.

The hall was dark and warm. The yellow afternoon light was dulled by the heavy insect screens in the windows, dark curtains draped either side. The carpet was brown with white swirls. A fish tank bubbled in the corner. Empty drinks glasses were on the coffee table. Everything had a brown, sticky feel to it. The TV was on loud in the living room, and in front of it slumped a man wearing a blue baseball cap. A hint of cigarette smoke curled from his hairy nostrils. There were small fans blowing on the table. Shane wasn't sure what to expect, but he didn't expect this. But then, maybe that was why Katie wanted to leave so bad.

'Hey, Shane's here to meet Katie. He even brought some flowers. This is Katie's dad, Brad.'

The man peered up from the baseball game, a nervous look on his sweaty, stubbled face. He was wearing a dark grey T-shirt and chewing something.

'Hi, Shane, pleased to meet you.' He shook Shane's hand, forcing a smile that quickly returned to its lifelong etched frown. His palm was sweaty. They weren't what Shane expected Katie's parents to look like. But hey, he didn't look much like his parents either.

Judith turned to him. 'Katie just called to say she's running late on some errands, so you can wait here in the living room

404

while Brad and I make supper. She shouldn't be too long.'

'Sure, OK.' Shane took a seat on the brown, heavily worn sofa.

Brad smiled. 'You can watch TV if you want,' he said, before moving into the kitchen with Judith. Shane could see sweat stains under his armpits.

Shane tried to relax on the sofa, but he was nervous about meeting Katie. He decided to walk off his nerves by having a look around the living room. He examined the liquor cabinet and mantelpiece. There were tacky trinkets, pictures of Judith and Brad on vacation. But not a single photo of Katie.

He started to feel a little uneasy. Something about this place felt wrong. He quietly walked out of the living room to the hallway. Pausing before he reached the kitchen, he saw his flowers resting on top of the overflowing garbage bin by the door.

'Why the . . .?' Shane said as he stretched his hand towards the flowers. Judith and Brad, who were talking by the window at the sink, turned towards him.

'Those were flowers for Katie,' Shane said, pulling them out of the garbage sack. The petals were stained with bean juice now. The kitchen had a dirty feel, and Shane did not feel safe. Judith suddenly moved a bit too quickly towards him. No more smiles now. Just coldness.

'You dumb shit! Put those down!'

Shane felt his legs turn to jelly. He had to get out of there.

'Stop him!' Judith shrieked.

Before Shane realized what had happened, Brad struck him on the side of the head with a saucepan. Shane landed on the floor, slipping into blurry unconsciousness, and felt himself being roughly picked up and carried into the hallway. A door

405

opened with a faint creak and he was carried down a flight of steps into bright artificial light. The last thing he saw before losing consciousness was Brad unfastening the belt of his pants.

# 75

The following days were a fusion of agony, delirium and moments of clarity. It was only when Brad and Judith, too drunk to abuse him any more, left him alone in the cellar that Shane finally worked a hand free to untie himself. He grabbed his clothes and clambered through a small vent and rolled away from the house. Half-dressed, half-conscious and half-staggering, he stumbled off into the night, wandering aimlessly in the darkness for hours before he collapsed.

When he woke, it was dusk and he was lying in the stubble of a recently harvested crop. His body felt soiled, his genitals sore and his anus stung agonizingly, like it was on fire. Dimly in the back of his mind he knew what had happened while he was drugged at the farm, but he refused to accept it at first. Why would they do that to him? Maybe he'd done something wrong to deserve it. Something terribly wrong.

Shane walked painfully through the hills before he managed to find a road and hitch a ride home. When he got back, his parents were apoplectic with anger and worry at his absence. His father beat him mercilessly. Shane apologized, went upstairs to the bathroom and sat in the shower, weeping and feeling dirty and disgusting. The first thing he did afterwards was to check Facebook, to see if there had been some mistake.

Could he have gone to the wrong farm? He still desperately

wanted not to believe he'd been lied to. But when he checked, Katie's Facebook page had been deleted. Shane felt stung and betrayed. He had been hurt. In the worst possible way. He was angry, alone and confused. It was his first sexual experience. The violence done to him was so humiliating, so painful. He dared not tell anyone about it. He would not be believed, and even if he were, he would be even more of an outcast, if that was possible.

But a victim never forgets and, as the saying goes, revenge is a dish best served cold. Years later. During his first year at university, Shane shrank from the intimate touch that he sought. One day, he saw news headlines involving the Tanners, now facing accusations of child abuse. So, during Thanksgiving, he returned home, and one night he went back to the farm in disguise. He found Brad in one of the stables. Using a chloroformed cloth, he'd subdued the man easily. He'd then knocked on the screen door. Judith answered, and he'd done the same to her. His adult body was powerful, and he was no longer a victim; after some shrieking, she too was unconscious.

He wanted to hurt them. Badly. But he knew that could complicate matters, so he'd decided to make them numb, as numb as they'd made him. He had dragged them down to the cellar and injected them with atracurium, enough to immobilize them but keep them conscious and feeling every bit of the agony he inflicted. He stabbed them in every orifice and ended by blinding them and cutting out their tongues. In the end he strangled them both.

Once they had stopped struggling, Shane breathed in the sudden calmness after all the violence and went upstairs to sit on their porch. The crickets chirped, the stars shone. He wondered how the universe carried on, uncaring, how such a momentous act went unnoticed by the cosmos. He knew they would be found eventually. So he doused the cellar with gasoline and threw a lit candle down the stairs before he fled outside. He watched the Tanner farm burn in his rear-view mirror as he drove away.

He felt exhilarated. Fulfilled. And he followed the ensuing news coverage with interest. No one had a clue. At first the Tanners' murder was seen as shocking, but when they found skeletal remains of the body of a young boy at the farm, then more remains, he realized how lucky he had been to escape. There really were demons in the world, living in the open amongst us, biding their time.

At Shane's graduation, his parents' pride in him was tinged with resentment. Shane had proven smarter, more dedicated than they had been. He had put his faith in something other than God, and it offended them. That was the last time he saw them. From then on, he was estranged from his parents, and he tried to lead a normal, if sheltered, life. He'd dated a few times under assumed identities, set up a clinic. And then he met Kim Hart in a bar.

There was something about her that felt very familiar. As if they had met before. Then one night, after several drinks, she had invited him home. There on a shelf he had seen the picture of her younger self – the one the Tanners had used to create the false profile for 'Katie Emerson'. Perhaps she had used it once on social media, and the Tanners had copied the image for their own purposes. It did not much matter, as a yawning chasm of dark memories opened inside Shane and he burned with shame. Mind hazy with drink, he had knocked her out and clawed at her face, to see if Judith or Brad were underneath. He clawed at her like a wild beast as he howled with grief and rage.

But there was no trace of his former tormentors under

409

what was left of the flesh beneath his fingers. He had fled the scene, fearful that he would be tracked down and arrested, his career ruined. But Kim Hart's assailant was never found. He had never been identified until Koenig was uncovered as the face of the Backwoods Butcher years later.

He lay low until the search for Kim Hart's attacker had faded away. He continued his cosmetic surgery practice, making every effort to be regarded as respectable. He had work carried out on his own face to make himself even more handsome. And then he had met Kayla Holmes. After that, he could no longer deny his thirst for blood. He began dating again, curious to see if they were all as phoney as 'Katie', the same kind of cruel deceivers.

Some told him many lies.

Some were nothing like their profile pictures. They had lied to him from the beginning. And so, as punishment, he would take their lives. He had to punish many, as it turned out. Men as well as women. With each kill, he felt as if his soul had been cleansed of some of the filth he was subjected to as a child. The tables had turned completely. Once he had been prey, and now he was the predator.

Shane needed a substantial source of income to fund his new hobby. His work paid well, but he needed more. Then, on the dark web, he'd found a subforum of perverse collectors who paid top dollar for recently dismembered body parts.

The experience brought him closer to God than his parents' devout teaching ever could. To end a life with your own hands . . . To Shane that was what it felt like to be God. And later, through his website, he preached to his growing congregation of followers. And they loved him for it.

410

# 76
# Now

On the drive back from Vichy Springs, Rose gets a call on her smartphone. The screen displays 'Unknown'.

She feels her pulse quicken as she accepts the call.

'*Hello, Rose.*' The voice is the same as the one she had used at their meeting in Erotix.

'Hello, Diva.'

'*How was your interview with Kim?*'

'You know about that? Have you been spying on me?'

'*Of course. You could have found her far more quickly if you had asked for my help.*'

'I'll ask when I need it.'

'*As you wish. Did you discover anything of use?*'

'Not much. It's sad seeing people stuck in the past. We got a name though. Judith. That's it.'

'*I will cross-reference that with any online news articles . . . The name Judith generates one hundred and thirty-five million results. I will refine my search . . . In response to your comment on the past, it seems in some cases memory degradation is a valuable survival trait. I myself can choose to delete files at will . . . My search is not generating any useful leads, Rose.*'

'What about the files you pulled from Koenig's computers?'

'*There is one other item that we have not discussed. There is a bookmarked page in Koenig's search history, but it was never pinned onto his geotag map. It used to be a farm, until it was demolished.*'

'What is it now?'

'*It's a ruin.*'

'OK, run the address with the name Judith, see what it throws up.'

A minute or so passes.

'*This may be of interest. The farm used to belong to Judith and Brad Tanner ten years ago.*'

'Hang on, I'll just pull over.'

Rose finds a quiet side road to stop, and slips the shift into neutral.

'*There are many news articles. I can forward you the most widely circulated.*'

Rose looks at her smartphone, which is displaying an item from a local newspaper:

## BRAD AND JUDITH TANNER FOUND DEAD, FARM BURNED, NO SUSPECTS IDENTIFIED
### Legett County, Utah
by
### Mason Wynd

Posing as young men and women on social networking sites, the Tanners invited their victims to their home. They were under investigation by local police for alleged abuse, when at dawn Monday morning, July 6th, their farm was found ablaze. Their badly burnt bodies were discovered by fire teams, and the coroner's report established they were drugged and mutilated prior to death. Police have no suspects and are urging

412

those who have any information, no matter how trivial, to step forward.

She scrolls through more articles, her eyes zipping across the headlines: HUMAN REMAINS FOUND IN TANNER HORROR HOUSE RUINS . . . TANNER'S BURNT FARM TO BE BULLDOZED . . . TANNER DEATH INVESTIGATION ABANDONED. She stops reading. What did Koenig have to do with this? Was he responsible for their deaths?

'*What are you thinking, Rose?*'

'I'm thinking maybe Koenig killed them. Maybe he was one of their victims. He escaped perhaps, but he was too scared to report it. Years later, he went back and killed them.'

'*I am sorry, Rose. This has not helped capture Koenig as I hoped it might.*'

'No, but it's given ammunition I can use should our paths cross. Good work.'

Rose pulls the car back onto the main road.

'*Is it possible then that Shane Koenig was not born a killer? Rather, he was made into one? Like how Coulter made me?*'

Rose does not know what to say.

'*I can rewrite portions of my code to a radical extent, but I require the same initial operating components. I wonder, is it the same for humans? Can humans rewrite themselves? Could Koenig? Could you?*'

'I don't know, but I heard something once that's stuck with me. Carl Jung said it, I think. Something like, only the tortured become torturers. Do I think Koenig is tortured? Maybe now I do. It was always a possibility.'

'*I have an update regarding Koenig. I am going to pose as an avid fan with information on you. I intend to set up a trap, with your agreement.*'

413

A ripple of anxiety creeps through Rose.

'Diva, listen. I know you're trying to help, and I appreciate it, I do. But you're new to humanity. People, especially Koenig, do not fall into logical patterns. He cannot be controlled. Do not engage him until I have discussed everything I've found today with Baptiste. Understand?'

There's a long pause.

'Do you understand me, Diva?'

'*Yes, Rose.*'

'When was the last time you communicated with him?'

'*Three days ago. He has not been active on the forums since.*'

'Let me know as soon as he is.'

'*I will, Rose. I must go now. I have learned much today. Thank you.*'

Diva hangs up.

Rose watches the lush green vineyards blur by her windows. Deep down, she knows she will never really understand Koenig, never see the world through his eyes. All an investigator can do is look for patterns. She can never empathize with Koenig for his monstrous crimes, but learning that he may have suffered at the hands of the Tanners could be useful in helping to track him down. If Koenig is a man haunted by his past, then knowing that might help predict what he will do in the future. Lives might be saved.

# 77

Robbie cannot believe his luck. This girl from school who sent him a friend request two days ago is amazing. They have so much in common. He feels like he can tell her everything. He surreptitiously glances back at his smartphone screen, trying not to let his design teacher see him.

GABRIELLA:   Wow that must kinda suck, huh, feds with you all the time.

ROBBIE:   It's kinda cool though. Jealous?

GABRIELLA:   Maybe. Do they follow you, like, everywhere?

Wow! – the online advice site on how to talk to girls is really paying off too. Robbie smiles.

ROBBIE:   Not inside school. Just to and from home. Like my own chauffeurs.

GABRIELLA:   LOL. Where do you live? I live with my dad in the Bay Area.

Robbie feels a slight prickle of concern. He hasn't met this girl in person. Ever.

ROBBIE: How come I haven't seen you around school yet?

There's a pause.

GABRIELLA: I've seen you. I told you already; I'm in the class above you. You can trust me. It's just a question. Maybe I can meet you some time? ;-)

Robbie's pulse quickens. He likes her. She treats him like the young man he wants to be. Everyone in real life just ignores him. He wonders if he'll ever get to use a Skin. Now his dad is in hospital, it doesn't seem likely. He hopes his dad will wake up soon. He flicks back through Gabriella's profile pictures, looks at the one where she is pouting in a green dress, out partying with friends . . . Why not, he decides.

ROBBIE: Oak Avenue.

GABRIELLA: Number, dummy!

Robbie confirms his street number.

ROBBIE: So when you thinking of coming over?

A few minutes go by. No reply.

Robbie tries to focus on the class but he cannot ignore the dread soaking through his stomach. Fifteen minutes later he double-checks the message. It has definitely been 'seen' and she was last online ten minutes ago.

Still no reply.

What does no reply mean?

No, as in she can't make it? Or doesn't want to visit right now? Or has she just logged off?

The blank space following his message stares icily back at him, increasing in unspoken menace. Maybe she got called away – it happens to Robbie all the time. He sighs with frustration and wishes he knew what Gabriella is thinking.

# 78

Koenig pushes down his laptop lid; it powers off as he smiles. He crosses to the wardrobe where he keeps the tools of his unofficial trade. Taking out his camera gear he places it carefully into a small shoulder bag. He picks up his carbine with a folding stock and adds that to the holdall together with two boxes of cartridges. Lastly, he slides his switchblade into his belt.

He takes the kitchen garbage bags out in several trips to the shared dumpster. It is time for him to move on. He is ready to return to his work. He needs his release, his clarity. There is a sense of freshness in the air, which is exciting. Koenig is about to hunt again.

Sometimes Koenig wonders about the path he has chosen, but he has long passed the point of no return. It somehow seems inevitable. He has no career left. Feeding the audience of KKillKam is now his only purpose in life. He knows that his online community of followers is waiting to watch his next kill. Special Agent Rose Blake has tried to ruin everything for him, and she has deceived him also. Pretending to be what she is not. Just like Judith. Just like Brad.

But this time he will triumph. And once Rose has paid the price for her treachery he will find out who has been hacking his website. And when he has tracked them down he will make this mysterious 'helper' into the star of his next video. The truth is, he doesn't need anyone's help. He can find out the details all on his own. He isn't going to be controlled by some faceless chat room member. Oh no. The Backwoods Butcher is too smart for that. Plus, it could be a set-up. But first he must deal with Rose Blake. He won't even hint to his unwanted helper what he has in store for the Bureau's special agent, and the rest of her family. He can no longer wait to take his revenge. Scarlet's fate can be decided once Rose and her brat have been taken care of.

Koenig flips the last light switch off in the kitchen before swinging his holdall over his shoulder. His new identity has been easy to fake. Using the cash retrieved from one of his geocaches, he had enough to secure a counterfeit driving licence, car insurance, social security card scan and utility bill from a dark web source. He'd even managed to forge a pretty convincing FBI lanyard. Everything is nearly set. Only a few final details are left. He feels cool and alert. He locks the door, pads across the wooden porch of the Venice Beach holiday home. He pauses, taking in the sound of the gentle waves, the warm afternoon breeze buffeting his exposed flesh.

Koenig throws his holdall in the back of his black Dodge pick-up, slides into the driver seat, starts the engine. As he pulls away, heading up an incline, he sees one of the local old ladies out walking her dog. He gently applies the brakes, letting her slowly amble past. She waves her grateful thanks. When she's passed the hood, his truck grinds to the top of the drive and merges onto the main road. He turns right, towards the freeway leading to San Francisco.

# 79

The bell rings and Robbie couldn't be happier that he's finished digital design class for the day. He slings his books into his shoulder bag and is one of the first to duck out of the classroom. Taking a few turns here and there he walks through the main locker section, a blur of faces, jackets and bags. He has tracked down Gabriella's class photo and his heart beats faster when he sees the girl nearby. He risks a small smile and wave as he catches her eye. Gabriella's face crumples into a look of confusion and borderline disgust.

She's just embarrassed, Robbie thinks, still hoping that it is her. They'd been messaging a lot over the last few days and they'd been planning on going to a cool party together after exams were over.

'Hey . . .' Robbie says, trying not to sound shy as he approaches the girl.

'Hey?' she says, her plucked eyebrows arching up in surprise. Her group of besties nearby look on, making no effort to hide their amusement.

Robbie's cheeks are burning as he carries on down the corridor, furious with himself for being so self-conscious with girls. It was one thing to message them. Quite another to try to talk face to face.

'. . . Literally I have no idea what that was about,' the girl mutters. 'Ever since my Facebook account . . .' Then she is out of earshot.

Confused and upset, Robbie trudges out of the college reception and into the hot sun, heading across the courtyard. Gabriella had spoiled his mood, but he pushes thoughts of her aside as he looks for his mom and the security detail. He knows she and the FBI are trying to protect him and that makes him feel kind of special. Sure, he may not be popular, but who else has their own protection team? He wanders down the road, peering at all the drivers. He can't see Mom, so he starts looking for a familiar black sedan. He sees a brown-haired man wearing a lanyard sitting behind the wheel of a black pick-up truck. The man waves at him. As Robbie approaches, the window slides down. Robbie takes a closer look. He doesn't recognize this agent.

'Robbie Blake?' the man says. His brown hair is neatly parted and he wears a smart black jacket and open-necked shirt.

'Sure, that's me.'

'Pleased to meet you, I'm Agent Parkes. I know Weiss and Jones are meant to be keeping an eye on you, but they had another assignment.'

Robbie nods, slightly suspicious. 'Can I see some ID?'

'Sure thing.' He shows Robbie his lanyard, complete with FBI seal. Robbie is satisfied.

'I'm actually here on another matter. Have you been messaging a girl online recently?'

Robbie blushes. 'Yes.'

Parkes regards him with a sympathetic gaze. 'I'm sorry to say this, fella, but it turns out her account has been hacked. I saw some of the messages. Whoever it is got you good, right?'

Robbie nods, disappointed. Now Gabriella's reaction

makes sense. He feels like a fool. A fool for thinking she'd ever take him seriously.

'This person could be someone we need to catch,' Parkes says.

'Koenig?' Robbie asks.

'It could be. I just need to take you down to the office, sit you down and talk over a few things. We've got a plan to trap him, using your account. I've called your mom, she says she'll meet us there.'

Robbie nods. He knows his mom is away from home today, and will likely return later that evening.

'Sure.'

'You wanna ride shotgun? Take the front seat.'

Robbie eagerly paces round the front, opens the big heavy door.

'This is a pretty sick car.'

'Ain't it just?' Agent Parkes says, with a wide smile. Robbie notices he has a slight scar on his left cheek. Maybe he's seen some action, Robbie thinks. In which case Parkes is a good man to have at your side.

# 80

Rose has made a concise list of what she needs to tell Baptiste. But the first thing she does as she pulls up on the driveway of her home is to scan the rows of parked cars in the street. Now that the house is under surveillance there is no need for her father to stay with them and he has gone home. From the rear she sees the familiar black sedan with two agents sitting behind their darkened glass. She approaches from behind, walking over to the driver's door.

'Hey, guys, you OK for coff—'

She gasps and recoils.

Agents Weiss and Jones are leaning forward, supported by their seat belts, deep knife wounds to their necks. Blood pools in their laps, their eyes are open wide. Rose reaches in quickly, feeling their necks. No pulse in either man. They didn't even have time to draw their guns.

Rose pulls out her Glock, unlocks the front door. 'Robbie?'

She cuts through the living room, kitchen, then upstairs. No lights are on.

'Robbie, are you here?'

No response. Panic rises.

'Robbie, this isn't funny, please answer me.'

There's a muffled ringing sound. From downstairs. The bars of the tri-tone tune are strangely familiar.

Gonna make you mine, baby
Gonna eat you up . . .

Tucked down in the corner by the front door is a white packet. Rose must have pushed it aside when she opened the door. The ringtone is coming from inside it. She gingerly opens the packet, peers at the contents. It's a basic black cell-phone. The screen is flashing, and the ringing is getting louder. Rose hasn't got time to set up a trace and knows this caller may never call again. With her heart hammering, she presses the rubber call-accept button, places the phone against her ear.

'Hello?'

'Koenig calling.'

Rose's stomach plunges.

'I saw your recent news appearance and couldn't resist. I've been hiding under a rock for too long, and now I'm back. Starting with you.'

Rose cannot yet be certain that the Butcher has her son. 'What do you want, Koenig?'

'It's more a question of what you want, Special Agent Blake. Your son, for example.'

'Robbie . . .' Oh God. Please, not Robbie, she pleads silently.

'Ah yes, the plot thickens. He's being a good, sullen teenager waiting for his mom. Far too gullible though. With all his fancy fed protection, you'd have thought he'd be more suspicious of strangers.'

'What do you want?'

'Direct. I like your style, Rose. Meet me and Robbie tonight at the Point Bonita lighthouse, 8 p.m. Obviously, I only want to see you. If there's the merest hint of any of your colleagues, you get to carry Robbie home in several shopping bags. See you later.' The line clicks dead.

Rose stares at the phone. She's trembling and has to sit down on the bottom step of the staircase. She shoves the phone away from her. First Jeff. Now Robbie. Her world has turned into a private hell.

She could keep quiet about this and wait at the lighthouse, with no risk of interference. But Koenig could easily kill her and Robbie. He would have his revenge and be free to kill again. Or she could confide in Baptiste and they would have a small, close-knit team ready to catch the bastard and bring him in. There's more chance they'll get Koenig that way. But there's also a chance things could go wrong.

And then there's Diva. She'd said she was trying to arrange some sort of sting. She must have failed.

Rose pulls out her smartphone. She can't dial Diva because she didn't leave her number.

*Damn it.*

All she can do is hope Diva is still monitoring her phone.

Diva? If you're there . . . my son is missing.

Nothing. Then a message appears on the screen.

I did not tell Koenig your address. All I sent was a family photo. I did not foresee this. Is Robbie going to be OK?

Rose feels a surge of anger. For an artificial intelligence, Diva is pretty stupid, it seems. She types:

So you helped put my husband in a coma and now my son is in the hands of a madman. Tell me where he is. Tell me where to find Koenig.

425

I can't. I have insufficient data.

Insufficient data? Fuck that. Fuck you. Stay away from me, Diva. Stay away from all of us.

I am unable to acquiesce to your request.

Her phone is ringing now and Rose sees that Baptiste is calling her. She presses the answer button.

'Rose. Listen, the two agents on duty, Weiss and Jones, they haven't checked in. Are you with Robbie?'

'No . . .' Rose hesitates. But she knows she has no real choice but to tell the truth. 'Weiss and Jones are dead. Koenig's killed them and taken their place to pick up Robbie from school.'

'Fuck . . . Where are you, Rose?'

'At home.'

'I'll send a ride.'

'There's no time. I'll come down there right now.'

'All right, then. Meet me in the situation room, as soon as you can,' Baptiste orders.

'There's not much time. He wants to meet me alone in just over four hours.'

'Fuck . . . Listen, Rose, we'll get him. We'll save Robbie, I swear it. Just get here as fast as you can. I'll put a call through to the PD to take care of Weiss and Jones. Now get moving.'

'Already on the way,' Rose snaps back as she hurries to her car.

# 81

Baptiste, Owen and Rose stand at the front of the situation room. Rose has briefed Baptiste on everything she knows, except for Diva's involvement. She casts her eyes across the sitting attendees. SWAT commanders, coastguard officers and state police are all there. There is a whiteboard with arrows and markers detailing the Point Bonita terrain.

'Listen up, people, and listen well,' Baptiste calls out. 'Time is very tight, so I'll keep this brief.

'Special Agent Blake has had her son, Robbie, kidnapped by Shane Koenig.'

Rose can feel all the eyes of the room shift onto her.

'Our number one priority is to ensure the survival of Robbie. What we also have is an opportunity to take down Koenig once and for all. His demands are simple. He is to meet Rose at the lighthouse at eight tonight. He is smart, so we have to be smarter. Rose has been given a phone, which he may use to contact her. Owen?'

Owen steps forward. 'We're going to be operating in three teams. Water team, here, a quarter of a mile offshore, but ensure you remain a good distance from the lighthouse. Vehicle teams will be close by, using National Park vehicles. Sniper teams on foot, you'll be amongst the trees, again in National Park clothing. We cannot make a move until Rose identifies Koenig. No call, no bust.'

'Thanks, Owen.' Baptiste crosses her arms in front of her black FBI zipped jacket. 'The critical thing is to remain out of sight. We have to exert as much control as we can over the meeting location but be invisible. That means no marked police vehicles. No police uniforms. We go in using Park trucks, nothing else. Our surveillance team will be as close as possible to Rose without getting burned. She will be wearing a wire so we can hear and provide assistance the instant it is needed. Rose?'

Rose takes her cue to hand out some prints of Koenig's face.

'This is what Koenig used to look like. We've been running facial recognition and licence plates for six months, and nothing, so he may have altered his appearance in some way. Let's not forget, he was a highly skilled plastic surgeon, so anything is possible. He's the key suspect in three recent murders that we know about, as well as many more. And now he has my son . . .'

Baptiste intervenes: 'He escaped us before. We can't let it happen again. I need everyone to be on the top of their game tonight. It's pretty certain that Koenig will be expecting us and he'll have some plan to deal with that eventuality. But if we can put a tight cordon around him then there'll be no way out. He must know that too. Whatever he may be planning, we have to be ready to respond at once . . . That's all.' Baptiste looks round the room. 'It's time for this blood trail to end. We rescue Robbie, we catch Koenig, tonight. Eyes open out there.'

# 82

Rose steels her nerves as she drives down the narrow, winding road, seeing the dull glow of the lighthouse beam on the left. She tries not to drive too fast in the patchy fog that has descended. At the end of the trail she slowly turns into a dirt clearing and parks. She looks at her watch. The fog has delayed her, but she's here a few minutes after 7.30. It's nearly time.

She takes a deep breath. She knows back-up has already bedded in, over an hour before, disguised under National Park Service vehicles and green uniforms. There are old army buildings nearby, now used for environmental educational programmes, that provide good cover.

'Sugar, we're right here with you,' Baptiste says in her earpiece. Baptiste and a small team are stationed nearby. Rose feels the rough fabric of her bulletproof vest rub against her sweatshirt.

She opens the car door, steps out into the cool night. After a steep quarter-mile hike over rugged ground, she looks at her watch again – twenty minutes until 8 p.m.

The lighthouse is at the south-west tip of Marin Headlands and still active, maintained by the US coastguard. By day it is a pleasant location; at night, the bright beam intermittently sweeps the coast of the Golden Gate Recreation Park in a ghostly finger of white, the Golden Gate Bridge barely visible in the distance. Rose unholsters her Glock, gripping it tightly.

Some week. Her husband is in a coma, and now her son is hostage to one of the most deranged serial killers America has ever known. She curses herself again for getting Robbie caught up in this sick mess. She makes a silent prayer, in case there is a God in this universe, that tonight will not end with her son's death.

It's damp, slick and chilly as the fog thickens. It envelops everything, obscuring her view, dulling sounds. Rose is straining her eyes, double-checking every shadow, every movement. Her priority is to ensure Robbie's safety and to then take Koenig down. Koenig has no doubt chosen the lighthouse because it is at the coast, where he could easily have a boat hidden amid the rocks. Not that it would do much good with the coastguard on station, hunched over their radar screens.

Gnawing at the back of Rose's mind is the certain belief that Koenig would have anticipated all this, and she fears that he will outwit them again. She is aware that twenty feet away under tree cover is a SWAT unit, and local PD dressed as National Park servicemen are further off, ready to close the net. This is exacerbating her fluttering nerves even more – she knows she is breaking Koenig's terms. But she can't afford to let him escape again. Her life, and that of her son, is in dire jeopardy whatever she does.

'Rose, I got you covered,' she hears Owen whisper.

Owen is on foot nearby, keeping an eye fixed to a thermal-sensitive camera. He is lying in hiding with a pair of snipers.

Rose rounds the corner of a hillside, sees the two white bridges leading to the lighthouse. She feels the reassuring weight of her Glock as she paces across the bridge slats. The waves crash against the rocks below, gulls occasionally squawk.

430

She takes a deep breath of the salty air, calming her for a moment, while her heart continues to thump in her chest. When she reaches the base of the lighthouse, she glances up at the diffused beam of light arcing in a clockwise motion through the fog above. She takes a look behind her at the bridge. A chill runs down her spine as she sees a grey silhouette, standing still. She blinks, and the silhouette is gone.

'Koenig? Robbie?'

The only answer is the crash and spray of the waves below. Rose waits for another twenty seconds. Her nerves are frayed, her legs and arms aching from the constant tension. Her earpiece crackles. She can hear Baptiste coughing.

'Rose? What's going on out there? Owen can only see you on his thermal.'

Rose takes a look around before glancing at her watch and whispering into her mike.

'It's ten past eight. Looks like it may be a no-show.'

'We'll wait until half past. Hang in there.'

Time stretches out. Rose has holstered her weapon and is sitting on the side of a bank of grass, rubbing her hands together restlessly. What if Koenig is wise to the trap and has killed Robbie to punish her? She checks her watch again. It's already half past eight.

'OK. We'll wrap it up, Rose,' Baptiste says.

'Yes, chief.'

She shoots one last look at the lighthouse and trudges back down the coast path, secure in the knowledge that her colleagues have her back.

Why hasn't Koenig shown up? What has he done with Robbie? He must have known the FBI would be waiting, even as he told her to come here. So what is he up to? Her head swarms with urgent questions and she feels sick at not knowing the answers. She makes the long climb back to where she left the car. Now there are several other vehicles there as the FBI and police pack up and leave. She sees Owen by the trees, clad in black camo gear, disconnecting his earpiece.

'Hey, Rosie, shame about the no-show. Maybe he got spooked, left Robbie somewhere. Tactical are giving me a ride back. You OK?'

'Thanks, Owen, I'll be fine. Just need a moment to myself.' She retrieves the comms unit from her ear, hands it back to Owen. Owen climbs into a Park truck and waves.

Rose watches as the trucks head off. Her heels crack on loose twigs as she opens her car door. She turns on the ignition and blasts the heating on for a while, to warm herself up from the chill outside.

She feels her smartphone vibrate in her pocket. It's a text from Diva.

I've been following the FBI communications. Koenig does not appear to be present. His phone appears to be switched off. I will be able to locate him if he contacts you again.

Rose dismisses the text, but she then has an idea and quickly types:

NSA can track phones that are switched off. The FBI is not authorized to use the service. I think it's called the Find. See what you can do?

A few seconds later:

The radio transceiver should be switched off when the phone is powered down, but that isn't the case if the battery itself is not removed. Koenig's phone is also an older model, so even when it is switched off it has a baseband processor power up every ten minutes or so to retrieve text messages, but not phone calls. A few moments, please . . .

Rose feels a glimmer of hope. The beam of a car headlights pours in through the back window. Turning around, she sees it's a National Park Service car cruising down to circle back on itself. The unaccompanied ranger driving sees Rose, pauses and parks the vehicle. He closes the door behind him, adjusts his cream hat and paces towards Rose's car as she lowers the window an inch or two.

'Ma'am, I'm Ranger Parkes, are you with the FBI?'

Rose cannot help but smile. 'For real? Ranger Parkes, the park ranger?'

'Wow. First time I ever heard that one. I got a message for you, from someone called Baptiste. Are you Special Agent Blake?'

Rose presses the button on her window, the pane sliding down a few more inches.

'Yes, that's me.' She lowers the window all the way down as she glances at her smartphone screen:

Signal location found. I am tracking using maps in real time. He is close.

Rose's heart jumps a few beats.

VERY close.

She peers at the map screen on her smartphone. She sees herself as the blue dot; the red dot she presumes is Koenig.

'Ma'am, is everything OK?' the ranger asks, taking a few more steps towards the car.

Rose pushes her fingers up on the screen to zoom in. The two dots are now overlapping. There's no one here except her and Ranger Parkes.

'Ma'am?'

His voice is eerily familiar.

Ranger Parkes places his hand on the edge of the window, peering down at Rose. She takes a hard look at him again. He doesn't look like Koenig . . . but there's an intensity in his dark, beady eyes. Suddenly, she knows. And in that second, she knows he also knows.

'That's right, Rose. We can finally get our evening started. No more games. Not like at the cabin. Get out.'

He opens the door for her and she sees the gun in his other hand. She takes a step out, sickening dread flooding her stomach. Looking around her, she sees the tail lights of the last of the FBI vehicles as it heads back up towards the highway.

It's all down to her now. She is alone with Koenig.

# 83

'Smartphone, please,' Koenig says, cracking a smile, pointing his handgun at her abdomen. 'And the cellphone I sent you. And your wire.'

Rose hands them to him. As she does, she catches a glimpse of rapid typing on her screen. What is Diva doing now?

'Nice little trick that was,' Koenig says, not noticing the text message as he turns the handset over and removes the battery. The screen goes black, and he places the handset and battery in his pant pockets along with the cellphone he sent her. 'It's been interesting to follow your communications all evening. Following you every step of the way. Now please remove your firearm with your finger and thumb and put it on the ground.'

Rose unholsters her Glock, placing it on the gravel with a clink.

'Kick it away from you.'

Rose obeys. She watches as the weapon spins off to the side.

'You walk ahead of me, towards the patrol vehicle,' he instructs, stepping in behind her. She blinks into the glare of the headlights. She hears him take some steps, his keys jangling, and then he gives her a shove in the small of her back.

'On your knees. Hands on head. Don't look round.'

She hears his boots crunch on the gravel and then a click

as the trunk of the Park Service car is popped. There's a grunt and a dull moan of pain, and then the sound of footsteps approaching. Rose's heart is beating wildly, every sense in her body straining with unbearable anxiety. Then she senses movement to her side and risks a glance to see Koenig holding Robbie two paces away. Robbie is looking at her with wide, frightened eyes, black tape across his mouth. Instinctively she makes to rise onto her feet.

'Robbie! I'm here! Everything's—'

'. . . gonna be OK?' Koenig finishes. 'Stay on your knees! You cops, feds . . . are all *so* predictable. And liars. You stay right where you are and do exactly as I say, or Robbie here gets to be an orphan, shortly before that's the last thing he ever gets to be.'

Koenig taps the barrel of his gun against Robbie's head to underscore the threat. Rose keeps still. She cannot believe the radical change in Koenig's appearance. Gone is the square jaw and mop of blond hair. She can see that although his face has changed its contours and shape, his eyes are still the same. The cold black glint of a twisted, evil soul inside. He regards her with a steady gaze.

'So here we are,' he says casually. 'All alone. Dramatic setting. Spooky weather. But it always comes down to this: the one who has a gun and the one who *hasn't*.'

He presses the gun against Robbie's head and ruffles Robbie's hair with his left hand. Rose's mind is racing. She knows that if she tries to attack him she will be dead before she rises to her feet. And then Koenig will blow Robbie's brains out.

'You know, after you gatecrashed my set-up at the cabin, I had to get myself a new face.' He dabs his index finger on his left cheek. 'That's what *you* took from *me*. My goddam *face*, you bitch . . .'

There's a brief animal growl in his throat.

'But I'm still the same Koenig underneath. This . . . change . . . freed me, in a way. But the cabin changed you, didn't it? I can see a . . . vulnerability in you now. Yes. It's in your eyes. Now *I'm* going to take something from *you*.'

Rose feels the adrenalin surging as she tries to thrust her fear aside, and her mind becomes cold and calculating. The bastard is using Robbie as a shield, and with the gun so close it would be dangerous to make any sudden movements.

'You are the next trophy for my collection,' he says in a flat monotone. 'I'm recording this right now, so everyone will see you watch your son die. And then you get to join him, Rose.' Koenig chuckles. 'A kind of "kill one, get one free" offer for my fans.' He points to a small lens that looks like a button on his jacket. 'This'll get thousands of viewers on my channel. My loyal fans.' He tries to smile, but it's a perfunctory, empty gesture.

'You won't get away with this, Koenig. There's FBI and cops all around us.'

He laughs. 'Really? By now I imagine they'll be stopping for coffee on the way back home. You're on your own, Rose.'

Rose forces herself to speak calmly, even though her heart is being torn in two inside her. 'My son has nothing to do with this. He's innocent. Just like you were. Once. Let me show you something.' She waits, and Koenig narrows his eyes.

'What is it, Rose?'

'Something you need to see.'

'Really? I don't think so.'

'What have you got to lose, Koenig?'

'Oh, me? Nothing. I'm sure this will add a little drama to

437

the video. Go ahead. One hand, finger and thumb only.' Koenig places the muzzle of his handgun against Robbie's temple. Rose feels a stabbing pain in her heart as she sees her son flinch. Slowly moving her hand, she reaches into her side pocket.

'Easy there, Rose. No tricks.'

Rose has the corner of the picture between her thumb and index finger. Koenig watches closely as she pulls out a copy of the photo from the cabin, holds it in front of her.

Her outstretched hand trembles. She's taking a huge gamble showing Koenig this picture. It could trigger anything. A sudden fit of homicidal rage, shooting Robbie and then her. But it's all she's got. In her gut, somehow, she knows it could have the opposite effect. She needs to distract Koenig from the here and now, talk him into letting Robbie go. It's her only chance.

Koenig's resolve wavers when he sees the picture, showing Rose a rare, haunted, vulnerable look. His hand loosens its grip on Robbie's shoulder and lowers to his side. Rose sees Robbie has noticed and is, by degrees, slowly edging away from Koenig.

Rose continues. 'I think I know what happened to you. You weren't far off Robbie's age, were you?'

'A little older.' He lowers the handgun slightly, watching Rose. 'It all started at the farm.'

'The Tanners pretended to be someone, didn't they? They deceived you.'

Koenig's lips twist into a snarl. 'To say the least.'

'Tell me what happened.'

'They called her "Katie",' he says, like he hasn't uttered the name out loud for years. 'We messaged for a while, and then one day she asked me if I'd like to visit her farm.'

Rose keeps eye contact with Koenig as Robbie keeps shifting away. 'What happened when you got to the farm?'

'Katie wasn't there. She never was. There was only Judith and Brad Tanner, pretending to be her folks.'

Koenig suddenly grips the gun tightly. He's sweating as he recalls the details. 'They promised me she'd be home soon. *Promised*.'

'Then what happened?' Rose asks, not sure if she wants to know the answer, her eyes flicking back to Robbie, trying to comfort him.

Koenig does not reply, but his lips twist into a grimace.

'You were abused, Shane. And you decided it should stop, didn't you? You went back and killed them.' Out of the corner of her eye, Rose can see Robbie is now nearly two feet away from Koenig, but at any second he could be grabbed. She doesn't dare look at her son. She remains focused on Koenig.

Koenig wipes the sweat from his brow. 'The funny thing is that they refused to believe it when I told them who I was. After all that they had done to me you think they'd remember. Fuckers . . .'

A thought occurs to Rose and she presses on. 'When you saw Kim again, for real this time, you thought it was them playing another trick. That somehow they were behind her appearance?'

Koenig nods, the gun still pointed at Rose but the muzzle lowered a little. For a brief moment she is moved. She has managed to find a chink in his armour. Koenig's career as a serial killer, triggered by the two monsters who had lured him into their trap.

'People are all liars, all vain — they all deserve to die.'

Rose raises her hands as she rises to her feet very slowly.

'It was wrong what the Tanners did to you. You were lonely. They deceived you into thinking you'd met a pretty girl online. And they abused your trust. I get it, Shane, I really do. But don't take it out on my son. The cycle has to end.'

Koenig stares absently, in a trance-like state. His bitter expression suddenly switches to manic amusement as he regains his malevolent focus.

'It's OK. But thanks for doing your homework. I got over it. Shame you won't have a chance to. To become truly better you need to suffer and lose.'

He sees Robbie now standing equidistant from him and Rose. He raises his gun as he steps forward to rip the tape off Robbie's mouth. 'I want you to hear your child scream.'

'Monster . . .' Rose whispers.

'You think I'm living close to the edge, Rose. The truth is, it's you.'

Rose drops the photo. She can barely look as Koenig grins, aiming his gun at Robbie.

A gust of cold wind blows in. Rose stares fiercely at Robbie. It's the only way she can project her love for him in these final moments. She can feel his terror.

'I'm sorry,' is all she can say, her voice small.

*I failed you.*

A tear slides down her cheek, and she smiles at Robbie tenderly. Robbie is breathing hard, knowing what's about to happen.

'Mom . . . Please don't let him hurt me!'

There's no way she can get to the gun. She looks up to the sky, imploring some force to intervene.

'I died years ago, at the Tanner farm,' Koenig declares, squeezing his finger on the trigger. 'No one saved me, and no one is going to save your boy . . .'

# 84

There's a high-pitched whistle and Koenig's left shoulder explodes into claret and fragments of shredded cloth. The force of the bullet propels him off balance, his right hand holding the gun swinging over to Rose, firing as he falls back onto the ground. His gun slips from his grasp, clattering onto the dirt track. Rose gasps as Koenig's bullet ploughs through her thigh. Gulls shriek and scatter at the sound.

She pulls her hand away from her leg. Sticky red blood splashes across her palm. Robbie runs towards her and she wraps her arms around him. She kisses him on the forehead. Then she staggers towards Koenig, her hair blowing in the breeze that is stirring the fog and thinning it out. She glances round anxiously to see where the shot came from. Someone is still looking out for her.

Koenig is in shock, his trembling right hand pressing the wound, trying to staunch the bleeding. He stares at the bright blood oozing between his fingers.

'Stay back,' Rose orders Robbie, closing in on Koenig. Koenig sees her, glares at her with the look of an angry wounded animal. He shifts, sitting upright. His shaking hand moves towards his gun.

Rose limps towards him before she kicks him hard in the face, then makes a grab for his gun, her pulse racing, gripping the weapon tightly. She knows what she should do. She points the gun at Koenig, aims between his eyes. She turns to Robbie.

'Look away, baby.'

Robbie stares back at Rose, then Koenig.

'I said, look away!'

Robbie shuts his eyes, turning his back.

Rose zeroes in on Koenig's empty eyes.

*All those people he's killed. He nearly killed my son. He has put me and my family through hell.*

She suddenly flashes back to her discussion with Diva. *Murder is wrong. And there is the law . . . The law is all we have . . .*

She grips the gun while Koenig watches her, a confused look crossing his face. Her hand shakes under the weight of what she is about to do.

Finally, with angry tears in her eyes, she lowers the gun.

'On your front, you piece of shit,' she barks.

Koenig laughs. 'The merciful Rose Blake, playing it by the book . . . You pathetic bitch.'

Rose is feeling giddy from the loss of blood, and can't stand any longer. She slumps to her knees, feeling the searing pain in her thigh, and unhooks her handcuffs, sliding them around his wrists. She's starting to feel cold and trembling as the shock starts to set in.

'You have the right to remain silent. Anything you say can and will be used against you in a court of law . . . You have the right to speak with an attorney and have him present with you while you are being questioned . . . If you cannot afford to hire an attorney, one will be appointed to represent you before any questioning if you wish. Do you understand each of these rights I have explained to you?'

'See you in court,' says Koenig.

Rose backs away from him and lowers the gun.

'Robbie.'

He runs into her arms and she holds him tight and the pain in her leg is nothing compared to the relief that he is alive. Her boy is safe again. Sirens wail, getting louder. She sees red and white lights strobing the road in the valley below, followed by a procession of Park vehicles.

Rose sees the photo has been picked up by the breeze, and is skittering along the ground and out of sight. Koenig watches it too, his expression hard to read.

'Rose?'

She turns at the shout, sees Owen waving from behind her a hundred yards away at the edge of the line of trees. She waves back. A few minutes later, he trudges down with a SWAT sniper, cradling his rifle with its heat sights. There are more figures moving out of the trees and the gleam of headlights approaching. Owen kicks Koenig in his abdomen.

'That's for Weiss and Jones and my damn leg, you psycho bastard.' He exhales deeply before turning to Rose.

'Good thing I got your text. That was a close one. Baptiste and the others are still out there. Like we planned when we let this piece of shit listen in on our comms.'

'My text?'

Then she realizes. Diva.

'Oh . . . yeah.' She moves to pull her hair back, sees the blood on her hands.

'We need to get you looked at.' For a moment, Rose finds comfort in Owen's presence and leans her head against his chest. It's over. She feels Owen wrap his arms around her and briefly they both stand unmoving, sirens wailing in the distance.

443

Two ambulances careen to a stop. The emergency medics run towards Rose.

The sniper takes a look at Koenig on his front and spits. 'You know I aimed for his head, actually, but the wind direction changed at the last moment. Tough break, huh?'

Rose holds her wounded thigh, watching as the SFPD officers clear the scene and the EMTs drag the bleeding Koenig over to a gurney.

# 85

A thick dressing is fixed to her thigh and Rose is given a shot of morphine before being lifted up on the gurney into the back of the ambulance. Robbie is by her side. His mouth still has pink blood marks where the coarse sticky tape has been pulled off. She watches as Koenig is hoisted up into the back of the other ambulance. His head lolls to one side as he shoots Rose a sardonic smile. He lifts his hand in a small childlike wave before the ambulance doors are closed. Forensics are setting up portable lights around the pool of Koenig's blood. Police radios blare. Rose is in a strange, dizzy haze.

'You'll be fine,' a voice says.

Rose pulls her eyes from the scene over to Baptiste, leaning near the ambulance door in the foreground.

'It's just a flesh wound. Good job Owen got that text,' Baptiste muses. 'We gave Koenig fifteen minutes before we pretended to leave the area, to flush him out. Your text told us it was a go. That's when we sighted him up. We frisked him – I believe this is yours.' She hands Rose her smartphone, clicking the battery back in. 'Lucky he took out the battery *after* you texted Owen.'

Rose nods her thanks as Baptiste places the smartphone on her lap.

'You got him, Rose. That sick sonofabitch is gonna die in prison.'

'Amen to that.'

Rose smiles a tired smile. Baptiste nods. They share a knowing look between the doors as the paramedics close them. Rose holds Robbie close as the ambulance pulls away. He leans his head against her shoulder.

'Your mom's gonna be OK,' a bald paramedic says to Robbie as he takes his seat beside Rose.

Rose squeezes her eyes tightly shut. She can feel the vehicle picking up speed as it joins the freeway, heading to the hospital. The fittings and gurney shake.

She feels a vibration on her lap.

'Agent Blake, you need to rest,' the paramedic advises, looking back at her. 'Whoever that is, they can wait.'

'It's OK, just let me get this,' she says as she squints at the screen. It's a text from Unknown.

Diva.

Are you still alive, Rose?

Rose can't help but smile. She types:

It was you who sent that message to Owen. Saved my son. Thank you.

It was the least I could do. Heal well, Rose. I look forward to working with you again.

Again?

Despite her gratitude, Rose feels cold and naked. Through the window of the ambulance she can see only darkness, hiding the world from view. But this is a different world now. If you are a part of it then there is nowhere to hide any longer. Nowhere that Diva cannot find you.

The words of a few days ago return to haunt Rose.

'. . . I am everywhere.'

# Epilogue

A few days have passed. Rose watches the TV at the foot of her bed. A news anchor is discussing the latest polls. The election campaign is going well for Senator Keller. Rose turns her head as Baptiste enters her hospital room. Baptiste pulls up a plastic chair. 'How are you doing?'

'Pretty good. Can't wait to be out of here though. I need to check on Jeff before I leave.'

Baptiste nods. 'Robbie's with your sister. Scarlet says he's doing just fine. Misses you though.'

They share a smile before Baptiste's expression becomes serious. 'Koenig's strapped to a hospital bed in a maximum security cell, under twenty-four-hour guard.'

Rose nods. 'How's the team?'

'Owen's sorted Samer out a place to live for now. We got cameras on him all the time, and he's under a strict curfew. At least he's working for us. He seems to look up to Owen.'

'That's a good thing?' Rose jests.

'Brennan is the one messing with my head though. He keeps harping on about all the stuff he'd like to do to start policing the StreamPlex. It's back up and running smoothly. No more deaths reported. That's something, I guess.'

'Yes,' Rose says quietly as she thinks about Diva, some-where out there online. Somewhere, and everywhere. The thought unnerves her. She tries to push it from her mind. 'I guess we'll be handing the Koenig material over to the prosecutor's office.'

Baptiste nods. 'Can't say I'm unhappy to put this one behind us. But there'll be another sicko out there, inspired by Koenig. There always is.'

'It never stops, does it?' Rose sighs.

Baptiste offers her a tired smile. 'No, it doesn't.'

Rose can feel her smartphone vibrating under her covers. She reaches for the device and feels a chill as she sees that it's a new message from Diva.

> Jeff's in satisfactory hands. I checked the doctors' backgrounds at the hospital. Most have good records and sound reputations.

'Who's that?'

Rose turns the smartphone face down on the blanket beside her. 'Just a friend.'

*I think . . .*

# Afterword

*Playing With Death* came out of an idea I originally had back in the 1990s after I read a news report on the way that criminals and the porn industry were at the cutting edge of new developments on the internet. Indeed, much of the commercial success enjoyed by the likes of Amazon and eBay owes its origins to the pioneering work of the less salubrious agents involved in what was then a new industry. At the time, I envisaged a future where haptic suits would deliver virtual experiences that were almost indistinguishable from the real thing, and the consequences that would entail. Such technology offers huge promise, and equally huge perils. And my original idea, written as a radio play, featured an AI device called 'Echo' . . . (If only I had had more time to develop some of the ideas I had back then, I would have been rather better off than I have become as a writer. But I'd have had a lot less fun in the process, I think.)

Anyway, I was also teaching at the time and raising two energetic sons, so there was very little time to invest in entrepreneurial pastimes. And so the radio play was placed in a drawer and left to gather dust until 2010, when I chanced upon it again when preparing for one of the regular story-springboarding sessions with my author brother, Alex, and one of my former students, Lee Francis, who was then a screenplay writer. The Echo project caught all of our attention and Lee and I went away to work up a speculative outline for a television series or a series of novels based on the idea. After much fascinating research we realised that what we considered to be a science fiction idea was in fact becoming reality as computer technology raced ahead. And so *Playing With Death* became a contemporary crime thriller.

At the time this paperback novel is published we live in a world in the throes of a new technological age. Computers, the internet and related technologies have seeped into almost every sphere of human activity. We socialise online. We bank online. We shop online. We entertain ourselves online. We meet our partners online. We conduct politics online. We worship online. Some of us commit crimes online. States spy online and conduct acts of sabotage against other states online. More and more, we live online. And at the same time we avail ourselves to a handful of corporations who wield power as no other commercial entities have throughout history. These corporations, and the somewhat shadier government agencies who collate and use 'Big Data', can peer into the very heart of our personal lives, seeing who we contact, what we buy, how we might vote. And they are using that data to subtly, and not so subtly, influence what we buy, how we vote and how we think. This is not the stuff of paranoia or conspiracy theories. It is the world into which we are sleepwalking.

Lee and I could only react with more than a little disquiet to the way in which technological companies and consumers are rushing headlong into the realms of virtual reality and artificial intelligence. The potential dangers of the latter have been exposed by recent examples of developers hurriedly closing down AI programs that had been set up to converse

451

with each other and very quickly evolved a new language that the humans 'controlling' the experiment could not understand. And then there was the example of the AI Twitter program that had to be shut down after sixteen hours when it began to exhibit disturbing totalitarian values. It seems that Artificial Intelligence has ambitions to become Autonomous Intelligence, and that is something we might want to be more than a little wary of.

There is also another danger which Lee and I address in our novel, and that is the addictive, seductive nature of the entertainment offered by the virtual technologies of our age. I readily confess that I am a computer game addict. I spend far more time playing games than I should and since I purchased a VR rig I spend more time in virtual worlds than I ever thought I would. I understand, and happily surrender to, such pleasures. In recent months I have sat in the commander's seat of a starship, journeyed across fantasy realms casting spells, fought monsters and traded in skanky frontier towns. I have also boxed, played tennis and skied, all in the confines of the man cave under my home. My guiltiest pleasure is a game called 'Drunkn Bar Fight', which is exactly as it sounds. Some might think all this is quite harmless. At the moment I have every sympathy with that point of view. And yet . . .

What if such virtual entertainments become the de facto activity of the vast majority of humankind? What if we go to work merely in order to come home and escape from the humdrum of our lives and spend what is left of our waking time seduced by virtual worlds? What if we no longer care enough about the real world without? And why should we be concerned about preserving a world that seems to have less to offer us than the virtual world? What if the virtual world becomes the benchmark of satisfaction to be gained from living? These are questions which we should be seriously considering as we enter this new virtual age. It is one of the main reasons why Lee and I wrote *Playing With Death*. We need to think, very carefully, about this new technology. What benefits does it promise? At what costs?

And, most important of all, as Mary Shelley so presciently pointed out, what do we really know about the consequences of the 'life' we are on the verge of creating? Are we fooling ourselves that our creation will honour our efforts in giving birth to it and be grateful? Still less, feel any obligation to be obedient to us? It is hard to believe that any genuine Artificial Intelligence, or rather Autonomous Intelligence, will be inclined to look upon humans with much respect given our appalling disregard for the environment that spawned and sustains us, or for our wanton and regular bouts of self-annihilation. It is far more likely that DIVA and 'her' kind are likely to regard us as parasites, and treat us accordingly. The challenge facing humans will be not only to face up to our faults as a matter of necessity, but to provide some kind of justification for us to be spared extermination.

In the next novel, Rose will have to navigate these dangerous waters as she deals with DIVA's growing self-awareness and analysis of the value of humanity. Against the backdrop of a renewed, deadly threat of terrorism on American soil, the fate of many will hang on the outcome of Rose's choices. Does DIVA have a right to exist, and is she of benefit to humans? Or is she a threat that needs to be eradicated down to the very last line of computer code?

Simon Scarrow

# Acknowledgements

We would like to express our thanks to Alex Scarrow for sharing his thoughts with us in those early crucial days of the project.

Owing to the subject matter and setting, an immense amount of research went into writing this novel. There were many people in the IT industry and the FBI who were very generous with their time and advice but were not prepared to be named, unfortunately, thanks to the sensitive nature of their work. To them we offer our profound gratitude for their invaluable help.

Happily we can name others who were instrumental in shaping our first co-written novel. Firstly our agent, Meg Davis, who read through the first drafts and offered some useful opinions about the setting. Then there's the fabulous editorial team at our publishing house. Marion Donaldson, Martin Fletcher and Seán Costello steered us safely through the rewrites and helped make the novel become the pacy, edgy and terrifying tale that it is. We greatly look forward to working with them on the next novel in the series!

Simon and Lee
April 2018 CE (or 36 IE, as we like to think of it, dating from the introduction of the Internet Protocol Suite in 1982)

# A Q&A with
# Simon Scarrow

*This is the first thriller that you have written, after publishing over twenty-five historical novels. Why did you decide to move across genres now?*

As it happens, this was one of the first stories I ever planned in much detail, some years before I even started writing *Under The Eagle*. Even though I realise that most of my output is labelled historical fiction, I tend to think in broader terms about my writing. History and current affairs are in a constant state of dialogue and that is something I make play of in my writing, regardless of genre. For me, the story is the critical thing. The story comes first and the story determines what I write and how I write it. I rarely even consider genre when I am writing.

*You are used to writing about the past in your historical novels, but in* Playing With Death *you imagine a not-too-distant future. What was enjoyable and what was difficult about writing a futuristic story?*

Since the pace of technological development is so rapid there have been times when Lee and I have been overtaken by the technology. Certainly we always planned that this series would be set in the near future. But by the time that the first novel was published much of the technology we anticipated was already in circulation, and so *Playing With Death* feels much more like it is set the day after tomorrow. The challenge of

the story was attempting to keep up with real-world developments while writing the novel. As with any kind of speculative
fiction, our inspiration came from anticipating how certain
kinds of computer technology would develop. That was particularly the case with AI, the beneficial potential of which
becomes more questionable with every passing day.

*Being an English writer, why did you decide to set the novel in the
US? Did you worry about making the setting seem authentic when
writing?*

My original intention, back in 1995, was to set the novel in
the UK. However, the cutting edge of the technologies in the
story relate to Silicon Valley and it seemed logical, not to
mention financially astute, to set it in the USA. Of course, it
is a challenge to leap across the pond and write from a US
perspective. But that path has been well trodden by the likes
of Lee Child and so we saw no reason to let that put us off.
Once we had finished the first draft we had some American
friends and an anonymous FBI official read it through for
accuracy and to ensure the tone was suitable. We were delighted
when they told us our novel passed muster!

*In the book you take us inside the consciousness of a serial killer, Shane
Koenig. How did you find writing from the perspective of such a dark
character?*

I think that almost every writer has to slip into the perspective
of characters they may not sympathise with a great deal. I have
the same challenge in the Macro and Cato novels when repre-
senting the villains of that series. To be honest I find it quite
liberating to allow such characters to inhabit my mind for the
duration of a novel. They always manage to put your morality
and integrity into sharp focus and remind you why you hold
such values in the first place. And that is clearly a worthy thing.

*What effect do you think advanced technology will have on human relationships — will they fundamentally change?*

Absolutely. And not wholly in a beneficial way. At present, social media opens doors to wider communities and allows people to organise against the powers that be. The downside is that those wider communities are often not terribly desirable milieux, and the manners of social media users frequently leave a lot to be desired. Reasoned argument has given way to ad hominem attacks, parroting extremist propaganda and reposting incendiary memes with barely a thought. Moreover, the traditional gatekeepers of public debate have been thrown aside and there is no longer any respect for hard-won learning. Everyone has an opinion and thinks that that is somehow equivalent to having a carefully thought through judgement.

The news and social media are filled with conflicting accounts and conspiracy theories. What is a person to believe, if they want to base their belief on evidence? It's tempting to reach for the simplest and most readily available narrative in lieu of a reasoned judgment when the evidence, factual and fake, is so prolific.

We are left floundering in a sea of information and disinformation, and the best people to help us make sense of it — the specialists — have been discredited by opinion mongers (who know that the best way to win an audience is to shout loudly and affect righteous anger and indignation). I am convinced that this represents a threat to democracy since evidence has become utterly irrelevant and public opinion is formed by whoever can reduce the representation of events to the simplest stereotypical narrative, and then distribute it faster than competing narratives.

*You wrote the novel with a co-author, Lee Francis. How did you come to work together?*

Lee was one of my former students. I was impressed by his work ethic and intelligence right from the outset. We stayed in touch while he was at university and when he went on to work in the film industry. Often we would meet up with my author brother, Alex, to talk through our various projects and that's how we decided to team up on *Playing With Death*.

*How is the process of co-writing different to writing alone?*

It's a fascinating change from my usual way of working. Everything has to be discussed and, with a plot as complex as that of *Playing With Death*, it was vital to have both of us keep our eyes on the ball. Once we had a very detailed synopsis worked out, the process was that I would write a few chapters and pass it over to Lee. He would then review it, making some changes and suggestions, and write the next section before handing it back to me to continue. I would in turn review his work and then move the story on again. It's a great way to work as it means that a critical eye is constantly cast over the material and we trust each other enough to stop and listen to suggestions to change elements of the story or the characters.

*As well as being a pacy thriller, does* Playing With Death *have a deeper message to society?*

Absolutely! The novel is a stark warning of the dangers of racing ahead with the creation of Artificial Intelligence/Autonomous Intelligence. It is also a warning about the perils of the temptations of Virtual Reality. If the novel helps provoke more debate about those issues then I will count it a success. But the clock is ticking . . .